One Bad Idea

A Novel

SABRINA STARK

Copyright © 2019 Sabrina Stark

All rights reserved.

ISBN-13:

9781796303216

CHAPTER 1

I stared up at the stranger. "Excuse me?"

Standing in the mansion's open doorway, he gave me another annoyed look and repeated, "She's not here."

I gave him a look right back. I didn't care that he looked dangerous – and not only because of the tattoos. I *also* didn't care that he was looking at me like I was some kind of annoying bug, to be flicked off the sleeve of his faded red hoodie.

Hell, I didn't even care that the guy wore no shirt, that his hoodie was fully unzipped – *or* that his abs looked like something out of my deepest, darkest fantasies.

Really, I didn't.

The guy was a total ass, and he was standing between me and my best friend, wherever she was.

Already, I'd given my name – Allie Brewster. *And* I'd told why I was here – to pick up the friend who'd called me for a ride.

And what had the guy given *me*?

Jack squat.

I tried again. "But she told me she was here." I glanced around. "At this address."

"Yeah? Well maybe she told you wrong."

I bit my lip and tried to think. She'd also mentioned a public beach, but that was crazy. I'd gotten Cassidy's desperate call late last night. *She wouldn't've seriously slept outside? Alone? Would've she?*

Fearing the worst, I asked, "What about the beach?"

"What about it?"

I made a sound of frustration. "Where is it?"

He looked at me like I was the biggest idiot on the planet and then flicked his head toward the side of the house, as if I *hadn't* noticed that the whole street – with its glorious mansions and manicured lawns – was sitting on some of the finest beach-front property I'd ever seen.

Through gritted teeth, I said, "I meant the *public* beach."

"There isn't one."

"But there *has* to be."

"Sure, if you drive maybe ten miles."

I shook my head. "I meant nearby, like within walking distance." When his only reply was a bored look, I added, "She said there *was* one."

"Yeah? Then she gave you a load of crap."

I was glaring now. "She's not a liar."

He crossed his arms, making his ab muscles shift annoyingly fine above the waistband of his tattered jeans. "I never said she was."

My teeth were grinding now. *Where the hell was his shirt?* He should've been wearing one. After all, *I* never answered the door shirtless. Okay, maybe it wasn't exactly the same thing, but I didn't care. My friend was in trouble, and this guy was no help at all.

I yanked my gaze upward and shot back. "Yes, you did."

"I did what?"

"You implied that she was a liar."

"I don't deal in implications," he said.

I gave him a stiff smile. "That's an awful big word for a guy with no shirt."

He looked down and frowned, as if noticing his bare chest for the very first time.

Well, that made one of us.

In happier news, my comment had obviously found its mark, because the guy was still frowning. In spite of everything, I almost smiled. *Take that, Hoodie Man.*

He looked up and muttered, "Shit."

"What? You didn't realize you were shirtless?"

"No, I didn't realize you'd be such a pain in the ass. And where the hell is my pizza?"

What? I squinted up at him. *Pizza? Was he on drugs or something?* Anything was possible, given his semi-scruffy appearance. And that wasn't the only thing that made me pause.

The guy wasn't much older than I was, which put him somewhere in his late twenties. *Wasn't he a little young to look so jaded?* Plus, he'd been rude from the get-go.

In reply to his question, I said, "I don't know. Where the hell are your manners?"

His jaw tightened. "Manners are for pussies."

Well, that was nice.

"And," he continued, "you knocked on *my* door, not the other way around."

"For the last freaking time," I said, "I didn't knock. I rang the bell." Not that it really mattered, but the guy was getting seriously under my skin.

He looked past me, searching the street for who-knows-what. Finally, his gaze landed on the vehicle that had carried me here – an ancient pickup that guzzled gas like Uncle Joe guzzled beer at ball games.

Still looking at the truck, the stranger said, "No wonder you're cranked. You won't make dick driving *that* thing."

I didn't bother looking. That "thing" wasn't even mine. I wasn't even supposed to be driving it. But that was a problem for another time, probably *after* I was arrested for grand theft auto, assuming that Stuart – my jerk of an ex-boyfriend – made good on his threat.

In front of me, the stranger was saying, "So, where is it? In the truck?"

I gave a confused shake of my head. "Where's what?"

"My pizza, just like I said."

I felt my gaze narrow. He was messing with me. I was almost sure of it. "Oh, please," I said, "like a normal delivery person would knock on the door – *without* pizza, mind you – and demand to see her best friend."

From the open doorway, he flashed me a sudden grin. "I thought you rang the bell."

That grin – so damned cocky – sent a bolt of heat straight to my core. Worse, from the look in his eyes, he darn well knew it.

I was so distracted by his smile that it took me a moment to realize that he'd just made fun of me. "Hey!" I said. "I was speaking metaphorically."

"About what?"

As if he didn't know. "About knocking on the door."

He shrugged. "So was I."

I opened my mouth, intending to say something sharp and cutting. The only problem was, nothing came to mind. In truth, the guy had a point, and really, did it matter whether I'd knocked or rang the bell?

No. It didn't.

And I was wasting precious time.

After all, I'd driven ten hours for a reason, and it wasn't to exchange insults with whoever this guy was.

I mean, it was pretty obvious that he didn't *own* the house. If I were being generous, I might assume he was the owner's son or grandson. And if I were being less than generous? Well, let's just say that if he were robbing the place, he was a total dumb-ass to be opening the door at all.

I glared at up at him. Speaking very slowly and clearly, I said, "Where is she?"

The words had barely left my mouth when an electronic ringing sounded from somewhere near my feet. With a gasp, I turned to look. The noise was coming from my cell phone, which I'd set face-down on the fancy brickwork of the top step.

The phone was attached to my charger, which I'd plugged into the outdoor electrical socket before ringing the doorbell.

Yes, I was bumming a charge.

It wasn't the kind of thing I normally did, but my phone had died hours ago, and Stuart's pickup was seriously lacking in charging ports.

Desperately, I dove for the phone and yanked it free of the cord as I checked the display. *It was her. Thank God.*

I answered with a frantic, "Cassidy?"

But it wasn't Cassidy's voice on the other end. It was a different female, a stranger, who seemed absolutely determined to make me crazy.

Just like *him.*

CHAPTER 2

I'd been on the phone for less than a minute, and already, I wanted to scream – profanities mostly, because it was pretty darn obvious that the caller knew a lot more than she was letting on.

In a sly voice, she asked, "Cassidy who?"

My jaw clenched. "McAllister, like I just told you."

At this, her tone grew snotty. "Hey, you called *me*, remember?"

The comment was annoyingly similar to what the guy in the doorway had told me just a few moments ago. Now, doubly irritated, I mimicked his voice in my head. *"You knocked on my door, not the other way around."*

Jerk.

At the thought, I glanced toward the doorway and felt myself frown.

He was gone.

Odder still, he hadn't bothered to close the door.

My frown deepened. Maybe he *was* robbing the place.

On the phone, the girl was saying, "Did you hear me?"

I yanked my gaze from the doorway and murmured, "What?"

She sighed in obvious irritation. "I said, *you* were the one who called *me*."

I shook my head. "I did not. You called *me*."

"When?" she demanded.

"Just now."

"Yeah, well you called me like a dozen times last night." She gave a little sniff. "And just so you know, I didn't appreciate it."

On this, she might've had a point. I *had* called a dozen times, but I'd been totally justified. Very late last night, I'd gotten a frantic phone call from a number that I didn't recognize. But I *had* recognized the caller's voice. It was my best friend, Cassidy, calling me at our apartment.

Unfortunately, I hadn't been home at the time, so she'd left a message – a very scary message.

In a hushed tone, she'd practically begged me to drive down here and pick her up.

Even under normal circumstances, I would've been worried. But this situation was anything but normal. She'd been calling from Florida while I'd been ten hours north in Nashville, where both of us had been living until Cassidy's sudden move just last week.

Even at the time, I knew she'd been making a terrible mistake, moving in with the monster she called her mom. I'd told her so, too – not that she'd listened.

But that wasn't important, not anymore. Now, I just wanted to find her safe and sound.

Into the phone, I said, "Who is this, anyway?"

Sounding snippier than ever, the stranger replied, "Gee, I don't know. Who are you?"

Who was I? I felt my fingers clench. I was the chick who was going to slap her silly if she didn't give me some answers, and fast. My friend was in trouble, and I was wasting precious time on this stupid guessing game.

Unfortunately, I wasn't within slapping distance, and if I pushed too hard, she'd probably just hang up and refuse to answer when I called back.

In the nicest voice I could muster, I said, "I'm a friend of Cassidy's."

She gave a mean little laugh. "Cassidy who?"

Oh, for God's sake. "Listen, I've had enough of the games. She called me last night, from *your* number, begging me for a ride."

"Oh, please. She didn't sound like she was begging to me."

My breath caught. "So you were there when she called?"

"Maybe."

"So…?" I prompted.

"So…what?"

Through gritted teeth, I replied, "So, where was she?"

"At a party – not that she was invited."

I paused. *So Cassidy had crashed a party?* That didn't sound like her at all. I asked, "Are you sure?"

"Of course I'm sure. It was totally rude."

I'd known Cassidy for years. She was polite to a fault, usually to her own detriment. Trying to keep my temper in check, I said, "Okaaaaay. When was the last time you saw her?"

"I dunno."

By now, I was gripping my phone so tightly, it was a wonder it didn't snap in half. I took a deep, calming breath and said, "Was it today?"

"Hardly."

"So, it was last night."

"Maybe."

I took that as a yes. "When you saw her, what was she doing?"

"Aside from using *my* phone?"

"Yes," I gritted out. "Aside from that."

"Mostly, she was calling for a ride."

Obviously.

And hadn't we covered this already?

Desperate for more information, I said, "And…?"

"And what? You got my message, right?"

I froze. "What message?"

She gave a loud sigh. "You don't seriously expect me to repeat it?"

My jaw clenched. "Well, since I didn't hear it the first time, yeah, that would be really nice."

"Well, this is just great," she said. "I go to all the trouble to call you back, and you just ignore the message."

"I wasn't ignoring it," I told her. "My phone was dead, so if you left a message, I didn't get it."

"It *couldn't* be dead," she shot back. "You called me like a million times."

Somehow, we'd gone from a dozen to a million in the blink of an eye. *Talk about exaggeration.* I hadn't even meant to call *her*. Rather, I'd been trying to reach my friend.

I was *still* trying, not that I was having any luck.

But arguing the details would only waste time. Working like hell to stay calm, I explained, "Yes. I *did* call you – from a truck stop in Alabama, where I took five minutes to charge my phone. *That's* when I left those messages."

"So, why didn't you answer when I called back?"

Wasn't it obvious? "Because my phone died like ten minutes later."

Again, her tone grew snippy. "They sell chargers at truck stops, you know."

"I *know* they do," I said. "But my vehicle doesn't have a charging port."

"Oh come on, they all do." She gave a little snicker. "Unless your vehicle's older than dirt."

The vehicle *was* old, vintage actually, and it wasn't even mine. But none of this was important. I sighed. "Just tell me the message, okay?"

"Why?" she said. "It's too late now."

Oh, no. That sounded bad. "What do you mean?"

"What do you *think* it means?"

What was this? A trick question?

I shoved a hand through my long blond hair and tried to think. This wasn't as easy as it should've been. I'd been awake for over twenty hours, and half of those hours had been spent on the road, driving a semi-stolen pickup across unfamiliar terrain.

Into the silence, she said, "It *means*, you should've followed my advice."

"What?"

"Yeah," she said. "And if you didn't bother to listen, it's not *my* problem, so *don't* call me again."

And with that, she hung up.

More confused than ever, I pulled the phone from my ear and studied the display.

Sure enough, I had two missed calls and two messages. Frantically, I hit the play button and listened with growing trepidation to the voice of the person who'd just hung up on me.

After giving her name – Morgan Fletcher – she got right to the point. "Listen," she said in the message. "If you're planning to get your roommate, you might want to hurry, because she's drunk off her ass and making a spectacle of herself."

I shook my head. *No. That couldn't be true.* Cassidy wasn't remotely a partier, and she hated drama more than anyone I knew.

There was a brief pause before the voice continued. "No, it's *more* than a spectacle. You want the truth? She's whoring herself out for drinks and gas money."

I swallowed. *What?*

"It's disgusting," she was saying. "There's these two rich guys who own the place, and she's all over them, promising the lewdest things for a little cash. And just so you know, they like to share." Her voice grew shrill. "So if you're planning to pick her up, get your ass in gear and just do it already before I call the police!"

And then, she was gone – or rather, her voice was.

I stood there for a long, silent moment, wondering what planet I was on, because there was no way on Earth that message could be true.

And yet, a little voice in my head whispered that Cassidy's mom *was* a partier, and would've done exactly the sort of thing the stranger had described. Even worse, Cassidy had been living with her for the past week.

Cripes, for all I knew, that monster had dragged Cassidy to the party and put crazy ideas into her head – or more likely, drugs into her drink. *Date rape drugs?*

Oh, God. Maybe the story *was* true.

Now, I was desperate to hear the second message.

There was only one problem. The phone was dead. *Again.*

Shit.

I should've left it plugged in, even if it meant that I had to huddle next to the outlet to talk. But I hadn't. And now, I was totally screwed.

No. Cassidy was screwed. *Literally?* I sure as hell hoped not. My gaze drifted to the open doorway, and I felt my eyes narrow.

If Cassidy was in there, I was going to get her – or kill someone trying.

CHAPTER 3

Bracing myself, I stepped through the open doorway. The place was more like a palace than a house, but I couldn't appreciate any of it. I stopped to call out, "Cassidy? Are you here?"

No one answered, not even the idiot who'd originally come to the door.

I looked around. *Where was he?*

Maybe he'd skirted out through the back?

I frowned. If so, what did that mean? Was he, even now, making his way down the beach with a bunch of jewelry and a wad of stolen cash?

It wasn't completely outside the realm of possibility.

As I glanced around, I tried not to worry that if such a thing *had* happened, I was probably in danger of getting blamed for whatever was missing.

But I wasn't going to let *that* stop me, not with Cassidy in trouble.

Still calling her name, I strode deeper into the house, keeping a sharp eye out, not only for my friend, but also for any sign that I was on the right track.

Supposedly, there'd been a party here last night, but I saw no signs of it – no empty drink cups, no dirty dishes, no mess at all.

Instead, I saw expensive-looking furniture, obscenely high ceilings, fancy woodwork, and through the stunning patio doors, a breathtaking view of the ocean.

Whoever owned this house, they had money. *Serious* money.

I thought back to that awful message. The chick, whoever she was, had mentioned two rich men who apparently owned the place. I saw no sign of *them* either, but I *did* hear something – a sudden clank from a nearby room.

My breath caught, and my palms grew sweaty. Still, I picked up the pace and strode toward the sound.

A few seconds later, I pushed through a wide swinging door and stumbled to a stop at the sight of the same guy as before.

I stifled a gasp. Now, he appeared to be wearing nothing at all, or at least nothing that I could see. His chest was bare – well, except for all those muscles and tattoos. And I saw no sign of the red hoodie.

As far as the jeans he'd been wearing earlier, I had no idea whether they were on or off. He was standing behind a tall kitchen counter – granite of course – and he was…What the hell? Making a sandwich?

I blurted out, "What are you doing?"

He looked up and said with a distinct lack of enthusiasm. "What, you never saw lunchmeat before?"

Heat flooded my face. Oh, I'd seen lunchmeat before. I just prayed I wouldn't be seeing *his* meat, because that kitchen counter was the only thing that stood between me and whatever was below his waist.

I just didn't know if his "meat" would be on full display or covered by clothing. Desperately, I glanced around, but saw no sign of discarded jeans.

That was good, right?

Regardless, I had a sneaky suspicion that his meat would dwarf the stack on the counter.

At the thought, I gave myself a silent kick. *Why was I even thinking of this?*

More annoyed than ever, I said, "I know sandwich stuff when I see it." I don't know why, but I couldn't bring myself to say the m-word. *Meat.* Or doubly-embarrassing, man meat.

Good Lord.

Oblivious to my discomfort, the guy said, "Yeah? Then why'd you ask?"

By now, I was so lost in my own confusion that I couldn't even remember the question. But it didn't matter. There was only one thing I desperately needed to know.

I took a single step forward and demanded, "Where the hell is she?"

He returned his gaze to the partially made sandwich. "Out. Just like I said."

I blinked. "You never said she was out."

He was still looking down. "Yeah? What'd I say?"

I tried to think. "You told me she wasn't here."

"Yeah. Because she's out." As he spoke, he began stacking the meat – ham, turkey *and* bacon – onto some sort of Kaiser roll.

I made a sound of frustration. "Out with who?"

"My brother."

His brother? That couldn't mean what I thought it meant? *Could it?*

In the message, the caller had mentioned two rich brothers who'd been on the receiving end of Cassidy's offers to – I felt myself swallow – sell her body for drinks and gas money.

But *those* brothers were supposedly rich, and the guy in front of me was – well, annoying mostly. On top of that, he was way too young to own a house like *this*, unless a very rich relative had died on the sudden side.

Maybe it wasn't *totally* impossible. For all *I* knew, the guy could've killed the relative himself – because he was just that awful.

I was still thinking when he looked up and said, "You wanna take over?"

I gave a confused shake of my head. "Take over what?"

"Making the sandwich."

I felt my jaw clench. "I'm not making you a sandwich."

A quiet scoff escaped his lips. "You're telling *me*."

"What?"

"I'm just saying, I *know* you're not making it. But you could."

Slowly, as my teeth ground against each other, I looked down to the kitchen counter. The sandwich was mostly made. In fact, all it needed now was maybe a squirt of mayo, a dash of mustard, and the top bun. Surely, he could handle *that*.

I gave a snort of derision. "It's almost done."

"I know," he said. "So you're getting off light."

"What?"

"I mean," he said, "I've done most of the work already, so really, you should feel lucky."

I wanted to throttle him. *Lucky?*

What a total jackass.

Within the last twenty hours, I'd lost my job, crashed my car, *and* driven halfway across the country in a vehicle that wasn't even my own. On top of *that*, I'd just spent my last forty dollars on gas, and I had no idea how I'd be filling the tank to get home.

But all of this would be nothing if only I could find my friend.

And what was this guy doing? *Taunting me.*

I frowned. Or maybe he was stalling.

Either way, I'd had just about enough.

Speaking very slowly and deliberately, I said, "Where. Is. Cassidy?"

He grinned. "Why? You worried?"

Just like earlier, that grin did funny things to my insides. This would've been bad enough under normal circumstances, but now, it was doubly annoying, because that warm funny feeling was followed by a bolt of guilt so strong it should've toppled me over.

I was a monster.

My friend was in trouble, and here I was, going all weak-kneed, just because some lunkhead smiled at me.

For some reason, it was the final straw. "Of course I'm worried!" I yelled. "She's in trouble. I just know it."

If he was startled by my sudden outburst, he gave no sign. "You're telling me," he muttered.

I froze. "What?"

"I'm just saying, my brother's got that look."

"What look?"

Now, he was frowning, too. "Trouble."

"Trouble for who?" Again, I felt myself swallow. "Her?"

He shrugged. "So, you're *not* gonna finish it?"

"Finish what?"

"Making the sandwich."

It was then that something snapped. I strode forward and grabbed the sandwich off the counter. With an embarrassing little scream, I hurled it onto the floor and stomped on it, good and hard.

It felt squishy under my shoes, and I stifled a disgusted shudder even as I yelled, "How's *that* for finished?" I gave it another stomp, and then another. "Asshole."

When he made no reply, I kept on stomping until it felt more liquid than solid. The whole time, I didn't even bother looking down, because let's face it, the sight would *not* be pretty.

While the guy watched in silence, I gave it one final stomp and glared across the counter. "Well?"

This whole time, he'd shown no reaction – not even surprise. Somewhere in the back of my mind, I couldn't help but wonder if this sort of thing happened to him a lot.

With a personality like his?

Definitely.

When he *still* said nothing, I threw up my hands. "Aren't you gonna say something?"

He paused for another long moment. The kitchen was very big and way too quiet. The only noise I heard was the sound of my own ragged breathing.

Finally, looking annoyingly calm, the guy leaned over the countertop and studied the mess on my side of the floor.

I should've been embarrassed, but I was too far gone to care.

The only upside was that the movement revealed that yes, he *was* wearing pants, thank God. They were the same tattered jeans that he'd been wearing when he answered the door.

They looked good on him, too – hugging his tight hips and displaying a set of ab muscles so fine it gave the term "washboard" a whole new meaning.

The bastard.

Was I staring? I *felt* like I was staring, which made me feel ten times worse, not because I cared what the guy thought of me, but rather, because drooling over some jackass would do nothing to help my friend.

I shook my head. "You know what? Forget it. I'll find her myself."

And with that, I turned on my heels, intending to stride out of the kitchen with my head held high. There was only one problem.

The floor sandwich.

It was surprisingly slippery. Or maybe it was my shoes. Either way, I lost my footing and slid sideways, hard and fast, until something caught me in mid-slide.

Him.

CHAPTER 4

I couldn't see him, but I could feel his hands on my hips, steadying me, even as I struggled to find my footing on the slippery floor. His hands were strong, but surprisingly gentle as they kept me from sliding further into the mess of my own making.

Okay, now I *was* embarrassed. Slowly, I turned my head to look.

He asked, "You okay?"

He was leaning across the countertop, with his bare stomach pressed tight against the cutting board where he'd been prepping his sandwich. The last time I'd seen it – meaning the cutting board, *not* his stomach – it had been stacked with cheese, extra bacon, and the top half of the Kaiser roll, the one that might've topped his sandwich, if only I hadn't just destroyed it.

I saw no sign of these things now. All I saw was *him*, looking almost human, even as his muscles corded under the effort of holding most of my weight while I stared at him like a total idiot.

I snapped, "I'm fine."

He gave me a dubious look and held on tight while I found my footing enough to mutter, "You can let go now."

Slowly, he did and then smiled when I stepped back, more carefully this time, and muttered a disgruntled thanks, along with an obviously false claim that I really hadn't needed his help anyway.

To my infinite surprise, he didn't argue. Instead, all he said was, "If you wanna look, be my guest."

My gaze dipped to his abs. He was standing upright again, and his bare torso looked annoyingly fine in spite of the fact that it was now slightly marred by shiny smudges of what could only be bacon grease.

Unfortunately for me, the new sheen only further accented the lines and ridges of his flat, defined stomach. I felt my tongue dart out between my lips as I stared stupidly across the counter. And then, with a little gasp of horror, I sucked in my tongue, realizing far too late that he meant that I could look for Cassidy – not for signs of bacon on his body.

And now, I'd been caught staring. As heat flooded my face, I told myself that it was surely was the thought of bacon, and *not* him, that had me licking my proverbial chops.

It wasn't *that* far-fetched. I mean, seriously, I hadn't eaten since Nashville. And in truth, I had a real thing for bacon.

Was it any wonder that I'd be drooling at the sight of, well, *not* him, that was for sure.

He asked, "You hungry?"

Absently, I mumbled, "What?"

His mouth twitched at the corners. "If you want, you can have my sandwich."

Slowly, I looked down at the mess on the floor. It wasn't a sandwich anymore. I didn't know what it was, but I *did* know that it wasn't anything I'd ever put in my mouth.

I looked up and gave him my sweetest smile. "No. That's *all* yours. I insist."

Without waiting for his reply, I turned away, more carefully now, and picked my way out of the kitchen, trying like hell to ignore the fact that I could hear his footsteps following directly behind me.

Just outside the kitchen door, I paused in mid-step and looked down at my sneakers. I frowned, considering what might be stuck to the bottom of them.

The house was clean and nice, well, except for the kitchen anyway, and I hated the thought of tracking sandwich goo all over the place.

As my face flooded with new embarrassment, I made a move to slip off my shoes, only to pause in mid-motion when I heard a low chuckle behind me.

I whirled to look. "What's so funny?"

"You."

I glared up at him. "Oh yeah? Why's that?"

He glanced down at my sneakers. "Because it's a little late for that, don't you think?"

"Late for what?"

He gave me a crooked smile. "Worrying about messes."

The comment grated on me – and not only because it was true. It was because, somehow, the guy had known exactly what I'd been thinking.

I squared my shoulders and said, "I just don't want to slip, that's all." And then, with a look of defiance, I deliberately shoved off my shoes and kicked them to the side.

The guy spared them half a glance. "That'll show me."

Whether it would or not, I didn't care. In truth, I was mostly surprised that I hadn't flung both of them in his face, because he definitely had it coming.

I spent the next half-hour stomping through the house – well, as much as I *could* stomp in just my socks. The whole time, the guy followed after me, making smart-ass comments and refusing to take any of this seriously.

For what felt like the millionth time, he said, "Is that her?"

Unlike the first few times, I didn't bother turning to look, because if I did, he'd only shrug and say something stupid like, "Nah, just a lamp."

Or a chair.

Or a bed.

Yes, we *had* made our way upstairs.

The only break I had from his stupid commentary was when he paused at random intervals and tapped at his cellphone. Maybe he was texting someone to call the police. Or maybe *I* should call the police – except that sometime during this whole misadventure, I'd come to an unbelievable conclusion.

Probably, this *was* his house.

Damn it.

Now, I didn't know what to do, except keep on looking – if not for Cassidy, then at least for some clue on where she might've gone. Already, I'd been through most of the downstairs and a couple of bedrooms on the second floor.

Unfortunately, I'd seen nothing to indicate that she'd been here at all.

From inside the third bedroom, I whirled to the guy and said, "At least tell me this. Do you have any idea where she is?"

Standing in the open doorway, he said, "Yeah. Out."

I rolled my eyes. "Gee, thanks for the help."

"How about this?" he said. "You find her phone, I'll give you a clue."

I paused. "So, her phone's here? In the house?"

He gave another shrug. "Could be."

I made a sound of frustration. "You *do* know you're no help, right?"

At this, his expression turned serious. "And *you* know, you're taking a big chance, right?"

"What do you mean?"

"I mean, I could be anyone." He was frowning now. "Does anyone know you're here?"

The question sounded vaguely ominous. "What?"

"I'm just saying, you barge in here, at a place you don't know, with no one watching your back?"

Embarrassingly, I knew what he meant. Maybe I *had* been stupid, but it hadn't started out that way.

I lifted my chin. "So?"

"So, for all *you* know, I could be some psycho nutjob."

I gave him a stiff smile. "*Could* be?"

Ignoring the obvious insult, he glanced around the bedroom. "You do this a lot?"

"No," I snapped. "I don't do this a lot. In fact, I wish I weren't doing it now."

"Yeah, that makes two of us."

I was glaring again. "And what does *that* mean?"

He gave me a look. "You've gotta ask?"

Something about that look set me off. "Fine. You want me to find her phone?" My fingers clenched. "Oh, I'll find her phone, alright."

I stalked toward the nearest dresser and yanked open the top drawer. I reached inside and dug through the clothes, not caring that a whole bunch of them tumbled to the floor.

I was even less careful with the second drawer. Maybe I *wanted* to make a mess. Maybe I wanted to make him pay. Or maybe I didn't know what I wanted, except to drive him half as crazy as he'd driven me.

When I turned to glare at him, he leaned against the doorjamb and crossed his arms. "I'm just saying, you should be more careful."

I forced a laugh. "What? With the clothes?"

"No. With yourself." An edge crept into his voice. "I could be someone a lot worse than me."

I forced another bark of laughter. "As if *that's* possible."

But *he* wasn't laughing. "You think it's not?"

In the back of my mind, I knew exactly what he meant. He was a complete stranger and half-naked. As for myself, I was upstairs in an unfamiliar house – a house where my best friend had apparently gone missing.

But the truth was, when I'd first arrived, I'd been far too angry and worried to care. *And now?* I was still angry, but some of the worry had faded, probably because the guy's attitude – as annoying as it was – had made the whole thing seem more stupid than sinister.

Was I making a mistake? Somehow, I didn't think so.

And in spite of what the guy might believe, this wasn't the kind of thing I normally did, even under better circumstances. Cripes, I'd never even had a one-night stand, so his warning – if that's what it was – was totally unnecessary.

And besides, this was none of his business. All I said in reply was, "I'm not afraid of you, you know."

"Yeah? I wish I could say the same."

Well, that was nice.

In retaliation, I turned away and yanked open another dresser drawer. I reached inside and tossed a wad of clothing over my shoulder, praying that something whacked him in the face, even as I demanded, "What does *that* mean?"

"I mean, you're pretty scary for someone so small."

I was definitely on the short side, so I knew what he meant, except for the part about me being scary. I wasn't scary. I was merely going insane. And it was all *his* fault.

Without bothering to look back, I told him, "If you think I'm scary now, just wait."

"For what?"

I bit my lip. "I don't know, but you're gonna regret it."

"Hell, I *already* regret it."

Yeah, you and me both, asswipe.

I yanked open the next dresser-drawer and started flinging aside more clothes – shorts, T-shirts, socks and even a few unmentionables, many that were decidedly feminine.

But they weren't Cassidy's. Of this, I was absolutely certain, because *this* stuff was beyond expensive, and Cassidy – like me – didn't have that kind of money.

From behind me, the guy said, "If you think she can fit in that dresser, you're nuts." He paused. "Well, unless we chopped her up or something."

I stiffened. *Was that a joke?* If so, it wasn't funny. And besides, as he darn well knew, I *wasn't* looking for Cassidy – not at the moment, anyway. I was looking for her phone – and yes, the opportunity to make the stranger a little crazy, too.

Still, I wasn't about to let his comment pass. I turned to him and said, "I swear to God, if you did *anything* to her, I will kill you. Slowly."

He smiled. "Hell, you're killing me now."

With a few choice words, I moved away from the dresser and strode toward the closet. I began shoving aside clothes in search of who-knows-what. *My friend? Her phone? My sanity?*

By now, I had no idea. In truth, I was hardly thinking at all.

A day without sleep will definitely do that.

As I continued shoving aside clothes, the guy said, "Hey Velma, you wanna check the bookcases, too?"

Velma? It took me a moment to realize that he was referring to that Scooby Doo cartoon character – the bookish one with the big eyeglasses.

Whatever.

Still rummaging through the closet, I told him, "You don't *have* any bookcases, dumb-ass. I checked for those first."

"That's not true," he replied. "We've got a whole library downstairs."

They did? I hadn't seen it. But then again, the house was big – *very* big, with too many rooms to count.

Was it any wonder that I might've missed a few?

From the open doorway, he said, "So who's the dumb-ass now?"

Deciding that was a rhetorical question, I kept my attention on the clothes even as I threatened to shove a Scooby Snack up his ass.

Whether he heard me or not, I had no idea. By now, the closet was a total mess, with clothes falling off the hangers into rumpled heaps at my feet.

And yet, I kept on going and refused to be distracted, even when he said, "Found her."

Sure he did.

I called over my shoulder. "Oh shut up. I'm not falling for that again."

"Suit yourself," he said. "If you want me, I'll be in the library."

Without bothering to look, I yelled, "As if you can read!" Under my breath, I added, "Idiot."

But then, a moment later, I heard a voice – a new voice, standing eerily close. It was Cassidy, who said in a soothing tone, "Allie?"

CHAPTER 5

With a little gasp, I whirled around, and there she was – Cassidy, my best friend and former roommate.

No, I reminded myself – not my *former* roommate. She was my *current* roommate. After all, that's why I was here, wasn't it? To take her back home?

Beyond relieved, I soaked up the sight of her. She looked perfectly fine, thank goodness. Wanting to be sure, I eyed her up and down, taking in her black yoga pants, the pale pink T-shirt, and her long dark hair, without a single strand out of place.

Finally, something in my heart eased. *She was definitely okay.*

Tears pricked at my eyes, and I wanted to lunge forward and wrap her in my arms. *And* I wanted to throttle her for making me worry. Before I could stop myself, I'd already blurted out, "Where were you?"

She bit her lip. "Um, out?"

From somewhere down the hall, my shirtless tormentor yelled, "Told ya!"

God, what a jackass. So he'd *known* she was fine? And he hadn't bothered to tell me anything useful? I wanted to strangle him. Instead, I turned and hollered back, "Oh, fuck off!"

As the words rang through the house, I stifled a gasp. Okay, I *did* tend to curse when I got angry, but normally, I cursed in private, where I wouldn't make a total spectacle of myself.

Too late for that now.

Turning back to Cassidy, I murmured, "You weren't here."

She glanced away. "I know. I was getting..." She cleared her throat.

"…uh, pancakes, actually."

I stared at her. "Pancakes? Are you freaking kidding me?"

At the mere thought of breakfast, my stomach gave a low rumble. *I hadn't had pancakes.* Come to think of it, I'd eaten nearly nothing since dinner yesterday.

Before leaving on my impromptu road trip, I hadn't had the time. And *after* leaving, I couldn't afford much of anything to eat, not with that stupid truck guzzling gas like there was no tomorrow. And I *still* didn't know how on Earth I'd be paying for fuel to get home.

Knowing Cassidy, she'd be willing to pay for every gallon if she could. But knowing her mom? Cassidy was dead-broke by now.

And how did I know this?

It was because Cassidy was always broke whenever her mom bounced back into her life. The woman really *was* awful.

But that wasn't important, not now. Somehow, we'd figure everything out. We always did, right?

As my thoughts churned, it slowly dawned on me that Cassidy was eyeing me with obvious concern.

It was easy to guess why.

No doubt, I was a total mess.

On the inside of the closet door, there was a full-length mirror. I gave my reflection a sideways glance and wanted to cringe at the sight.

I looked even worse than I'd imagined.

My long blond hair was in a tangled disarray, with only half of it contained in the loose ponytail that I'd whipped it into however many hours ago. My rumpled clothes – long black shorts and a dingy grey sweatshirt – were way too big and not even my own. As for my eyes, they were red-rimmed and glassy, with dark circles underneath.

Good grief. I looked like a druggie, fresh off a bender.

But this wasn't all my fault.

When I'd left Nashville, I'd looked perfectly normal. I'd even been wearing my own clothes, *not* the ill-fitting extras that I'd found in Stuart's gym bag.

Now, ten hours later, my reflection was living proof that the drive had *not* been fun. Even the one thing I'd splurged on – a small hot chocolate with extra whipped cream – had ended up mostly on my lap, thanks to the lack of cup holders in the truck. *Thus, the need to change my clothes.*

In happier news, I was here. And Cassidy was safe. That's all that counted, right?

In front of me, she was saying, "Gosh, Allie. I'm *so* sorry."

I tried to smile. *I* wasn't sorry. I would've driven twice as far if that's what it took. I whispered, "You're okay?"

"Uh, yeah," she stammered. "I called. Didn't you get my message?"

"Of course I did. Why do you think I'm here?"

She winced. "Actually, I meant the *second* message, the one telling you that I was alright."

I gave a confused shake of my head. "What?"

"Yeah. In fact, I left *two* second messages – one at the apartment, and then another on your cellphone. You didn't get either one of them?"

I tried to think. She must've left them *after* I'd pulled away from that truck stop, the one where I'd bummed a charge for my cellphone. That was the last time I'd been able to make or receive any calls – at least until showing up here, where I'd spent most of the *new* charge, the one I'd bummed on the front porch, talking to that chick with the attitude.

As I stared stupidly at my friend, I considered that awful voicemail, the one informing me that Cassidy was selling her goodies for gas money.

Finally, I gave a low scoff. Just as I'd suspected, the message was a big, steaming pile of crap. And yet, like a total idiot, I'd still stepped into it with both feet, barging into some stranger's house like a crazy person.

Looking back, it was a wonder the guy hadn't called the police – or at the very least, tossed me out on my ass.

Judging from his physique, he was certainly more than capable.

Still, I had to wonder, why on Earth had he left open the door?

Cassidy's question hung between us. *Did I get her messages?* I tried to laugh. "Do I *look* like I did?"

"But how did you get here?"

Wasn't it obvious? "How do you think?" I said. "I drove."

She frowned. "But I thought your car was in the shop."

I hesitated. It wasn't just in the shop. It was totaled, thanks to that incident with the cement truck. The only upside was that I hadn't actually been inside the car at the time, thank God, or *I'd* be the pancake, hold the syrup.

But in my first frantic voicemail to Cassidy, I hadn't mentioned any of this, mostly for lack of time. Now, I regretted mentioning my car at all. And I *especially* regretted telling her that I wouldn't be able to pick her up.

All of it was a huge mistake – and one I would've surely corrected sooner, if only I hadn't had such a hard time getting my hands on a vehicle.

And then, by the time I did, my phone was as dead as a doornail. On top of that, I'd been racing against the clock – not only to help Cassidy, but also to avoid getting busted in a truck that I wasn't supposed to be driving.

The whole thing was a giant mess, and I'd be facing a load of grief when I returned to Nashville – assuming that I wasn't arrested somewhere along the way.

As these thoughts swirled in my head, I considered how horrified Cassidy would be if she ever found out the truth. And she'd feel guilty, too. She always felt guilty, even when she shouldn't.

In reply to her question, I looked away and mumbled, "I uh, borrowed something."

"Sorry, could you repeat that?"

I looked back to her and sighed. "I borrowed a pickup. You didn't see it when you came in?"

She gave me a perplexed look. "In the driveway?"

"No. On the street."

"Honestly, I was pretty focused on the house."

I gave her a rueful smile. "Yeah. Me, too."

Just then, a noise near the bedroom door made us both turn to look. In the open doorway stood a guy who looked eerily familiar. This was the first time I'd seen him, but I was pretty sure that I'd met his brother – the jackass who'd answered the front door.

They had the same dark hair, the same muscular build, and the same dangerous eyes. But at least *this* guy was wearing a shirt.

From the open doorway, he gave us a long, inscrutable look. As he did, I felt myself squirm in embarrassment. It was beyond easy to guess what he was thinking. *"Who's the psycho in the closet?"*

Cassidy gave him a tentative smile. "Oh, hi."

He didn't smile back. "Hi."

Feeling more self-conscious than ever, I glanced around. So did Cassidy.

The room was a total mess, with open drawers and clothes scattered across the floor. As I watched, Cassidy's gaze landed on the final drawer that I'd ransacked. It was overflowing with lacy undergarments, most with price-tags still attached.

From here, I couldn't see the tags, but I'd gotten a decent look earlier. All of the stuff was incredibly expensive, and I couldn't help but wonder if I'd be expected to pay for it.

Technically, I hadn't ruined anything – well, except for the shirtless guy's sandwich, but that was a different matter entirely.

Cassidy turned back to the new guy and summoned up a reassuring smile. "Don't worry," she told him. "I'm gonna clean everything up. You won't even know we were here, honest."

I bit my lip. This was easy for *her* to say. She hadn't seen the sandwich.

The stranger still wasn't smiling. But he wasn't frowning either. *That was good, right?*

He replied, "I wouldn't count on it." And then, he turned his cool gaze on me.

I felt myself swallow. I wanted to say something, but I didn't know what. I mean, what *could* I say?

Oops?

He asked, "You need anything?"

The question caught me off-guard. It was surprisingly thoughtful, which had me rethinking my conclusion that the two guys were brothers. Based on their personalities, they hardly seemed related at all.

As I considered his question, I reached up to rub the back of my neck. There were a lot of things that I needed – food, gas money, and cripes, even a bathroom. But it seemed beyond rude to ask for anything at all after making such a mess.

I mumbled, "No. I'm fine." Under my breath, I added, "*Now*, anyway."

He gave me a dubious look. "You sure about that?"

"Sure." I cleared my throat. "I mean, what would I need?"

His gaze dipped to the hem of my sweatshirt. "I dunno. A shower, breakfast, clean clothes?"

I snuck another quick glance in the mirror and spotted a coffee-colored stain just above my waist. *Damn it.*

I heard myself sigh. If he thought *these* were dirty, he should see what happened to my *first* set of driving clothes.

Now, *those* were dirty.

I was still trying to think of something relevant to say when Cassidy turned to me and asked, "Are you sure? There's a private bathroom, and…" She perked up. "I have some things you can borrow."

Now, *that* confused me. Why would she have extra things so readily available? *Was she living here?* I snuck a quick glance at the guy in the doorway. *Maybe he and Cassidy were a thing?*

On one hand, I could totally see it. They were both very good-looking, and he'd been surprisingly nice, all things considered. Plus, they'd just returned from breakfast in spite of the fact that it was now early afternoon.

But I knew Cassidy. Like me, she preferred to take things slow. She'd been living in Florida for only a week, which meant that she'd known the guy for just a few days at the most.

It was way too soon for her to be moving in, regardless of the guy's looks or money, which he obviously had in abundance.

There was definitely more to this story, and I made a mental note to start asking as soon as we returned to the truck, assuming of course that it hadn't been towed away.

I still hadn't replied to Cassidy's offer of clothing and what-not. I was seriously tempted, and yet, I forced myself to decline, if only to spare everyone further embarrassment.

Finally, I looked to the guy in the doorway and said, "I guess I should apologize for barging in." I couldn't help but wince. "And I might've been a little rude."

He gave an easy shrug. "Forget it. Knowing my brother, he had it coming."

From somewhere down the hall, the first guy called, "I heard that!"

The guy at the door turned his head and called back, "You were meant to hear it, jackass, so quit your bitching."

In spite of everything, I almost smiled. If he and Cassidy were a thing, I'd totally approve, not that she needed my approval. It was just that I could totally see them together, and Cassidy was way overdue for something good in her life.

When I turned to give her a questioning look, she whispered, "They're brothers."

"I know," I teased. "He just said so."

She smiled. "Oh. Right."

From the doorway, the guy looked back to me and said, "Let me know when you change your mind." And with that, he turned and walked away, leaving me and Cassidy alone.

I felt my eyebrows furrow. Obviously, that last comment had been directed at me. But I wasn't planning to change my mind. Mostly, I was planning to leave – the sooner the better. And yet, I'd be smart to at least use the bathroom before hopping back into that truck.

Cassidy said, "Come on. Let's talk in my room, okay?"

I frowned in confusion. "*Your* room?"

"Just for last night," she clarified. "But it'll give us someplace to talk." She reached for my hand and gave it a gentle tug. "Now, come on."

Maybe it was exhaustion. Or maybe it was stupidity. Either way, I let her lead me down the hall, and then, in the private bedroom, proceeded to make her feel awful – even though that had never been my intention.

CHAPTER 6

Sitting in the small armchair beside the bed, I tried to laugh. "But then, I remembered Stuart's extra car key – the one he keeps hidden under his bumper." I hesitated. "Wait, does that make it a *truck* key? It probably does, right?"

Yes, I *was* rambling.

From nerves? Or lack of sleep?

Probably both.

Cassidy, who was sitting on the edge of bed, stared at me in obvious horror. "Wait, are you staying you took it without permission?"

I hesitated. "The key?"

"No," she said. "The truck."

"Well, yeah." I forced a shrug. "I had the key, so..." I let my words trail off, like this should explain everything.

Apparently not.

Cassidy was still staring. "You *stole* it?"

"No. I borrowed it, just like I told you."

Cassidy paled, looking like the pancakes weren't sitting so well.

Damn it. I'd meant for the story to be funny, not worrisome. Oh sure, it hadn't felt funny at the time, but surely we'd look back *someday* and laugh, right?

I just prayed I wouldn't be laughing from some jail cell in Tennessee.

What Cassidy *didn't* know was that I'd omitted the most concerning details, including all of the messages that I'd received from my ex, promising to send the police out after me.

Like he knew them personally or something.

Then again, his brother-in-law *was* a deputy sheriff in Memphis, so maybe Stuart really *did* have connections.

But I couldn't think about that now.

Now, the most important thing was returning the vehicle to Stuart's driveway – and fast. And then, I'd just have to smooth everything over, that's all.

It shouldn't be *too* hard. After all, Stuart had borrowed *my* vehicle plenty of times without permission. In contrast, this was the first time I'd ever done it to him.

Of course, my timing could've been a teeny bit better, considering that, unlike him, I'd done the borrowing *after* our horrendous breakup.

To Cassidy, I mumbled, "Hey, I left a note."

She gave a weak laugh. "Well, that's good. What did it say? 'I'm taking your vintage truck to Florida'?"

No. It hadn't. In truth, the note had been a bit short on details, mostly because I hadn't wanted him to flip out.

It hadn't worked, and I had the text messages to prove it. I also had a whole bunch of voicemails, which I'd listened to at that truck stop in Alabama. I'd even called him back and promised that I'd return the truck tomorrow.

From there, the conversation had gone decidedly downhill, especially when he informed me that I'd be dealing with the police, not him, in the future. True to his word, I hadn't heard from him since.

I was still mulling all of this over when Cassidy said, "He doesn't know the truck's here, does he?"

I sighed. "Not *exactly*. I mean, I didn't tell him *specifically* where I was going, just that it was an emergency." I glanced away and muttered. "And besides, he was sleeping. I didn't want to wake him."

Cassidy made a scoffing sound. "How thoughtful of you."

"Oh, shut up."

"Alright, forget last night," she said. "Did you at least call him this morning?"

No. I hadn't. Our conversation from the truck stop was bad enough, and besides, I hadn't the time – or a charged cell phone for that matter.

Now, I tried to make a joke of it. "Are you kidding? He'd just tell me to bring it back."

But Cassidy wasn't laughing. "Well, obviously."

"And besides," I said, "my phone died in Alabama. I couldn't call him even if I wanted to."

And I *hadn't* wanted to.

Yes, I was worried about the consequences, but not nearly as worried as I'd been for Cassidy's safety. Her mom really *was* awful – and not the normal kind of awful either.

Based on little things I'd seen and heard, I was almost certain that her mom was surviving like she always had – by trading sex for money. If that's what she wanted, it was fine by me, as long as she didn't force Cassidy along for the ride.

But the thing that *really* set me off last night was that tense phone call from Cassidy herself. I knew her all too well. She wouldn't've asked for me to travel ten hours to pick her up if she weren't in serious trouble.

Now, a resigned sigh escaped my lips. "But what did you expect? You sounded scared. And I *know* how your mom is. You think I'd just give up because I couldn't drive my own car?"

On the bed, Cassidy looked ready to cry. "I knew you'd come if you could, but God, Allie, I'm so sorry. I shouldn't've asked you in the first place." Now, she was literally wringing her hands. "It was incredibly stupid, and now I'm worried you're gonna get in trouble."

Hoping to ease her worry, I joked, "Did you just call me stupid?"

From the look on her face, she wasn't amused. "No. I called *me* stupid. For leaving that message, the first one, I mean."

"That wasn't stupid," I told her. "Now, moving down here? *That* was stupid." I leaned forward. "But calling me to take you home? That was smart, like the smartest thing you've done all month."

Finally, she gave me the ghost of a smile. "When do you need to be back to work?"

Oh, crap.

For a moment, I debated lying. But that would just make her worry in another way. Finally, I admitted, "I, uh, don't."

She blinked. "What?"

"I was fired, actually."

Her jaw dropped. "What, why?"

I waved away the question. "Long story. It's not important."

"It is, too," she insisted. "You were so excited to get that job. And you've only had it for what? A month?"

Actually, it had been five weeks. In truth, it had been the best *and* worst job I'd ever had. On the upside, I'd been working as the personal assistant to some bigtime country music producer. As a huge country music fan, the job had seemed like a dream come true. On the downside, however, my boss had been a total nightmare.

In fact, he'd been such a nightmare that he'd refused to give me any time off to get Cassidy, even when I'd explained that she was in serious trouble.

And then, when I'd informed him that I was going anyway, he gave me the proverbial heave-ho which meant that I was now officially unemployed.

Still, I tried to look on the bright side. At least I wouldn't be working eighty hours a week anymore. So that was good, right?

In a quiet voice, Cassidy asked, "What happened?"

I gave a casual shrug. "Nothing. The job sucked anyway."

"Don't tell me...." She cringed. "You were supposed to work today?"

"Oh, you know how that guy was." I tried for another laugh. "I was supposed to work *every* day."

Her eyes filled with tears. "Oh, Allie. I'm *so* sorry."

That wasn't what I wanted to hear – not because I didn't appreciate her concern, but rather because I didn't want her to feel bad. She hadn't forced me to do anything, and besides, if I had to do it all over again, I wouldn't change a thing.

And I told her so, even as she stood and made her way to the nearby dresser, where she dug through a small stack of clothing. She pulled out a pair of shorts, a little yellow T-shirt, and even a bra and panties, both with the tags still attached.

And then, she hustled me toward the private bathroom, insisting that I take at least an hour to shower and rest.

The showering part was easy. But as for resting?

It didn't happen.

And why?

It was because I spent most of that time arguing with the jackass who'd answered the door.

CHAPTER 7

Freshly showered and dressed, I was standing alone on the front porch, staring at the empty electrical socket.

I felt my brow wrinkle in confusion. *My phone – where was it?*

Before barging into the house, I'd hooked it back up to the charger and then tucked it behind a potted plant, intending to retrieve the phone and charger before getting back on the road.

But then, in all the commotion, I'd forgotten both of them, at least until after getting out of the shower.

Now, I'd returned, but the phone and charger were gone. The charger, I could replace. *But the phone? Not so much.*

Especially without a job.

I bit my lip. Maybe Cassidy had spotted the phone on the way in and snatched it up?

No. If that were the case, she surely would've mentioned it. With a pang of new worry, I glanced around and then did a double-take.

What on Earth was he doing?

Earlier, I'd parked the truck out on the street. I'd even locked it, too.

Now, the truck was still there, but the passenger's side door was wide open, and my shirtless nemesis was leaning with his ass against the side of the truck while talking on his cell phone.

Technically, he wasn't *completely* shirtless, but he might as well be. The red hoodie was back, not that he'd bothered to zip it up.

When he saw me gaping, he should've been embarrassed – not because of his clothing, but rather because he'd obviously just broken into my vehicle.

But this guy – he didn't look embarrassed at all. Instead, he looked annoyingly at ease, leaning against a truck that wasn't even his own – or mine, for that matter.

I hollered out, "Hey! What are you doing?"

In reply, he held up an index finger, signaling for me to wait.

I felt my jaw clench. *Wait, my ass.*

I stomped down the front steps and stalked across the front lawn. I stopped within spitting distance and glared up at him. "Hey!" I repeated. "That's not your truck."

Ignoring me, he said into his phone. "Sorry, not gonna happen."

I made a what-the-hell gesture with my hands and moved closer. "You heard me, right?"

Ignoring *this* too, he focused all of his attention on whatever the caller was saying. And then, he frowned. "Yeah, but you're not dealing with *her*." An edge crept into his voice. "You're dealing with *me*."

I stifled a sudden shiver. Even when I'd destroyed his sandwich, he'd never sounded – or looked – quite so ominous.

But I wasn't going to let that stop me. I squared my shoulders and hissed, "We need to talk."

In response, he turned away, facing the truck instead of me.

That's when I spotted it – my own cell phone, tucked into the back pocket of his tattered jeans.

My mouth fell open. *What an ass.*

And no, I wasn't talking about his backside, which admittedly, was pretty darn nice.

I gave a small shake of my head. *What on Earth was wrong with me?*

Shrugging off the distraction, I focused on the phone.

Probably, I should've been happy to see it, but all I felt was irritation. For all I knew, he'd been planning to keep the thing, if only to make me crazy.

The guy had obvious boundary issues. Already, he'd helped himself to the truck *and* my phone. *What next? My panties?*

As soon as the thought crossed my mind, I felt an embarrassing rush of heat flash across my face and then, even worse, settle southward. The topic of my panties was so far removed from the situation at-hand that it didn't even make sense.

Plus, the panties in question weren't even my own. They were borrowed, which made the whole idea doubly ridiculous.

Into the phone, he was saying, "Go ahead. Call if you want. But I'm still the one you'll be dealing with."

I cleared my throat. "Hey! Remember me?"

When he didn't even flinch, I sidled up beside him, making myself impossible to ignore.

And yet, the ignoring continued.

I cleared my throat again. "Well?"

Finally, he pulled the phone away from his ear and studied the display. Speaking more to himself than to me, he said, "Guess he hung up."

I gave a snort of derision. "Yeah, I can see why."

Finally, he gave me a smidgen of his attention. "Meaning?"

I glared up at him. "I'm just saying, you weren't very nice."

"Good," he said. "I wasn't trying to be."

Yeah, whatever.

I crossed my arms. "Speaking of which, what are you doing?"

He gave me a look. "Aside from being hassled?"

I almost laughed in his face. "*You're* being hassled? Oh, please." I pointed toward the open passenger's side door. "You broke into my truck."

He didn't even look. "You think?"

I wanted to throttle him. *So much for an apology or explanation.*

"And," I continued, "you took my phone." I thrust out my hand, palm up. "Are you gonna give it back?"

"Yeah."

And yet, he didn't.

"Well?" I demanded.

"In a minute."

I thrust my hand closer. "No. *Now.*"

"Sorry, I'm waiting for a call."

What? I gave a confused shake of my head. "So?"

"So, I'll give it back in a minute, just like I said."

"But—"

Just then, a ringing sounded from his back pocket. "Hold that thought." He reached back and pulled out – yup, sure enough – *my* phone. He glanced at the display and told me, "Sorry, I've gotta take this."

Un-freaking-believable. "You're kidding, right?"

But no, he wasn't. I watched in stunned silence as he answered the phone – *my* phone – with a bored. "Yeah?"

By now, I didn't know what to think. Obviously, the call wasn't for me. What did that mean? Had he given my number to some stranger? And if so, how did he get the number in the first place? It's not like it was scribbled on the side of the phone or anything.

This was just terrific.

And now, he was ignoring me again.

I wanted to lunge for the phone and rip it from his clutches. But he was practically twice my size, and unless he was willing to actually let go, the effort would be a total waste. Plus, I'd be risking serious damage to the phone.

With a sigh of frustration, I looked toward the house. *Maybe the brother could help?*

At the thought, I almost rolled my eyes. *Yeah, right.* Like I could even ask such a thing after trashing his house.

I looked back my tormenter and hissed, "You're an ass. You know that, right?"

If he heard me, he gave no sign. Into the phone, he was saying, "Yeah, you could do that. But I wouldn't recommend it."

Even through my rage, I couldn't help but wonder, *do what?*

After another silence, he said in a dangerously low voice, "Because I know where you live."

I sucked in a breath. *Holy crap.* Was he threatening someone? On *my* phone?

I seriously hated this guy.

I waited with growing fury as the conversation continued.

"Here's the deal," he was saying. "I'll pay you double the value, plus a replacement. And in return, *you're* gonna stop being a whiny little bitch."

My fingers clenched. *What a total bastard.*

"And," the guy continued, "you're gonna forget it happened. No more cops. No more grief. Not today. Not tomorrow. And not fifty years from now." His voice grew a shade darker. "Or else."

Now, that was *definitely* a threat.

Obviously, the caller had taken it the same way, because the jerk was saying, "Or what?" He paused for a long, dreadful moment. "I'll be paying you a visit, that's what." He smiled. "And if you think *she's* a pain, you ain't seen nothing yet."

The conversation ended a moment later with him telling the caller that someone would be there in a half-hour to handle the details.

What details he meant, I didn't even want to speculate.

Aside from throttling him, the only thing I wanted to do now was recover my phone *and* get him away from the truck.

The phone part was easy. But the thing with the truck? *That* turned out to be annoyingly complicated.

CHAPTER 8

When he finished talking with whoever, he held out my cell phone, saying, "Told ya."

I snatched it from his hand. "Told me what?"

"That I'd give it back."

"What, you want credit or something?" My chin lifted. "Maybe you shouldn't've taken it in the first place."

"Yeah?" He gave a casual shrug. "Maybe you shouldn't've left it outside."

I shoved my cell phone into the front pocket of my borrowed shorts. "I didn't leave it 'outside,'" I told him. "I left it on the porch."

"Same difference, you ask me."

"Except I *didn't* ask, did I?" I glanced around. "And where's my charger?"

He pointed vaguely toward the front door. "Kitchen counter, near the fridge."

I turned and looked toward the house. *So he'd taken the charger inside? Why?* Surely, it couldn't've been just to be nice.

When I turned and gave him a questioning look, he said, "What, you need directions?" The corners of his mouth twitched. "Turn left at the sandwich."

Stupidly, I wanted to giggle. *And* I wanted to scream. He was doing this on purpose. I just knew it. I gave him a stiff smile. "What, you didn't eat it?"

At this, he had the nerve to laugh. It wasn't a big laugh. It was more of a chuckle really. Still, I liked the sound. *And*, I hated the fact that I liked it.

I was definitely losing my mind. And *he* wasn't helping.

Sometime in the last minute or two, he'd gone back to leaning his ass against the truck. This would've been annoying enough, but with him, it was *doubly* annoying because he looked so stupidly good doing it.

His hair was wavy and thick. His mouth was full and lush. And his eyes? They were dark and intense – the kind of eyes I might've gotten lost in, if only they weren't connected to the most obnoxious person I'd ever met.

It didn't help that his body was just as annoying. His legs were long. His hips were tight. And his whole upper body was too maddening for words, partly because I was seeing way too much of it.

His hoodie wasn't *wide* open, but it was open far enough to give me another good look at his tattooed torso. His pecs were firm, and his stomach was flat, except for all of those interesting ridges and valleys of tight muscles. Even as far as the tattoos, they'd never been my thing. *But on him?* Let's just say, I was reconsidering their appeal.

I blinked. *Damn it.* I'd gone all fuzzy again.

At least I hadn't been staring.

Had I?

In my stupefied state, I had to remind myself that my phone wasn't the only thing he'd grabbed without asking.

There was the truck, too.

The reminder was the perfect cold splash to the warm, funny feelings dancing in my stomach. I gave him a no-nonsense look. "So tell me, how'd you get in?"

"In what?" he asked.

I pointed toward the open passenger's side door. "That."

"You mean the truck?"

Through gritted teeth, I replied. "Of course I mean the truck. What else would I mean?"

He shrugged. "You tell me."

Oh, I wanted to tell him, alright. Unfortunately, calling him names would only waste time. "Well?" I demanded. "How'd you get in?"

He flicked his head toward the truck bed. "Through the slider."

I gave a confused shake of my head. "The slider?"

"The rear window."

"Oh."

"It slides open. You know that, right?"

I *hadn't* known.

But so what?

Even now, I didn't know much about the truck at all, except that it guzzled gas, drove like a brick, and had no air conditioning whatsoever.

Oh yeah – and if Stuart made good on his threats, that godawful truck would be the thing that landed me straight in jail.

In front of me, the guy was saying, "You should've locked it."

"Oh, so it's *my* fault you broke in?"

"I didn't break in," he said. "I crawled in. Big difference."

"It is not."

"Sure it is," he said, giving the window a quick glance. "You see anything broken?"

"Oh come on. You know what I mean."

"I'm just saying—"

"Well, don't," I snapped.

None of this was going how I'd anticipated. It's not like I'd expected him to grovel at my feet or anything, but seriously, shouldn't he be at least a *little* ashamed to be caught in the act of, well, whatever he'd been doing.

When he made no reply, I pointed toward his hips. "Maybe you should get your ass off my truck."

At this, his eyebrows lifted. "*Your* truck?"

Now, *that* made me pause. *Oh, crap.*

Did he know something? In what I hoped was a casual tone, I asked, "What do you mean by that?"

"I mean, the truck's not yours."

I felt myself swallow. *So he knew? How?*

In the back of my mind, I had visions of police cars screeching up to the house, and then – I gave a hard swallow – one of them leaving with me in the back, cuffed and stuffed like a common criminal.

The image was more than a little disturbing.

And he *still* hadn't answered my question.

I made a sound of frustration. "Are you gonna answer or not?"

Amusement danced in his eyes. "You're awful bossy for someone so little."

I felt my gaze narrow. "Are you calling me short?"

"No. I'm calling you fun-sized."

What was this? Another so-called joke? If so, I was in no mood. And yet, I couldn't help but wonder what he meant. *Fun sized? Like what? One of those bite-sized candy bars?*

Candy bars were sweet.

And delicious.

Everyone loved candy bars.

Was this some sort of come-on?

No. Definitely not.

The whole time I'd been here, he'd shown exactly zero interest in me – not that I *wanted* him to show interest. After all, I wasn't interested in *him* either.

Not one bit.

Really, I wasn't.

Deliberately, I changed the subject. "Alright, if you're so smart, whose truck is it?"

He flashed me a wicked grin. "Mine."

Annoying or not, my shoulders sagged in relief. It was an obvious joke. Or maybe he was hoping to goad me into flipping out again. Either way, I was just glad that he hadn't mentioned the real owner – a guy with no sense of humor whatsoever, especially when it came to his "sweet baby."

Yes, that *was* Stuart's favorite pet name.

For the truck.

Not me.

Just the thought of my ex was enough to make me feel slightly nauseous. He'd made some pretty serious threats. Would he make good on them?

Maybe.

Maybe not.

Either way, I needed to get back to Nashville – and fast.

Deliberately, I sidled around the Shirtless Wonder and climbed into the passenger's side of the truck. I turned in the seat and shut the so-called slider. And then, I locked it for good measure.

As I did, I watched the stranger from the corner of my eye. He was still leaning against the truck. But now, he was leaning forward, toward the truck bed, watching me through the rear window.

He looked beyond amused, and for the life of me, I couldn't figure out why – unless it was purely to annoy me.

With my hand too low for him to see, I flipped him the bird and said a silent prayer that he'd be gone by the time I returned with Cassidy. At that point, we could simply hop into the truck and drive away, leaving all of the madness behind.

Little did I know, the madness had barely begun.

CHAPTER 9

I'd just crawled onto the bed when the bedroom door flew open, and Cassidy rushed in, looking surprisingly excited.

With a happy smile, she breathed, "I've got the best news."

Cassidy didn't know it, but I'd only returned to the bedroom ten minutes ago, after relocking the truck and retrieving my charger from the kitchen.

I'd found it exactly where he'd indicated, which only confirmed what I'd suspected all along. He hadn't been doing me a favor. He'd brought the charger inside for one reason – and one reason only.

It was to make me parade past the floor sandwich.

Yes, it *was* still there, reminding me of my tantrum. Who knows, maybe his twisted script called for me clean it up.

I hadn't. And I wasn't planning to.

Take that, Shirtless Guy.

Cassidy's steps faltered. "Oh. Sorry. Did I wake you?"

Hardly.

I sat up and shook my head. "Actually, I was just getting up."

As if I'd slept at all.

Forget sleep. I couldn't even relax. Turns out, the quiet room had been the perfect place to obsess over the mess that I'd be facing in Nashville.

No job? Check.

No money? Check.

No guarantee that I wouldn't be arrested? This was a check so big, it seemed to fill the whole room. But surely, Stuart had been bluffing, right? I mean, once I returned the truck safe and sound, he'd calm down and be reasonable. *Wouldn't he?*

Cassidy shut the bedroom door behind her and said, "Well? Don't you want to know what it is?"

I was almost too distracted to think. "Sorry, what?"

"My news."

"Oh. Right." I summoned up a smile. "Sure. What is it?"

She bounded forward and announced, "I've got a lead on this incredible job."

My stomach sank. "Really?"

She nodded. "Yeah. And it's really, really good."

I almost didn't know what to say. If she meant a job here, I'd be insanely happy for her. And yet, it would also mean that this whole trip had been for nothing.

When I made no reply, her smile faded. "What's wrong?"

"Nothing." I rubbed at my aching eyes. "I'm just a little tired, that's all." Trying to sound more enthused than I felt, I asked, "So, what kind of job is it?"

She brightened. "It's a personal assistant job, you know, like yours in Nashville." She hesitated. "I mean, the one you *had* in Nashville."

The reminder did nothing to ease that sick feeling. "Oh?"

"Yeah. But this one pays *a lot* more, and there wouldn't even be weekend work." She paused. "At least, not normally."

"Oh. That's nice." *And it was.* In truth, I could hardly imagine. Back in Nashville, I *never* had weekends off. Come to think of it, I never had weekdays off either.

Near the bed, Cassidy was saying, "So it's a total dream job, right?"

"Sure," I said. "I mean, it sounds like one." Reluctantly, I asked the question that I'd been dreading. "So...where is it?"

She gave a happy laugh. "Here."

Shit. "Oh."

At something in my expression, her smile faltered. "Aren't you happy?"

"Sure," I repeated. "I mean, it sounds like a great opportunity."

"I know." Looking happier than ever, she flopped onto the nearby chair and said, "That's why I couldn't wait to tell you."

I gave a nervous laugh. "The way you talk, it's a sure thing."

"It could be," she said. "And it's *really* good."

It felt like the tenth time she'd said that, and I tried to look enthused. But I simply wasn't feeling it, and not only because of all the trouble I'd taken to get here.

Over the past week, I'd been missing her like crazy, even if we hadn't parted on the best of terms. She was my roommate, my best friend, and the sister I never had. If she took a job *here*, when would I see her again?

Probably not any time soon, especially if Stuart made good on his threats.

As she rattled off the pay and benefits, I had to admit, the job *did* sound pretty incredible. I was happy for her. Really, I was. Back in Nashville, she'd been working as a waitress at a sports bar. She was way overdue for a lucky break.

Still, in the back of my mind, I was trying to come up with some sort of plan. Interview or not, I needed to get back, like *now*.

But today was Sunday. Even if Cassidy's interview was first thing tomorrow, I'd be taking a huge risk if I waited.

But what if I left, and she *didn't* get the job? Would I need to come back to get her? *Could* I come back?

With no money? No vehicle? I felt myself swallow. *No freedom?*

Yikes.

I was so lost in my muddled thoughts that it took me a moment to realize that Cassidy had just asked me a question.

I gave a little shake of my head. "Sorry, what?"

She leaned forward in the chair. "So, how long will it take?"

"For what?"

She laughed. "For you to get ready."

I still wasn't following. "For what?"

She gave me a perplexed look. "For the interview."

I blinked. "What do you mean?"

"I'm just saying, he's waiting for you *now*."

"Who?"

"Jax, the guy who needs a personal assistant."

"Who's Jax?"

"He's the tall, dark-haired guy you met earlier. And just so you know, I mean the nice one." She made a face. "Not the other one. *His name is Jaden, by the way.*"

So the Shirtless Wonder had a name. Go figure.

Cassidy said, "But forget him. I told Jax you'd be right down. He's waiting in his office, meaning his *home* office. It's right downstairs."

More confused than ever, I reached up to rub my temples. "Wait, why would he be waiting for *me*?"

"Weren't you listening?" she said with a happy laugh. "*You're* the one with the interview."

CHAPTER 10

Turns out, Cassidy wasn't exaggerating. The job was seriously incredible – so incredible, in fact, that I was getting excited in spite of myself.

Fifteen minutes earlier, while practically dragging me down the stairs, Cassidy had told me something that had shocked me to the core. Turns out, the guys who owned the house – *this* house – were the Bishop Brothers.

This wasn't just a reference to their last name. It was the name of their international brewing company, one that I was surprisingly familiar with, thanks to my love of their main product.

Yes, I liked beer – theirs in particular.

The guys were a total legend, and with good reason.

A few years earlier, they'd picked up a local brewery that was on the verge of going under. After some serious rebranding and fine-tuning, they'd taken the market by storm.

They hadn't stopped with beer either. Today, they had so many brands and products, they could probably stock a full bar with just their own stuff – rum, vodka, you name it. Plus, their daiquiri mixer was seriously to die for.

On the other side of the desk, my interviewer – a guy I *now* knew as Jax Bishop – was looking a little surprised, "So you're familiar with our business?"

"Oh yeah." I leaned forward in the chair. "I love your stuff."

His eyebrows lifted. "Is that so?"

"Well, yeah. I especially love your beer." I felt color rise to my cheeks. "But it's not like I drink it all the time or anything. Weekends mostly. And, uh, at ballgames, too."

Damn it. I was oversharing, wasn't I?

I didn't normally do this, but my excitement was getting the best of me. Oh sure, the whole truck thing was still hanging over my head, which meant that regardless, I'd need to return it as quickly as possible – hopefully *without* a jail-related detour.

But now, rather than looking at my future with dread, I saw a tiny sliver of hope.

Who knows? Maybe this little adventure would turn out to be the best thing that had ever happened to me – and Cassidy, too.

She and Jax seemed to have a genuine spark. If we stayed in the area, she'd have the chance to get to know him better. Plus, she and I could be roommates again. She liked warm weather, and I'd always dreamt of living near the beach. With a job like this, I could actually afford it.

And besides, I was long overdue for a change.

As Jax listened, I went on to tell him how much I admired their company and products. To drive the point home, I even mentioned that their daiquiri mix was so good, it made other brands taste like swill in comparison.

I finished by announcing, "And I'm not just saying that, either. I really mean it."

Now, he looked dangerously close to smiling. "Good to know."

Suddenly, I wanted to smile, too. I liked this guy – not in a romantic way. But rather, I admired everything that he'd accomplished, especially at such a young age. And more importantly, he'd rescued my friend.

Obviously, he was the reason I'd found her safe and sound, rather than in serious trouble. And he liked her. I could tell, which only proved that he had terrific taste.

Still, there was one thing that confused the heck out of me.

The guy in the hoodie – the guy I *now* knew as Jaden Bishop – he was a total jackass. No matter how hard I tried, I couldn't imagine him being half of the dream-team that I'd admired for so long.

Maybe I should've recognized the brothers on my own, but then again, it's not like I'd ever expected to meet them in person.

When we moved on to discussing my qualifications, I was already prepared. Even without a resume, I was able to rattle off a list of previous responsibilities that aligned surprisingly well with the duties of this job, at least according to what Jax had told me – not that he'd shown me a description or anything.

While discussing my experience, I glossed over my most-recent job and focused mostly on the job that I'd had before that. It was another assistant position, this one for a commercial builder.

I concluded by saying, "And I'm sure he'd give me a good reference. Do you want his number?"

He studied my face. "No."

I paused. "Really?"

"Tell me," he said, "this builder, was he your most-recent employer?"

I tensed. Now, *that* was a dangerous question. I hesitated for a long moment before saying, "No. He wasn't."

Slowly, Jax leaned back in his chair. "Right."

Something in his demeanor suggested that he knew a lot more than he'd been letting on. I tried to think. *Had Cassidy told him that I'd just been fired?*

If she had, I couldn't blame her. I mean, it's not like I wanted to lie about it. It's just that, well, I was kind of hoping that it wouldn't come up *quite* so soon.

Still, I wanted to be honest with him. After all, if I got this job – and I only prayed that I did – I'd be the guy's personal assistant. It was a close working relationship, one that required trust both ways.

"Alright," I said. "You want the truth?" I took a deep, calming breath and just said it. "Actually, I was fired."

He gave me an inscrutable look. "Is that so?"

"Yes. It is. And I don't want to make excuses or anything…" I paused, wondering how much I should say.

He made a forwarding motion with his hand. "But?"

I sighed. "But I'd been working for twenty days straight, without a single day off, and—"

"And you'd had enough?"

"No." I hesitated. "Well, yes. But that's not what got me fired."

"So, what did?" he asked.

"An argument, actually." *And this was putting it mildly.* "You see, he wouldn't give me the day off, meaning today, even after I practically begged him." My voice picked up steam. "I even offered to work double the hours tomorrow."

Jax frowned. "But what about the drive?"

"You mean the drive back to Nashville? What about it?"

"When were you planning to sleep?"

I tried to laugh. "Who needs sleep, right?"

When he made no reply, I added, "The thing is, Cassidy needed me. So when my boss said no, I, uh, well, you know…" I gave a loose shrug and let the sentenced trail off.

A ghost of a smile crossed his features. "You told him to fuck off."

I froze in my seat. *He knew?*

He couldn't've heard it from Cassidy, because I hadn't yet told her. I asked, "Did you, uh, call him or something?"

"I might've."

Obviously, that meant yes. The call must've happened sometime within the last hour. And yet he'd *still* interviewed me for the job? That was a good sign, right?

Reluctantly, I asked, "What else did he say?"

"Nothing good."

I almost cringed. "How bad was it?"

"He said you were temperamental."

My jaw dropped. "Seriously?"

"*And* a pain in the ass."

What the hell? If anyone had been a temperamental pain in the ass, it was my old boss. As for myself, I'd been the epitome of professionalism until my very last day. And even then, I'd only lost it when he'd backed me into a proverbial corner.

Bracing myself, I asked, "Was there anything else?"

"Yeah. He called you scary."

Okay, now that was just insulting.

If I weren't so distressed, I might've laughed. Yes, it's true that I'd lost my temper on my way out the door, but I'd been at my wit's end.

And he'd been utterly heartless.

But what did it matter? The damage was obviously done. Still, I wasn't going to slink away without letting Jax know the rest of the story.

"Alright," I said, sitting up straighter in my chair. "You want the truth? I don't regret it. I *needed* to get here. Cassidy's mom – you don't know her, but…" I hesitated. "Well, let's just say, she's …"

Silently, I searched for the perfect description.

A call girl?

A prostitute?

A psychotic selfish bitch who'd rather sell out her own daughter than deal with a smidgen of inconvenience to herself?

I chewed on my bottom lip. *Damn it.* I couldn't say any of these things – not without violating Cassidy's privacy, especially if she liked this guy.

Finally, I looked away and mumbled, "Well, I just needed to get here, that's all."

So much for making a good impression.

I was still looking away when he said something that caught me completely off-guard. "You're hired."

My head snapped in his direction. "What?"

"You're hired," he repeated.

I gave a confused shake of my head. "I am?"

He smiled. "What, you don't want the job?"

I *did* want it, so very badly. And, with a rush of excitement, I told him so with as much grace as I could muster.

A minute later, we were discussing my start date when a ruckus sounded from somewhere inside the house.

Startled, I looked around. *What the heck was going on?*

I had no idea. But whatever it was, it sounded bad – *and* it was headed our way.

CHAPTER 11

More confused than ever, I looked toward the office door. It was shut, but I could still hear the yelling. Sure enough, it was getting closer.

I couldn't make out what was being said, but the loudest voice was definitely female – and *not* Cassidy's, thank goodness.

But I *did* hear the Shirtless Wonder – aka Jaden Bishop.

Well, that explained the yelling.

After all, he *did* that have that effect on people.

I was just turning back in my seat when I heard Cassidy call out, "Wait! I think he's in a meeting."

Again, I whirled toward the door. *Oh, crap.* So Cassidy *was* involved?

A moment later, the doorknob rattled, and from the other side, Jaden hollered out, "Hey, asshole! Open up! We need to talk."

"Yeah!" the unknown female echoed. "Like now."

From behind me, Jax called back to his brother, "Ten minutes."

Jaden yelled, "I'm not waiting ten fucking minutes."

"Yeah," the female hollered. "Me neither!"

I was still twisted in my seat, looking at the rattling doorknob. *What the hell?*

From behind his desk, Jax called back, "Yeah? Well, too bad."

I turned back to face him. He looked surprisingly calm, all things considered. I whispered, "Is something wrong?"

Probably, it was a stupid question. After all, something had to be wrong, or there wouldn't be crazy people yelling outside the door.

Jax gave a tight shrug. "Nothing I can't handle."

His calmness was only slightly reassuring. And yet, I said a silent prayer of thanks that I'd be working for *him* and not his godawful brother, who even now, was muttering, "The guy's off his rocker."

Cassidy told him, "He is not. Whatever he did, I'm sure he had his reasons."

At this, the unknown female scoffed, "So what's the reason? You?" Her voice rose. "Are *you* Morgan's replacement?"

Morgan? The name sounded vaguely familiar, but I couldn't seem to place it.

Cassidy was stammering now. "I, uh…No. Definitely not."

I felt my eyebrows furrow. Were they talking about the job? The one I'd just accepted?

I was still staring at the door. And *they* were still bickering. I didn't like it, not with Cassidy out there alone. She needed backup, and I knew just the person.

Me.

I made a move to stand, intending to march out there and join her side.

I'd barely budged when Jax said, "Wait."

I turned to look. With his gaze still on the door, he got to his feet, saying, "I'll handle it."

"But—"

"It's a family thing," he said. "Not your problem."

That's what *he* thought. In a way, Cassidy *was* family, *my* family. I said, "But what about Cassidy?"

"Don't worry, I've got this." From the look in his eyes, he meant it, too. And for the briefest instant, I almost felt sorry for whoever was on the other side of the door.

Almost.

But not quite.

As I watched, Jax strode away from his desk. The resulting breeze scattered the paperwork on his desktop, but he didn't even pause.

Outside the door, the argument was still going strong. Cassidy was saying, "I know what you're implying, and I don't appreciate it."

The woman yelled, "Yeah, well *I* don't appreciate you getting my daughter fired."

I sucked in a breath. *Her daughter?*

So *that's* why she was angry?

Finally, I understood. Her daughter must've been Jax's previous assistant. She'd been fired, and now, she was being replaced.

By me.

Cassidy shot back, "If she was fired, it was her own fault."

"*If* she was fired?" the woman yelled. "She *was* fired. You know it. I know it. And Morgan knows it. And *how* do I know this? Because she's crying on my damn couch."

Morgan. There was that name again. Where on Earth had I heard it?

And then it hit me. *Holy crap.* She was the chick who'd left that terrible voicemail – the one claiming that Cassidy was drunk and disorderly – and oh yeah, selling her goodies for cash.

And now, that chick's mom was giving Cassidy a hard time?

Unable to stop myself, I stood. As I did, I happened to glance down at Jax's desk. Amidst the scattered paperwork, I saw something that made the blood drain from my face.

Oh, no.

It was simple sheet of paper, nothing spectacular really. And yet, it changed everything.

I almost wanted to cry.

Apparently, I'd just made a horrible mistake.

And now, somehow, I'd have to fix it.

CHAPTER 12

By the time Jax opened the door, I was standing at his side. If he was surprised to see me, he didn't show it.

From the open doorway, I glared at the woman who'd been giving Cassidy such a hard time. She looked to be around sixty years old, and was very petite with short red hair. She wore tan shorts, a white cotton blouse, and a scowl so big, it might've knocked me backward if only I weren't so angry myself.

But I *was* angry. Her last comment – the one about her daughter crying on the couch – had gone completely unchallenged.

Apparently, we were supposed to feel guilty.

I didn't.

And I didn't want Cassidy to feel guilty either.

I told the woman, "Yeah? Well maybe your daughter's a horrible person. You ever think of that?"

Her face flushed with obvious anger. "What?"

I took a single step forward. "Yeah, I said it. Because it's true. Do you know, when I called last night, she told me that my friend was whoring herself out for drinks and gas money?"

From a few feet away, Cassidy gave a little gasp. "What?"

"Yeah," I said, turning to face her. "And just so you know, the word 'whoring' was hers, not mine."

Cassidy turned and gave Jax a long, worried look. I could see why. He looked like he wanted to kill someone. I only prayed that it wasn't me or my friend.

I looked back to Cassidy and tried to explain. "Last night, I called you right back—"

"But wait," she said. "How could you? I didn't have my phone."

"I know," I said. "That's why I called the number you left that message from."

"Oh." Her mouth tightened. "What else did she say?"

Reluctantly, I glanced around. I *so* didn't want to reveal it, especially in front of both brothers, not to mention the crazy redhead.

My gaze landed on Jaden, leaning sideways against the wall. He was wearing the same jeans as before, along with a black T-shirt that sported a skull on the front.

So he *did* own a shirt? *Go figure.*

Unfortunately, he looked annoyingly good in *that*, too. *How unfair was that?*

I looked back to Cassidy and muttered, "Nothing."

"No," Cassidy insisted. "Tell me."

"Alright, fine." I lowered my voice. "She said the two brothers would be sharing you."

Cassidy was staring now. "And you believed her?"

"No. Of course not." I bit my lip. "It's not that I believed her, but there's the thing with your mom and, well, you know what I think of *her*."

Of course, Cassidy knew. A week earlier, we'd had a huge argument about it. I'd known that Cassidy was making a terrible mistake, moving down here to give her mom another chance.

A chance to what? Ruin her life?

In the heat of the moment, I'd said some things that weren't very nice, even if they *were* true. Her mom was a liar. And a user. And way too interested in Cassidy's looks, which yes, were beyond stunning.

Based on what I knew of her mom, I'd had visions of Cassidy being pimped out or pressured into a hard and fast lifestyle – one that she'd never want for herself.

Still, in hindsight, losing my temper hadn't accomplished a single thing, except to create a giant rift, one that I was desperate to mend.

Now, standing in the quiet hallway, I gave Cassidy a pleading look. *Say something. Please?*

But she didn't. And neither did anyone else.

Around us, the silence grew and twisted, taking on a life of its own, until I wanted to crawl away and hide. The last twenty-four hours had not been kind. And even the job, the one I'd been so excited to get, was now a total impossibility.

I couldn't accept it.

I stiffened my spine. No. I *wouldn't* accept it.

Hell, I'd be smarter yet to sabotage it, to make Jax see that I was the worst candidate in the whole world. And then, he could hire his first choice – Cassidy.

Just before coming out here, I'd seen *her* name on the scattered paperwork. This had revealed a sickening truth. The job was supposed to be *hers*, not mine.

I felt myself swallow. *It wasn't too late, was it?*

I was still thinking when someone finally broke the silence. It was Jaden, saying, "So, were we taking turns? Or doing you at the same time?"

I turned to stare. I was so lost in thought that it took me a moment to realize that he was referring to that stupid message, the one claiming that the brothers would be sharing Cassidy.

My stare turned into a glare. *What a total ass.*

From beside me, Jax told him, "Say that again, and you'll be getting a fist in the face."

Jaden shrugged. "Dude, chill. It was just a question."

I was still glaring. What was he doing? *Goading his brother on purpose? Or was he seriously that dense?*

Now, Jax was telling the redhead, "Yeah. I fired her. And I should've fired her weeks ago."

The woman made a sound of protest. "But—"

"But nothing," Jax said. "If you wanna do her a real favor, you'll go back and tell her that instead of crying on your couch, she should get off her ass and find a job she can handle."

The woman gave Jax a pleading look. "I'll have a talk with her, okay? Just give her another chance. She'll do better, I promise."

"No," Jax said, "she won't, and she's out of chances." His tone left no doubt, especially when he added, "You should know, I've already hired her replacement."

Oh, crap.

I had to undo this.

But already, Cassidy was smiling up at him. "You did?"

When he made no reply, she turned and gave me a questioning look. My mouth opened, but I didn't know what to say. Desperately, I wanted to pull Jax aside and ask him what the hell he'd been thinking.

Too soon, Jaden demanded, "Don't *I* get a say in this?"

Jax didn't even hesitate. "No."

Jaden frowned. "And why not?"

"Because you hired the last one, and you did a shitty job."

From the sidelines, the redhead said, "Hey! That's my daughter you're talking about."

Jax turned to look, and his expression softened. "I know. But I'm done. And when you have time to think about it, you'll see it's best for her, too."

But apparently the redhead didn't agree. After a few choice words, she turned and stalked away, leaving a trail of profanity in her wake.

In spite of everything, I had to give her credit for one thing at least. That was some pretty creative cursing.

A moment later, the sound of the front door slamming echoed through the house. I was still looking toward the sound when the jackass said, "Hey blondie, you never said."

Blondie? He must mean me. After all, I was the only blonde here.

I turned and gave him an annoyed look. "I never said what?"

"With your friend," he replied, flicking his head toward Cassidy, "was it supposed to be a three-way? Or were we taking turns?"

It was then that a torrent of thoughts collided in my brain. He was so stupidly insufferable. I'd just about had it. And more to the point, I needed something – a spectacle so big that I'd be fired on the spot, or more accurately, not hired, considering that we hadn't yet signed the paperwork.

So I did the only thing I *could* do. With a little scream, I took a flying leap in his direction.

CHAPTER 13

I never made it. Before I could tackle him, someone tackled *me*. That someone was Cassidy, who tumbled with me onto the hard wooden floor.

As we hit, I hollered out, "What the hell are you doing!"

She held on tight. "I'm saving you."

Already, I was sprawled face down on the floor, with Cassidy on top of me. I tried to squirm away. "From what?"

"From making a fool of yourself, that's what."

At this, I grew very still. I'd been *trying* to make a fool of myself. That was the whole point. But I hadn't wanted to make a fool of *her*.

That would ruin everything.

Damn it. None of this was going how I'd planned.

From somewhere above us, Jaden said, "If they kiss, you owe me a beer."

I wanted to scream. *God, how I hated him.*

Cassidy shifted above me. "We can't kiss," she told him. "We're not even facing each other." *Dumbass.*

She didn't say it, but the implication was obvious.

Against the floor, I muttered, "I'll give him something to kiss."

I could only imagine how ridiculous we looked. For my own sake, I was beyond caring. But it wasn't *me* I was thinking about. As quietly as I could, I hissed, "I'm fine. You can get up now."

At first, I wasn't sure she'd heard me. But then, after a long tense moment, she finally let go and pushed herself up. As she got to her feet, I flopped over on my back and tried to think.

What now?

As I gazed up at the ceiling, I was vaguely aware that all three of them were staring down at me – not that I could blame them. I knew I was making a terrible impression, but that had been the whole idea.

I had to work with what I had, right?

Even though I'd just had a job interview, I wasn't dressed in business attire. Rather, I was wearing the same clothes I'd borrowed earlier – shorts and the yellow T-shirt.

My hair felt tangled, and my bare legs felt hot against the cool wooden floor. I was tired and hungry, and stupidly conscious that I couldn't lay here forever.

And yet, I was seriously tempted.

With a look of obvious concern, Cassidy extended me a helping hand. I started to reach out, but then paused when I caught sight of Jaden.

He was staring at me like I was some sort of demon who'd come to claim his soul. I almost scoffed out loud. *As if he had a soul.*

When Cassidy nudged her hand closer, I finally took it. As she helped me to my feet, I gave her what I hoped was an apologetic smile. "Sorry," I whispered. "I guess I blew it, huh?"

I sure *hoped* I blew it.

That *was* the plan, after all.

Cassidy turned and gave Jax a questioning look. As she did, I snuck a quick glance at Jaden. Or rather, it was *supposed* to be a quick glance. But his gaze locked on mine, and suddenly, I couldn't make myself look away.

His eyes were dark and dangerous and filled with something new – something I couldn't quite decipher. With a slow shake of his head, he asked, "Who the hell are you, anyway?"

But it was his brother who replied. "She's Allie Brewster." His voice hardened. "Your new assistant."

I blinked. *Huh?*

Jaden's assistant?

Not Jax's?

With a muttered curse, Jaden glared at his brother. "You're joking, right?"

In reply, Jax looked to me and said two terrifying words. "Welcome aboard."

CHAPTER 14

After delivering this job-related bombshell, Jax turned and stalked back into his office.

Beyond confused, I scrambled after him, with Jaden and Cassidy close on my heels.

Cassidy called out, "Wait, I thought she'd be working for *you*."

Jaden said, "Yeah, what the hell?"

Jax stopped and slowly turned around. He gave his brother a serious look. "I already have an assistant."

Cassidy spoke up. "You do?"

"Yes," Jax replied. "I do." He flicked his head toward his brother. "Morgan was *his* assistant, not mine."

I looked from brother to brother.

Oh, crap.

This was no joke.

And now, I didn't know what to do.

Desperately, I'd wanted Cassidy to get the job. But there was no way I'd ever want her working for such an insufferable jackass.

She'd be miserable. I just knew it.

Again, I asked myself that terrible question. *What now?*

Jaden was still glaring at his brother, "So we'll switch, not a big deal."

At this, I perked up. *Yes. A switch.* For once, I totally agreed with the jackass. It would be the perfect solution.

But Jax wasn't buying it. "We *can't* switch," he replied. "You know it. And I know it."

Cassidy broke in, "Wait, why can't you switch?"

Jax said, "Ask my brother. He knows."

Cassidy turned to Jaden. "Well?"

Ignoring her, he stepped closer to Jax and said, "I swear to God, I'll get you for this."

Again, I looked from brother to brother. *Another threat – how nice.*

"No," Jax told him. "You won't. Because this makes us even."

"For what?" Jaden demanded.

"For hiring Morgan in the first place."

Jaden gave a dramatic groan. "Shit, this again?"

"Hell yeah," Jax said. "I told you not to, but you did anyway."

Jaden crossed his arms, making his muscles pop in ways that were stupidly distracting. "So?"

"So, it's *your* bed," Jax said. "*You* lie in it."

"No way," Jaden retorted. "She's a fuckin' psycho."

Obviously, he meant me. I rolled my eyes. *Gee, you destroy one little sandwich.*

I was standing on the outskirts now, desperately trying to come up with a plan. I couldn't simply refuse the job. That would be way too obvious, especially to Cassidy.

But I *could* make myself as unappealing as possible.

It shouldn't be too hard, right?

After all, Jaden had just called me a psycho. This meant I was halfway there. *One brother down, one to go.*

Maybe I *was* crazy, because in that moment, I almost believed that somehow, I could still turn the situation around.

If I were deemed unsuitable, Jax would surely return to his first choice. He liked Cassidy. I could tell. He wouldn't stick *her* with his brother. *Would he?*

No. He'd switch. Maybe not right away. But he would eventually.

I almost smiled. *One switcharoo coming up.*

While the three of them argued back and forth, I reached up with one hand and further messed my hair. And then, I subtly reached down, twisting my shorts until they were saggy and crooked on my hips.

Cassidy was still glaring at Jaden. "Hey! She is not. She's perfectly lovely. And really smart, too."

When they turned to look, I was as ready as I'd ever be.

My posture was slumped, and my expression was dull. My clothes were crooked, and my hair was a mess. If I could've, I would've summoned up a burp so big, it would've made Uncle Joe proud.

But my stomach was empty, and I was no Uncle Joe. So I had to settle on the next best thing, looking like your basic slack-jawed, dim-witted slob.

And no, I didn't mean Uncle Joe, who happened to be as smart as a whip.

For a long moment, no one moved, not even a twitch. But then, Cassidy gave me a desperate smile. "Go on," she urged. "Tell him. You'll be great at this."

Showtime.

Channeling my inner slob, I reached up and scratched at the exposed skin just above my shorts. Maybe I didn't have a beer-belly, but I could *act* like I had one, right? I kept on scratching and made no reply.

Cassidy's smile faded.

Jaden looked beyond disgusted.

My gaze shifted to Jax, and I held my breath.

With a no-nonsense look, he said, "By the way, it includes a company vehicle."

Damn it.

Cassidy beamed up at him. "Really?"

Looking decidedly unenthused, he replied, "Really."

From a few feet away, Jaden protested, "But Morgan didn't get a vehicle."

"Yeah, well," Jax muttered, "she didn't show the same initiative."

I blinked. *Initiative?*

Okay, I'd shown plenty of initiative during the actual interview. But afterward, after spotting Cassidy's name on the paperwork, I'd shown no initiative at all. In fact, I'd shown just the opposite.

What was I missing?

Almost in a daze, I turned and stared toward the front door. The whole vehicle comment was a grim reminder that regardless of what happened here, I'd still need to leave right away.

The sooner I returned to Nashville, the sooner I could stop worrying about that stupid truck.

Sounding happier than ever, Cassidy gushed, "That's great! So what kind of vehicle is it?"

Jax replied, "An old Ford pickup."

Huh?

No freaking way.

I whirled to face him.

Cassidy gave Jax a perplexed look. "What?"

"Yeah," he said, "Jaden bought it a couple hours ago."

I felt my jaw tighten. *It? Meaning Stuart's truck?*

Again, I looked toward the front door. In my mind, I could still see him – not Stuart, but Jaden, leaning against the truck, claiming that the vehicle was his.

So that hadn't been a joke?

I reached into my pocket and yanked out my cell phone. I scrolled through the display and felt my gaze narrow.

Sure enough, the last incoming call had been from Stuart.

So *that's* who Jaden had been talking to?

Finally, so many things made sense – the truck being wide open, that strange phone call, the talk of someone dropping off paperwork – I sucked in a breath – and all of those veiled threats.

In my mind, I could still hear them.

"You're not dealing with her. You're dealing with me."

"I know where you live."

"No more cops. No more grief. Or else."

He'd also called Stuart a whiny little bitch. On that, I had to admit, he had a point.

Slowly, I turned back around. Jaden was still there, giving me that look again – the one I couldn't quite figure out.

In that moment, I couldn't even be sure whether he'd just done me a huge favor or had been messing with me all along.

The next day, I *still* didn't know, which was part of the reason I stopped by their corporate headquarters on a last-ditch effort to make everything right.

CHAPTER 15

"You can't quit," Jax said. "You haven't yet started."

Technically, this was true. Yesterday at his house, we'd agreed that next Monday would be my official starting date. In theory, I'd be using the time until then to get settled into the new apartment.

But now, I had other plans. I'd be spending that time looking for a different job and convincing Cassidy to take this one.

Unfortunately, the first step – getting Jax to agree – wasn't going anything like I'd hoped.

It was nearly noon, and we were talking in his massive office at the Bishop Brothers' corporate headquarters. I hadn't had an appointment, but he'd agreed to see me anyway – a promising sign, or so I'd thought.

From his visitor's chair, I gave him a pleading look. "I know I haven't started. But that just makes it easy, right?"

He frowned. "Easy for what?"

I leaned forward in the chair. "For me and Cassidy to switch."

With something like a scoff, he looked away and said something too low for me to make out.

I shook my head. "Excuse me?"

He looked back to me and said, "Not gonna happen."

"But why not?"

"Because I hired *you,* not her."

"I know," I said. "But she was your first choice." I paused. "I mean, I saw the paperwork. You *did* offer her the job, right?"

He leaned back in his seat. "I did."

"And?"

"And she turned it down."

I made a sound of frustration. "I know. But she only did that because she felt bad about me losing my job in Nashville. You *do* know that, right?"

This wasn't mere speculation either. After leaving their house yesterday, I'd actually confronted Cassidy about it, telling her that I'd seen the paperwork with her name, not mine.

I'd even tried to talk her into rethinking her decision to turn it down. But she'd absolutely refused, telling me that she would've sucked at this job, anyway.

This wasn't true. She was good at everything she tried. This was such a great opportunity. She should've taken it for herself.

Hell, she could *still* take it.

From behind the desk, Jax said, "I know what you're thinking."

"What?" I asked.

"That if you refuse, it'll go to her."

"Well yeah. Why wouldn't it?"

"Because I wouldn't do that to her."

I felt my brow wrinkle in confusion. "But you already did."

He stiffened. "I know."

"So, what's changed?"

"Nothing." Abruptly, he stood. "Take the job. Or not. Your choice."

"But—"

"But nothing. If you don't want it, let me know. I've got a list of candidates a mile long."

Now, *this* I believed.

Probably, I should've given up, but my own stubbornness wouldn't let me. As I stood, I said, "But she'd be better than all of them. And she's *really* great with people. Trust me, everyone loves her."

From the look on his face, this wasn't what he wanted to hear. "If that's the case," he said, "she deserves better than my brother."

I felt color rise to my cheeks. "I didn't mean—"

"I know what you meant," he said. "But it doesn't change the facts."

"What facts?"

"That he'd chew her up and spit her out." His frown deepened. "My brother, he's..." Jax paused, as if searching for the right thing to say.

He should've asked *me*. I had lots of descriptions that were just perfect.

A jackass?

A rude, obnoxious piece of work?

A total tool?

I was in serious danger of finishing the sentence on his behalf when somewhere behind me, a familiar male voice said, "Pissed."

I whirled to look. Sure enough, there he was, Jaden Bishop, standing in the open doorway.

He eyed me with a distinct lack of enthusiasm, even as I marveled at his appearance. Yesterday, he'd been dressed casually and then some. But today, he wore a dark business suit that looked like it was tailor-made just for him. And of course, the suit looked obnoxiously terrific, accenting his wide shoulders and long, lean legs.

Cripes, he even wore a tie, which *also* looked good.

Damn it. This was so unfair.

As for myself, I was wearing a plain navy dress – one I'd purchased just this morning, using the last available credit on my nearly maxed-out card. The dress was loose and long, falling nearly to the floor.

Ugly as it was, I'd picked the style on purpose. *And why?*

It was because I was wearing sneakers, that's why.

But *Jaden* wasn't wearing sneakers. No. He was wearing leather loafers that perfectly matched his suit.

Well, goodie for him.

As I stared stupidly across the distance, I tried to reconcile the Shirtless Wonder with the perfectly respectable looking guy leaning against the door jamb.

Absently, I murmured, "Pissed?"

"Yeah," Jaden said, giving his brother a hard look. "Pissed. As in 'pissed off.'"

I wasn't following. "What?"

He looked back to me and said, "You wanna know what I am?

That's the word."

Apparently, he was doing what *I'd* wanted to do – completing his brother's sentence.

Now, I was doubly irritated. After all, the word "pissed" hadn't even been on my list.

From behind the desk, Jax gave a low scoff. "Yeah, what else is new?"

"I'll tell you what's new," Jaden replied. *"Her."* His dark gaze shifted back to me. "Unless you're here to quit?"

I felt my eyes narrow. He *wanted* me to quit. That much was obvious. I gave Jax a sideways glance, wondering what he'd say.

I had, after all, attempted to quit just a few moments earlier, assuming that Cassidy could take my place.

Apparently, that wasn't an option, which meant that I'd be stupid to walk away now, especially if I wanted some way to pay the rent – not just for me, but for Cassidy, too.

That settled it.

I gave Jaden a slow, evil smile. "Me? Quit?" Deliberately, I widened the smile until my face literally hurt. "I wouldn't dream of it."

As the words echoed out between us, I realized that I actually meant it. If Cassidy truly couldn't take my place, I was determined to make this job work, if only for a year.

The money aside, it would be a terrific addition to my resume. These guys were bigtime – even more bigtime than the music producer back in Nashville. Regardless of how I felt, I'd be a fool to not jump at this opportunity.

Jaden was staring now. "Now *that's* fucking scary."

I ditched the smile and blinked innocently in his direction. "What?"

"That look." He turned to his brother and said, "You saw it, right?"

I almost rolled my eyes. He wasn't scared. He was just being an ass.

Still, I couldn't resist tweaking him just a little. "If you think that's scary, you should taste my coffee."

In reality, I made great coffee, but a little fear would do him good – or so I thought, because as it turned out, the joke was on me.

"Yeah?" he said. "Well, I don't drink coffee."

I felt myself frown. "Tea?"

"No."

"Well, what *do* you drink?"

Jaden gave a low scoff. "Don't you know?" He smiled. "The blood of my enemies." And with that, he turned and strode away.

I looked back to Jax. After a long, perplexed pause, I said, "He was kidding, right?"

Jax gave a tight shrug. "If you wanna quit, now's your chance."

That was no kind of answer, but I didn't complain. Already, I'd been seriously pushing my luck, and I knew the end of the road when I saw it.

So, I did the only smart thing I *could* do. I told him to expect me on Monday, just like we'd originally planned.

And then, I returned back to the apartment, where I found a *different* jackass waiting out front.

CHAPTER 16

As I pulled up to the apartment, I felt myself frown. Parked on the street out front was a vintage Chevy pickup with Tennessee license plates.

My stomach clenched. *No. It couldn't be. Could it?*

Florida was a long way from Tennessee, and I knew of only one person who'd be driving such a vehicle.

Praying I was wrong, I parked a couple of car lengths behind it and cut the engine. Through the front windshield, I gave the unfamiliar truck a good, long look. It was fire-engine red with classic lines and ultra-wide tires.

Based on its style, the truck was at least three times my age. And yet, it looked nearly brand new. No doubt, it was worth a small fortune.

I saw no driver – or passenger, for that matter.

Wondering where they were, I looked toward the place that I now called home.

Our new apartment was located on the second floor of a stately old Victorian house that had been converted into two separate units.

Cassidy and I had been living in the upper unit for only a day, and already, we loved the place. It was nice and roomy, with oversized bedrooms, tons of character, and our own private balcony.

The apartment had even come furnished.

Best of all, it was located on a quiet side street only a block from the beach.

Even now, I could hardly believe that such an amazing place had been within my budget, even *with* my newly inflated salary.

Reluctantly, I looked away from the house and scanned the quiet city street. *Where was the driver of that truck?*

A moment later, I had my answer when a blond head popped up in the truck's driver's seat.

I stifled a groan. *Yup, it was him, alright.* I couldn't see his face, but I was nearly certain.

My suspicions were confirmed within two seconds when the driver's side door swung open, and Stuart got out, looking slightly rumpled. He was tall and lanky with longish blond hair and light blue eyes. There was a time I'd loved looking into those eyes, but those days were gone.

As far as boyfriends went, he wasn't the worst I'd ever had, but he was far from the best. We'd been together for nearly six months until our bad breakup just a few weeks ago.

Since then, we'd barely spoken at all – unless I counted all of those tense exchanges regarding his beloved truck, the one I was currently driving.

Now, he was heading in my direction.

Still, I made no move to get out. *What on Earth was he doing here? Had he come for his truck?*

It seemed unlikely, given the fact that he didn't own it anymore, unless – *oh, crap* – what if Jaden had pulled a fast one?

I could almost see it, him telling everyone that he'd purchased the truck, only to laugh his ass off as I was hauled off to jail.

But surely even Jaden wouldn't be that awful, would he?

I needed time to think, but already, Stuart was rapping on the driver's side window. Reluctantly, I rolled down the glass and gave him a perplexed look. "Stuart?" In confusion, I cocked my head to the side. "What are you doing here?"

He smiled. "I came to get my stuff."

The smile caught me off-guard. "What stuff? Your gym clothes?"

"Forget the clothes," he said. "I'm not here for an old sweatshirt."

"So, what *are* you here for?" My stomach was still in knots, but I tried not to show it. "You, uh, don't mean the truck, do you?"

He made a scoffing sound. "Why? I've got a new one."

Something in my shoulders eased, and I almost sighed with relief. So Jaden *hadn't* been lying?

Thank God.

I looked toward the shiny red truck. "Wow, that was fast."

"Yeah, tell me about." Stuart's face broke into a happy grin. "That sweet baby? It's got eight cylinders under the hood."

I hadn't been talking about the truck's driving speed. I'd been talking about the speed of Stuart's purchase of a replacement vehicle. But the last thing I needed now was an argument. "Oh. Well, that's good."

His smile faded. "You don't even know what I'm talking about."

Okay, maybe I didn't know exactly what a cylinder was, but I *did* know that more cylinders equaled more power.

Forcing a smile, I said, "I know that eight is bigger than seven."

This was meant to be a joke. Even *I* knew that cylinders came in pairs, which meant there was no such a thing as a seven-cylinder anything. My smile faltered. Or at least, I was *pretty* sure there was no such thing.

Stuart gave a snort of derision. "Seven? Goes to show what *you* know."

God, what a douchebag. Stuart had no sense of humor. This was probably the main reason we'd broken up. Or maybe, he just didn't get *my* humor.

Now, my smile was long gone. He *always* made me feel like this – stupid and awkward, even when it came to the littlest things.

Outside the truck, he was saying, "You never got me at all."

He was right. I didn't.

I *still* didn't. And I especially didn't get why he was here. He'd claimed it was to get his stuff, but aside from the truck itself, I knew of nothing so valuable that he'd drive ten hours to get it.

And now, he was giving me the rundown on his new "sweet baby." I heard words like "filter canister" and "thermostat housing." By the time, he got to "engine displacement," I'd already checked out.

When he finished, I said, "Wow, that's quite a truck."

He gave a slow, satisfied nod. "I know, right?"

This was so entirely surreal. The last time I'd communicated with him, he'd been threatening to have me jailed. Now, he was acting like we were best truck buddies or something.

It was more than a little unsettling. Abruptly, I said, "What stuff are you talking about?"

He blinked. "What do you mean?"

"You said you were here to get your stuff."

"I know."

"Well?" I said, glancing around. "What stuff is it? Like paperwork or something? I could've mailed it, you know."

He frowned. "What, aren't you glad to see me?"

I gave him a look. *What an asinine question.* Of course I wasn't glad to see him. Our breakup hadn't been friendly. *And*, he'd been a rotten sport about the whole truck thing, too.

I didn't want to argue, and yet, I couldn't stop myself from saying, "Well, you *did* threaten to have me arrested."

He scoffed like this was nothing. "Yeah, because you deserved it, making off with my truck like that."

I felt my gaze narrow. "You *do* remember that you borrowed *my* car all the time, right?"

"Yeah, but that's when we were together."

Okay, on this he had a point, but not when you factored in quantity and inconvenience. Through gritted teeth, I said, "You borrowed it at least twenty times."

"So?"

"Without asking."

"So?" he repeated.

"So, half the time, you left me stranded."

"Oh come on," he said. "You had a roommate. I didn't."

Now, it was my turn to say it. "So?"

"So, she was there to give you a ride."

"Not all the time, she wasn't."

"Yeah, but it all worked out." With a little smirk, he added, "I don't know why you're so riled up now."

I gave him an annoyed look. "Well, *I* don't know why *you* threatened to throw me in jail."

At this, he looked away and mumbled, "I wasn't gonna do it

personally or anything."

I wasn't even sure what that meant. When he looked back, I said, "And you *do* realize it was an emergency, right?"

"Jeez, let it go," he said. "You weren't even arrested."

I did my best Stuart impression. "So?"

"So, if anyone should be mad, it's me. You drove it like what? Five hundred miles? I mean, it's not like you just took it to the store."

I sighed. Maybe he was right. And besides, I didn't care enough to argue with him. Mostly, I just wanted him to leave, so I could go inside and nap. Between all the driving and drama, I'd slept only a few hours in the last two days. Now, it was seriously catching up with me.

I muttered, "Fine. Let's just forget it, alright?"

Stuart smiled. "Is that an apology?"

"What?"

"An apology," he repeated. "You know, for taking the truck."

I didn't smile back. "I dunno, did *you* ever apologize for taking *my* vehicle?"

"No." He straightened. "But that was different, just like I said."

I gave him a long, cold look. If he was waiting for an apology, he'd be waiting a long time.

"Alright," he said. "I'll tell ya what. Make me a sandwich, and we'll call it good."

My jaw clenched. *What. The. Hell.*

Of all the things, he might've suggested, why that? Why now? Until recently, I had nothing against sandwiches. In truth, I *loved* sandwiches. I even loved *making* sandwiches. Until our breakup, I'd made plenty of sandwiches for both of us.

But now, just the thought of a sandwich was enough to make me feel nearly homicidal.

At something in my expression, Stuart gave a nervous laugh. "I'm just saying, I could use some lunch."

Through gritted teeth, I said, "We don't have any groceries."

"Why not?"

"Because we just moved in yesterday."

"Then how about a nap?"

I gave a confused shake of my head. "What?"

"A nap," he repeated. "I've got a long drive ahead. I could use the rest, you know?" He leaned forward and lowered his voice. "And you and me, we could catch up."

I leaned back. *And here, I thought the sandwich idea was bad.* "Are you hinting that we should..." I didn't even want to say it.

He smiled. "Hey, I'm game if you are."

I almost didn't know what to say. I was still searching for the perfect comeback when I heard a sudden screech of tires from somewhere behind me. Startled, I whirled to look.

Through the truck's back window, I saw a sleek red sports car that hadn't been there before.

I gave a little gasp.

And why?

It was because the driver of that vehicle was already getting out. *And who was it?*

It was Jaden Bishop, my new boss.

CHAPTER 17

I couldn't help but stare. He was still wearing the suit and tie, but somehow, he didn't look half as civilized as he had back in the office. His eyes were dark, and his mouth was tight. Without bothering to shut his car door, he began striding toward us.

What the heck?

I looked back to Stuart and did a double-take. His face was pale, and his eyes were wide. He glanced around as if searching for a hole to hide in.

Under his breath, he urged, "Lemme in, alright?"

I was so surprised, I could hardly think. "In what?"

His voice rose almost a full octave. "The truck, the truck."

I couldn't fathom why he'd say it twice, but I had no time to ask him – or to let him in, because already, Jaden was standing right beside him, blocking the driver's side door.

Unless Stuart wanted to bolt for the passenger's side, he *wasn't* getting in – not without going through Jaden anyway.

As if trying to play it cool, Stuart gave Jaden a shaky smile. "Oh, hey."

Jaden's voice was flat. "What are you doing?"

Stuart swallowed with an audible gulp. "Nothing."

Jaden took a single step toward him. "Is that so?"

Stuart stepped back. "Uh, yeah. Totally."

From inside the truck, I asked, "What's going on?"

It was Stuart who answered. "Nothing."

It was the same thing he'd just told Jaden. I hadn't believed him then, and I didn't believe him now.

Obviously, *something* was going on. *But what?*

I looked to Jaden. "Well?"

And of course, he completely ignored me. He was still focused on Stuart, who even now, was backing up another step.

Stuart held up his hands in mock surrender. "Hey, I was just leaving."

I felt myself frown. Okay, it's not like I'd been happy to see Stuart. But I'd been even *less* happy to see Jaden, who, if anything, was a bigger jackass than my ex. *And that was saying something.*

Already, they'd traveled several paces beyond my driver's side door. If they kept on going, they'd eventually end up at Stuart's new truck.

And then what?

Honestly, I had no idea.

I shoved open my truck door and climbed out of the vehicle. I strode toward them, calling out, "Will one of you *please* tell me?"

Without looking, Jaden replied, "Tell you what?"

I made a sound of frustration. "What you're doing here for starters."

With his gaze still on Stuart, Jaden replied, "I'm checking on my investment."

Okay, that made zero sense. "What investment?"

"You."

I stopped moving. *Did he just call me an investment?*

Talk about insulting.

Plus, I had no idea what he meant.

I looked to Stuart. Although he was still facing my direction, his eyes were glued to Jaden. With another step backward, he mumbled, "Yeah, well, I'd better get going, huh?" He gave a nervous laugh. "Long drive and all."

As for Jaden, he took another step forward, moving with slow deliberation, like he had all the time in the world.

But to do what?

That was the million dollar question.

I stalked toward them and stopped not quite between them, since there was no room and all, but directly next to them. I looked from

Stuart to Jaden and back again.

"Well?" I repeated.

Stuart cleared his throat. "Yeah, well, I'd better get going."

Hadn't he already said that?

He looked like a gazelle, who wanted to bolt, but didn't quite dare, lest he become instant dinner.

I looked to Jaden. "How about you? Do *you* need to get going?"

In a dangerously low voice, he replied, "Me?" He gave Stuart a cold smile. "Nah. I've got all day."

The smile did nothing to ease my worry. "To do what?"

His smile vanished. "Whatever it takes."

Well, that was informative. With a little huff, I said, "Will you *please* look at me?"

Slowly, Jaden turned his head in my direction. "Yeah, what?"

That's when Stuart made his move. Channeling his inner gazelle, he turned and bolted for the red truck. Moving faster than I'd ever seen him, he yanked open the driver's side door and practically dove inside. A split-second later, the engine roared to life, and the truck squealed away, leaving me staring after it.

I kept watching even as it rounded the next corner and disappeared from sight.

Well, that wasn't strange or anything.

I looked back at Jaden and demanded, "What was that about?"

In reply, all he said was, "See you Monday." And with that, he turned and strode back to his own vehicle.

I watched in stunned silence as he climbed inside and drove slowly off, leaving me staring after him.

Beyond curious, I tried calling Stuart.

He didn't answer.

I left a message.

He didn't call me back.

I sent a few texts.

I received none in reply.

It wasn't until Cassidy came home an hour later that I had any insight at all. But weirdest thing was, it didn't make me feel any better.

CHAPTER 18

"So then," I continued, "he says, 'See you Monday' and drives off."

Cassidy frowned. "Just like that?"

"Yeah. Just like that."

We were sitting in the living room of our new apartment. A full hour had passed since that scene outside, and I still had no idea what had truly happened.

On the nearby sofa, Cassidy looked just as confused as I felt. She said, "And you *still* haven't heard from Stuart?"

"No. And I've called him like ten times."

"Maybe his phone's dead," she suggested.

"Maybe." I paused. "But it was all so strange. Like for starters, how did either one of them know where I live?"

"Well, with Jaden, that's easy," she said. "I mean, you *do* work for him."

"So?"

"So you probably filled out some paperwork, right?"

I shook my head. "Not yet. I'm supposed to be doing that on Friday."

"Oh." She paused for a long moment and then perked up. "Wait, I know. It was *their* realtor who showed us the apartment. Jaden probably got the address from her."

Now, this made sense. Yesterday, before leaving their house, Jax had set us up with his own personal realtor to help us find an apartment. And that realtor had shown us exactly one place, *this* place.

Apparently, she'd been so certain that we'd take it, she hadn't planned on showing us anything else. And of course, she'd been totally right. We'd pounced on it like kittens on yarn, especially after she mentioned that the property owners were offering two key incentives – the first month's rent for free and a complete waiver on the security deposit.

In truth, I still couldn't believe our good luck.

"Okay," I said, "but what about Stuart? How would *he* know where I live?"

"You didn't ask?"

"I didn't have time," I said. "Honestly, I didn't even *think* to ask until he was already gone."

Cassidy leaned forward on the sofa. "Wanna know what I think?"

"What?"

"I think he's got a tracking device on the truck."

"Stuart?" I had to laugh. "Oh, please, he's not that devious."

"He doesn't need to be devious," she said. "These days, they're super-cheap." She gave a little frown. "He probably has an app right there on his phone. And as you know, he *did* love that truck."

Oh, crap. She could be right. If she was, what would that mean? *That Stuart could find me anywhere, any time?* It was a distressing thought.

"But wait," I said. "The truck wasn't even here when Stuart showed up."

"So?" she said. "It was parked here all last night, right there in the driveway." She rolled her eyes. "Even Stuart would've known what *that* meant."

Well, there was that.

Slowly, I turned and looked toward the front of the apartment. From here, I couldn't see the truck, but her theory *did* make a lot of sense – except for one thing. I turned back to her and said, "But if that were the case, he would've found me yesterday." I forced a laugh. "Or sent someone else to find me."

"What do you mean?" she asked.

"Well, I didn't want to worry you, but…" I bit my lip. "…yesterday, he threatened to call the police. I was almost sure he meant it, too. But then, he didn't. So, I guess I should be thankful, huh?"

Cassidy made a face. It was the same face she always made

whenever I said something nice about Stuart. "How do you know he *didn't* call the police?"

"That's easy," I said. "They never showed up."

Cassidy gave a quiet scoff, but said nothing in reply.

I gave her a perplexed look. "What?"

"Okay, fine," she said. "I didn't want to tell you, but actually..." She winced. "They did show up."

My jaw dropped. "What? When?"

"While you were in the shower."

I looked toward the rear of the apartment.

Quickly, Cassidy added, "I don't mean here. I meant at Jax's house, yesterday."

I was staring now. "You're kidding."

"I wish."

"And you didn't think to tell me?"

She gave me a faint smile. "I didn't want you to worry."

At the thought of Stuart's treachery, I sat back in my chair. "That jerk."

"You don't need to tell *me*," she said. "I never liked him, you know."

My head was spinning as I considered his recent visit. "Do you know, when he was here, he acted like the whole truck thing never happened? I mean, yeah, he wanted me to apologize, but other than that, he was all friendly and stuff."

Cassidy's gaze narrowed. "*How* friendly?"

"Get this," I said. "He suggested we 'nap' together."

"Do you mean nap-nap, or..."

"No. I mean the *other* kind, where you don't sleep."

"Oh." She was making that face again. "God, what an ass. What did you tell him?"

"Nothing. That's when Jaden showed up, acting all crazy."

Cassidy gave a rueful laugh. "Good thing, too."

I wasn't following. "How so?"

"I'm just saying, he probably did you a favor."

I couldn't help but scoff. "Jaden? Oh, please."

But even as I said it, I recalled him talking to Stuart yesterday on my cell phone. Among other things, he'd told Stuart to leave me alone. *Or else.*

Come to think of it, he'd also mentioned something about the police, hadn't he?

And now, I didn't know what to think. Apparently, Jaden had known a lot more than I'd realized. Heck, when it came to the whole truck thing, he probably knew more than *I* did.

I looked to Cassidy and said, "Hey, a question. Yesterday, did he know the police stopped by?"

"You mean Jaden?" Cassidy nodded. "Oh yeah. He was the one who dealt with them."

"Dealt with them how?"

"I don't know," she said. "That's all I know. He dealt with the police *and* the truck."

"Oh."

It suddenly struck me that he'd gone to an awful lot of trouble on my behalf. In fact, he'd gone to *extra bonus trouble*, if I considered him showing up here to get rid of Stuart.

But that wasn't for *my* benefit. That was for himself.

Right?

He'd called me his "investment." That didn't sound warm and fuzzy. It sounded cold and businesslike.

Then again, I was his assistant, even if he wasn't terribly happy about it.

Cassidy and I were still trying to sort things out when a knock sounded at the apartment door. I looked to Cassidy and asked, "Are you expecting someone?"

She shook her head. "No. Are you?"

"Not me." As I made my way to the door, I mentally ran through the list of potential visitors. *Stuart? Jaden? Jax? Cassidy's godawful mom?*

But it wasn't any of those people. It was someone I'd never met – an older guy in a business suit, who introduced himself as the Bishop Brothers' head of security and then promptly informed me that he needed the keys to the truck.

"For what?" I asked.

"Mister Bishop's orders."

Mister Bishop? At the whole "mister" thing, I almost wanted to snicker. Even so, it wasn't lost on me that I probably *would* need to start addressing both of them in a more formal manner. They were soon to be my employers, after all.

Cassidy joined me at the door. "*Which* Mister Bishop?" she asked. "Jax or Jaden?"

Without cracking a smile, he said, "Jaden."

Reluctantly, I asked. "Is this some sort of repo thing?"

His brow wrinkled. "Excuse me?"

"I mean, is he taking back the truck?"

It wasn't that far-fetched. Technically, the truck belonged to *him*, not me. *Was he was taking it back until my actual start date?*

The guy looked at me like I was nuts. "Back to where?"

I tried again. "I mean, are you taking it back until Monday?"

"No," he said. "I'm taking it for a security check."

"Oh." With mixed feelings, I dug out the keys and handed them over.

As the guy turned to go, he said over his shoulder, "I'll be back in an hour."

Actually, he was back in fifty-three minutes. As he handed me the keys, I asked, "So, did you find anything?"

"Sorry, can't discuss it," he said. "You'll have to ask Mister Bishop."

This time, I knew which brother he meant. Obviously, he was talking about Jaden who – as I learned one week later – didn't care for that "mister" thing at all, at least from me.

CHAPTER 19

Standing in the open doorway to my new office, Jaden gave me an annoyed look. "*What* did you just call me?"

From behind my desk, I cleared my throat. "Um, Mister Bishop?"

Even to my own ears, it sounded strange and oddly obscene. Worse, I didn't even know why. After all, that's what everyone else called him, and it never sounded funny when *they* did it.

"Call me that again," he said, "and you're getting a new office." His voice hardened. "In the basement."

Well, this was just great. I'd been on the job for barely three hours, and already, he was threatening to banish me to the underworld.

It was a discouraging thought. But then, I felt my gaze narrow. "Wait a minute. Does this building *have* a basement?"

It was eleven o'clock, and I'd just finished with my orientation and corporate tour, courtesy of Louise in Human Resources. The building was sixteen stories high and served as the headquarters of *Bishop Brothers International*, my new place of employment.

During the last few hours, I'd visited all sixteen floors, where I'd been introduced to the heads of marketing, accounting, quality control, and more. I'd even had a tour of the mail room, which was located on the ground level – meaning the *first* floor of the building and definitely *not* in the basement.

Afterward, I'd been delivered to my own office, which was directly across from Jaden's. As far as offices went, I counted myself lucky. It was large and luxurious, with a comfy chair and beautiful desk. It even had lamps and pictures on the wall, plus my own little conference table nestled off to the side.

No basement office would look like *this*.

In reply to my question, Jaden said, "Yes. There is."

So there was a basement? I wasn't quite sure I believed him. "Really? What's down there?"

"What, you wanna find out?"

Today, he was wearing another business suit. This one was dark gray, but not nearly as dark as his eyes. His tie was red, and his shoes looked very expensive.

Funny, he looked almost civilized. But I knew better. Underneath that polished exterior were a whole bunch of muscles and tattoos – not to mention a heart made of stone.

As for myself, I was wearing a classic black dress. It was short, but not too short, and form-fitting, but definitely not tight.

It might've been just my imagination, but I was almost certain I saw a flicker of surprise in Jaden's eyes when I'd shown up looking perfectly respectable.

Really, I was just glad the movers had arrived on schedule, delivering all of my belongings from Nashville. Everything had been perfectly packed, too, courtesy of the moving allowance that had been included in my employment package.

If Jaden had asked – which he didn't – I might've told him that I had a surprisingly good wardrobe, thanks to my previous employer, a guy who felt that image was everything.

The only downside was, my wardrobe had cost me a small fortune, which meant that my credit cards were nearly maxed as a result.

Now, I was determined to pay them off – and quickly, too. But in order to do that, it was pretty important that I survive my first day without getting fired.

In reply to Jaden's question, I summoned up my sweetest smile. "I'll pass on the basement tour, but thanks for the offer."

He gave a low scoff. "You wouldn't thank me if you saw it."

I didn't doubt this for one minute. If there really *was* a basement, it was probably one of those electrical-mechanical things that housed no people, just stuff.

And now, I didn't know what to say. I was still searching for a snappy comeback when he said, "By the way, you've got a lunch meeting at eleven-fifteen."

I glanced at my watch and stifled a gasp. That was only four minutes from now. "Really? With who?"

"Me."

CHAPTER 20

From the other side of the table, Jaden asked, "So, did you bring it?"

"You mean the description?" Nodding, I reached for the slim folder that I'd brought with me to the restaurant. "Sure, I've got it right here."

Back at the office, when I'd asked him if I needed to bring anything to this impromptu meeting, all he'd said was, "Yeah. Your job description."

Thanks to my orientation with Louise, I actually had one. From what I could tell, it was the same description that I'd seen on Jax's desk during that initial interview.

The duties were pretty straightforward – answer phones, schedule meetings, make reservations, handle travel arrangements, and so on. There was nothing on the list that I couldn't handle, and I was determined to prove Jaden wrong for thinking otherwise.

Across from me, he held out his hand. "Lemme see it."

When I handed it over, he gave the sheet a quick glance and then – *What the hell?* – ripped it right in half.

I stared across the table. "What are you doing?"

In reply, he tore the sheet again and then tossed aside the pieces. "This stuff?" he said, flicking his chin toward the destruction. "It's nothing."

I frowned. "So I'm *not* supposed to be doing those things?"

"Oh, you'll be doing them." His gaze met mine. "But that's not worth what you're getting."

I sat very still in my seat. I wasn't quite sure what he was getting at, but I didn't like the sounds of it.

Very carefully, I said, "Are you referring to my salary? Like you expect something extra?"

For some reason, the word "extra" felt like it was loaded with all kinds of innuendo. *Would a blowjob in his office count as an extra?* Because if it did, he had the wrong girl.

Oh, it's not like I disliked that sort of thing. In fact, I enjoyed it quite a bit. But I sure as hell wasn't going to crawl under his desk just because I was being paid or because he expected it.

And I couldn't help but notice that he'd phrased it oh-so carefully, too, in that "Gee-she-must've-misunderstood" sort of way, in case I lodged a formal complaint.

What an asshole.

He leaned back in his chair. "What do *you* think?"

Oh, so *that's* how he was playing it? I gave him a stiff smile. "If you're talking about a blowjob under the desk, you can forget it."

He looked at me for a long silent moment. And then, he gave a snort of derision. "Dream on. I can get *that* any day of the week."

Huh?

Okay, yes, I realized that no doubt, he *could* get that – and a whole lot more – any time he wanted. But this wasn't the thing that surprised me. It was his odd reaction.

And "dream on" – seriously?

What did he think? That I sat around dreaming about his cock?

Talk about arrogant.

And now, the jackass was laughing. "What, you've been thinking about my 'desk'?" He said desk like it was the filthiest word imaginable.

"I, uh…" *Holy crap.* What if I *had* totally misread it? If so, I'd just made a complete ass of myself. But if not, he *had* to be gaslighting me, making me think that *I* was the crazy one.

I straightened in my seat. "I don't like to play games," I told him, "so if you meant something else, you might as well tell me."

Just then, we were interrupted by the waitress coming to take our orders. She was tall and statuesque, with stunning blue eyes and the kind of cleavage that guaranteed no one would notice – meaning her eyes, of course.

Five minutes earlier, when she'd delivered our drinks – soda for me and a beer for him – she'd been all kinds of flirty, too, like she'd be willing to serve up her panties if only Jaden asked.

But he *hadn't* asked. In fact, he hadn't paid her much attention at all.

Still, the whole thing had been pretty darn annoying – not that I was jealous or anything. But still, how did she know that we *weren't* a couple?

I mean, for all she knew, I could be his lunch date.

After I murdered him, that is.

He looked to the waitress and said, "She'll have a sandwich."

My jaw clenched. "Are you seriously ordering for me?"

And a sandwich of all things?

I knew exactly why he'd said that, too. I almost rolled my eyes. *Ha-freaking-ha.*

And now, he looked ready to laugh. "What, you wanna do it?"

My chin lifted. "Yes. As a matter of fact, I do."

"Just so you know..." He grinned. "...they make a good pastrami."

Through gritted teeth, I said, "I don't *want* a sandwich."

He shrugged. "Eh, your loss."

Actually, it *was* my loss. I loved pastrami. In fact, I'd been planning to order pastrami until he'd ruined everything by choosing it on my behalf.

The jerk.

And now, no one was saying a word, not even the waitress, who stood there, giving me an expectant look.

Jaden said, "She's waiting for your order."

"Oh." *Of course she was.* I knew that. Or, rather, I would've known that if only Jaden hadn't thrown me off-kilter.

Now, feeling more self-conscious than ever, I gave the menu a nervous glance. I didn't even know what I wanted, not anymore. *And why?* It was because I'd stopped reading after pastrami.

I heard myself say, "I'll have the chicken."

The waitress frowned. "You mean the grilled chicken sandwich?"

Oh, God. Another sandwich? My mouth watered at the thought. But if I ordered a sandwich now, I'd never hear the end of it.

Damn it.

I forced myself to say, "No. But thanks. I'll have the *other* chicken." I tried to smile. "Please."

She was still frowning. "You mean the chicken dinner?"

It was a little early for a chicken dinner, but whatever. I gave a jerky nod, only to die of embarrassment when she informed me that they didn't serve dinners until after four.

I gave Jaden another look. Did he know this? *Probably.* It suddenly struck me that there had been a whole lot of sandwiches on the lunch menu – and not much else.

The jackass.

I blurted out, "Salad. That's what I'll have."

The waitress gave me a perplexed look. "The chicken salad?"

I gave a distracted nod. "Sure, thanks."

When she looked to Jaden, he ordered a pastrami on rye. *Of course.* I *loved* pastrami on rye. He probably knew this, too.

I don't know how he knew, but it couldn't be a coincidence.

Probably, he *also* knew that I loved beer. Maybe *that's* why he'd ordered it – to taunt me with that frosty mug of liquid bliss, knowing that I'd never order beer on the job, especially on my very first day.

Fine. Whatever.

It was a little early for beer and pastrami, anyway.

When the waitress left, Jaden leaned across the table and said in a low voice, "That's a sandwich, you know."

Oh, so now he was rubbing it in?

I gave him a stiff smile. "I *know* it's a sandwich. I've *had* pastrami before."

His mouth twitched. "I meant the chicken."

I blinked. "What?"

"The thing you ordered. Chicken salad. It's a sandwich."

I shook my head. "No."

He nodded. "Yeah, comes on a croissant."

Heat flooded my face. "Oh." Coming from Nashville, I was well versed in the uses of chicken salad. And yet, I hadn't even thought to ask – or check the menu, for that matter.

I was definitely off my game. Of course, it didn't help that the whole "blowjob under the desk" thing was still hanging out there, like undies on a clothes line.

As I mentally reeled them back in, I waffled between demanding to know what he meant by "extras" or praying that he'd just drop the matter entirely.

My gaze shifted to the tattered remnants of my job description. *What on Earth had he meant?*

I was still staring at the torn pieces of paper when he said, "And just for the record, that's not the way I work."

I looked up. "Sorry, what?"

"Extras," he said. "And the thing with the desk." His expression grew serious. "That's not in the description, written or otherwise."

"Oh." *I was saying that a lot lately, wasn't I?* But he made me feel so stupidly tongue-tied.

"And," he continued, "if anyone gives you that kind of trouble, you tell me. I'll handle it."

I looked at him for a long moment, waiting for the punchline.

None came.

In fact, he looked deadly serious.

Before I could stop myself, I'd already said, "You mean like you handled Stuart?"

"Him?" Jaden scoffed. "No. The guy's a douche."

Yes. He was. But I so didn't want to admit it. "Well, we're broken up now, so…" I didn't bother finishing the sentence.

Jaden gave me a penetrating look. "Does *he* know that?"

"Sorry, what?"

"Stuart – does he know you're broken up?"

What kind of question was that? "Of course he knows."

Again, Jaden leaned back in his seat. "Uh-huh."

What did that mean?

I said, "Why do you ask?"

"It seems to me, he forgot."

"Forgot what? That we're not together?"

"Yeah. That."

This whole conversation had gone way off-track. Really, this was none of his business, and I was tempted to tell him so. But I didn't, because it was a topic that I'd been hoping to bring up myself. I shifted nervously in my seat. *No time like the present, right?*

CHAPTER 21

Sitting in the quiet restaurant, I took a deep breath and just asked what I'd been dying to know. "That thing last Monday – what was that about?"

Jaden said, "What thing?"

"Oh come on, you know what. At my apartment, there I am, outside talking with Stuart when *you* show up – out of nowhere, I might add – and scare him off."

"Was that a problem?"

I studied his face. Weird, he looked genuinely curious.

And, as far as his question, I didn't have a good answer. Finally, I murmured, "Well, it *was* strange."

"Yeah? You wanna know what's more strange?"

"What?"

"Him. Calling the cops for something he could've handled himself."

Now, I didn't know what to say. Obviously, he was referring to the fact that Stuart had reported me to the police.

"Yeah, well, I didn't *know* he actually called them. I mean, he *threatened* to, but I thought he was bluffing."

Jaden gave a low scoff. "No, you didn't."

"Oh, so now you're a mind reader?"

"I don't need to be," he said. "It was obvious."

"By what?"

"Your face."

Feeling suddenly self-conscious, I reached up to touch the side of my cheek. My skin felt excessively warm, but that was completely irrelevant. "What about it?" I asked.

"I'm not talking *now*," he said. "I'm talking when you showed up at the house. You kept looking at the truck, like you were waiting for trouble."

"I did not," I protested.

"And," he said, "once you got inside, you kept looking toward the front door, like you were waiting for the swat team to bust through it."

I tried to scoff. "No, I wasn't."

"And," he continued, "you looked scared shitless."

Okay, now that was just plain insulting. "I wasn't scared," I told him. "I was annoyed."

"Yeah." Again, he looked ready to laugh. "With *me*."

Whatever the joke was, I didn't get it. I gave a hard nod. "Exactly."

"But me, you *weren't* scared of."

It was simple statement. And it was true. I *hadn't* been scared of him. I'd even marched into his house and – my face suddenly felt a few degrees warmer – destroyed his lunch, too.

But he totally had it coming. And plus, I'd been too annoyed to be scared.

Across from me, Jaden said, "It was a dick move."

"Sorry, what?"

"Calling the cops."

"Oh, so you're an expert in dick moves, are you?" As soon as the words left my mouth, I wanted to take them back, not because they were rude, but because the words "dick" and "move" were just a little too suggestive, considering the rest of our conversation.

I cleared my throat. "I'm just saying, you're no angel yourself."

"Damn straight," he said.

I hesitated. *Wasn't he supposed to argue the point?*

Guess not.

I waved away the distraction. "But you never answered my question. Outside my apartment – why'd you show up?" Before he could answer, I added, "And, how'd you know Stuart was there?" My voice picked up steam as I tossed out yet another question. "And that security guy, what was that about?"

Part of me didn't expect an answer to any of these questions, but hey, it didn't hurt to ask, right?

"I'll tell you," Jaden said. "But first, I've got a question of my own."

"What?"

"Where do you think he got the truck?"

I stared across the table. "Who do you mean? Stuart?"

"Yeah." Jaden's mouth tightened. *"Him."*

Obviously, he meant the classic red truck that Stuart had driven to my apartment. I hadn't asked Stuart where he bought it, mostly because I hadn't cared. "I don't know," I admitted. "From a dealer, I guess."

"Guess again."

I gave it some thought. "From a private collector, maybe someone in Tennessee?"

Jaden replied, "Now, you're only half wrong."

I gave him a challenging smile. "Or maybe I'm half *right*."

"Fair enough," he said. "But which half?"

Now, this was easy. In my mind's eye, I could still see that red truck parked in front of my apartment. The Tennessee license plate was a dead giveaway. "The Tennessee part."

Jax gave a low scoff. "Now you're *all* wrong."

"What?"

"He bought it *here* in Florida, from a private collector."

I shook my head. "But it had Tennessee plates."

"Not a couple weeks ago, it didn't."

"What do you mean?"

"I mean, we switched them out."

"Switched what? The plates?" And then, I sat back as Jaden's full statement caught up with me. "Wait a minute. Who's 'we'?"

"You can't guess?"

I could. I just didn't want to. "Don't tell me *you* were the private collector?"

"Alright."

"Sorry, what?"

"I won't tell you."

"But you *were*?" I was staring again. "So *you* were the one who sold him the truck?"

"It wasn't a sale. It was a trade." Jaden gave a tight shrug. "Other than that, good guess."

It hadn't been *that* good, considering that it took me a few tries to figure it out. "But how?" I asked.

"The usual way," he said. "Draw up the papers, deliver the goods, call it a deal."

"But that's not what I meant. I'm just saying, he doesn't even live here."

"So? We handled it over the phone."

Now, this made *some* sense. After all, I'd overheard part of their conversation, or rather, *conversations*, as in plural. And now that I thought about it, there'd surely been a few more calls that I *hadn't* overheard.

"But how did he get here?" I asked. "I mean, *I* had his old truck so…"

"So he flew."

"On such short notice? But isn't that expensive?" I tried to laugh. "I bet Stuart just *loved* that." I hesitated. "Wait, he *did* pay for the flight, right?"

"In a manner of speaking."

"What does *that* mean?"

"It means, I wanted the problem to go away."

Now, I wanted to cringe. "So *you* paid for the flight?"

"More or less." He gave another shrug. "I sent the jet to pick him up."

"The jet?" I swallowed. "As in *your* jet?"

"Mine and Jax's," he clarified. "Or the company's, depending on how technical you wanna get."

Holy crap. I'd never actually flown on a private jet, but I *did* know they weren't cheap to operate.

As I tallied up everything that my little truck adventure had cost him, I was having a hard time catching my breath. And to think, he hadn't even griped about it, or demanded payment, or tried to make me feel guilty.

In fact, he hadn't mentioned the truck at all until I'd started asking.

I heard myself say, "Why?"

"Why what?"

"Why would you do that?"

"Like I said, I wanted the problem to go away."

"But surely there were cheaper ways," I said. "I mean, the truck could've been delivered, right?" Under the table, I was wringing my hands. "Or was that even more expensive?"

"Don't know, don't care."

"What?"

"I wanted to see for myself."

"See *what* for yourself?"

"What kind of pussy calls the cops on girl trying to rescue her friend."

My breath caught. "Oh." I sat back in my seat. Of all the things I'd been expecting him to say, this wasn't even on the list. It was surprisingly chivalrous and more thoughtful than I ever would've imagined.

In a very quiet voice, I said, "Thank you. For everything, really."

He frowned. "Don't."

"Don't what?"

"Don't thank me."

"Why not?" I asked. "You did me a huge favor."

"No. I didn't."

"But—"

"I wasn't doing it for you."

A new rush of heat flooded my face. And here, I thought the whole blowjob thing had been awkward. But for some stupid reason, this exchange felt ten times worse, because I had no idea what to say.

Into the silence, I stammered, "Oh. Right. I mean, I know. You were probably doing it for Jax, right?"

"No." He paused as if thinking. "Sure, he told me to handle it. But I wasn't doing it for him."

"Then who?"

"Me."

I stared across the table. "I don't get it. Why you?"

His gaze met mine. "Why not?"

Huh?

That was no kind of answer, and now, I didn't know what to say.

Happily, I was saved the trouble when the waitress appeared with two sandwiches – the chicken salad for me and the pastrami for him. As she set them on the table, she looked to Jaden and practically cooed, "Can I get you anything else, Mister Bishop."

"No. We're good." Almost as an afterthought, he added, "Thanks."

When she left, I couldn't resist saying, "*Mister* Bishop?"

"Yeah, so?"

"Well, you told me not to ever call you that."

"Yeah, but she's not you."

I wasn't quite sure what that meant, but I didn't dare assume anything. If he were anyone else, I might think this was a gesture of friendship or maybe something more.

But this was Jaden Bishop. And for the most part, we hadn't been friendly. Besides, he was still my employer.

Stalling, I picked up my sandwich and took a little nibble. It was amazingly good. Still, it was no pastrami.

I looked up and gave his sandwich a longing look as he took his first bite. But then, our eyes met, and I felt a little flutter deep in my stomach. In the end, it wasn't the *sandwich* that made my mouth water. It was *him*.

Damn it.

CHAPTER 22

Back at the apartment, Cassidy was saying, "So Stuart got that truck from *Jaden*? You're kidding."

"I wish." I gave a shaky laugh. "Or maybe I *don't* wish. Actually, I don't know what to think." I shoved a nervous hand through my hair. "He's the most confusing person I've ever met."

She frowned. "Stuart?"

"No. Jaden. I mean, most of the time he's a total jerk, but then, I see hints of something more. Like with the whole truck thing, it was actually pretty nice."

"Jaden Bishop? Nice?" She laughed. "You're kidding, right?"

Was I? I gave it some thought. He was definitely a smart-ass. And he'd scared the crap out of Stuart. But in reality, I'd never seen Jaden do anything cruel, unless I counted him giving me such a hard time when I'd first shown up on his doorstep.

And even then, he'd been annoying more than anything.

Plus, unlike Stuart, he *hadn't* called the police.

When I explained all of this to Cassidy, she said, "But I don't get it, why would *Jaden* call the police?"

"You know, for that whole scene at the house."

She bit her lip. "Oh. Yeah, there *is* that."

Cassidy still didn't know about the incident with the sandwich, and I had no plans to tell her. The way *I* saw it, she'd been embarrassed by me more than enough already.

She asked, "But what about the license plate? How did Jaden explain that?"

"He didn't, but I think I figured it out." As she listened, I told her my theory – that they'd simply transferred the plates from Stuart's *old* truck to Stuart's *new* truck.

"But wait," Cassidy said, "so what kind of plates are on *your* truck?"

"Technically, it's not my truck," I reminded her. "It's Jaden's."

"Oh, you know what I mean."

I did. So I went on to tell her that when I actually looked, I discovered that the truck I was currently driving was now sporting Florida license plates.

Looking perplexed, Cassidy glanced in the general direction of the driveway. "Really? I didn't notice."

"Yeah. Me neither until I checked. I mean, it's not like I spend a lot of time looking at the back bumper."

"So when did he switch them?" she asked.

"I don't know."

"Maybe that security guy did it."

I shrugged. "Maybe."

"You don't know?"

I shook my head. "I was going to ask, but…" I sighed. "It just got all weird and awkward. Like get this, I try to thank Jaden for the whole truck thing, and what does he say? He tells me that he did it for himself, and *not* for me."

"Were those his exact words?"

"More or less," I said. "And after that, I didn't want to talk about it."

"Why not?"

"Because it was embarrassing."

Little did Cassidy know, it was even *more* embarrassing when I started having all those warm, fuzzy thoughts. It didn't even make sense. After all, it's not like I liked him or anything.

"Anyway," I continued, "we spent the rest of lunch talking about my job."

Cassidy snickered. "As in blowjobs under the desk?"

I glared at her. "I already told you, it's not funny."

"Yes, it is."

When I'd first told her the story, I'd thought she was going to die laughing, especially when I told her what Jaden had *really* meant by "something extra."

Not only was this extra task perfectly respectable, it wasn't even that complicated – or so I thought at the time.

But the sad truth was, it was a lot harder than it sounded, especially the next afternoon, when I had to do it for the very first time.

CHAPTER 23

In the executive suite, the twenty-something redhead was glaring down at me. "I *know* he's in there."

I crossed my arms. "No, he's not."

She gave a little stomp of her foot. "He is, too!"

Just like the waitress from yesterday, the redhead was tall and statuesque. *Was it just a Florida thing?* I mean, I fully realized that I wasn't tall, but I'd never felt quite so short until now.

Of course, it didn't help that she was wearing heels at least three inches tall.

I straightened to my fullest height, not that it did much good. "If you'd like to leave your name," I said, "I'll make sure that he gets the message."

Even as I said it, I wondered who this chick was and why she'd been trying to barge into Jaden's office – until I'd thrown myself in her path, that is.

Inside the building, we all wore badges – well, except for Jax and Jaden. But *she* wore no badge, and already I'd tried several times – unsuccessfully – to get her name.

Towering over me, she gave a little huff. "And just so you know, you're in *my* seat."

What seat? I glanced around. I wasn't even sitting. I was standing outside Jaden's office door, blocking her from barging in.

I felt my gaze narrow. "What was that? A short joke? Because I've heard better."

She looked at me like I was crazy. "What are you getting at?"

"I'm not sitting. I'm standing. So if that's a joke, it's totally nonsensical."

She gave a snort of derision. "I'm not here to 'joke' with you. I'm here to see Jaden."

Yes. She was. I knew this because she'd told me like ten times already.

I gave her a no-nonsense look. "And *I'm* here to tell you that he's *not* in." I wasn't even lying. It was late afternoon, and I hadn't seen him since early this morning.

She pursed her lips. "You really don't get it, do you?"

"Get what?"

She turned and pointed toward my office. "*That's* my seat."

"Excuse me?"

"That seat," she repeated, pointing again for emphasis. "It's mine. And *your* ass is in it."

I peered around her and studied my desk. And then, I looked back to her.

Finally, I realized why her voice sounded so familiar. This *had* to be Morgan, Jaden's previous assistant, the one who'd been so snippy when I'd been desperate to reach Cassidy.

I considered what I knew. Morgan had been fired, and quite recently, too. I still didn't know the full story, but I *did* know that she was nothing but trouble. After all, this was the same chick who'd told me that godawful story about Cassidy and the brothers.

Now, *I* was the one glaring. *Would it be unprofessional to tell her exactly what I was thinking?*

Probably.

Damn it.

I tried to look on the bright side. Now that I knew what she looked like, maybe I'd get lucky and run into her at the grocery store or something. And then, I could give her a peace of my mind without jeopardizing my job.

But that would have to wait. So instead, I gave her my sweetest smile. "It's not there now."

"What?"

"My ass," I helpfully added. "Since you seemed so concerned and all."

Her eyes narrowed, and her nostrils flared. She moved closer, until she was looming over me like a vulture, looking to pick a carcass clean. "Listen here, *chickie*," she said. "I don't give two shits about your ass, unless you're talking about moving it the hell out of here."

Well, that degenerated quickly.

Now, with her standing so close, I had to crane my neck to stare up at her. Still, I refused to back down. Still smiling, I gritted out, "And *I* don't give 'two shits' who are you are or what you want. He's not in, just like I said."

"Oh, please," she scoffed. "I know how this works. I used to have your job, remember?"

"Yes. I do." I summoned up another smile. "And how'd that go?"

"What do you mean?"

"I'm just wondering, how'd you do in the job?"

Her jaw clenched. "You've got a lot of nerve, you know that?"

Yes. I did. But Jaden's instructions had been very clear. My primary responsibility, in addition to the things on that list, was to, as *he* put it, keep people off his ass – and out of his office.

At the time, it sounded like nothing at all. But now, as I guarded his office door, I was wondering if I deserved a raise.

The funny thing was, I might've been guarding the door for nothing. I mean, it could be locked for all *I* knew. After all, it's not like I tried the doorknob.

Morgan gave another little huff. "So, are you gonna move or what?"

"Sure," I said. "As soon as you do."

"Excuse me?"

"When you leave, I'll move."

"Oh yeah? Well, I'm not leaving." She threw back her shoulders. "So there."

"So there?" In spite of everything, I almost snickered. "Well, I guess you showed *me*."

"What, you think it's funny?"

I made no reply even though yes, the situation *was* pretty ridiculous.

But nearly a half-hour later, I didn't feel like laughing at all.

And why?

It was because she still hadn't left.

Instead, she just stood there, vulturing over me in that predatory way of hers, even as I held my ground – refusing to step aside *or* look away. By now, my neck was stiff and my spine was twitchy.

If by some mishap, I died at my post, she'd probably feast on my flesh and spit out the bones. She certainly seemed the type.

But what about Jaden?

If he came in and found her picking at my carcass, would he care?

Or join in?

Yes, my mind *was* wandering, but what else could I do?

She and I hadn't spoken for at least twenty minutes, and I couldn't help but grudgingly admire her persistence. If she admired mine, she sure as heck wasn't showing it. Mostly, she glowered and huffed, as if hoping to menace me into submission.

Dream on, sister. I had four older brothers. If I wasn't scared of *them*, I wasn't going to be scared off by the likes of her.

Still, in the back of my mind, I had to wonder, how long this would last. The executive suite was spacious, but secluded, with only the office of Jax and his assistant nearby.

Jax was out of town, and I hadn't yet met his assistant. For *I* knew, she was out of town, too. This meant that I was on my own – for now, at least.

With Morgan blocking my view, I didn't see Jaden enter the suite. But I *did* hear him, saying, "What are you doing?"

In unison, Morgan and I turned to look. At the sight of my boss, she practically squealed, "Jaden! Thank God you're here."

CHAPTER 24

Already, she was bounding toward him, all legs and heels. As for Jaden, he stood and watched with an expression that suggested he wasn't nearly as happy to see *her* as she was to see *him*.

With another squeal, she threw her arms around his neck and held on tight, even when he made no move to return the embrace.

Now, she was practically hanging off him, which was quite a feat, considering that with the heels, she was just a few inches shorter than he was.

As she held on for dear life, Jaden repeated his question. "What are you doing?"

Without letting go, Morgan replied, "She's being a pill, that's what. Do you know, I've been here for like two hours? And she totally refused to let me in."

I made a scoffing sound. "Oh, please. It was a half-hour, tops."

Thirty long minutes, not that I was complaining – yet.

Morgan let go of Jaden and whirled to face me. "That's a total lie." She looked back to him and announced, "And she cursed me out, too."

My mouth fell open. "I did not!" In fact, I'd been pretty proud of my self-control. After all, this was no grocery store.

She was glaring again. "You did too. You said, 'ass.'"

"Yeah, because you said it first."

Jaden's voice cut through the noise. "Morgan."

She turned to look. "What?"

"I wasn't talking about *her*. I was talking about *you*." He gave her a hard look. "What are you doing here?"

"I came about the job," she said. "You said you'd help me get it back."

I stiffened. *What the hell?* My gaze darted from her to him. *Was that true?*

No. It couldn't be.

Already, she'd proven herself a liar. *Why should this be any different?*

I waited for Jaden to correct what she'd said.

But he didn't. All he told her was, "I said we'd talk about it tonight."

Tonight?

Was there something going on between them? I recalled how angry Jaden had been when he'd learned that Morgan had been fired. *Was that because they were an item?* I wanted to ask, but really, it was none of my business.

After all, he was my boss, not my boyfriend.

But as far as the other thing – what she'd said about my job – now that *did* concern me. And yet, I'd die before giving her the satisfaction of asking when she could overhear.

Like an idiot, I was still standing with my back against Jaden's office door. I gave a silent scoff. *No need for that now.*

With as much dignity as I could muster, I left the door and strode toward my own office. Unlike Jaden's, my office had not only a glass door, but also a big interior window. Together, they gave me a clear view of the executive lobby as well as into Jaden's office – well, when his door was actually open, that is.

Unlike mine, his office was very private.

He and Morgan were still talking in the lobby area. Or, rather, *she* was talking, but more quietly now, in a low, breathy voice that made it nearly impossible for me to catch what she was saying. But I did hear words like, "*so* rude" and "totally awful."

Was she talking about me?

Probably.

I shut my office door behind me and reclaimed the seat behind my desk. And then, I turned my attention to the meeting notes that I'd been transcribing until *she'd* tottered in.

My computer faced the executive lobby, where they were still talking. As I worked, I kept glancing up in their direction. I didn't want to, but I couldn't seem to make myself stop.

From my current vantage point, I saw much more of his face than of hers. His eyes were hard, and his mouth was tight as he listened stiffly to whatever she was telling him.

She was talking louder now, probably because I'd shut my door. I still couldn't decipher what was being said, but her tone and body language – with lots of arm waving and foot-stomping – suggested a whole lot of frustration.

Good.

After all, I knew the feeling.

Deliberately, I returned my attention to my computer and tried like crazy to focus on my actual job. I'd been at it for just a few minutes when she suddenly yelled, "But you're not even listening!"

I looked up just in time to see Jaden stride past her, heading toward his private office. She followed on his heels for like three steps until he turned around and said something too low for me to make out.

Her face fell, and she stopped moving. And then, after exchanging a few more words back and forth, she turned and stomped toward the lobby door. She yanked it open, stepped through the doorway, and then gave the door a good, hard yank.

The way it looked, she'd been trying to slam it. Unfortunately for her, the door had one of those slow-shutting mechanisms, which meant that in spite of a pretty good swing on her part, the door still came to a slow and easy stop.

I almost smiled. *How unsatisfying.*

For her, that is.

As for Jaden, he stalked back into his office and shut the door behind him.

I watched that door for a long moment, debating what to do next.

Should I barge in and demand to know if he was, in fact, trying to replace me?

Or should I wait and see how it played out?

My goal was to keep this job for at least a year. Today was only my second day.

I wasn't a gambling person, but it wasn't hard to figure out that my odds of keeping the job were a whole lot greater if I kept my head down and mouth shut.

Yes, I decided. That's exactly what I was going to do – nothing. Well, nothing except for my job.

I gave a slow nod.

Yup. That was definitely the way to play it. Nice and cool.

There was only one problem – Jaden.

What he did just a couple of hours later only added to my confusion.

CHAPTER 25

It was five o'clock, and I was standing in the building's main lobby, staring at my unexpected visitor. With a confused shake of my head, I asked, "What are you doing here?"

He gave me a toothy grin. "You can't guess?"

No. I couldn't.

My visitor was Bryce Rogers, my old boss. His mane of silver hair was perfectly coiffed, and he was wearing a black business suit, along with a white shirt and black Texas tie.

I glanced around, wondering what I should do. It was the end of the business day, and all around me, employees were filing out, heading toward the main doors.

My visitor gave a hearty chuckle. "What's the matter?" he drawled in that country way of his. "Cat got your tongue?"

Funny, he hadn't been chuckling the *last* time I'd seen him. Rather, he'd been red-faced and yelling, telling me that if I actually walked out of his office, I shouldn't bother walking back in, because my ass would be fired.

He hadn't cared that Cassidy was in trouble.

He hadn't cared that I'd worked three weeks straight without a single day off.

He hadn't even cared that I promised to make up the time – for free – if only he'd give me a day off to bring Cassidy back home.

No. All *he'd* cared about was his dry cleaning. And his correspondence. And the dinner party he'd been planning for the following Thursday.

Bryce was a country music producer who specialized in artists that were up-and-coming – mostly because a shocking number of them were too naïve to realize what a turd he was behind that big ol' smile of his.

Funny to think, I'd been just as naïve as the rest of them. Like an idiot, I'd actually believed that working for him would be my ultimate dream job. I loved country music. I loved the thought of meeting the artists up close and personal. Cripes, I even loved that smile of his, until I realized that he only used it when he wanted something.

I felt my gaze narrow. "No, the cat *doesn't* have my tongue. I'm just wondering what you want."

He gave another chuckle. "Who says I want anything?"

"Well, you're here, aren't you?" I glanced toward the nearby bank of elevators. When the building's receptionist had called to inform me that I had a visitor, I'd been skeptical right from the get-go.

I'd been living in Florida for only two weeks, and I had no local friends other than Cassidy. Plus, I hadn't been working here long to have any appointments.

At first, I'd been nearly certain that the receptionist had meant to call someone else. But then, when she gave me Bryce's name, I practically flew from my desk in order to head off whatever trouble he was bringing with him.

After all, we hadn't parted on the best of terms.

And yet, he was still smiling. "The truth is," he drawled, "I'm here to make you an offer."

I eyed him with suspicion. "What kind of offer?"

His grin widened. "Your old job back."

I couldn't help it. I laughed. "Oh, please. You're kidding, right?"

His smile faded. "What makes you say that?"

"Because you fired me."

"Eh, moment of weakness." He shrugged. "*You* said some things, *I* said some things…"

This was true. We'd both said things that I'd be embarrassed to repeat. And yet, I couldn't regret what I'd told him in the end. Maybe I'd done most of the cussing, but *he'd* said some things that were truly scary, including his final parting shot. *"Leave now, and I'll make sure you never work in this town again."*

At the memory, I lifted in my chin. *Hah!* I wasn't *in* that town. I was in *this* town – in a different state, a different market, *and* in a totally different kind of business.

By some miracle, I'd actually landed on my feet – no thanks to him. I gave a bitter scoff. "Speaking of 'saying things', thanks *so much* for the reference."

His brow furrowed. "What reference?"

As if he didn't know. "When Jax Bishop called you last Sunday, you told him all kinds of awful things – things that weren't even true."

"Aw come on," he said. "They weren't *that* awful."

I was glaring now. "You called me temperamental."

"Yeah, well…"

"And a pain in the ass."

He reached up to tug at his tie. "I'm not sure I put it *that* way."

"And," I said, "scary."

At this, he gave a weak chuckle. "You want the truth? You're lookin' a little scary now."

The five weeks I'd worked for him had been five of the most miserable weeks of my life. I didn't mind the hard work or long hours. And I didn't even mind all of the menial tasks. But I *did* mind that I almost never got a day off, not even when I was sick or had an emergency.

To think, I'd even worked the day I'd gotten food poisoning from that godawful salmon that *he'd* insisted I try. The salmon had come from the fridge in his office. Looking back, I was probably just his personal guinea pig to see if the salmon had gone bad.

And just for the record, it had, *bigtime.*

My stomach roiled at the memory.

In front of me, Bryce edged closer and said, "You feelin' okay? You're looking a little green around the gills."

Gills? Did *salmon* have gills? I didn't even want to speculate. With a little shudder, I said, "I'm fine. But I think you should leave."

He frowned. "But you haven't heard my offer."

"Yes. I have." I straightened. "My old job? I don't want it."

"Then how about a promotion?"

Now, I was staring. Just two weeks ago, he'd been all too willing to see me gone. Now, he wanted me back?

It made no sense.

Abruptly, I asked, "And what are you doing here, anyway?"

He glanced around. "I figured this was the best place to talk."

This was just like him, too. Obviously, he didn't care one whit that by coming here of all places, he might be jeopardizing my new job. On top of that, he was totally missing the point.

"I don't mean here in the lobby," I said. "I mean here in Florida."

"Recruiting trip."

At least *this* made sense. He did that sometimes – flew out to wherever in hopes of signing a new act. *Talk about bad luck.* I mean, what were the odds that he'd be recruiting someone *here*, where I now lived?

Regardless, I'd heard enough. "Well, good luck with that," I said, turning away.

A hand on my arm made me stop. When I turned to look, Bryce said, "In case you missed it, *you're* the one I'm recruiting."

"What?"

He looked away and mumbled, "I miss you."

I was staring again. I didn't even know what he meant. There had never been anything romantic between us, and as far as friendship, there was less than nothing there.

But if this was just a job thing, why would he phrase it like that?

Now, I didn't know what to say.

I looked down to my arm. He was still holding on. I didn't like it. His hand was cold, and his grip was just a little too tight. I gave my arm a quick tug.

He didn't let go. "I flew a long way," he said. "So it seems to me, the least you can do is listen."

I gave a hard scoff. "And the least you can do is—"

From behind me, a familiar male voice said, "Fuck off."

At this, I almost groaned out loud. I whirled to look. Sure enough, there was Jaden, standing within arm's reach. *Where on Earth had he come from?*

It took me a moment to realize that my arm was now free. I turned back to Bryce, who even now, was summoning up his heartiest smile. He looked to Jaden and said, "And you are…?"

Jaden didn't smile back. In a low voice, he said, "The guy who's gonna toss you out on your ass."

Suddenly, Bryce wasn't smiling anymore. "Now, listen here—"

"No," Jaden said. "You listen." He flicked his head toward the front entrance. "Get out."

"But—"

"Now."

Bryce gave a shaky laugh. "Or what?"

Now, Jaden *did* smile. The smile was cold and predatory, even as his voice remained eerily calm. "Stick around and find out."

I looked from Jaden to Bryce and back again. One was my current boss. One was my former boss. I wasn't friendly with either one of them. And yet, I found myself edging just a little bit closer to Jaden.

It made me feel funny, like I was letting him fight this battle on my behalf. But then I remembered that Jaden *wasn't* the chivalrous type. Even with the truck thing, he'd flat-out told me that he'd done it for himself, and not for me.

Was this for him, too?

Probably.

And really, I couldn't blame him. This was *his* company. We were standing in *his* lobby. And I was *his* assistant – unless Bryce ended up getting me fired, that is.

I gave Bryce a pleading look. "Listen, you really should leave."

He said, "I will if you consider my offer."

Damn it.

This wasn't the place to be discussing it. Still, I needed to set him straight once and for all. Through gritted teeth, I said, "I'm not interested, just like I told you, okay?"

"So, you still got my number?"

"Yeah, but —"

"So gimme a call when you're free. We'll do dinner, have a talk. What time do you get off work?"

See, this was the thing about Bryce. He never took no for an answer. This was fine enough when he was trying to recruit a new act.

But it wasn't fine now. I *had* a new job *and* a new boss, who, even now, was watching us with an expression that made me just a little bit nervous.

I leaned closer to Bryce and practically hissed, "I don't want dinner."

"Drinks then?"

Oh, for God's sake.

Abruptly, Jaden's voice cut through the noise. "Listen. *Asshole*. She's mine. Not yours. So get the fuck out."

I whirled to face him. *She's mine?* If I weren't so distressed, I might've rolled my eyes. But this was no eye-rolling matter. I couldn't afford to lose this job.

And knowing Bryce, that's exactly what he was gunning for.

I'd seen the way he negotiated. He played dirty – not in a rough-and-tumble sort of way, but in a slick, sneaky sort of way.

My worst fears were confirmed when Bryce said to me, "Or better yet, lemme give you a ride. We'll talk in the car."

I turned and gave Jaden another nervous glance, only to feel myself pause. Now, he was smiling for real.

I felt my brow wrinkle in new confusion. *What the heck?*

As I watched, Jaden looked to Bryce and asked in a friendly sort of way, "So, where'd you park?"

Bryce glanced toward the lobby's main double doors. "In the garage. Why?"

Obviously, he meant the massive multi-level parking garage that was attached to the building. It was the same place I'd parked – just like everyone else who worked here.

Jaden gave a slow nod. "Good choice." He was still smiling. "You know what? Let's you and me talk."

Bryce replied, "About what?"

"Let's call it…" Jaden paused as if thinking. "…a negotiation."

At this, Bryce perked up. He *loved* to negotiate. "Oh yeah?"

"Sure, why not?" Jaden moved forward and wrapped an arm over Bryce's shoulder, buddy style. "C'mon, I'll walk you out."

Bryce gave Jaden a sideways glance. With the difference in their heights, he had to crane his neck to do it. But soon, even this was impossible as Jaden yanked him closer saying, "Good thing you stopped by."

"Oh yeah?" Bryce gulped. "Why's that?"

"Always better to talk in person, right?"

Now, Bryce was decidedly off-kilter, with his head mashed against Jaden's shoulder and his legs struggling to find their footing.

As I watched, Jaden turned and began guiding Bryce toward the side exit.

Bryce was saying, "But that's not the way I came in."

"Shortcut," Jaden replied.

"But—"

"I insist," Jaden said, moving faster now.

Unsure what else to do, I scrambled after them. "You know what?" I forced a laugh. "I'm sure Bryce can find his own way out."

Jaden paused and slowly turned to look over his unoccupied shoulder. His gaze met mine, and I stifled a shiver.

He wasn't smiling anymore. "I'll see you in the office."

"Wait, what?"

"Upstairs."

"But—"

"Five minutes," he said. "See you then."

Next to him, Bryce croaked out, "You know what? I think she's right." He gave a nervous chuckle. "And, uh, I've got another appointment, so…"

Ignoring this, Jaden began moving again, yanking Bryce along with him as he made for the emergency exit – the one that led to a narrow stairwell before opening out into the garage.

An alarm sounded as Jaden pushed open the door and gave Bryce a good shove. I heard myself gasp. The last thing I saw was Bryce, poking his head around the doorway, only to be yanked out of sight by a large hand, gripping his Texas tie.

And then, they were gone.

The door swung shut behind them, and the alarm grew silent. I was left staring at nothing of interest as my fellow employees milled past me, heading toward the main doors.

I stood motionless, watching the spot where I'd last seen them. I was seriously tempted to scramble out after them, but I'd seen that last look – the one Jaden had given me just before heading out the door.

If I valued my job, I'd do exactly what he said.

I *did* value my job, and more to the point, a part of me – a very small and petty part of me – wanted to snicker at Bryce's undignified departure.

Was I a bad person?

Maybe.

Still, I stood there for another long moment, wondering if they'd ever reappear.

They didn't.

So I did the only thing I *could* do – I returned to my office to wait.

For what, I didn't know.

But knowing Jaden, it wouldn't be dull.

CHAPTER 26

I spent the next half-hour pacing up and down the executive suite. As I moved, I kept glancing at my watch. *So much for returning in five minutes.*

It felt like forever before Jaden finally strolled in, looking like he didn't have a care in the world.

I stopped in my tracks. "What happened?"

"With what?"

As if he didn't know. "With Bryce."

"You saw what happened," Jaden said. "I walked him to the garage, end of story."

I didn't believe that for one minute. "Yeah, but I didn't see *all* of it."

"Eh, you weren't missing much."

"But you were gone thirty minutes."

"So?"

"So you said you'd be back in five."

"Yeah, well, I made a stop on the way back."

"Where?"

His only reply was a long, silent look. From the set of his mouth, it was easy to guess what he was thinking. *Just who worked for who around here?*

I cleared my throat. "I'm just curious, that's all."

"Alright," he said. "I stopped at Accounting."

That sounded harmless enough, but that *wasn't* what I was desperate to know. "So…" I bit my lip. "…what happened down there?"

"Not much." Jaden's mouth twitched like he just might smile. "They gave me the new sales figures, had some cake from Rhonda's party…"

"What?"

"Chocolate," he said, "since you look so curious."

I wasn't curious. I was frustrated. I didn't even know who Rhonda was or why she'd have a cake. *A birthday? A promotion? A welcome back from wherever?*

I had no idea. I was so distracted, I couldn't even care. I felt my jaw clench. From the look on Jaden's face, he knew exactly what he was doing.

He was messing with me.

As usual.

Through gritted teeth, I said, "I *meant*, what happened with Bryce?"

"You already asked that." There was no trace of a smile now. "And I answered." With that, he strode past me, heading toward his own office.

I turned and scrambled after him. "But wait, I've got something to say."

He stopped and turned around. "Yeah, what?"

I froze. Now that I had his attention, I wasn't quite sure what I wanted to tell him. I wasn't even sure what he deserved.

A thank you?

Or a kick in the pants?

Under any other circumstance, I might've told him that I didn't need anyone to stick up for me, that I could've handled Bryce on my own, and that Jaden should've minded his own business.

That very last point was the sticky one. This *was* Jaden's business, literally.

Reluctantly, I asked, "Am I in trouble?"

"No. But you're gonna be."

I stiffened. "Why?"

He glanced down at his watch. "Because I've got plans at six."

I glanced at my own watch. It was 5:50. Still, I couldn't seem to let the subject go. "I just meant, am I in trouble for the Bryce thing? For the fact that he came here, I mean." Before Jaden could reply, I quickly added, "And just so you know, I didn't invite him here."

"You think I don't know that?"

"Actually, I don't know *what* you know."

"I know he had his hand on you." Jaden's gaze darkened. "And I know you didn't like it."

He was right. I hadn't. I *especially* hadn't liked that Bryce had refused to let go when I'd tried to pull away. Still, there was something I needed to know. "You didn't hurt him or anything, did you?"

Jaden gave me a hard look. "What if I did?"

I swallowed. "So you did?"

"That's not what I said."

"But you implied it."

"Yeah? And *you* didn't answer my question. So I'll repeat it." Speaking very clearly, he said, "What if I did?"

By now, I was practically chewing on my bottom lip. "Well..." I stammered, trying to collect my thoughts. "...I guess on some level, I wish he would've just left on his own."

"Yeah, but he didn't. So then what?"

"I, well..."

"Wish I'd minded my own business?"

"I don't know," I admitted.

"Yes, you do."

"What do you mean?"

"I mean, you didn't *want* me to let it go."

The objection came automatically. "I did, too."

"Oh yeah? Then why didn't you stop me?"

"From what?"

"From showing him the door."

I tried to laugh. "You didn't *show* him. You dragged him."

"Yeah? And you made no move to stop it."

I almost scoffed out loud. "Are you serious?" I made a point of looking Jaden up and down, taking in his broad shoulders and considerable height, especially compared to me. And then, I forced a laugh. "As if I could."

"Meaning?"

"I'm just saying, you're a lot bigger than I am."

"Yeah. I am, which is why I handled it. And I'll tell you something else. You were glad I showed up."

Now, I did scoff. "I was not." This was actually true. I'd been horrified to see him, mostly because I dreaded the thought of getting fired. And yet, there was a part of me that, yes, might've been the teeniest bit relieved.

But I had no idea how to say this, or even if I should, so I gave a useless shrug and said nothing else.

Jaden gave me a penetrating look. "And you wanna know *how* I know that?"

"How?"

"Because I've seen you in action."

"What does *that* mean?"

"It means, you don't give two shits about provoking someone twice your size."

I sputtered, "What?"

"You know it. And I know it. So don't give me that story and think I'll buy it." He gave a low scoff. "I can smell bullshit a mile away."

"Oh yeah? Well maybe you're forgetting something."

"What's that?" he said.

"You're my boss."

"So?"

"So, it's not like I'm gonna be all rude or anything."

His eyebrows lifted, but he made no reply. He didn't have to. We both knew what he was thinking. Technically, I was being at least a little rude now. But that was hardly the point.

I tried again. "I don't mean *now*," I clarified. "I meant in the lobby. Like, what was I supposed to do? Tell you to butt out? Follow you into the garage? Try to 'rescue' him?" I forced another laugh. "I can just imagine."

"Imagine what?"

"Well for starters, your reaction."

"Yeah? You wanna know what *I* can imagine?"

"What?"

"You not giving a rat's ass what I thought, not if you liked the guy."

I opened my mouth, intending to say something sharp and cutting.

But words failed me as I considered the truth of what he'd just said.

Not too long ago, *Bryce* had been my boss, and I hadn't hesitated to tell *him* where to go when a friend's safety was at stake.

But that was different.

Wasn't it?

I honestly didn't know. Somehow, this felt a million times more complicated for reasons that I couldn't quite understand.

I clamped my mouth shut and looked away.

Into the silence, Jaden said, "By the way, he rescinded his offer."

I turned to look. "What?"

"The job offer – he had a change of heart."

Well, that was a shocker.

I heard myself say, "Can I ask you something?"

"No."

"Sorry, what?"

"No," he repeated. "I'm done." And with that, he turned away, heading deeper into his office. As I watched, he leaned over his desk, yanked open the top drawer, and grabbed his keys.

I glanced at the clock. It was nearly six. Apparently, my time was up.

Already, Jaden was striding past me, heading out the way he'd come. I watched in agitated silence as he pushed through the suite's door and disappeared from sight.

I wasn't sure what just happened, but I knew that I didn't like it. And for once, it wasn't because of anything he'd done. It was because of myself.

The conversation hadn't gone anything like I'd been hoping. Even as frustrated as I'd been, I'd meant to at least offer some sort of thanks, and maybe an apology for bringing trouble into the workplace.

Now, I couldn't help but sigh. This was only my second day on the job, and already, I felt like I'd failed somehow.

Tomorrow, I vowed, I'd make things right, or at least as right as they could be, considering who I was dealing with.

Unfortunately, I never had the chance.

And why?

It was because Jaden never showed.

CHAPTER 27

From behind my desk, I said, "So, do you know where he is?"

Standing in my office doorway, the tiny sixty-something redhead gave a derisive snort. "Aren't *you* supposed to know?"

I bit back a sharp reply. The visitor was Darla, who I'd had the displeasure of meeting at Jaden's house right after my initial job interview.

That was two weeks ago, but I remembered it like yesterday. She was Morgan's mom and hadn't been happy to see her daughter fired, which meant that she'd been equally thrilled to see *me* take her daughter's place.

And now, she was here in the executive suite, giving me a look of pure loathing. Even worse, it was just the two of us.

I gave her a stiff smile. "Actually, I didn't realize he was going to be out."

"But you're his assistant," she said. "You should know these things."

Yes. I should.

But Jaden hadn't mentioned it, which meant that I knew nothing, except that he wasn't here *and* that he wouldn't be back until Monday. Or at least, that was my best guess, based on the limited information that I had.

This morning, I'd arrived early, only to discover that Jaden's electronic calendar had been cleared of everything for the rest of the week. Only Jaden and I had access to the thing, which meant that he'd cleared all of those appointments himself.

It was beyond strange.

As far as instructions, the only thing I saw was a message in the notes section, saying, "*If anyone complains, reschedule.*"

I'd received no complaints – mostly because I hadn't yet contacted the participants to inform them that their meetings were off.

No, the only thing *I'd* received was this little visit from Darla, who'd just marched into the executive suite to inform me that Jaden wasn't here.

As if I couldn't figure that out on my own.

It was just past eight o'clock, my usual starting time, and already, the day wasn't looking so great.

In front of me, Darla was saying, "You're not a very good assistant, are you?"

Well, that was nice.

From Cassidy, I'd learned that Darla was some sort of friend of the family, which made my position doubly precarious. Even now, it's not like I could say exactly what I was thinking.

I almost sighed out loud. It was so much easier when I'd been *trying* to get fired.

Then again, I hadn't succeeded at *that* either.

I forced another smile. "Should I let him know you stopped by?"

"Why?" she scoffed. "I'll probably see him before *you*."

I gritted my teeth. "Alrighty then."

She frowned. "What?"

"Nothing." Deliberately I pushed back my chair and stood. "Well, thanks for stopping by." I gave the door a pointed look. *Off you go.*

Her eyebrows furrowed, and she made no move. "I'm not 'stopping by.' I'm here to stay."

Now that we were both standing, it suddenly struck me that we were almost exactly the same height. It was funny to think that she had such a tall daughter. Then again, my own parents were on the tall side, too, which only proved that trends didn't always run in the family.

Unfortunately, when it came to personality, Darla and Morgan were cut from the same cloth – the bitchy one, with lots of barbs and digs and what-not.

I was so lost in my thoughts that it took me a moment to realize what she'd just said. *She was here to stay?*

I felt my brow wrinkle in confusion. "Excuse me?"

"I'm not 'stopping by,'" she repeated. "What do you think this is? A social call?"

Obviously, it wasn't – not that I needed *her* to tell me.

Darla was wearing a no-nonsense black dress with a polka dot scarf. Clipped to the scarf was an official company badge, which meant that she actually worked here.

Heaven help me.

Which department, I had no idea, but I *did* know that the sooner she returned there, the better.

Very carefully, I said, "But don't you need to get back to your desk?"

Her mouth tightened. "Oh, so *you're* my boss now?"

"No," I said. "But I *do* need to get back to work…" Again, I gave the door a pointed look.

She crossed her arms. "Are you expecting someone?"

"No. Why?"

"Because you keep looking at the door." Her eyes narrowed. "Or is that some sort of hint?"

Yes. It was.

But she obviously wasn't taking it.

Bummer for me.

I made a sound of frustration. "Look, I'll just be honest. I don't know what you want, or why you're here. I already told you that Jaden isn't in today, so—"

"You told *me?"* She was glaring now. "Don't you mean, *I* told *you*?"

"Fine. But just so you know, I'd already figured that out on my own."

She gave another snort of derision. "If so, it's the *only* thing you've figured out."

I stiffened. "And what does *that* mean?"

"It means, you're in my daughter's seat."

Oh for God's sake. This again?

I'd heard a similar statement from Morgan. By now, I felt like tossing that stupid chair out the window – except that I didn't *have* a window, unless I counted the interior one that faced Jaden's office.

I gave her my snottiest smile. "I can't, because I'm standing."

She looked at me like I was crazy. "What are you talking about?"

I pointed to the chair behind my desk. "You see that thing? My butt *isn't* in it."

She didn't even look at the chair. "You *know* what I meant."

I widened my eyes in mock confusion. "Do I?"

"If you don't, lemme spell it out. Sitting or not, you're in Morgan's spot. And by the time she and Jaden get back from Miami, it would be nice if you were gone."

I froze. So that's where Jaden was? *Miami? With Morgan?*

The news hit like me a slap to the face. I wasn't even sure why. Yesterday, he'd mentioned plans at six o'clock. In my mind, I'd imagined dinner plans or some sort of business meeting.

I *hadn't* imagined him hopping a plane to Miami with Morgan. A quiet scoff escaped my lips. *No.* He wouldn't even *need* to hop a plane. Miami was just a few hours away by car. And even if he did want to fly, he had his *own* plane, ready to take him wherever at his convenience.

Well, goodie for him.

In front of me, Darla smiled. "I see I've got your attention."

I gave her a look. "Is there anything else? Because I really do need to get back to work."

She didn't move. And neither did I. The visual standoff lasted way too long for my comfort.

I said a silent prayer. *Just go already.*

But she didn't.

Instead, she turned in the wrong direction, heading not toward the exit, but rather toward the half of the suite that belonged to Jax.

Beyond confused, I moved toward my office door and peered in that direction. I watched in silent confusion as she entered the office directly opposite Jax's.

Oh, crap. That was the office of his assistant. Was *she* Jax's assistant?

No. She couldn't be.

Could she?

CHAPTER 28

The morning dragged slowly on, even as I made a slew of phone calls to cancel or reschedule Jaden's appointments. As I worked, I was overly conscious of Darla, sitting – or whatever she was doing – in that neighboring office.

From my own desk, I couldn't see her, and yet, I was obnoxiously aware of her presence, especially at mid-morning, when a gaggle of coworkers barged in with cake and coffee – not plain old coffee-pot coffee either, but rather the good kind, probably with chocolate and whipped cream.

Either way, I knew it was the good stuff, because I recognized the logo on the cups. The logo belonged to an upscale coffee shop within walking distance of the office, so even though I couldn't actually *see* what was inside those cups, it was easy enough to imagine.

As for myself, I hadn't even *had* coffee this morning. And why? It was because I'd been too anxious to get to work, in hopes of smoothing things over with Jaden.

It was stupid, really.

To think, I'd actually felt guilty for not acting more gracious about the whole Bryce thing.

Meanwhile, no one was offering *me* coffee, much less a slice of cake or a friendly hello, even as the laughing and talking continued until nearly lunchtime.

I saw no sign of Jax, but that was no surprise. From what I'd learned just yesterday, he'd be out of town all week, attending some conference in London.

Better than Miami.

With Morgan.

When I finished rescheduling Jaden's appointments, I turned my attention to some meeting notes that Jaden had asked me to type up whenever I had the chance. There was a whole stack of them, written by hand on pale pink notebook paper.

The handwriting was big and bold, with loopy letters and personal observations scribbled in the margins – mostly related to what the attendees were wearing or what kind of cell phones they were using, as if that mattered.

Obviously, the notes had been taken by Morgan, back when she'd been sitting in my seat. I paused. Or was it *her* seat? Probably, it depended on who was talking.

Regardless, the notes were a jumbled, crazy mess. Some had dates at the top. Some didn't. Some listed the participants. Some didn't. Some were legible, and some looked like they'd been written by a drunken mental patient.

Already, I'd shut my office door to drown out the party in the neighboring office. It did little good, and by noon, I had a raging headache.

I didn't bother with lunch. I wasn't hungry. Plus, I hated the thought of scuttling out, leaving Darla to do who-knows-what in my absence.

I was so distracted that it took me a moment to realize that my office phone was ringing. Startled by the unfamiliar tone, I stopped typing to study the digital display.

It was an outside call from an unknown number. Whoever it was, they weren't calling Jaden. They were calling me.

Or more likely, they were trying to call Morgan, in which case, they'd probably tell me to get out of her chair.

That was, after all, the thing to say, wasn't it?

Still, I forced a smile into my voice and answered with a cheerful, "Allie Brewster, how may I help you."

After a long silence, Jaden said, "What's wrong?"

At the sound of his voice, I practically jumped in my seat. I shouldn't't've been surprised. I mean, of course, it was perfectly natural for him to call and check in, even if he *was* on some sort of impromptu vacation.

Still, it begged the question, where was he now? *On the beach? Or in a hotel room? Was Morgan lying next to him, naked and ready?*

I gave a mental eye-roll. *No.* Even if it *was* that type of vacation, he'd surely delay the call until *after* Morgan had put on some clothes. *Wouldn't he?*

And yet, the image lingered. She was naked. He was naked. Cripes, even the imaginary bellhop was naked, because hey, as long as my imagination was running wild, I might as well go full-weirdo, right?

Stupidly, I still hadn't answered his question. *What was wrong?* I rubbed at my eyes. "Nothing."

"You're lying."

My grip tightened on the phone. This was just like him – Mister Blunt, even when calling from the beach – or wherever he was.

But it wasn't *him* I was frustrated with. Mostly, I was frustrated with myself. Somehow, I'd let him get under my skin. And if that weren't bad enough, I was doing a sorry job of hiding it.

But then again, I'd never been great at hiding my feelings, even now, when I didn't know what exactly those feelings were.

But there was no way I'd admit any of this because, for one thing, he wouldn't want to hear it. "Everything's fine," I lied. "Were you calling about the appointments?"

"What appointments?"

"The ones you canceled, on your calendar, I mean."

"Fuck the appointments."

No. Fuck Morgan. And fuck you.

Damn it. Why was I so bothered? It made no sense. I didn't even like him.

Really, I didn't.

When I made no reply, he said, "Tell me."

"Tell you what?"

"What's wrong."

I forced another smile. "Nothing."

"Alright," he said in a carefully controlled voice. "How about this? What's going on?"

"You mean here at the office?" I glanced around. "Nothing much. I rescheduled the appointments, and..." I hesitated. "Well, it's just me and Darla, so it's pretty..."

I bit my lip. *Pretty what?*

Weird?

Stressful?

Quiet?

Not hardly. Right on cue, a burst of laughter rang through the walls.

On the phone, Jaden asked, "Did you say Darla?"

"Yup. I sure did."

"And she's there *now?*"

"Actually, she's been here all morning." I forced a smile so big, my face almost hurt. "Bright and early."

In a barely audible voice, he muttered, "Fuck."

I paused. "Excuse me?"

"Five minutes," he said.

"Sorry, what?"

"Five minutes," he repeated. "I'll call you back. You gonna be there?"

"Of course." I glanced at the clock. Forget five minutes. I'd be here for at least five more hours – five *long* hours if the afternoon was anything like this morning.

After we hung up, I heard a phone ring from somewhere outside my office. The ring was followed by a sudden silence that seemed to fill the whole suite.

I heard nothing at all for several long moments. And then, the parade of visitors began streaming past my office, heading toward the suite's main door. One by one, they filed out, taking the remainder of the cake with them.

I saw no sign of Darla, and for some reason, that made me just a little nervous.

What on Earth was going on?

I had no idea, but it was pathetically easy to guess that the mystery caller had been Jaden.

Just what had he told her?

CHAPTER 29

When my phone rang again, I jumped in my seat. A quick glance at the display confirmed that it was Jaden, calling me from the same number as earlier.

Still, I went through the basic greeting, only to hear him say without so much as a hello, "If she gives you any grief, let me know."

"Who? You mean Darla?" I didn't want to jump to conclusions, but she *had* been the last person we'd discussed.

On the phone, he replied, "Her or anyone else."

It was a noble sentiment, which only put me further on edge. *Jaden, noble? Oh, please.* I gave a nervous laugh. "How about you?"

"What about me?"

"What if *you* give me a hard time, should I let you know, too?" *Good grief. What the heck was I saying?*

"Why?" he said. "You planning on it?"

"No." Already, I was kicking myself for saying something so completely nonsensical. "It was just a joke."

"Good." And with that, he hung up.

I sat there for a long moment wondering what had just happened. Obviously, it had been a mistake to try to make light of whatever was going on, but the truth was, I was having a hard time thinking of him as my boss.

Maybe it stemmed from the way we'd met, with him standing shirtless at the door. Maybe it was the fact that he hadn't wanted to hire me. Or maybe it was just lingering tension related to yesterday's incident with Bryce.

Regardless of the reason, everything was just so strange. Of course, that dream I'd had last night wasn't helping.

What dream?

Well, let's just say he was missing more than his shirt.

Deliberately, I pushed away the distraction and returned my attention to the notes.

They really *were* a mess, even if it was vaguely entertaining to read that Felicia's blouse was "super-ugly" or that Frank's pants were "too tight for his gut." I had to wonder, was I supposed to transcribe these little observations, too? Or should I just stick with what had actually happened in the meeting?

In the end, I split the difference – transcribing the meeting notes *without* the commentary, but adding them back in as footnotes at the end of each document.

Who knows, maybe Jaden *did* want to know that Bob's tie was "seriously ugly."

I was nearly finished with the notes when a loud knock sounded at the door. I looked up and saw Darla glaring at me through the glass.

Damn it.

Still, I tried to smile as I called, "Come on in."

She pushed open the door and said, "I'm not coming in. I'm just letting you know that I'm leaving for the day."

On instinct, I glanced toward the clock and felt my eyebrows furrow. It wasn't even four o'clock.

Darla said, "What, you're checking up on me?"

"Sorry, what?"

"I saw you look at the clock."

Oh, for crying out loud. "Was I not supposed to?"

She pursed her lips. "Well, I can't say I'm surprised."

I sighed. "Okay, what am I missing?"

"I'm just saying, I know you're a tattle-tale."

"A tattle-tale?" I had to laugh. "What are we? In grade-school?"

She crossed her arms. "Did you, or did you not tell Jaden that I was causing a ruckus?"

"I didn't tell him anything."

She gave me a look. "You sure about that?"

"I just mentioned that you were here – *and* only because he asked." She gave a little sniff. "Likely story."

I'd had just about enough. I pushed myself up and said, "If you've got a problem with me, why don't you just say so?"

"Alright," she said. "I've got a problem with you." She gave me a smug smile. "There, you happy?"

"Thrilled."

"Yeah, and you're a little snot, too."

I *so* didn't want to argue with her. "Listen," I said, "I know we got off on the wrong foot—"

"You're telling me," she snapped. "And just so you know, my daughter's not a 'horrible person.'"

"Okay, fine, I'm sorry, but what she did *was* pretty terrible."

Darla lifted her chin but made no reply.

I tried again. "She lied to me about my friend. I was worried sick. Don't you think that's at least a *little* terrible?"

"No," Darla said. "What *I* think is that you and your friend are all hot and heavy for my boys."

I blinked. "Your boys? You don't mean—"

"Who? Jax and Jaden? Yeah, that's exactly who I mean."

Now, I was seriously confused. "So, you're their mom? Really?"

"I might as well be," she said. "And just so you know, they were doing perfectly fine before you and your hussy friend showed up."

I felt my gaze narrow. "Cassidy's *not* a hussy."

"Yeah? Well, my daughter's not a terrible person. So now you know how *I* feel."

"But that's totally different," I said. "Cassidy hasn't done anything to you."

"Wanna bet?" Darla gave snort of disgust. "She got my daughter fired."

"That's not true," I protested. *Or at least, I was pretty sure it wasn't true.*

"Sure it is," Darla said. "If it weren't for your friend, Morgan would still be here. And *you* wouldn't be in her seat."

Cripes, again with the seat?

This time, I didn't bother pointing out that I was actually standing.

As Darla launched into another series of complaints, I recalled what Jaden had told me on the phone, that if anyone gave me trouble, I should let him know. But I hated the idea of letting him fight my battles.

As it was, he'd already fought my battle with Bryce.

And with Stuart.

Plus, there was the little matter of him being in Miami with, holy hell, his *sister*?

As Darla went on, I desperately tried to assemble the pieces of their family puzzle. Thanks to Cassidy, I knew that Jaden's brother had actually dated Morgan for a while.

So they couldn't be *real* siblings.

What did that mean?

Were they step-siblings?

If so, where did the Miami trip fit into all of this? *Was it romantic? Or some sort of family getaway?*

The questions were still swirling in my head when Darla said, "You're not gonna land him, you know."

"Who?"

"You know who," she said. "I see the way you look at him."

Okay, this was beyond ridiculous. "If you're talking about Jaden," I said, "there's nothing to see. And besides, you've only seen us in the same room *one* time for like five whole minutes."

"Yeah, and I heard how *that* went."

"What do you mean?"

"I mean, after I left, you tried to jump him."

Obviously, she was referring to the scene at his house, where I'd taken a flying leap in his direction. But it wasn't the way she made it sound.

And besides, that was mostly for show anyway.

When I made no reply, she gave me a smug smile. "I see you've got no answer to *that.*"

"What do you want me to say?" I threw up my hands. "It was just a misunderstanding, that's all. And honestly, it's not like I was throwing myself at him."

"Says you."

"No. Says everyone who was there."

"I'm just saying, he deserves a nice girl."

I didn't bother hiding my disbelief. "You can't be serious."

"Why not?" she demanded.

"Because..." I almost didn't know how to say it. I had to remind myself that Jaden was my boss, and she was his, well, I didn't know what, but I did know that she wouldn't appreciate my insights on *any* of this.

Finally, I muttered, "You know what? I'm not discussing it."

"Good," she said. "Then you can listen."

"To what?"

"To some friendly advice."

I gave a bark of laughter. "Friendly? Seriously? You're one of the least friendly people I've ever met."

"Yeah, well you're no prize yourself. At least I don't go around jumping people."

Well, there was that.

But in my own defense, I really *wasn't* the violent type. That whole spectacle at Jaden's house was unlike anything I'd ever done. And even then, I'd been motivated mostly by concern for Cassidy.

I felt my gaze narrow. "Yeah, well you would've done the same thing in my shoes."

She straightened. "Honey, your feet are too big for my shoes."

I looked down. My feet were actually on the small side. With the desk between us, I couldn't see *her* feet, but judging from her height, our feet were probably similar in size.

But what did this have to do with anything?

I muttered, "Better big feet than a big mouth."

"Yeah, well you've got one of those, too."

"What?"

"I'm just saying, I heard you were yelling so loud, you rattled the windows."

Gee, you flip out one time...

I gave her a look. "Is there a point to all this?"

"No point," she said. "I'm just warning you, that if you think you can weasel your way into his pants, you're wrong."

"His pants?" I sputtered. "Seriously?"

"Dead serious."

"Trust me," I said. "His pants are safe."

"They'd better be," she said. "He's a nice young man. And he deserves a nice girl." Her gaze narrowed. "And honey, you're not it."

And with that, she turned and strode toward the exit, leaving one final parting shot in her wake. "See you tomorrow."

CHAPTER 30

Cassidy was laughing. "A nice young man? Seriously?"

I nodded. "Swear to God."

I'd been home from work for only twenty minutes, and I'd spent most of those minutes griping about my crappy day at the office.

On the sofa, Cassidy was still laughing. "Oh, my God, I can't even imagine."

"Can't imagine what?" I asked.

"Jaden being nice *or* young. He's one of the most jaded people I've ever met."

"Yeah, well, according to Darla, *I'm* even worse." I kicked off my shoes and sank deeper into the armchair. "Can you believe, she called me a snot?"

Cassidy snickered. "No."

I gave her a look. "What does *that* mean?"

"Nothing," she said. "But you've got to admit, you *were* pretty snotty when you met her."

"Well yeah," I said. "But she totally had it coming. And now, she's acting like *I'm* the crazy one, when it's so obvious that Jaden is ten times crazier than I could ever be."

Cassidy leaned forward. "Hey, if you ever want to make him *really* crazy, you know what you should do?"

"What?"

"Mention marriage."

"What do you mean?"

As I listened, Cassidy went on to tell me a little more about the night she'd met both brothers for the first time. They'd been wearing tuxes, and she'd assumed they were on their way to a wedding.

But it wasn't until Cassidy had mentioned the possibility of it being *Jaden's* wedding that she'd gotten a real rise out of him.

Now, sitting on the sofa, she did a fairly decent imitation of him, saying, "Marriage? Me? God, no." She laughed and continued in her own voice. "Or however he put it. I'm just saying, he was *so* horrified, like I suggested he have sex with a donkey or something."

I frowned. *Well, that was an image I didn't need.*

Still, I saw what she meant. "You want to hear something *really* horrifying?" I said. "Think of the poor gal who *does* end up with him." I gave a little shudder. "I can't even imagine."

And yet, I *could* imagine other things, like the honeymoon. To my extreme annoyance, the thought induced a shiver of a different kind, a warm shiver that went all the way to my toes.

I tried not to think about it.

On the sofa, Cassidy was saying, "It's a good thing he's so against it then."

"Yeah. No kidding." But the topic *did* remind me of something. "Hey, a question... Is Darla their mom?"

Cassidy's brow wrinkled in confusion. "No. Why do you ask?"

"Because, get this, Darla called both of them 'her boys.'"

But already, Cassidy was shaking her head. "No. They *can't* be related."

"Why not?" I asked.

"Because Jax and Morgan were a thing."

"I know," I said. "But maybe they're step-siblings."

Cassidy gave it some thought. And then, after a long moment, she said, "No. Definitely not."

"How can you be sure?" I asked.

"Because neither brother referred to Morgan as their sister. And even with Darla, it's not like she told Jax, 'You fired your sister.' She said, 'You fired my daughter' -- or something to that effect."

I saw what Cassidy meant. "If you find out," I said, "will you let me know?"

Cassidy laughed. "You'll probably find out before I do. I mean, *you* work for them. *I* don't."

At the reminder, I felt that all-too familiar pang of guilt. "Yeah, but you could've."

"Oh, forget that," she said with a happy smile. "Guess what?"

"What?"

As I listened, she went on to tell me that she'd just found a job. Starting tomorrow, she'd be working as a waitress at a bar and grill located within walking distance of our new apartment.

She looked glad, which made me feel glad, too. After congratulating her, I said, "But why didn't you tell me right away?"

"Because," she said, "the Jaden thing was a lot more interesting."

On this, she had a point. It *was* interesting, like a train-wreck, with lots of screaming and twisted metal.

As we chatted back and forth, Cassidy also mentioned that she'd gotten the job out of the blue, without even applying.

I asked, "But how is that possible?"

She shrugged. "I've been making the rounds. I'm guessing someone knew someone. Funny how that works, huh?"

It *was* funny, even more than Cassidy realized – as I learned later that same week.

CHAPTER 31

It was late Friday afternoon, and I was beyond eager for the week to end. The last few days had been quiet, but stressful, with both brothers out of town and Darla working in the neighboring office.

By unspoken agreement, the two of us weren't talking – not even a basic good morning to start off each day.

Obviously, she wanted me to feel unwelcome and was doing a pretty good job of driving the point home. She still had visitors, but there was no cake, and no large, noisy crowds. And yet, it was pretty obvious that she'd told everyone far and wide that I was someone to be avoided at all costs.

By the end of the week, I was almost anxious for Jaden to return. Oh sure, he was rude and unpleasant, and a giant smartass, but at least he never acted like I didn't exist. And for that, I was grateful.

How pathetic was that?

Each day, he checked in by phone. And each day, I told him that everything was fine. Whether he believed me or not, I had no idea.

I didn't ask what he was doing or if he was having fun in Miami with the horrible person who may or may not be his own step-sister.

Instead, I gave him a daily rundown of his messages, along with notes from the meetings that he'd asked me to attend on his behalf.

It was funny in a way. When I'd first met him, I'd assumed that he was just as shallow as he looked. But now, after only a few days on the job, it was beyond obvious that he was a real driving force in the company's success.

I could tell by the messages – from suppliers, from advertisers, from distribution centers, and on and on – that he was more than just some figurehead or namesake. Already, I felt slightly embarrassed that I'd assumed he was some muscle-bound pretty boy with no ambitions other than to drive people crazy.

Still, I had to admit, he was obnoxiously good at that, too – driving people crazy, that is. Or maybe it was just me.

Even from Miami, he delivered little pokes and prods over the phone – the crack about me being pint-sized and the veiled references to trucks, sandwiches, and psychos on doorsteps.

Maybe I *was* a psycho, because I was almost starting to look forward to his calls. I liked sparring with him, and I had a sneaky suspicion that he felt the same way – probably because everyone else seemed so afraid of him.

It was no wonder.

I had, after all, seen how he'd acted with my ex-boyfriend, and more recently, my old boss. In truth, he *had* been a little scary.

It was nearly five o'clock when Darla appeared suddenly in my doorway and said, "How's your friend?"

I almost fell out of my chair. She'd been utterly silent – to me, anyway – for three whole days, and now she wanted to pass the time?

I wasn't buying it.

Even now, she had several visitors hanging out near her office. If she only wanted to make conversation, she wouldn't be bothering with *me*.

So obviously, there was something more to her simple question. *But what?*

Carefully, I said, "If you mean Cassidy, she's fine. Why do you ask?"

Darla gave me a look that was all innocence. "Do I need a reason?"

No. What you need is a giant kick in the pants.

But I didn't say it. For one thing, she was wearing a dress. And for another, I'd been working here for only one week, including today. It seemed a little soon to be joking about violence in the workplace. Plus, knowing Darla, she wouldn't take it as a joke.

Rather, she'd use it as one more thing to make everyone avoid me. I could practically hear it now. *"She threatened to kick me. Can you believe it?"*

At the door to my office, she demanded, "Are you gonna answer or not?"

I gave it some thought. "Nope."

She was glaring now. "Why not?"

"Because I figured the question was rhetorical."

She placed her hands on her hips. "Well, it wasn't."

I sighed. "Alright, fine." Using my overly patient voice, I said, "No. You don't need a reason to ask about her, but I know that you're not fond of her, so it *is* a bit curious."

Darla gave me a thin smile. "Yes. It *is* curious, isn't it?"

Something in her tone was setting off warning bells. I asked, "What do you mean?"

"I mean," she said, "it's *really* curious that your friend was offered a job when she didn't even apply. Don't you think?"

I leaned forward in my chair. "Wait, how did you know that?"

She smiled again. "I know lots of things."

My gaze narrowed. "Like what?"

"Well, for starters, I know who owns the place where she works."

"Really? Who?"

Darla made a show of looking around. "Who do you think?"

Oh, no. "Don't tell me...*they* own it?"

"Maybe. But you didn't hear it from *me*."

"But..." I was trying to think. "...how'd you know that Cassidy was hired?"

"Oh, I know lots of things."

No doubt, she did.

"Great," I snapped. "Are you gonna share any of them?"

With feigned innocence, she asked, "Like what?"

I gave her a look. "Like whatever you know about Cassidy's job."

Darla said, "I know she didn't get it on her own."

"So, how *did* she get it?"

"From a phone call."

"Sorry, what?"

"Jax called the manager on her behalf."

I sat back. "He did?"

"And not only that," Darla said. "He *ordered* the guy to give her a job." With her thumb, Darla pointed over her shoulder to Jaden's office. "They fought about it, you know."

"Who fought?"

"Jax and Jaden."

"But why would they fight?"

"Because," Darla said, "Jax wanted to find your friend an even *better* job, something here at corporate."

I felt my gaze narrow. "And Jaden didn't?"

Darla was smiling again. "No. He didn't."

What a jerk.

Against my better judgment, I said, "But why?"

Her smile vanished. "Because Jaden knows what I know."

"Which is…?"

"That your friend is trouble, and so are you." Her chin lifted. "If you ask me, she's lucky she got any job at all."

I pushed myself up from my chair. "No. *They're* lucky to get someone so qualified."

Darla made a sound of disbelief. "Is that so?"

"Definitely." My voice rose. "Cassidy's incredible, and really nice, too – which you'd know if you gave her half a chance."

"Why would I bother?" she said. "She'll be gone before you know it." Her eyes narrowed to slits. "And so will you."

My jaw tightened. "Is that a threat?"

"Oh, please," she said. "I don't need to 'threaten' either one of you. You're a psycho, and your friend's a hussy. You'll be sinking your own ships without any help from me."

It suddenly struck me that Darla's visitors had grown eerily silent. No doubt they were listening to every word, which only added to my discomfort.

I glanced at the clock. It was officially past five, and I'd heard just about enough. I yanked open my bottom drawer and grabbed my purse. I slung it over my shoulder and made for my office door, praying that Darla would move aside before I got there, because if she didn't, I was seriously tempted to bowl her over and be done with it.

Happily, that wasn't necessary. She moved away just in time and then silently watched as I locked my office door behind me.

As I did it, she gave a little laugh. "I have a key, you know."

"What?"

"A key," she repeated. "I can go in there any time I want."

I wasn't quite sure I believed her. But even if it *was* true, there was nothing I could do it about it now. So instead, I turned away and marched out of the executive suite with my head held high.

From somewhere behind me, I heard the sound of snickering. It might've been Darla. Or it might've been one of her visitors. I didn't know, and I didn't bother to look.

Instead, I kept on going and didn't stop until I reached my truck – or rather, Jaden's truck, as I reminded myself for the millionth time.

Driving back to the apartment, I said a silent prayer that next week would be a whole lot better – or at least, not quite so terrible.

I didn't mind a little stress, and I was fine at sticking up for myself.

It was just that now, I felt so seriously outnumbered.

On the phone, Jaden had told me to let him know if anyone caused me trouble. But Darla was, at the very least, a sort of mother figure to him. There was no way he'd choose me over her.

And as far as the other people who worked there, I couldn't exactly complain that I was being given the cold shoulder. And besides, what would I say? *"People don't say 'hi' to me."*

It was a pathetic complaint if I'd ever heard one.

And regardless, I wasn't the complaining type. In reality, I was more of a confront-it head-on type of person.

This was probably a good thing, because long before Monday, I had my chance -- except the person I confronted wasn't Darla.

It was Jaden, who had the nerve to show up where?

On my own doorstep, that's where.

CHAPTER 32

It was nearly nine o'clock at night, and I'd just woken up from a long, restless nap. I wasn't normally the napping type, but the work week had taken its toll, and I'd been hoping that if I slept for a few hours, I might be able to get a fresh start for the long-awaited weekend.

No such luck.

I woke feeling just as irritated as I'd been before going to sleep. Cassidy was at work, which meant that I was on my own.

Probably, this was a good thing.

I'd surely be horrible company for anyone unfortunate enough to cross my path. I was still upset, not only at Darla's rudeness, but also because of what she'd told me about Jaden sabotaging Cassidy's chances for a better job.

Why would he do such a thing?

Did he hate both of us that much?

Probably.

It shouldn't've been a surprise. After all, he'd tried to stop Jax from hiring *me*, too.

Now, the jerk was my boss, and I wasn't even sure how I'd face him on Monday. To think, I'd actually been looking forward to his return.

What a joke.

I'd just gotten out of the shower when I heard a knock at the door to the apartment. I gave a muttered curse. I wasn't expecting anyone, and now, I had to throw on whatever clothes I had handy, unless I *wanted* to answer the door naked, which I surely didn't.

In truth, I didn't want to answer the door at all.

But I knew myself all too well. If I didn't see who it was, I'd be on pins and needles all night, wondering who it was or if they'd return.

I poked my head out of the bathroom door and called out, "Be there in a minute!" And then, I threw on the first clothes I laid my hands on – a pair of shorts and a little black T-shirt. My hair was wet, and my arms and legs were pink from the shower, not that it mattered. It's not like I planned to impress whoever was rude enough to show up uninvited on a Friday night.

Besides, I had a pretty good guess who it was. Probably, it was Cassidy's mom, who was one of the most thoughtless people I'd ever met.

But as it turned out, my guess was totally wrong. When I peered through the peephole, who did I see?

Jaden.

The jackass.

I whispered, "Shit."

Through the peephole, I swear, I saw the hint of a smile, almost like he'd overheard the quiet curse. Maybe he had. Regardless, he surely knew that I was home.

Still, I refused to make him feel welcome. Not bothering to hide my irritation, I called through the door, "Who is it?"

He didn't even flinch. "If you don't know, look again."

"What do you mean?"

"The peephole," he said. "It's there for a reason."

I looked again, not that I needed to. Mostly, I was stalling while I got a grip on my temper.

Jaden was dressed in a suit and tie, and looked almost civilized. But I wasn't fooled, not one bit. If *anyone* was a psycho, it was him, *not* me, regardless of how nicely he was dressed.

I unlocked the door and yanked it open. And then, I greeted him with nothing but a long, cold stare.

Yes, he was my boss, but this was my home, and he was totally uninvited.

It would be a mistake to make him feel like this was okay. It definitely wasn't. I was off the clock, and if the jackass thought it was perfectly fine to stop by unannounced, I was determined to correct that assumption one way or another.

He met my gaze with one of his own. But where mine was cold and challenging, his was filled with obvious amusement.

It was easy to see why.

I was a disheveled soggy mess.

I snapped, "What's the matter? You never saw anyone wet before?"

His eyebrows lifted, but he made no reply. Belatedly, it hit me that such a statement could be taken in multiple ways. One of those ways was decidedly obscene.

My pink skin grew a shade pinker. I didn't need to look. I could feel it as plain as day, the warmth creeping upward and then – *damn it* – back down again as I considered the ramifications of what I'd just said.

Just a few nights ago, I'd dreamt of him. And yes, the dream *had* made me embarrassingly wet – and not in the showery sense either.

Maybe I *was* a psycho. After all, he wasn't even my type.

When he made no reply to my stupid comment, I blurted out, "From the shower."

He looked at me for another long moment. "Is that a question?"

"What?"

His mouth twitched. "Am I supposed to answer?"

I froze. *Oh, right.* I'd asked if he'd ever seen anyone wet before. But I didn't *want* an answer, mostly because I was afraid of what it might be.

"No," I said. "I'm just wondering why you're here." My gaze narrowed. "*And* why you didn't think to call first."

"Was I supposed to?"

What kind of question was that? "Well, it would be polite."

He gave a tight shrug. "Alright." He reached into the pocket of his pants and pulled out his cell phone.

I made a sound of annoyance. "It doesn't count if you call when you're already here."

He held up a finger. "Hang on. I'm making a call."

I rolled my eyes. "Very funny."

True to his word, he scrolled through his contacts and then tapped at the screen, presumably at my name. I crossed my arms and gave him the snottiest look I could muster.

That look faded when I heard the telltale sound of ringing. I almost groaned out loud. *Oh, crap.* The ringing was coming from *him.*

I tried not to cringe. *He had my phone? But how?* Suddenly, I recalled my hasty departure from the office. I'd grabbed my purse, which contained my keys. But looking back, I couldn't recall grabbing my phone.

And now, it was still ringing from somewhere in pants. *Was it in his pocket?* I sure hoped so.

He smiled. "So....you want *me* to get that?"

I looked toward his pelvis. "Well, *I'm* not going to."

With his free hand, he reached into his pocket and pulled out my cell phone. He answered with a bored, "Allie's phone, how may I help you?"

With a sound of frustration, I lunged forward and yanked the phone out of his hand. Like a slippery fish, it slid out of my grasp and surely would've tumbled to the floor if only Jaden hadn't reached out and caught it in mid-air.

What was he? A secret ninja or something?

He held out the phone in my direction, obviously waiting for me to take it.

I snatched it away, more carefully this time, and then watched in silent annoyance as he tucked his own phone back into his pocket while eyeing me with clear amusement.

Now, I didn't know what to do.

I *had* to thank him, but I hated the thought. Plus, I'd just made a fool of myself, yet again. I mumbled, "I guess I should thank you, huh?"

"Nah." He grinned. "Your warm welcome is thanks enough."

My so-called welcome had been anything but warm, as both of us knew. I glanced down at my phone, still in my hand. "Where was it? On my desk?"

If so, I knew exactly where. At work, I kept my cell phone to the left of my computer screen, close enough to grab if anyone called, but mostly hidden from prying eyes.

Jaden replied, "Good guess."

It wasn't *that* good, but I didn't bother correcting him. Instead, I frowned as I realized something. "Wait a minute. You were in my office?"

"Is that a problem?"

Was it? Technically, some might say that it was *his* office because the whole building belonged to him and his brother. Still, something about this was distinctly unsettling.

Choosing my words very carefully, I said, "Well, I guess I *am* curious, since I locked the door."

"Yeah? Well, it wasn't locked an hour ago."

I felt my jaw clench. So Darla hadn't been kidding? She really *did* have a key?

This posed a whole slew of other questions. *What had happened after I left?*

Had she gone through my drawers?

Scrolled through my phone?

No. That, at least, was impossible since I'd recently added a password.

But the rest of it was a strong possibility. I looked to Jaden and asked, "Was it unlocked or open?"

"You mean the door?" he said. "It wasn't shut, I can tell you that."

Lovely.

So not only had Darla snooped in my office, she'd left the door wide open so others could snoop, too.

How nice.

And now, I felt more awkward than ever. By returning the phone, Jaden had done me a favor. And he was being a pretty good sport about it, too.

As for myself, I'd been a terrible sport from the moment he'd knocked. Still, the unexpected visit wasn't the only thing that had set me off. It was the recollection of what Darla had told me about Cassidy's job.

I was *so* tempted to call him on it. And yet, I hated the thought of giving him the satisfaction. Plus, what did it matter? It's not like he'd ever change his mind or give Cassidy a break.

Rather, he'd just go on being his awful self, except for times like this when he was surprisingly decent.

He was the most confusing person I'd ever met.

And now, neither one of us was talking. I couldn't help but wonder, what was he waiting for?

Was I supposed to invite him in?

The thought was obnoxiously appealing and repulsive all at the same time.

He was trouble, plain and simple.

So why was it, I wondered, that I couldn't stop thinking about him, even when I shouldn't?

Obviously, I'd lost my mind, that's why.

Finally, it was Jaden who broke the silence. "So, are you gonna tell me?"

"Tell you what?"

"Why you're so pissed off."

I stifled a curse. This was just like him, blunt to a fault. Normally, I was fairly blunt myself. But this was so embarrassingly complicated, especially when it came to my job.

Obviously, he and Darla were closer than I'd originally realized. If it came down to a choice, I knew which way he'd go. Plus, I was a brand new employee – and even worse, one he hadn't wanted to hire in the first place.

Even about Cassidy, what was I supposed to say? *Why'd you sabotage my friend?*

No matter how I sliced it, I could only lose if I complained now. I reminded myself that it wasn't just my own job on the chopping block. The brothers owned the place where Cassidy worked, which meant she could be fired just as easily as she'd been hired.

But I had to tell Jaden *something*. He had, after all, just asked.

Finally, I said, "It was just one of those weeks, that's all."

He gave me a dubious look. "If you think *last* week was bad, just wait 'til the next one."

My stomach sank. "Why?"

"Because," he said, "your boss is back, and we both know he's an asshole." And with that, he turned away, leaving me staring after him as he descended the stairs that led to the front porch.

Watching him go, I shoved a nervous hand through my damp hair. *Was* he an asshole?

At that moment, I couldn't be sure either way. But I *did* know one thing for sure. In a million years, I'd never figure him out.

When he disappeared from sight, I shut the apartment door and wandered to the bathroom, where I planned to run a comb through my hair and try to pull myself together.

That didn't happen. And why? It was because when I looked into the bathroom mirror, I realized with a start which shirt I'd grabbed in my rush to get dressed.

It was the shirt that Cassidy had given me as a joke on my last birthday, after I'd cursed up a storm one too many times.

And what did the shirt say?

I talk dirty.

In the mirror, the letters were reversed, but the message was clear enough. I squeezed my eyes shut and tried not to look. It did no good. My entire reflection was burned into my brain – my wet hair, my pink skin, and the decidedly obscene message.

What if he thought I'd picked that shirt on purpose?

I shook my head. *But surely he wouldn't.*

Would he?

I tried not to think about it. After all, I wouldn't even be seeing him until Monday.

Unfortunately, when Monday came, I was even *more* stymied when I saw what my asinine boss had left on my desk.

CHAPTER 33

From behind my desk, I stared down at the thing. It was a joke, obviously. And to my infinite annoyance, I couldn't help but smile. It was a cardboard coaster from a restaurant that I'd never heard of – *Slappy's Sandwiches*.

It sported an outline of a sandwich – a tall one, made with a bun, not bread, like the sandwich that I'd destroyed in Jaden's kitchen.

I didn't even know if the restaurant was real, but it was funny and annoying all at the same time. I cursed under my breath. The fact that I was amused only fueled my irritation.

Technically, none of this was funny.

It was the beginning of a new week, which meant that I was facing five straight days of Jaden's barbs and Darla's hostility – or so I'd been thinking.

But the strange thing was, when I'd arrived bright and early, I'd seen someone else sitting at Darla's desk. It was a woman close to Darla's age, but with darker hair and thick glasses.

Her office door was shut, but I could still see her as plain as day through the window of Darla's office door. I gave the stranger a smile and a little wave, but received nothing in return. Either she didn't notice me or she was giving me the cold shoulder just like everyone else.

By now, I should've been used to it, but it did make me wonder, *Was Darla out sick or something?*

I didn't know, and saw no benefit of asking. So instead, I kept strictly to my own office, where I had more than enough to keep me busy.

Still, a half-hour later, I couldn't resist peering around my office doorway for another quick look.

The woman was still there, but now, she had her back turned as she talked on her phone. Probably, this was a good thing, or I'd feel like an idiot for peeping.

Unfortunately, a split second later, I *did* feel like an idiot when an all-too-familiar voice said, "Looking for someone?"

I gave a little jump. It was Jaden, who'd suddenly appeared in the open doorway to his office. Funny, I hadn't even realized that he was in.

When I'd arrived, his door had been partially open, but the office itself had been quiet and dark, with the lights off and shades drawn.

Now, I tried to look nonchalant. "I was just seeing who's here." I glanced past him toward his darkened office. "Do you always work with the lights off?"

"I dunno," he said. "Do *you* always get here early?"

I glanced at the nearby clock. It was half past seven. Officially, my workday began at eight, but I'd arrived early for a reason. I'd wanted to get here before everyone else, so I could see if anything in my office had been molested by Darla.

By now, I'd already given it a thorough inspection. Surprisingly, I'd found nothing missing or out of place. The only change at all had been the appearance of that stupid coaster, sitting in the exact spot where I usually kept my cell phone.

The coaster *hadn't* come from Darla. Of this, I was nearly certain – just like I was nearly certain that Jaden was the one who'd relocked my office after retrieving my phone.

But it couldn't have been as a favor to me. Probably, it was some sort of security thing. *Right?*

Regardless, the whole situation was slightly unsettling. I'd shown up expecting to be the first one here, not the clueless late arrival with no idea what was going on.

Without thinking, I gave Darla's office another sideways glance.

Jaden lowered his voice to a mock whisper. "That's Karen."

"Oh." Again, my gaze slid in her direction. She was still on the phone and still looking away. Quietly, I asked, "Is she filling in for Darla?"

"No," Jaden replied. "Darla was filling in for *her*."

I felt my brow wrinkle in confusion. "What?"

"You didn't know?"

I shook my head. "Was I supposed to?"

"I figured she'd mention it."

Who did he mean? Darla? I recalled all of the things that she *did* mention. Most were insulting, and none of them were particularly helpful.

I muttered, "It must've slipped her mind."

Jaden gave a low scoff. "I doubt that. And just so you know, she'll be filling in for *you*, too."

"Darla?" I stared up at him. "What do you mean?"

"When we travel," he said, "she'll be manning your desk."

At the idea of Darla sitting at my desk, possibly going through my things, and generally making trouble, I tried not to frown. "Oh. Well that's good."

In reality, I should've been jumping for joy. Without Darla, the office might actually be a reasonably pleasant place. But I couldn't begin think about that now, because the other half of his statement was belatedly hitting home.

When we travel?

Meaning him and me?

Yikes.

I'd known this from the job description. And yet, the thought of going anywhere with him was deeply unsettling.

Still, I tried not to dwell on it – not that day, nor any other day that week. I never did say anything about the coaster, because I knew all too well that its only purpose was to get a rise out of me.

I refused to give Jaden the satisfaction.

Instead, I responded with a little surprise of my own.

It was a flyer that I'd spotted at the grocery store. It advertised a cooking class for beginners – kids in particular. The illustration showed a cartoon child in a chef's hat, proudly holding a sandwich that was nearly as tall as him.

It was silly, really, but not any sillier than the coaster.

Late that Friday night, I placed the flyer directly to the left of Jaden's computer, similar to where he'd placed the coaster for me.

I felt myself smile. *Two could play at this game.*

I wasn't even sure what game we were playing, but as I soon learned, it was far from over.

CHAPTER 34

We did this for several weeks. Every other Monday, I'd come into work and find something completely ridiculous – and vaguely insulting – on my desk. There was that flyer for an anger management class, a sandwich recipe book, and this latest surprise, a Scooby Doo Christmas ornament.

As far as the ornament, I had no idea where Jaden had gotten it. Christmas was still months away, so it was impossible to believe that the thing had been an impulse purchase, made at the store while picking up something else.

No. This was premeditated.

Standing at my desk, I gazed down at the thing and felt an annoying smile tug at my lips. I knew exactly why he'd selected this particular item to torment me.

On the day we'd met, when I'd been rampaging through his house in search of my friend, he'd made a bunch of sarcastic comments referencing Scooby Doo's gang of amateur sleuths.

He'd called me Velma. Of all the characters, she was probably the smartest, but not terribly attractive. At the time, the description had only *half*-fit, because on that first fateful day, I'd been stupid *and* unkempt.

But Velma? She was almost never stupid.

Still, the comparison wasn't flattering, at least in the looks department.

And why did this matter?

It didn't. Or at least that's what I kept telling myself.

It's not I like cared whether Jaden considered me attractive. By now, he surely realized that I was no idiot, and really, that was the most important thing, right?

All modesty aside, I'd proven myself to be a perfectly competent assistant. I had a way of anticipating what he wanted and giving it to him long before he thought to ask.

As far as jobs went, this was the best one I'd ever had. There were only two problems. The *first* problem was that everyone avoided me like the plague, and the *second* problem was Jaden himself.

The first problem, I could deal with – and hopefully solve at some point. After all, I knew exactly why people were avoiding me.

It was because of Darla.

Although she didn't work for the company full-time, she was in the building way too often. Whenever I thought I was making a new friend, I'd eventually spot that person talking to Darla in some quiet corridor. And then, all too soon, they'd be giving me the cold shoulder just like everyone else.

I could only imagine what she was telling them.

But this, even as oppressive as it was, wasn't the thing that kept me awake in the deepest parts of the night. It was that second problem – my complicated feelings for my boss.

He drove me crazy in every possible way. He was blunt, sarcastic, and a total jackass. Unfortunately, he was also smart, insightful, and the most intriguing person I'd ever met.

Plus, he had an unexpected thoughtful streak that made it nearly impossible for me to truly hate him. There was the time he'd sent me home – with pay – because he'd overheard me coughing up a lung in my office. There was the time he'd given me a ride home when I'd accidentally locked my keys in the truck. And of course, there was that time he'd returned my cell phone rather than leaving it sitting on my office desk.

Unfortunately, he was *also* the guy who'd sabotaged my friend's job prospects and seemed to take a particular delight in driving me insane.

He was a mess of crazy contradictions, which in turn, was making *me* a little crazy myself. Even after a couple of months, I still didn't know what to make of him.

It didn't help that I was always fielding phone calls from women desperate to get his attention.

At first, I'd simply tell these women that they should try his cell phone if they were calling about a personal matter, at which point, they'd either inform me that they didn't have the number *or* that he wasn't answering.

Like the good professional I was, I never gave out his cell number, no matter how much they begged. This was, after all, part of my so-called extra responsibility of – as he'd put it – keeping people off his ass.

See? I was doing it for him.
Not me.
Really, I was.

As far as these female admirers, I didn't know whether they were women from his past or women who wanted to be in his future. Regardless, as time went on, I found myself getting increasingly annoyed at all of them, including Morgan.

Oh yeah. She was still in the picture.

She might've been fired from the job that I now held, but that didn't stop her from bounding into the office nearly every day and making the rounds – first to Jax and then to Jaden.

By now, I'd learned a little bit more about their family relationship, mostly from Morgan herself. Apparently, Darla had taken in both brothers when they'd been teenagers. Morgan was Darla's natural daughter, and had been smitten from the start.

The way it looked, she was *still* smitten. I didn't know how long she and Jax had dated, but I *did* know that she wanted him back. That much was glaringly obvious.

And while she was at it, she wanted Jaden, too.

I could see in the way she leaned over his desk, especially when wearing something low-cut. I could hear it in the way she laughed a little too loud when he said something funny. And then, there was the way she pouted a little too sexily whenever he informed her that he had to get back to work.

The sad thing was, Morgan was practically the only person – other than Jax and Jaden themselves – who was remotely friendly to me. I might've been thankful for her company, if only the conversations didn't consist mostly of her pumping me for information about Cassidy.

I knew why, too. Morgan was jealous of something between Cassidy and Jax. They weren't quite an item, but it was ridiculously easy to see that Jax was interested.

From Cassidy, I knew that they'd been running into each other at the coffee shop near our apartment. But I *also* knew that Jax didn't even drink coffee – and even if he did, he could get anything he wanted from a place a lot closer.

Cripes, he could even send out his assistant for whatever he wanted.

After all, that's what Jaden did. Even after all this time, I still didn't know if he sent me to sandwich shops on purpose to tweak me, or if he really did love them that much.

Regardless, I could recite most of the local sandwich menus by heart and had acquired my own personal favorites. Unfortunately, they tended to be the same ones that Jaden favored, which only made it more embarrassing whenever he happened to notice what I was eating at my desk.

Who knows, maybe he thought I was tweaking *him* by ordering the same thing.

I wasn't.

It's just that we had annoyingly similar tastes.

And I did love a good sandwich.

But it wasn't our shared love of sandwiches that had me lurking over his desk one Friday evening, long after everyone else had gone.

No. I was lurking because just this past Tuesday, he'd mentioned an extreme dislike of broccoli, and I'd found the perfect thing to get a rise out of him.

It was a broccoli shaped doggie toy – the kind that made squeaky noises when you squeezed it. The noise was surprisingly loud for such a little thing. *It would drive him nuts.*

I smiled as I set it in the traditional spot.

Take that, Broccoli-Hater.

In the back of my mind, I couldn't help but wonder what he did with the stuff that I left on his desk. *Did he keep it? Or toss it out?*

I didn't know, because we never discussed it.

Still, I did this every other week, just like he did the same to me in return. By unspoken agreement, we alternated weeks, leaving something every other Friday for the other person to find on the following Monday.

As I tiptoed out of his office, I took one final glance over my shoulder. The broccoli was sitting there, completely out of place, like a proverbial turd in a punchbowl.

It would be the perfect thing to start out his week – whether with a smile or a quiet curse. If he was anything like me, he'd probably do both.

I'd just returned to my own office to grab my purse and cell phone when a sudden burst of female laughter made me pause.

The laughter had come from just outside the executive suite. I turned to look just in time to see Jaden walk through the suite's door, looking slightly irritated.

Even more unsettling, he wasn't alone.

CHAPTER 35

Accompanying Jaden was a stunningly tall brunette wearing a form-fitting red dress and matching red heels.

I knew who she was. Her name was Victoria Landers, and she was an account executive with the advertising agency that handled most of the Bishop Brothers' promotional campaigns.

She worked out of New York, but had flown here just this morning for a meeting with Jaden. I knew this because I'd been the one to schedule the appointment *and* to greet her earlier today when she'd shown up a full hour early for their one-on-one meeting.

But this meeting had ended hours ago, which told me one important thing. Whatever was going on now was more of a social call. As if to prove it beyond all doubt, Victoria gripped his arm and gave a little laugh as she said, "I can't believe I left it."

Jaden's reply held no trace of laughter. "Yeah. You and me both."

She gave him a playful swat to the arm. "Oh, don't be grumpy. This'll give us a chance to talk before my flight."

Something in her tone suggested that talking wasn't the primary thing on her mind. As if to hammer the point home, she leaned her head closer to his and practically cooed,"…unless you want me to reschedule?"

I stiffened. *Reschedule what?*

The flight?

That's what it sounded like to me.

The whole thing was beyond awkward. It was long past quitting time, and the only reason I'd stayed so late was to leave that stupid chew-toy on Jaden's desk. Now, he'd not only discover it early, but also discover it in front of an audience.

An audience of her.

And me.

I wasn't sure which aspect bothered me more.

Until now, these little gift-exchanges had always been done in secret. It made it seem less strange somehow – like we weren't just a boss and employee, but something different.

Friends?

Sparring partners?

Or something more complicated?

I didn't know, and I hated the idea of finding out now, in front of someone who I didn't particularly like.

It wasn't that Victoria had been rude, exactly, but she'd obviously decided from the get-go that I was barely worth a hello. In contrast, she'd greeting Jaden like he was the juiciest morsel she'd ever seen.

Today was the first day the two of them had met in person. I knew this, because the purpose of today's meeting – in theory anyway – had been to give Victoria the chance to introduce herself as the newest member of the team handling the company's account.

The way it looked now, she was bucking for a more personal introduction after-hours. I bit my lip. Or maybe, that so-called introduction had already taken place.

After all, they weren't acting like two strangers. Plus, it wasn't lost on me that Jaden had been missing for most of the afternoon. His schedule had been empty, so I had no clue where he'd gone.

Basically, he'd just wandered off sometime around two o'clock, only to never return.

Until now.

Shit.

I should've realized that he'd be back. Even so, there was no way I could've anticipated him returning with a female companion. After all, he'd never done such a thing before, at least not in the time that I'd been working here.

Now, I wasn't quite sure what to do.

After first spotting them, I'd quickly sat down at my desk so it wouldn't look like I'd been standing there, staring. Now, I was trying to look busy – shuffling papers and glancing at my computer screen, as if I *weren't* embarrassingly aware that she sounded like two seconds away from suggesting a quickie on his desk.

Oh, God.

His desk.

Would they do it next to the broccoli?

The whole thing – stupid or not – made me feel just a little bit queasy, and *not* because I wasn't a huge fan of broccoli myself.

In my mind's eye, I could practically see it – him bending her over the desk with her face next to that chew toy. Or maybe she'd be on her back, and he'd be driving into her from above.

Damn it. Why was I thinking of this? It's true that I'd thought of similar things before, but in all of *those* thoughts, it was *me* on the desk, with him treating me as something a lot more than his assistant.

I hadn't *wanted* to think those things, but no matter how hard I tried to squash them, those X-rated ideas kept popping up like gophers at a golf course.

Regardless, I wasn't planning to act on any of those impulses, even if they *did* keep the days interesting.

But this current situation? Oh, it was interesting alright, but not in any way that I enjoyed. When they passed my office, I gave a little wave, not that either one of them seemed to notice.

Together, they entered his private office without a single glance in my direction. With a little giggle, she shut the door behind them, leaving me with a clear view of absolutely nothing except the door itself.

This was a good thing.

Really, it was.

Because whatever was going on in there, I *so* didn't want to see it. I sure as heck didn't want to hear it either. With quick jerky movements, I grabbed my purse and cell phone, intending to bolt for the exit and not look back.

But just as I was passing his office door, I heard a sound that made me pause.

It wasn't moaning or groaning, thank God. Rather, it was the telltale squeak of the broccoli.

My face flooded with embarrassment, even more so when her laughter rang out from behind the closed door.

I should've kept on going, but suddenly, my feet wouldn't cooperate.

I heard her ask, "What it this? A stressball?"

Jaden's reply, assuming there was one at all, was too quiet for me to hear.

"You know," she said in a sultry voice, "if you're tense, I can think of other ways to solve it. You know, I give great massages."

I almost scoffed out loud. *Oh, she wanted to massage him, alright.* And I knew exactly which part.

His dick.

With her vagina.

Whether that ever happened, I had no idea, because a split second later, I was rushing for the door.

I pushed through it hard and fast, and never looked back.

Still, the images haunted me like a bad dream. All of this was so incredibly stupid. I was his employee, not his friend, and definitely nothing more.

He owned the building.

And the company.

And me, at least when it came to my paycheck.

I needed to get a grip, and possibly a new job – not because I didn't love the one I had, but rather because I was having a hard time dealing with whatever was going on.

Hours later, I was still irritated, even after a steaming hot bath and two bottles of my favorite beer – *his* beer, at least according to its brand-name.

Damn it.

Sitting on the sofa, I glanced around the place that I now called home. I loved the apartment, truly I did. And I loved the city, too. Still, tonight nothing felt quite right.

The apartment felt big and empty. And the city surrounding it felt cold and lonely in spite of the balmy weather. Cassidy was working, and I had no other friends here at all – mostly because everyone at work treated me like I was some sort of human disease, to be avoided at all costs.

This totally sucked.

On top of everything else, Stuart, my ex-boyfriend, had called my cell phone several times today, demanding that I call him back.

What a joke. He hadn't returned any of *my* calls, even when I'd been so desperate for information. The whole thing was beyond depressing.

But I didn't want to spend my time sulking *or* talking with my ex. It was a Friday night, which meant that I had two glorious days ahead of me, days *without* Jaden Bishop and all of his confusing behavior.

What I needed tonight, I decided, was a change of scenery – something different to shake off the gloom. Who knows, maybe I'd even make a new friend or two.

It was such a lovely thought that I pushed myself up from the sofa, threw on my favorite sundress, and ventured alone into a local nightclub just a short drive from the apartment – where the only real thing I found was more trouble than I'd bargained for.

CHAPTER 36

Next to me, the guy in the dark blazer was saying, "C'mon, you're pulling my leg."

I laughed. "I am not."

The stranger was tall and good-looking in that classic sort of way. He smiled down at me. "Prove it."

"Why should I have to prove it?"

"Because," he said, with a glance at my drink, "I could get in trouble, contributing to juvenile delinquency and all."

I was still laughing. "Why? You didn't buy the drink. I did."

"Yeah, but I'm determined to get the next one." He gave me a boyish grin. "You don't want me getting in trouble, do you?"

I rolled my eyes. "Don't worry, you're completely safe."

"Oh yeah? Why's that?"

I lifted my glass in his direction. "Because I'm sticking to just one tonight." I smiled. "But thanks anyway."

"One drink?" he said. "Where's the fun in that?"

Technically, I was on my third drink if I counted the two beers at home, but that was hardly worth mentioning.

So instead, I glanced around. "Well, there *is* the music." In truth, the music wasn't that great, or maybe it just wasn't my style. But I *did* like the crowd. The club was located directly on the beach, and it had a good mix of people my own age, along with some quite a bit older.

As for my new acquaintance, he was somewhere in the middle – a decade or so older than myself, but a long way from retirement.

Regardless, I wasn't here to get drunk. I was here for a change of scenery. As it was, I'd been nursing my first drink for so long that the ice cubes had gone watery.

Now, the guy was eyeing me with mock concern. "I *still* say you're not twenty-one."

It wasn't that far-fetched. I did look a little on the young side, mostly because I was shorter than average. Even so, the guy was obviously joking, not that I minded.

Until now, I'd hardly laughed all day. "Do I need to remind you," I said, "they checked my I.D. at the door?"

"Yeah, but it could be a fake." He lowered his voice to a conspiratorial whisper "People do that, you know."

I *did* know. In fact, with a little help from an older friend, I'd actually gotten into quite a few nightclubs in the two years *before* reaching the legal drinking age.

At the memory, I almost snickered. "I *have* heard of such a thing."

"Uh-huh." The guy held out his hand, palm-up. "C'mon, let's see it."

"See what?" I asked.

"Your I.D." Now, he looked ready to snicker, too. "Just between us, I'm an expert."

"In what? Fake I.D.s?"

I'd been at the nightclub for almost an hour, and I was finally starting to relax, mostly because the guy's conversation – as ridiculous as it was – was keeping my mind off everything that had driven me here in the first place.

We were standing just a few feet away from the main bar, within sight of the crowded dance floor. The music was mostly techno – the generic kind that made it hard to differentiate one song from another.

I'd been hoping to dance, but not to *this* – which made me doubly glad for the guy's conversation while I passed the time.

With another laugh, he nudged his hand closer. "C'mon, show me, and I'll tell you a secret."

I eyed him with mock suspicion. "What kind of secret?"

"If you wanna know, fork it over."

I smiled. "Not without a hint."

"Alright." He made a show of looking around. "Guess who I

spotted in the men's room."

"Who?"

"A famous athlete."

"How famous?" I asked.

"Gold medal famous."

"You mean the Olympics?" Now, I was intrigued in spite of myself. "Really? Which sport?"

He gave me a playful wink. "Sorry, can't say if you're under-age."

Already, I was laughing again. "What does that have to do with anything?"

"Sorry, rules are rules."

I'd never been a huge sports fan, but I *was* curious what he'd say next. In the spirit of things, I reached into the pocket of my sundress and pulled out my license. But I didn't hand it over. Rather, I held it up, flashing it badge-style, so he could take a quick look. "See?"

He looked at the license and then at my face. "Are you *sure* this is you?"

"What? It doesn't look like me?"

"Well, you don't look twenty-five, that's for damn sure."

"Oh yeah? Well, how old are *you*?"

"Older than twenty-five."

"How much older?" I asked.

He lowered his voice and leaned a fraction closer. "Old enough to know what I'm doing."

I leaned back. "Sorry, what?"

He gave me another wink. "I'm just saying, I've got a few tricks up my sleeve."

I hesitated. I'd found the first wink charming, but the second one made me feel a little squirmy, especially when paired with the comment about tricks up his sleeve.

Something new in his demeanor suggested that the trick was mostly in his pants.

Eager to change the subject, I said, "So, who's the athlete?"

He gave a little swagger. "You can't guess?"

I stared up at him. "You don't mean you?"

Grinning more broadly now, he extended his index finger and shot me with an imaginary gun. "Bingo."

I wasn't quite sure I believed him. "So, you were an Olympic athlete? Really?"

"What, does that surprise you?"

I hesitated. "I just never met one before. So, um, what sport?"

"Polo."

I tried to think. "You mean water polo?"

"No." He frowned. "Polo-polo. With horses."

"Oh." I was trying to think. I didn't even realize that polo *was* an Olympic sport. Then again, I hadn't followed the Olympics since high school.

The guy was still frowning. "Is something wrong?"

"No, it's just that--" I paused in mid-sentence as I spotted a familiar figure in the crowd.

Oh, crap.

It was Jaden Bishop – my boss, my nemesis, and my own personal thorn in the side.

In further bad news, he was staring straight in my direction.

And he did *not* look happy.

Damn it.

Why was he *here* of all places? *And where was Victoria?* More than two hours had passed since I'd seen them together at the office. For all *I* knew, she was still there, squeezing the broccoli.

Naked.

Or maybe she was on some airplane, headed back to New York.

Or – oh, God – maybe she was here. *With him.*

I felt my brow wrinkle in concern. Across the club, Jaden was still frowning.

But why?

I didn't know. And I didn't *want* to know. Already, I'd had more than enough of Jaden Bishop for one day -- cripes, maybe even one lifetime.

Deliberately, I looked back to my new acquaintance. "Sorry, what were you saying?"

"Nothing," he said. "You were the one talking."

"Oh." I forced a laugh. "What was I saying?"

"Got me," he said looking suddenly annoyed. "You never finished."

It was actually kind of strange. Sometime within the last two minutes, he'd gone from Mister Friendly to Mister Disgruntled. For some reason, it reminded me of Jaden, and I didn't like it.

At the thought, I snuck another glance in Jaden's direction, only to feel my eyebrows furrow in confusion. *He was gone.* I scanned the crowd, but no saw no sign that he'd ever been there at all.

I almost scoffed out loud. This was just like him, too, to come in and get me all stressed out for no good reason.

I said a silent vow. *Not tonight.*

Next to me, the stranger said something that I didn't quite catch. *Maybe something about horses? Polo horses?*

I sighed. I had no idea.

I looked back to him and said, "Sorry, what?"

He looked down toward the floor. "I *said*, do you wanna see it?"

Obviously, I'd lost total track of the conversation. And now, I was almost afraid to ask. *See what?*

I was still trying to figure it out when a familiar male voice answered the guy on my behalf. "No," he told the guy, "she doesn't."

CHAPTER 37

I whirled to look. Sure enough, standing directly behind me was my troublesome boss, who frowned down at me like he'd just caught me humping a bar stool.

I stared up at him. "Excuse me?"

"I wasn't talking to *you*." He looked past me toward the stranger. "I was talking to *him*."

Oh, for God's sake.

As I watched, Jaden gave the stranger a hard look. "She's not interested, so fuck off."

I stifled a gasp. *What the hell?*

Now, I was glaring. "What's wrong with you?" When he made no reply, I turned back to the stranger and said, "I'm *really* sorry."

The stranger's gaze darted from me to the jerk standing just past my shoulder. The stranger made no reply, not that I could blame him. After all, this wasn't exactly normal.

Speaking loud enough for Jaden to hear, I said, "His manners really *are* atrocious."

From behind me, Jaden said, "Yeah. They are. But he's still leaving if he knows what's good for him."

My gaze was still on the stranger. *What could I say to make things right?* Words utterly failed, even as the guy started backing slowly away.

He looked scared to death, which made total sense.

After all, it was perfectly normal to be afraid of a crazy person.

I whirled back to the maniac in question and said, "Will you *please* butt out?"

"Sure," Jaden said, "as soon as he's gone."

Through clenched teeth, I said, "Just what's your problem, anyway?"

"Nothing that his leaving won't help."

Well, this was rich. Just a couple of hours ago, he'd been doing God-knows-what in his office. In contrast, I was doing something perfectly acceptable, and more to the point, *away* from the office.

This was none of his business.

I turned back to give the guy yet another apology, only to freeze in confusion.

He was gone.

But that was impossible. He'd been there just a moment ago. Silently, I scanned the crowd. Finally, I spotted him weaving his way across the packed dance floor, jostling random people as he went.

From what I could tell, he was heading toward the rest rooms. I kept watching. *No. Not the restrooms.*

The side exit.

A moment later, he plowed through the door like the place was on fire. This was oddly fitting, considering that the alarm sounded for like two seconds until the door swung shut again, leaving those standing near the door gaping after him.

A hard scoff escaped my lips. *Well, that was delightful.*

I whirled back to Jaden and demanded, "What was *that* about?"

"The guy's an asshole."

My jaw clenched. *Speaking of assholes.* "Well you *are* the expert."

"Yeah. I am."

I made a sound of frustration. By now, I'd just about had it. "In case you didn't realize it, I just insulted you."

"What? By calling me an asshole?"

I gave a tight shrug. That *had* been the implication, but it seemed beyond stupid to say it outright, unless I *wanted* to be unemployed.

Jaden practically snorted, "That's no insult."

"What?"

"Yeah. I'm proud of it."

Funny, he didn't *look* proud. He looked mostly pissed off.

If so, that made two of us. I was still glaring. "You *do* know we're not at work, right?"

"Hell, I know all kinds of things."

"Sure you do."

He gave me a hard look. "And what are you doing here, anyway?"

"What do you *think* I'm doing here?" I made a sound of disgust. "I'm having fun."

He gave me a dubious look. "Are you?"

Alright, that *had* sounded slightly ridiculous, but he was totally missing the point – as usual. "Okay fine," I snapped. "I *was* having fun 'til *you* showed up."

"Yeah?" His mouth tightened. "It didn't look like it to me."

I crossed my arms. "Is that so?"

"Yeah. You looked tense."

Well, maybe Victoria could give me a massage. Hold the broccoli.

But I didn't say it. Not only did I *not* want to give him the satisfaction, really, this was none of his concern.

And besides, I hadn't been *truly* tense until I'd seen Jaden, here of all places. "Of course I was nervous," I said. "I saw you giving me that look."

"What look?"

"That pissed off look."

"Yeah?" he said. "Well I saw *you* before you saw *me*."

"So?"

"So you didn't look like you were 'having fun'."

I tried to think. *When exactly had he spotted me?* Was it *after* that second wink? If so, Jaden might've been right about the fun factor, even though I'd never admit it in a million years.

Regardless, that was no reason for him to run the guy off like that.

"Well, guess what?" I said. "I don't care what you think." My voice rose. "And why should *I* be on the defense all of a sudden? *You* were the one who behaved like a total jackass."

As that final word hung between us, I sucked in a horrified breath. I'd just called my boss a jackass. *Shit.* To think that earlier today, I'd left the office without a peep, only to lose it here, a couple of hours later.

So much for self-control.

But it was too late to take it back now, and besides, maybe I didn't want to. I mean, it's not like he deserved an apology or anything.

Still, I felt compelled to remind him, "And just so you know, you're not the boss of me here."

His jaw tightened. "Yeah? Well I'm not *here* as your boss."

"Oh really? Then *what* are you here as?"

He looked at me for a long moment before muttering, "I don't know."

"Yeah? Well, that makes two of us, because I didn't appreciate it."

"You didn't appreciate what?"

"Oh come on. You know what. You scared that guy off for no good reason."

In front of me, Jaden looked anything but contrite. "You sure about that?"

"Of course I'm sure. I was there, remember?"

"Don't you mean you were *here*?"

"What?"

"*There* is *here*," he said. "We haven't moved."

I felt like screaming. "Why does that even matter?"

"I'm just saying…"

"Well don't." I felt my gaze narrow. "And besides, you're just trying to distract me."

"From what?"

My chin lifted. "From telling you exactly what I think."

"Yeah? And what's that?"

"That you were incredibly rude."

"Not as rude as *he* was."

"Who?"

"Derek, the Douchebag."

I paused. "Derek? Was *that* his name?"

"What, you didn't know?"

"No. I'd only been talking to him for like five minutes."

Jaden's expression darkened. "Is that all?"

"Yeah. Why?"

"Because the guy moves a little fast, don't you think?"

I had no idea what he meant. "What are you talking about?"

Jaden edged closer and said in a low voice, "His cock."

CHAPTER 38

Around me, everything seemed to fade into the background as that single word hit with a thud.

I studied Jaden's face. I didn't know what he was getting at, but he looked deadly serious. I gave a confused shake of my head. "What?"

"You heard me."

Yes. I had. But I didn't know what Derek's privates had to do with anything. And now, I didn't know what to say. *I mean, what could I say?*

Finally, it was Jaden who broke the silence. "What, you *wanted* to see it? After knowing the guy five minutes?"

"Wait, what—" And then it hit me. *No.* The stranger – Derek – he'd been offering to show me something. *Surely, it wasn't...?*

I gave a bitter scoff. In truth, I had no idea.

And *why* was that? It's because I'd been so distracted by Jaden giving me that look of loathing from across the room.

I looked away and muttered, "You know what? Forget it. I'm going home."

"Good," he said. "I'll walk you to your car."

"Good?" I said. "No, it's *not* good. You totally ruined my night."

"Is that so?"

"Yes. It is." I meant it too, but not in the way it sounded. In reality, the night had started to go downhill the moment Jaden had walked into the office with Victoria. But that *wasn't* what we were talking about now, and I had no intention of bringing it up.

For what felt like the millionth time, I reminded myself that he was only my boss. Nothing more. And besides, we weren't talking about Victoria. We were talking about the guy named Derek.

I sighed. "Look, I don't even know what he said, but I can tell you this, I can handle myself just fine. So, even if he *did* say something crude, it's not like you had to run over here and be such an ass about it."

"Don't you mean ass*hole*?"

"What?"

"You said 'ass', but you forgot the 'hole.'"

I gave him a thin smile. "Oh, trust me. I didn't forget."

Asshole.

And with that, I turned and began striding toward the exit. And what did he do? He started walking with me. I turned to glare at him yet again. "What are you doing?"

"Walking you to the car, like I said."

"I didn't drive a car. I drove a truck, as *you* of all people should know." Yes, I realized that it didn't really matter, but I wanted to prove him wrong about something, *anything*. He was too damned sure of himself, and I'd had just about enough.

He gave a loose shrug. "Alright, then I'll walk you to your truck."

"Hah! It's not my truck. It's *your* truck."

Take that, Mister Know-it-all.

To my infinite annoyance, he responded with yet another shrug. "Alright."

Alright? As a response, it was oddly unsatisfying. "Forget it," I told him. "I don't *need* you to walk me out."

His jaw tightened. "That's what *you* think."

"No. It's what I know." I was glowering again. "And besides, I think you've done more than enough already."

"Yeah? And you wanna know what *I* think?"

"Not particularly."

"I think you need to be more careful."

"Well, guess what?" I said. "I don't care *what* you think. I'm not at work, which means I *don't* have to listen to you."

"Yeah, but you should."

"Oh really?" I snapped. "Why's that?"

"Because this place is *full* of assholes."

I met his gaze straight-on. "Yeah. Tell me about it."

"If you're calling me an asshole, I already told you, I don't care."

"Well maybe *I* do." I looked around. "And just for the record, I didn't come here for a hard time."

"Alright. Then what *did* you come here for?"

"What kind of question is that?" I gave the crowd a quick glance. "Why does *anyone* come here?"

His mouth tightened. "I can tell you why *Derek* was here."

"Oh, please," I said. "Like *your* reason's any different."

"Meaning?"

I made a point of looking him up and down. He'd changed clothes since I'd seen him last. He was wearing tailored slacks and a dark button-down shirt. The sleeves of his shirt were pushed up, revealing the hard muscles and colorful tattoos that snaked up his forearms.

He looked very rich. And very sexy. And more than a little bit dangerous.

I knew exactly why he was here, and it wasn't to chat it up with his least-favorite employee – meaning me, of course.

I gave him a thin smile. "What? You think I won't say it?"

"Say what?"

"Why you're here."

"No," he said. "I think you don't *know* why I'm here."

"Oh, please. You're here to get laid." I almost rolled my eyes. *And if he did get laid, what would that be? The third time today?*

He replied, "Is that so?"

"Sure. I mean, why else you would you be here?"

"I dunno," he said. "Why else would *you* be here?"

"What do you mean by that?" I demanded.

"I mean," he said, "that you shouldn't be too quick to assume, considering that you're in the same place."

The implication was obvious, and I didn't appreciate it one bit. "For your information," I said, "I came here for a drink and maybe to dance."

"What, you don't have drinks at home?"

God, what a total tool. "You know what I mean."

"And," he said, "I didn't see you dance."

I scoffed, "How would *you* know?"

His eyebrows lifted. "So, you *have*?"

I glanced away. "No. But I could've."

"Then why didn't you?"

"Well, it *wasn't* because I wasn't asked, if that's what you're thinking." I didn't even know why I was telling him this. It was hardly relevant.

Just like so many other things, it really *was* none of his business.

His gaze skimmed my sundress, and I saw of flicker something that *wasn't* loathing. "Trust me," he said. "That *wasn't* what I was thinking."

"What does *that* mean?"

"It means, I'm sure you had plenty of offers."

I gave a bitter laugh. "Oh yeah, loads. Including one that was a lot more interesting than I realized."

I mean, it wasn't every day some stranger offered to show you his privates.

Jaden gave me a look that I couldn't quite decipher. "You'd better be talking about Derek."

My only reply was a tight shrug.

"Tell me," he said with the barest hint of a smile, "is there someone else that needs a talking to?"

It wasn't even a full smile, and yet, just like always, it made me go soft in the head. I heard myself ask, "About Derek, did he *really* say that?"

"You didn't hear?"

I shook my head. "I heard something about a horse, but..." *Oh, shit.* Now, I couldn't help but cringe. "He wasn't implying that he's, uh...?"

"Hung like a horse?" Jaden gave a hard scoff. "Yeah, that was the gist of it."

I blew out a long, shaky breath. "But how could *you* hear, and *I* couldn't? I was standing a lot closer than *you* were."

"Not *much* closer," he said. "Besides, I knew it was coming."

"What do you mean?" I asked.

"You think you're the first girl he's said that to?"

"Oh." I gave it some thought. I'd been talking to the guy for only five minutes. If he moved *that* fast, no doubt he'd already been making the rounds. I bit my lip. "Let me guess. He's *that* guy."

Jaden's eyebrows furrowed. "What guy?"

"The local creep, the one who comes across as perfectly normal for five whole minutes before asking for your undies."

Damn it. Undies?

Why had I called them undies? And now, Jaden looked ready to laugh.

I murmured, "Never mind." With a shaky laugh, I added, "I'm pretty sure I don't want to know."

Somehow, in the last couple of minutes, most of my anger had evaporated. Jaden was a lot of things, but not a liar. If anything, he was too blunt, too honest, and too prone to say exactly what he was thinking.

In that way, maybe we were more alike than I wanted to admit.

With a sigh, I glanced toward the main exit. Storming out had seemed like such a wonderful idea just a few moments ago.

But now, it felt like an admission of defeat – that I couldn't have a reasonably normal evening without it going to crap. *And what was I? Some kind of freak magnet?*

I was still mulling all of this over when Jaden said, "So, why *didn't* you?'

"Why didn't I what?"

He flicked his head toward the dance floor. "That."

"You mean dance?"

"You said that's why you came."

I *had* said that, and it was mostly true. Still, the primary reason I'd come here was to forget about *him*. But I'd never admit it, so all I said was, "I dunno…"

"No." His voice grew softer. "Tell me." Again, he looked toward the dance floor. "Why aren't you out there?"

I gave it some thought. "Well, at first I didn't want to leave my drink and then, well, it was just the music, I guess."

"What, you don't like it?"

"Not really," I admitted.

"What *do* you like?"

I gazed up at him and tried not to notice that his eyes were so stupidly compelling. *And*, he looked genuinely curious.

I heard myself ask, "Why?"

He shrugged. "Because I'll make 'em play it."

Now, I had to laugh. "Oh, so you're the boss of *them*, too?"

"Sure, why not?"

I glanced around. My favorite music was country, especially classic country. Growing up, it had been the only thing we ever listened to, and I still had a strong fondness for it.

But here in the club, the techno beat was still going strong. Stalling, I took a nervous sip of my watery drink.

I could only imagine how well country music would go over in a place like this, where they'd been playing nothing but techno ever since I'd arrived.

Finally, I forced a laugh. "Oh, I'm sure they'd just *love* that."

"Who?"

I glanced around. "Everyone."

He smiled. "Fuck everyone."

I gave Jaden a good, long look. Rumor was, he *did* fuck everyone. In truth, I could see why. He looked embarrassingly fuckable.

Even now, when I was so frustrated, it was beyond easy to imagine how I might look at him if he were a just another stranger – *and* if I were a different kind of girl.

But he wasn't a stranger, and I wasn't his type.

I was his employee, and I liked to take things slow. And besides, I absolutely loathed him, well, most of the time, anyway.

Unfortunately, this *wasn't* one of those times.

It was stupid, really. Just a few minutes ago, I'd wanted to strangle him. Now, I didn't know what I wanted. I just knew that I was still gazing up at him, and that I didn't want to look away.

The strangest thing was, he wasn't looking away either. "So tell me," he said, "what's your favorite kind?"

"Of music? Why do you want to know?"

He leaned a fraction closer. "Because I'm gonna ask you to dance. And I want you to say yes."

CHAPTER 39

I stared up at him. "Why would you do *that*?"

"Do what?" He looked completely serious. "Ask you to dance?"

I gave a silent nod.

"Say yes," he said, "and I'll tell you."

"But that's bribery," I protested.

"Is that supposed to bother me?"

"Yes. Definitely."

He shrugged. "Sorry."

He didn't *look* sorry. He looked completely unrepentant and too darn sexy, which he no doubt knew.

He was up to something.

I just knew it.

After all, this was Jaden Bishop. He wouldn't be asking anything just to be nice, and he sure as heck wasn't expressing some sort of interest in the likes of *me*.

I mean, we didn't even get along.

So, what was this? *An employee-boss thing?*

Stalling, I took another nervous sip of my drink, and then another. By now, the drink was mostly water, but I didn't care. I kept on sipping until it was completely gone.

As I did, Jaden just stood there, watching me with obvious amusement.

I asked, "What's so funny?"

"You."

I almost rolled my eyes. "I'm so glad I amuse you."

"Yeah. Me, too."

Was he joking? By now, I had no idea. I gave him the squinty-eye. "You're up to something, aren't you?"

"Who says I have to be up to something?"

"Me. That's who."

"So, are you gonna be answering any time soon?" He glanced toward the bar. "Or should I grab a beer while I wait?"

I lowered my empty glass and gazed up at him. How long *would* he wait? I was sorely tempted to find out, if only to torture him.

He did, after all, have it coming.

But then, inspiration struck, and I suddenly wanted to laugh. Forcing him to drink beer was no kind of punishment. *No.* What *he* deserved was something a whole lot worse – for him, anyway.

I felt a slow, evil smile cross my lips. "Country."

His eyebrows furrowed. "What?"

"You asked my favorite music. That's what it is. And *that's* what I wanted to dance to."

He frowned. "You're kidding."

Unlike him, I was still smiling. "Nope." I paused. "And not just regular country either, *classic* country."

The way I saw it, I couldn't lose. Either he'd tell me to forget it. Or I'd have the distinct pleasure of watching him make a fool of himself by requesting music that the D.J. would never play in a million years.

Jaden studied my face. "You're bluffing."

I gave him a look that was all innocence. "I have no idea what you mean."

"Uh-huh."

I looked toward the D.J. He'd been spinning the techno stuff ever since I'd arrived, and the way it looked, he was seriously getting into it.

In front of him, the dance floor was absolutely packed with bodies gyrating to the fast and steady beat. Even the lights screamed techno as they flashed in multiple colors across the floor.

I looked back to Jaden and asked as sweetly as I could, "Is something wrong?"

A low scoff escaped his lips. "No. But there will be if you turn me down."

"What?"

"Wait here," he said before turning and striding away. I watched in momentary confusion until I realized where he was heading — straight toward the D.J.

Holy crap. He wasn't seriously going to do it. *Was he?*

But yes, he apparently was. I stared stupidly as he strode through the crowd of dancers and approached the raised platform where the D.J. was spinning the music.

Now that Jaden was actually doing it, I didn't know what exactly I was feeling. Guilty? *No.* He truly *did* have it coming. Still, I bit my lip as I watched the D.J. lean down to exchange a few words with my obnoxious boss.

The D.J. frowned and gave the dance floor a worried look. Even from here, it was easy to guess what he was thinking. *You want me to play what?*

But then, he gave a short, jerky nod. *What the hell?*

And now, Jaden was heading back in my direction. As he strode closer, I tried to tell myself that he was just messing with me. Probably he'd requested some popular new dance song and was going to laugh his ass off when I expected a musical change on *my* behalf.

And yet, my gaze strayed nervously to the crowd. Let's say Jaden *wasn't* messing with me. What then? What would everyone do? They didn't look like the rioting type, but they'd surely be displeased at the change of tempo.

Would anyone dance?

Or would it just be me and Jaden?

Heaven forbid.

Oh, stop it, I told myself. This was obviously just a joke. After all, I'd seen the look on his face when I'd told him my favorite type of music. He despised it, just like he despised me.

And now, I was irritated all over again. The plan had been to make *him* squirm, not the other way around.

And why was it, I wondered, that it always ended this way? With him getting the best of me no matter what?

It was so annoyingly unfair.

By the time Jaden reached my side, I was a nervous fidgety mess.

Trying to ignore him, I snuck a quick glance at the bar, wondering if it was time to rethink that whole one-drink idea.

Jaden leaned closer to me and said, "Forget it."

I gave a little jump. "Forget what?"

"The drink," he said. "I'll buy you one after."

"After what?"

The question had barely left my lips when the music suddenly changed tempo, and I heard the first telltale strums of – oh, shit – classic country.

I gave a little gasp. *Damn it.* He'd actually done it.

The jackass had called my bluff.

CHAPTER 40

I gave the dance floor another long worried look. It was still packed, but now, no one was dancing. Mostly, they were exchanging confused looks with their partners or staring straight at the D.J., who announced in an overly hearty tone, "And this one's by special request."

When I looked back to Jaden, he flashed me a wicked grin. The way it looked, he was actually enjoying this.

The bastard.

Still grinning, he reached for my hand. "C'mon, they're playing our song."

I didn't move. The song was "I Fall to Pieces" by Patsy Cline. It was at least fifty years old, and yet, I'd heard it probably a thousand times while growing up.

Still, I'd never heard it like *this*, in a crowded club where the dance floor was emptying faster than a movie theatre during the closing credits. I paused. No, *not* the closing credits – a freaking bomb threat, because let's face it, some of the people looked just a little bit terrified.

I knew the feeling. But unlike them, I stood completely still, even when Jaden gave a light tug on my hand.

In a voice filled with mischief, he said, "You're not gonna back out on me, are you?"

I looked from him to the dance floor and back again. Maybe he *wanted* me to back out. Maybe that had been the plan all along. Maybe all he'd *really* wanted was the pleasure of saying, *"Hey, I tried, but you were a giant chicken."*

I felt my gaze narrow. If he thought *that*, he was in for a rude surprise.

With a wicked smile of my own, I replied, "I wouldn't dream of it." And then, I let him lead me toward the dance floor, even as I wondered just how far he'd take this.

Maybe he'd stop before we reached it. And then *I'd* have the pleasure of calling *him* a chicken.

No such luck.

With his hand still in mine, he led us straight to the center of the empty dance floor and pulled me slowly into his arms.

Damn it. He was officially calling my bluff.

Or maybe I was calling his.

Either way, there we were – one lone couple in a space so big, it could've held a hundred couples just like us. If Jaden was embarrassed, he didn't show it. Instead, he acted like all of this was perfectly normal – the empty dance floor, the music that didn't quite fit, and the fact that for once, we weren't arguing.

The song was slow but not sultry, at least not in the modern way. Rather, it was something else, something deeper than sex and more meaningful than the quick couplings that featured so prominently in newer music.

I loved the song. And, to my infinite annoyance, I also loved the way Jaden felt.

He was a lot taller than I was, and my body was stretched tight against his hard physique as we moved in time with the music. Even *more* annoying, I liked the way he moved, smooth and easy, as if this *weren't* so incredibly awkward.

By now, surely everyone knew who exactly had requested this song. After all, Jaden and I were the only ones dancing, even now.

He was a good dancer and held me just the way I liked, not too firm and not too loose. Or rather it *would've* been just the way I liked, if only a tiny part of me weren't secretly wishing that he'd hold me just a little bit tighter.

Damn it.

All of this was so unfair. Even when he was doing things right, it made me feel all wrong. Desperate for a distraction, I suddenly recalled that he'd promised to tell me something if I accepted the dance.

But what was it?

Finally, through the muddled haze of my disjointed thoughts, I remembered. I pulled back and gave him a challenging look. "So….you said you'd tell me why."

"Why what?"

"Why you'd ask me to dance."

He gave me a knowing smile. "Do I need a reason?"

The smile caught me off guard, and I stupidly smiled back. "Well, you'd better have a reason," I teased, "because you promised to give me one."

"Did I?"

"Definitely. That *was* the deal, right?"

"Alright. Here's a reason." He paused. "I wanted to ask you something."

"But why didn't you ask me *then*?"

"Because I didn't want you running off."

"Why would I run off?"

"Wasn't that what you were doing?" he said. "Heading for the exit?"

"Maybe," I admitted, "but not when you asked me to dance. By then, I'd already stopped."

"Yeah, but for how long?"

It was a good question, but I had no good answer. Storming off had sounded like the perfect plan until he'd distracted me by acting almost human.

Almost, but not quite.

And now, he was doing it again. *Just what was he up to, anyway?*

"So…?" I prompted. "What was the question?"

Suddenly, he wasn't smiling anymore. "You do this a lot?"

"Sorry, what?"

"That's the question." He repeated it, more deliberately this time. "Do you do this a lot?"

"Do *what*?"

"Come to clubs alone."

I stiffened. "No."

"But…?" he prompted.

"But nothing," I said. "I felt like going out, and I wouldn't've come alone except that Cassidy's working."

"So?"

"So, it's not like I know a lot of people here."

"You know *me*."

I wasn't even sure what that meant. Recalling the scene with him and Victoria, I gave a bitter laugh. "Well, you looked pretty busy, so…" I didn't bother finishing the sentence.

His gaze met mine. In a low voice, he said, "Not as busy as you think."

What was that? *A hint that nothing had happened?*

It sure sounded that way.

I murmured, "Oh. Well, uh, that's good." Stupidly, I added, "It was just one of those weeks, that's all."

His gaze warmed. "Yeah, well, your boss *is* an asshole."

Something in his eyes made my stomach flutter, and I heard myself say, "Not *all* the time."

He gave a quiet scoff. "That's what *you* think."

We were still staring into each other's eyes, even as we continued to move with the music. The whole time, I was obnoxiously aware that practically everyone was watching, waiting no doubt for us to be done already, so they could return to the regular music.

I couldn't say that I blamed them. This was, after all, not a country music place, which led me to ask a question of my own. "How'd you get him to do that?"

"Who?" he asked.

"The D.J. How'd you get him to play this song?"

"I just told him to play something classic country. It wasn't hard."

"Oh, really?" I laughed. "I doubt everyone agrees. You realize they're all staring, right?"

"They're not staring at *me*."

"Sorry, what?"

"They're staring at *you*."

I almost laughed. "Oh yeah? Why's that?"

His gaze grew a shade warmer. "Maybe they can't help it."

CHAPTER 41

I felt myself swallow. That sounded *almost* like a compliment. But this was Jaden Bishop. He didn't compliment anyone, at least not that *I'd* ever heard.

I tried to think. *Had he ever said anything nice to me before?*
No.
He hadn't.
Not really.

And yet, a little voice in my head reminded me that he had *done* a few nice things. *Surely that was more important, right?*

I'd never been one for flowery words or fake compliments. All of my life, I'd appreciated *other* things – things like loyalty, honesty, and courage.

At a sudden realization, I almost wanted to snicker. It took an awful lot of courage to be out here alone while everyone watched.

Or maybe that was just me. Maybe Jaden truly didn't care what anyone thought. It certainly would fit. After all, he sure acted that way.

Still, it *did* make me wonder something. I asked, "So how, exactly, did you get the D.J. to do it? And don't say you just asked, because if *I'd* asked, he would've laughed in my face."

"Yeah, but I didn't ask."

"Sorry, what?"

"I told him to. Big difference."

I gave him a look. "Okaaaaay. But it doesn't change the facts. If I'd 'told him to', he would've laughed or at least said no. So why'd he say yes to you?"

"Because I'm the boss."

I gave a nervous laugh. "Thanks for reminding me."

"I don't mean *your* boss," he said. "I mean *his* boss."

I blinked. "What?"

"I own the place."

Now *that* surprised me. "You do?"

"Well, me and Jax."

"Oh." Now, I didn't know what to think. All along, I'd assumed that Jaden was here for a good time. "So, are you here to work?"

"If by work, you mean check on my investment, yeah, that's exactly what I'm doing." He paused. "And I'm *not* talking about the bar." His expression grew serious. "So let me ask you again, why'd you come here alone?"

And there he was, the jackass that I loved to hate. "I already told you."

"Yeah. And your reason sucked."

I scoffed, "Is that so?"

"Yeah. It is. You shouldn't be here alone."

"Why not?" I demanded.

"Because you're new in town. You don't know the landscape."

"I know plenty," I said.

"Yeah? So who's watching your back?"

"What?"

"Your back," he repeated. "Let's say you disappeared, who would notice?"

My chin lifted. "Cassidy."

"Yeah?" His voice hardened. "When? Tomorrow morning?"

I saw what he meant, but he was just being paranoid, or rather, he wanted *me* to be paranoid.

I told him, "I wasn't *planning* to disappear."

He frowned. "No one ever does." He glanced toward the bar, where I'd been standing with that stranger – the guy whose name was apparently Derek.

In what felt like a change of topic, Jaden said, "What'd that guy tell you, anyway?"

"I don't know," I said, "because I didn't hear it. Remember?"

"I'm not talking about *that*," he said. "I'm talking about the other line of bull."

I wasn't following. "What line?"

"With Derek, there's always a line." He grimaced. "So, who was he tonight? A musician?"

I gave a confused shake of my head. "What?"

"Or," he continued, "was he pulling the old, 'I have a yacht' routine?"

"Oh please, we didn't discuss yachts."

Jaden gave a slow nod. "Right. So, it was the gold medal thing."

Damn it.

When I made no reply, Jaden said, "What sport? Polo? Or skiiing?"

"Well, it wasn't skiing," I muttered.

"So polo then."

"Maybe."

"And you believed him?"

"I don't know," I said. "I didn't have time to think about it. And besides, it's not like I could ask anyone."

"Exactly."

"What?"

"That's exactly my point. You don't know him. You don't know *anyone*, which means you shouldn't be here by yourself."

Well this was just delightful.

"You know what?" I said. "I've heard just about enough." The song was winding down, and I made a move to go.

But Jaden held on tight. "Not yet."

"Why not?"

"Because the song's not over."

"So?"

"So, I'm not done."

We were no longer moving. "Oh, you're done alright."

"No. I'm not." He gave me a hard look. "I've got one more thing to say."

"Oh yeah?" I snapped. "What's that?"

"It's a good thing he doesn't know where you live, because if he did, you'd probably find him on your doorstep when you got home."

I swallowed. "What?"

"Your doorstep," he repeated. "He's got this fucked-up habit of turning up where he's not wanted." Jaden gave me a tight smile. "So, unless you want him creeping around your door, I'm just saying it's a good thing I showed up when I did."

Suddenly, my skin felt ice cold.

Oh, crap.

Like an idiot, I'd actually shown the guy my license. It even had my new address. What if his goal *hadn't* been to discover my age, but rather to learn where I lived?

Jaden studied my face. "What is it?"

"Nothing." I tried to keep my tone neutral. "What are you saying? That's he's dangerous?"

"Not yet. But that's no guarantee."

"What does *that* mean?" I asked.

"It means, he hasn't done anything illegal." He paused. "Or harmful, as far as I know."

Just then, the song officially ended, leaving us standing there for a long moment in absolute silence until the steady beat of techno announced the return of the regularly scheduled program.

Still, neither one of us moved, even as the dance floor filled around us. His hands were still on my hips, but my fingers were no longer laced around the back of his neck. Rather, they were pressed tight against his chest.

In the heat of my anger, I'd meant to push him away. But somehow, I'd never done it. And now, through the fabric of his shirt, I could feel the heat of his body and the hardness of his pecs.

Even in my distracted state, I couldn't help but notice that he felt amazingly good under my palms and fingers. Once upon a time, I'd seen his bare chest, but I hadn't been prepared for the feel of him -- shirtless or not.

My heart was pounding now, and I wasn't even sure why.

Was it because some creeper might be waiting for me on my doorstep?

Or was it because I was having some pretty creepy thoughts of my own?

On that very first day, *I'd* been the one standing on a stranger's doorstep – Jaden's doorstep, to be exact. That was how long ago? A couple of months? It felt like longer.

Back then, I'd hated him. Maybe I *still* hated him. But now, there was something else, something that I shouldn't be feeling for a guy who was so completely impossible.

And oh yeah, he was my boss, too.

And a total horndog, at least according to his reputation.

At the recollection, I pulled back, and this time, Jaden actually let go. Silently, I turned and waded into the crowd, ignoring the people dancing to the new beat. When I was free of the dance floor, I made straight for the exit.

I didn't bother looking back even though I had a sneaky suspicion that Jaden might be following.

After all, he'd done that earlier, hadn't he?

But it didn't matter. I didn't want anything to do with him – or the way he made me feel. I pushed through the exit and stalked across the lonely parking lot, heading straight for my vehicle – or rather, *his* vehicle.

But that was just one more thing I didn't want to think about.

The air was balmy with a light breeze. Still, I stifled a shiver as I reached into my pocket for the keys to the truck. It was then that I spotted him, Jaden, watching from a few paces away.

So he *had* followed me?

Who's the creeper now, huh?

But of course, even in my agitated state, I realized that I was being terribly unfair. In truth, it was kind of nice to not be out here alone, especially with that Derek guy so eager to flash me his goodies.

Still, I *was* annoyed, mostly with myself. *And why?* It was because I was so unnaturally drawn to my impossible boss.

This didn't even make sense. *He was rude, obnoxious, and way too sure of himself.*

Plus, he was totally off-limits, and not only because I worked for him. He was the kind of guy who chewed girls up and spit them out. Oh sure, they might be smiling as it happened, but that didn't change a thing.

He was trouble.

And I'd be smart to avoid him, at least outside the office.

It was such a sensible idea, and yet avoiding him turned out to be a whole lot harder than I anticipated, as an event later that night so awkwardly proved.

CHAPTER 42

I'd been home for a full hour, but I wasn't the least bit tired. It wasn't even midnight, and Cassidy was still at work, which meant that I was once again home alone.

I felt too unsettled to sleep and too distracted to do anything else. In the end, I decided to do something that I'd been putting off all day – returning Stuart's numerous phone calls.

If I was lucky, I decided, he wouldn't even answer, which meant that I could leave a voicemail and be done with it.

No such luck.

He answered on the very first ring, saying, "Allie? Is that you?"

"Uh, yeah," I said. "I'm returning your call."

"Don't you mean *calls*?" he said. "I was starting to think you were avoiding me."

Talk about nerve. "Hey, you avoided me first."

"What do you mean?"

"I mean, after you took off from my apartment, I tried to get ahold of you for like a month. You never called me back."

"I did, too," he insisted.

"Oh yeah? When?"

"Today."

"Gee, thanks for being so prompt about it."

"What'd you expect?" Stuart said. "That guy's a psycho."

It was beyond easy to guess who he meant – Jaden, obviously. "Oh stop it," I said. "He is not."

"Wanna bet?" Stuart said. "He told me to stay the hell away from you. Or else." Stuart made a scoffing sound. "Like *I'm* the psycho."

Stuart wasn't a psycho, but he *was* annoying, especially now, when I was in no mood for his theatrics.

When I said nothing in reply, he said, "So, is it true? Are you really working for that guy?"

I wasn't sure I liked his tone. And besides, he wasn't the only one with questions. I asked, "Where'd you hear *that*?"

"From *him*, when I picked up the truck. So, *are* you?"

I saw no reason to lie about it. "Yeah, I'm his assistant, actually."

"Then you'd better quit," Stuart said. "The guy's nuts."

I rolled my eyes. "He is *not*."

"Oh yeah?" His voice rose. "Do you know, he threatened me?"

Yes. I did. In fact, I'd overheard some of those threats myself. And even if I hadn't, the sight of Stuart practically peeing his pants at the sight of Jaden would've been a terrific clue.

On the phone, Stuart was still complaining. "He acted like I was gonna hassle you or something."

"Yeah, because you *were* hassling me."

"I was not," he said.

Ignoring his objection, I said, "*And* you tried to have me arrested."

"What, you're gonna hold *that* over my head?"

I gave a bitter laugh. "Why wouldn't I?"

"Because you stole my truck. Remember?"

As if I could forget.

And now, I was regretting calling him back at all. "Look," I said, "if you were just calling to complain about Jaden, I don't want to hear it, okay?"

"But the guy's off his rocker."

I considered everything that Jaden had done to keep me out of jail *and* to keep Stuart off my ass. "He is not," I said yet again. "And besides, it seems to me, you made out pretty good with the whole truck thing, so just drop it, alright?"

"I don't believe this," Stuart muttered. "You're sticking up for him?"

Was I?

Yes. I guess I was.

But in this case, it was totally justified.

I sighed. "He was just trying to avoid trouble."

Sounding more peeved than ever, Stuart said, "Trouble for who?"

My heart gave an embarrassing little flutter as the answer hit home. *Me. That's who.*

After all, Jaden had received no benefit to himself.

I was silent for a long moment before saying, "Well, maybe he didn't want to see me arrested." I hesitated. "You know, because I'm his assistant."

This was only half true. In fact, I *hadn't* been Jaden's assistant when he'd first brokered that deal with the truck. But this was none of Stuart's business, and I saw no reason to spell it out for him.

"Oh, get real," Stuart said. "When I stopped by your place in Florida, I wasn't coming to *arrest* you."

"Right," I snapped. "You came for sandwiches and sex."

At this, he had the nerve to sound insulted. "I did not!"

I gave another sigh. "Look, I don't want to argue. So let's just part as friends and be done with it, okay?"

He grumbled, "*Friends* don't steal friend's trucks."

"Yeah, and they don't call the cops on each other either, but if *I* can forget it, why can't you?"

"Oh come on. *You* haven't forgotten," he said. "You're still mad. I can tell."

He was right. I was. But I didn't want to fight about it. In an obvious hint, I said, "Well, it's been nice talking to you—"

"But wait," Stuart said. "When are you coming home?"

What kind of question was that? "I *am* home."

"But what about your stuff? Aren't you coming back to Nashville to get it?"

"No. The movers did that."

"When?" he asked.

"Months ago."

"But what about your old apartment? You didn't just walk away, did you?"

"Of course not." *As if I'd ever do such a thing.* "Becka's assuming the lease."

"You mean your cousin?"

"Yeah. That's exactly who I mean."

A few months earlier, Becka had suddenly needed a place to stay and had moved in with me and Cassidy. With both of us now gone, Becka ended up keeping the place on her own. It was a total win-win, especially since my cousin wasn't really the apartment-sharing type.

Last I heard, she was loving having the place to herself.

As concisely as I could, I explained all of this to Stuart, and ended by saying, "See? So it all worked out."

"But what about your old job?"

"What about it?"

"Maybe you could get it back."

I stiffened. "Yeah, well maybe I don't *want* it back."

"But why not?"

"Well for one thing, I was fired, remember?"

"Yeah, but Bryce called me looking for you."

"Bryce Rogers? My old boss?"

"Yeah." Stuart's voice picked up steam. "And you know what I told him?"

I was almost afraid to ask. "What?"

"That he should fly down to Florida and hire you back, like in person.'"

"Wait a minute," I said. "So *you* were the one who told him where I was working?"

Sounding annoyingly smug, Stuart said, "I might've had something to do with it."

I sat back in my chair. All this time, I'd assumed that Bryce had figured out my new place of employment because Jax had called him for a reference.

Apparently not.

And for all I knew, Stuart had egged Bryce on. Knowing Stuart, I could totally see it. Maybe he couldn't send the *police* out after me, but he *could* send my old boss.

Now, I couldn't help but recall Bryce's ill-fated visit to my new workplace. He'd been so determined to get his way, even to the point of risking my new job.

But then, Jaden had scared him off...just like he'd scared off Stuart.

And then, there was the guy from the club.

This was beginning to be a habit.

Even now, I still didn't know if I was annoyed or grateful. Probably, I was mostly confused.

And now, Stuart was saying, "At least he wasn't a psycho like Jaden Bishop."

Through gritted teeth, I said, "For the last time, he's *not* a psycho."

Just then, the squeal of tires made me pause. I looked toward the front of the apartment. The way it sounded, the noise had come from the street directly below our front window.

Stuart said, "What was that?"

Already, I'd jumped from the chair and was striding toward the window. I shoved aside the curtains and looked out onto the street, only to hear myself gasp.

"What's wrong?" Stuart asked.

I *so* didn't want to say.

But I did know one thing. I might need to reevaluate my claim that Jaden *wasn't* a psycho.

CHAPTER 43

I was still clutching my phone and staring out the front window. In the street directly in front of our apartment, Jaden was leaning down toward the driver's side window of an unfamiliar white sports car.

The way it looked, he was exchanging a few words with the driver, whoever the person was. From here, it was impossible to see who, exactly, was behind the wheel, but unless Jaden was talking to himself, there had to be *somebody* there, right?

On the phone, Stuart asked, "What's going on?"

"Nothing."

Jaden was dressed in the same clothes that he'd been wearing at the club. In the dim streetlight, he looked dark and dangerous – and embarrassingly, sexy.

Stuart said, "It didn't sound like nothing. What was that? A car crash?"

I bit my lip. *What on Earth was he doing here?*

I didn't want to speculate, but it was pathetically easy to guess who might be driving that white car. I recalled Jaden's warning that the creep from the club had a tendency to show up where he wasn't wanted.

But that still didn't explain what Jaden was doing here. I mean, he had no idea I'd shown the guy my license. *Had he?*

Stuart said, "Allie? Are you still there?"

"Uh, yeah. But I've gotta go, alright?"

"Why?"

"Because something came up."

Or rather, something was going down – meaning me. With barely a goodbye, I ended the call and rushed toward the apartment door. And then, I practically flew down the stairway that emptied out onto the front porch.

I emerged outside just in time to see Jaden literally yank the guy out of his car through the driver's side window and then slam him back against the driver's side door. The guy gave a little scream – or maybe that was me.

Cripes, it was probably both of us, screaming in stereo.

Even now, I was rushing toward them, wondering what on Earth was going on.

Jaden was gripping the guy by the lapels of his jacket and saying something too low for me to make out.

Sure enough, it was the guy from the club.

Without breaking stride, I yelled, "What's going on?"

Jaden didn't even look, but the other guy's head snapped in my direction. When he spotted me, he called out, "Hey, it's me, remember?" He gave me a desperate smile. "I came to say hi, like you asked."

I stopped in my tracks. I'd asked him no such thing. I looked to Jaden, who still hadn't looked in my direction. Rather, all of his attention was focused on my unwanted visitor.

With a muttered curse, I started moving again, striding forward until I was standing directly beside them. I still hadn't replied to the guy's ludicrous claim that I'd invited him here.

He gave a nervous laugh. "So, how's it goin'?"

I had no idea what to say. I looked from the stranger to Jaden.

Finally, Jaden turned his head to meet my gaze. He said nothing, but his look said it all. *I told you so.*

Well, that was nice.

The stranger – or rather Derek – looked back to Jaden and gave a nervous chuckle. "So, are we cool?"

The statement was beyond ridiculous. Jaden was still holding the guy in place. His car window was still open. I was still watching in horrified silence.

And I wasn't the only one.

On neighboring porches, people had come out to look, not that I could blame them.

I muttered, "You can't be serious."

I wasn't even sure who I was talking to – Derek for making such a ludicrous claim or Jaden for acting like, well, a psycho, I guess.

Or who knows, maybe I was talking to myself. After all, I *was* feeling a little crazy.

In reply to my statement, Derek turned back to me and said, "Uh, yeah. You asked me to swing by." He gave me a pleading look. "Remember?"

Okay, this is where it got a little tricky. I didn't want to lie for the guy, but I sure as heck didn't want any trouble.

Correction – any *more* trouble.

I glanced around. Already, way too many people were watching. No doubt, someone had already called the police.

I looked back to Derek and said, "You should go."

I wasn't concerned for *him*. Mostly, I was concerned for Jaden. And yeah, maybe me, too.

The guy swallowed and gave a single nod. "Good idea."

I looked to Jaden, who still hadn't budged. Through gritted teeth, I said, "He can't go if you're still holding onto him."

Still gripping the guy's lapels, Jaden leaned forward and said something very close to the guy's ear. Whatever it was, the guy didn't enjoy it.

He gave another swallow, followed by a nod so hard, it was a wonder that his head didn't pop off.

Finally, Jaden released him.

Derek didn't waste any time. He turned and practically sprinted toward the front of his car.

What on Earth was he doing?

Running away on foot?

No. Apparently not.

As I watched, he circled the front of his car and made a beeline for the passenger's side door. He yanked it wide open, dove headfirst into the vehicle, and then scrambled into the driver's seat.

A split second later, the engine roared to life, and he was gone, leaving a patch of burned rubber in his wake.

He didn't even stop to close the passenger's side door.

The whole time, Jaden hadn't moved an inch. I looked to his feet, thinking it was a miracle that he hadn't been run over – or at least lost a toe or two, thanks to Derek's panicked driving.

Nervously, I glanced around. If anything, the porches were *more* crowded now. I gave a little wave to no one in particular and summoned up a shaky smile. "It's alright!" I called. "We're just visiting, that's all."

Visiting?

What was I saying?

Slowly, Jaden turned his head in my direction. It suddenly struck me that during this whole process, I hadn't heard him say a single word. But Derek certainly had, judging from the speed of his departure.

I asked, "What did you tell him, anyway?"

Jaden gave me a hard look. "That's not the question."

I felt my brow wrinkle in confusion. "Then what is?"

"The question is, what am I gonna tell *you?*"

CHAPTER 44

Cassidy asked, "So, what did he say?"

"Nothing useful," I said. "Basically, he chewed me out for showing the guy where I lived."

"But wait," she said, "how did Jaden know?"

I sank deeper onto the sofa. "He saw."

"He saw what?"

"Me showing the guy my license."

She gave a confused shake of her head. "And he didn't say anything about it at the club?"

"No." I was scowling now. "Can you believe it?"

It was nearly two in the morning, and Cassidy had just walked in from her waitressing shift, only to be accosted by me and my tale of woe.

And yet, I hadn't told her the *whole* story, mostly because I didn't want her to feel bad.

Oh sure, she knew that Jaden and I didn't always get along. And she knew that work could be a little rocky. But she had no idea that I was some sort of social pariah – or that the only reason I'd hit the club alone was in hopes of meeting people who didn't treat me like some sort of disease.

Pathetic or not, I was keeping those details private for a reason. I realized all too well that Cassidy had given up that job – *my* job – in order to do me a favor.

Now, I could only imagine how conflicted she'd feel if she knew what a mixed blessing it had all turned out to be.

Plus, everything was so obscenely complicated, and she had enough troubles of her own, including a psychotic mother and an equally psychotic aunt. The last thing she needed now was to worry about *me*.

I was fine.

I just needed to figure out the Jaden thing, that's all.

The first step? Getting him out of my system. Lately, I'd been thinking about him way too much, usually at the most inappropriate places, like at my desk or even worse, at *his* desk.

Tonight, I vowed, I'd change that for good. I'd simply give in to the temptation so I could get over it already.

Oh, I wasn't planning to sleep with him, not in real life or anything. But a nice little quickie on my own might be just the ticket to a saner future. I'd simply *imagine* being with him, have an orgasm or two, and then move on.

It would be like rebooting the computer or flicking the power strip off and on.

A reset.

It was the perfect solution.

I went to bed smug with my decision and woke hours later feeling embarrassed at what I'd done in the privacy of my own bed. I wasn't against pleasuring myself or anything, but doing it while imagining my boss – a guy who I didn't even like half the time – made me feel just a little bit awkward in the light of day.

Unfortunately, that didn't stop me from repeating the process the very next night, which happened to be a Sunday, just hours before I'd be seeing him again.

I spent most of those hours – including the one just before sunrise – pleasuring myself to the thought of doing him *in* his office, specifically on his desk.

So much for getting him out of my system.

When it came time for me to get ready for work, I crawled out of bed with a silent vow to end this once and for all.

Today would be a fresh start. *No more thoughts. No more temptation. Just pure professionalism.*

All of that changed when I walked into my office and saw what he'd left me sometime over the weekend. It was a pair of novelty socks designed to look like fancy cowboy boots. They were silly and adorable all at the same time. And I knew exactly why he'd picked them.

It was because of the country music thing.

Still, it was a bit strange. It wasn't his turn to leave something. Rather, it was mine, which is why I'd left that stupid broccoli. The change in schedule was a little unsettling, but for the life of me, I couldn't figure out why.

Was it because I still didn't know how I felt?

Or because I knew how I felt, and just didn't want to admit it?

In search of clues, I glanced toward his office. The door was open, but the area beyond was dark and silent. Of course, from previous experience, I realized this was no guarantee that he wasn't in.

Unable to stop myself, I pushed away from my desk and crossed the spacious hall that separated our offices. I stopped at his doorway and poked my head inside.

He wasn't there.

And neither was the broccoli.

A voice behind me made me jump. It was Jax, saying, "He's out of town."

I whirled to face him. "Oh?" I frowned in confusion. I hadn't seen anything on his calendar. "Is he away on business?"

Jax nodded. "Something came up in New York."

My stomach lurched. *New York?*

Where Victoria lived?

For some stupid reason, that *wasn't* what I wanted to hear. Trying to be nonchalant, I said, "So...Is it something with the ad agency?"

I wasn't being nosy. I was his assistant.

I should know these things, right?

After a long moment, Jax replied, "No. It's something else."

He didn't elaborate, and I didn't ask. Instead, I listened as he told me that Jaden would be out all week and that I should reschedule any appointments.

All of this was beyond confusing. *Why was I hearing this from Jax?* It's not that I minded, but it *was* odd. Normally I received such updates from Jaden himself, whether by phone, email, or in person.

But this time, I'd received nothing.

After thanking Jax for the update, I returned to my own office. Silently, I stared down at the socks that Jaden had left on my desk. I loved them more than I should have. And like everything else, they confused the heck out of me.

What were they, anyway?

A peace offering?

Or just another thing to drive me crazy?

At the end of the day, I still didn't know.

I spent most of that week wondering what Jaden was doing and who he was doing it with.

As usual, he checked in at least once a day, but our conversations were brief and business-like. He didn't tease me at all, and to my extreme annoyance I discovered that I missed it.

How messed up was that?

But it wasn't until he returned that things went seriously off the rails.

CHAPTER 45

"You're still here," Jaden said.

I practically jumped in my seat. I'd been facing away from my office door and hadn't seen him come in.

I hadn't *heard* him come in either, probably because with everyone else gone for the day, I'd been listening to music louder than I normally would at the office.

Now, I switched it off, and a sudden silence descended around us.

He was standing in my office doorway, wearing jeans and a dark T-shirt. His casual appearance caught me off guard, mostly because aside from that initial day, I'd seen him mostly in suits and ties.

Now, the sight of him in jeans brought back memories of the first day we'd met, when he'd been standing in a different doorway, giving me all kinds of grief for no good reason.

The way it looked, he was about to give me grief again.

And how did I know? He looked just as delighted to see me *now* as he'd looked on that very first day.

Today was a Friday, and we hadn't seen each other all week. In fact, our last encounter had been outside my apartment, when he'd scared off that Derek guy and then stuck around only long enough to chew me out for being so careless.

If his current frown was any indicator, I was moments away from getting chewed out again. For the life of me, I couldn't imagine why. I mean, I'd talked to him just this morning, and he'd been perfectly civil *then* – or at least as civil as he ever was.

I braced myself, waiting for the verbal storm that was headed my way.

But he said nothing even as the silence stretched out.

What was going on?

Finally, when I couldn't stand it another moment, I said, "Well, you might as well tell me."

"Tell you what?"

I tried to laugh. "Why I'm in trouble."

"You're not in trouble," he said. "I am."

I didn't get it. "Why are *you* in trouble?"

"Because you're still here."

I stared up at him. "Wasn't I supposed to be?"

He was still frowning. "It's almost seven."

Yes. It was. But I'd attended two meetings today on his behalf, and I'd been planning to finish compiling the notes while everything was still fresh in my brain.

Plus, I didn't *want* to go home.

At home, I had that embarrassing habit of falling into bed and thinking of him in ways that were decidedly unprofessional. Plus, I'd been planning to leave something on his desk, but had been waffling about whether or not I should.

It was a black T-shirt that featured a cartoonish white square labeled as Fe – the periodic element for iron. The square was holding an electric guitar and banging its long-haired cartoonish head. Underneath the illustration were the words, "Heavy Metal" in bold, gothic script.

I loved the shirt. And Jaden would look great in it, too. Still, I'd been hesitant to give it to him.

Leaving clothing seemed a little personal, maybe too personal, considering that he was my boss. But I'd been trying to mimic that whole country-music sock thing with something similar.

Unfortunately, Jaden didn't like country music. He liked metal. I knew this from the one time I'd been inside his car, where heavy metal seemed to be the only thing on his stereo.

In reply to his comment about it being nearly seven o'clock, I explained, "I was working on the notes."

"What notes?"

"From today's marketing meeting."

"Forget it," he said. "Go home."

Now I was frowning, too. Normally if someone's boss tells them to go home on a Friday night, that was a good thing, well unless you're getting fired, that is.

I didn't think I was getting fired, but his attitude was seriously confusing.

I asked, "Is something wrong?"

"Yeah. You're still here."

I felt my eyebrows furrow. That was like the third time he'd said it. And by now, it was getting hard to not take it personally.

I pushed myself up to a standing position. "What is it?"

"What's what?"

I was tired of beating around the bush. "Well, if you weren't my boss, I'd say, 'What's your problem?'" I hesitated. "But since you *are* my boss, I'll just ask…" I bit my lip. I had no idea how to phrase it.

What have I done to irritate you now?

Why are you in such a rotten mood?

And why are you giving me that look?

In the end, I only shrugged and let the non-professional phrasing speak for itself.

At least I hadn't asked, "What's your *freaking* problem?"

Or worse.

He made a forwarding motion with his hand. "Go on."

My teeth clenched. This was just like him, making me finish even though I didn't know what to say.

Still, I tried again. "I guess I'm just wondering why you're in a bad mood."

"So, you think I'm in a bad mood?"

"I *know* you're in a bad mood. I can see it all over your face. Did something happen in New York?"

"You could say that."

"Well?" I said. "What was it?"

"You."

"What?"

He shook his head. "This isn't working."

That sounded bad. Reluctantly, I asked, "What isn't working?"

After a long, terrible moment, he said, "It's not you. It's me."

I stiffened. *Talk about a cliché.* And here, I thought people only used that stupid phrase when they wanted an excuse to dump someone.

Was he dumping me?

He couldn't. We weren't even together.

And then, it hit me. "Oh, my God. You're about to fire me. Aren't you?"

CHAPTER 46

As the question echoed out between us, my stomach knotted and twisted. Still, I tried not to show it as I waited for his answer.

And if he did fire me?

What then?

I stiffened my spine. *Well, I wouldn't just slink away, that's for sure.*

But then, he slowly shook his head. "No."

Relief coursed through me, and I let out a long, shaky breath. "Well that's good."

But then, he spoke again. "You ever think of moving?"

The question caught me off guard. I didn't like it. And yet, I forced a nervous laugh. "Yeah, to Hawaii."

But Jaden wasn't laughing. "It's no joke."

At something in his expression, I grew very still. "What do you mean?"

His gaze locked on mine. "I'm gonna find you a transfer."

What the hell? I almost didn't know what to say. "To where?"

"I dunno. We've got offices all over the world. You can take your pick."

I gave a confused shake of my head. "What?"

"I'm just saying, there are a lot of nice places."

So he was shuffling me off?

Was that it?

Unbelievable.

Through clenched teeth, I said, "Nice. Places. Are you serious?"

He shoved a hand through his hair. "Or shit, I'll go."

I felt like I was losing my mind. "You'll go where?"

"I dunno. Maybe New York, Chicago." He shrugged. "There's always Miami."

Miami – that's where he'd gone with Morgan during my first week of work. By now, I'd already learned from Morgan herself that the trip hadn't been a vacation at all, but rather it was related to some work project she'd been finishing up. The way she'd talked, she and Jaden had barely seen each other during that whole week.

But all of that was ancient history. At the moment, Miami was the furthest thing from my mind.

In front of me, Jaden was saying, "Or London."

Was he serious? *He'd literally move to a different country to get away from me?* It sure sounded like it.

But why?

I studied his face. "What am I missing?"

"Alright, you want me to be blunt?"

I scoffed, "Aren't you always?"

"No." His voice grew quiet. "Not with you."

I almost rolled my eyes. "You're kidding, right?"

"Meaning?"

"Meaning you're blunt with me all the time."

"Yeah, but that's all bullshit."

"What's bullshit?" I demanded.

"For every one thing I say, there's ten I don't."

"Oh really?" I crossed my arms. "Like about what?"

His gaze met mine. "Your hair."

"What about it?"

"It's long."

"So?"

"And blonde." Again, his voice grew quiet. "And soft."

"How would *you* know it's soft?"

"I can tell."

Feeling suddenly self-conscious, I reached up and ran a hand through my hair. It *was* soft, but that was beside the point. Again, I said, "So?"

"So, I think about it."

I felt myself swallow. "You think about my hair?"

"And other things."

"Like what?"

"Trust me. You don't want to know."

He was wrong. I did.

And now, I couldn't help but scoff, "Oh yeah? Well what about *your* hair?"

"What about it?"

"It's all thick and…" I hesitated. "…luscious."

He was still frowning. "Luscious?"

"Yeah. And don't give me that look. It's not *my* fault your hair's luscious."

"Oh yeah? Then don't blame *me* for your legs."

I glanced down. I was wearing a skirt, but he couldn't see my legs *now*, unless he had superpowers and could see through my desk or something. I murmured, "My legs?"

"Yeah." He gave a tight shrug. "They look good in dresses. Shorts, too."

"Fine," I snapped. "Then don't blame *me* for your chest."

He looked down. "My chest?"

"Yeah, it's all hard and muscly and stuff. And those tattoos? They're a serious distraction."

With him in short sleeves, I could see a few of his tattoos *now* – not the ones on his chest of course, but the ones on his arms. They were right there, as clear as day, inked over the more intriguing lines of his sculpted muscles.

He gave me a look. "Yeah? Well mine sucks compared to yours."

I was almost too distracted to think. "My what?"

His gazed dipped briefly to my blouse. "Your chest."

I lowered my head to look. I wasn't terribly well endowed, but what I *did* have was pretty darn perky, especially now.

That one single glance from Jaden had hardened my nipples to the point of distraction, and I felt that familiar ache deep in my core.

When I looked up, Jaden was still frowning, but in a totally different way.

The frown looked eerily familiar – not because I'd seen it on *him*, but rather because I'd seen it on my own face way too often, usually in the morning after a night of Jaden-fueled fantasies.

My breath caught.

Holy hell.

He wanted *me*, too.

And he wasn't any happier about it than I was.

Talk about messed up.

I heard myself ask, "What happened with Victoria?"

"Victoria who?"

"Oh, please. You know who. That account executive you met last Friday. Did you see her in New York?"

"Yeah. I saw her."

I'd never been one to play games. "Then why'd you act like you didn't know who I meant?"

"Because I'm not thinking of *her*."

"You're not?"

"Fuck no." He gave a low scoff. "I haven't thought of her all week."

"But you said you saw her."

"Yeah. For five minutes. I spent the rest of the week upstate working on a new acquisition."

No doubt, he meant a new property or facility. But that *wasn't* what I wanted to talk about. "So, you weren't..." I wasn't quite sure how to put it. "...hanging out with her?"

"Hell no."

"Why not?" I asked.

"Why would I be?"

I cleared my throat. "Well, it just seemed like you were interested, that's all."

He gave me a look. "You sure about that?"

I gave it some thought. Actually, she seemed a lot more interested in *him* than he'd seemed in *her*. Cautiously, I said, "So, you didn't–"

"No."

"Why not?"

"You serious?"

I tried for a casual shrug. "Well, I *am* curious."

"Alright, you want a reason? I haven't wanted anyone in weeks."

"You haven't?"

It wasn't lost on me that the conversation had taken a decidedly personal turn. But there was no way I was changing course now – even if he *hadn't* yet answered the question.

I tried again. More softly now, I asked, "Are you serious? That you haven't wanted anyone?"

"No."

I blinked. "So you're *not* serious?"

"I've wanted *one* person."

Suddenly, I could hardly speak. "Really?"

He nodded. "And you know who she is."

I *did* know. I could see it in his eyes. And probably, he could see it in mine, too. I heard myself say, "Well, maybe if we got it out of our system…"

"Meaning?"

I cleared my throat. "I'm just saying, it's probably like an itch or something."

He gave me a look. "An itch."

I bit my lip. *Talk about unfortunate phrasing.*

"Not an itchy itch," I clarified. "I just mean like a mental itch, something that needs to be…" I paused, searching for the right word. Finally, I settled on "…resolved."

Resolved?

Oh, please.

The word didn't begin to describe how I felt. I'd been thinking of him way too much. I'd been dreaming of him every night. I'd been acting on those dreams too – but only in my secret fantasies.

I *knew* he was my boss, but there was nothing professional about the way I felt. He was like a cookie in the cupboard, something that I couldn't stop thinking about, regardless of all my good intentions.

As the silence stretched out between us, I felt my tongue brush against my upper lip. I didn't even realize I was doing it until his gaze drifted to my mouth, and I saw *his* lips part, just a fraction.

Now, I was absolutely certain. *He wanted me just as much as I wanted him.*

And that's when I knew.

I was going for that cookie.

After all, there were times when you just needed to eat it and be done with the whole thing. And then, bright and early the next day, you could get on with your life – start a new workout routine or take an extra lap around the gym.

It made perfect sense, right?

Tomorrow, I'd be extra good to make up for what I desperately wanted tonight.

Him.

I felt my lips curve into a slow smile. *Yes.* It was the perfect solution, or so I thought until, with two simple words, he slammed the cookie-cupboard shut.

"Forget it."

CHAPTER 47

I blinked. "What?"

"Forget it," he repeated.

I felt my brow wrinkle in confusion. *He was turning me down? Seriously?*

How humiliating was this?

My face burned with sudden embarrassment. "Oh."

Other than that, I didn't know what to say. In my wildest dreams, I never imagined that he'd pass up the chance for quick and easy sex.

After all, I knew his reputation. He was a horn-dog, plain and simple. *So why wasn't he a horn-dog with me?*

Was it because I worked for him?

Or was I simply not his type?

The thought of asking for clarification was too horrifying to consider, so instead, I yanked open my bottom desk drawer and grabbed my purse. *No need to stick around, right?*

I was just reaching for my cell phone when he said, "I know what you're thinking."

I stopped in mid-motion. "No, you don't." This was definitely true, because *I* didn't even know what I was thinking. I just knew that it wasn't good.

He said, "You think I'm turning you down."

What did *that* mean? He *wasn't?*

Well so what? He had his chance. And besides, quick and easy sex had never been my style anyway.

By now, the cookie had totally lost its appeal. *Really, it had.*

I tossed him a cold smile, along with the same two words he'd just used on me. "Forget it."

And with this, I grabbed my phone and hurled it into my purse. And then, I strode out of my office, brushing past him and heading toward the suite's main door.

With whatever dignity I had left, I'd simply march out with my head held high. Or at least, that was my plan – a plan that sounded just fine until he said in a low voice, "You're smart for leaving."

My steps faltered, but I resisted the urge to turn around. Without looking back, I said, "It doesn't matter. It was stupid, anyway."

His voice cut through the distance. "Yeah. It was."

Now, I couldn't help but stop. *What a jerk.*

With slow deliberation, I turned back to face him. He hadn't moved, and the gulf between us seemed impossibly large. For some stupid reason, my gaze drifted to his pelvis, and I felt myself swallow.

In his jeans, there was a distinct bulge that hadn't been there just five minutes ago.

Speaking of impossibly large.

Even if his words said one thing, his body was clearly saying another. I knew the feeling. Even now, my tongue was once again brushing against my upper lip. I sucked it back in and glowered at him for good measure.

He'd just called me stupid. Or at least, he'd called my suggestion stupid.

Was it stupid?
Yes. Definitely.
But did he have to say so?
No. He didn't.

I made a scoffing sound. "Thanks for rubbing my face in it."

Oh, God, even *that* sounded stupid, or at the very least, vaguely obscene.

"In what?" he asked.

My gaze drifted downward. *Well, not your massive cock, that's for sure.*

I almost cringed. *What the hell was wrong with me?*

Once again, I yanked my gaze upward and then gave him a look he totally deserved – one of scorn and impatience. Or at least, that had been my original intention.

But he looked so damned good, standing there, a dark and dangerous silhouette in the dimly lit office. His eyes were brooding, and his lips were full. And his body – *shit* – it was a body made for sin.

Already, I'd seen him shirtless, but I'd never seen him pantless before. And yet, my imagination was painting a glorious picture.

Deliberately, I looked away, trying to focus on our surroundings and *not* him.

The office suite was really nice. It even had a large sofa, right there, just a few paces away. It was big and oversized like, well, not his erection, that's for sure.

Damn it.

This whole thing totally sucked. I'd never felt this way about *anyone* before. He made me crazy in every possible way. He was sweet and horrible, sexy and repellent, tempting and...well, *more* tempting.

And now, I was looking at him again. Before I could think, I'd already blurted out, "You *know*, I don't even like you."

He didn't even blink. "Yeah? Good to know."

"And I bet you're not half as good as you look."

"You're right." Something in his gaze warmed. "I'm *twice* as good as I look."

Good Lord. The arrogance was stunning. And yet, my body responded, growing warm and ready deep in my core.

Still, I rolled my eyes. "Oh, please."

"Please?" he said. "Is that a request?"

"What? Like I'm *begging* you or something?"

He gave a tight shrug. "It wouldn't be the first time."

God, he was such a tool. "Well, aren't *you* full of yourself?"

And of course, this like everything else, sounded a whole lot dirtier than I'd intended. Or maybe it was just my thoughts that were dirty. I didn't want him to be full of *himself*. I wanted *him* to be filling *me*, assuming that I could take all of him, that is.

Then again, I always did like a challenge.

Slowly, I reached up and touched the side of my face. In reality, I wanted to slap it, like they did in those old-time movies when someone was acting completely nuts.

But then, like a predator on the prowl, he took a single step closer, and my hand dropped limply to my side.

In a quiet voice, he said, "It's only arrogance when you don't deliver."

The comment was beyond twisted. After all, he'd made it perfectly clear that he wouldn't be delivering anything *my* way.

Good.

And yet, when he took another step in my direction, I couldn't seem to make myself back away. If I had any self-respect, I surely would. And while I was at it, I'd tell him exactly what he could do with his arrogance and innuendos.

But I said nothing and made no move. Instead, I waited. For what, I didn't know.

Soon, he was standing within arm's reach. With him so close, I had to crane my neck to stare up at him. My heart was racing, and I was having a hard time catching my breath. Something was definitely going to happen. I just didn't know what.

When he spoke, his voice was nearly a caress. "You wanna know why I said to forget it?"

"Why?"

"Because you make me so fucking crazy."

The statement hung there between us, confusing me, twisting me, and finally, compelling me to ask in a breathless whisper, "Crazy how?"

He edged a fraction closer. "That's the question, isn't it? I've been asking it, you know."

My breath hitched. "You have?"

He gave a slow nod, even as his gaze drifted leisurely downward, skimming me from head to toe. In that same low voice, he said, "I've been asking, 'What the hell is it? Her tight little body? The sweetness of her mouth?'" Now, he looked almost ready to smile. "'That look she gets, right before flipping out?'"

"Flipping out?" My gaze narrowed. "What do you mean by–?"

He leaned forward and silenced me with a kiss. The kiss wasn't gentle, but then again, I didn't want it to be.

When I gave a muffled moan, his arms closed around me, pulling me close, even as I reached up and laced my fingers around the back of his neck.

I sagged against him, savoring the feel of his lean, hard body as his mouth moved so perfectly against my own.

I pressed tighter against him, savoring the feel of his erection surging against my stomach, teasing and taunting me, with its size, its hardness, and its promise of delivering something that I'd been craving for far too long.

I still wasn't sure what we were doing, or how far we'd go. I just knew that I didn't want it to stop.

But already, he was pulling back – first his lips and then his whole body. Soon, we weren't touching at all, and the world suddenly felt a million times colder.

I wanted to whimper out loud. Who knows, maybe I did.

His gaze met mine. "You really want this?"

I did – so very much. I felt myself nod.

His voice was low in the quiet room. "You know, I'm not the boyfriend type."

His eyes were dark and way too compelling. I murmured, "What?"

"I don't do relationships."

At this, I almost laughed in his face. "I wasn't asking for a relationship."

It was true. I wasn't. I didn't even like him, at least not enough to consider him more than a guilty pleasure.

Again, I thought of that proverbial cookie. Like Jaden, it was a quick indulgence, something to get out of my system. And then, I'd be free to move on to something a whole lot healthier.

I made a scoffing sound. "And what makes you think I'd even *want* one, a relationship, I mean. You're not even my type."

"Good. Because you're not mine either."

"Oh yeah?" I said, more curious than anything. "So what *is* your type?"

"Slutty."

Now, I did laugh. "Slutty? Seriously?"

"Hey, it works."

"With what?"

"My goals."

"Which are?" I asked.

"To stay unattached."

Maybe the comment should've bothered me. But it didn't. The last thing I needed now was to fall for a guy who I barely liked.

No, what *I* needed was to scratch that itch, to gobble up that cookie, and to get him out of my system so I could forget him and move on.

But then, I paused. *Would that even be possible?* I'd never done a one-night stand. And he wasn't some stranger in a bar. He was my boss, which meant that I saw him practically every day, unless he'd been serious about that whole transfer idea.

I didn't want a transfer. I wanted him.

Suddenly inspired, I said, "But let's get one thing straight. You're not my boss."

He gave me a look. "I'm not?"

"Not now, you're not."

"So you're quitting."

I lifted my chin. "Yes."

Now, he was frowning again. "Why?"

"Because," I said, "tomorrow you're gonna hire me back."

"Tomorrow's Saturday."

I almost rolled my eyes. "You know what I mean. I'm just saying, you're not my boss in the bedroom." I hesitated. "Or on the couch, or the desk—"

His lips twitched. "The desk, huh?"

My gaze drifted to his office door. Somewhere inside that office was one of the biggest desks I'd ever seen. It looked really sturdy, too. It even had one of those big leather writing mats to cushion the hardness.

In truth, I'd thought about his desk often, and in ways that were totally unrelated to business. In my fantasies, he'd done me on that desk at least a dozen times.

Would the reality match the fantasy? *Hard to say.* The fantasies had been obnoxiously good.

I gave myself a mental slap. We were getting off-track. I looked back to him and said, "And I only want to do this once."

Now, he looked almost ready to laugh. "You mean one time or –"

"One night," I clarified. And then, feeling incredibly self-conscious, I mumbled, "Not that it has to be one *time* during the night. I'm just saying…" *Cripes, what was I saying?*

He eyed me with mock innocence? "Yes?"

I made a sound of frustration. "Well, I guess I'm saying, I just want to get you out of my system, that's all."

He gave a low scoff. "Good luck with *that*."

Whatever. "Do you have to be so cocky *all* the time?"

"Cocky, huh?"

"I'm not joking," I said. "I mean it. Afterward, it might get awkward, and I don't want it to be."

"Yeah? Why's that?"

I *so* didn't want to say. But as long as I was laying my cards on the table, I just put it out there. "Because I don't want to lose my job."

He stiffened. "You think I'm gonna fire you?"

"Isn't that what you were just doing?"

"No. I was trying to spare you."

"From what?"

He gave a rueful laugh. "From watching me go nuts."

I couldn't resist saying, "Oh, please. You've been nuts from the first moment I met you."

"You're telling *me*."

I was pretty sure I'd just been insulted. But I refused to let myself get sidetracked. "I'm just saying, if we get it out of our system, I don't want to feel all funny after."

"If you feel funny," he said, "someone's doing it wrong."

"I'm not kidding," I told him. "If we do this…"

His mouth was twitching again. "This?"

"You know what I mean. I'm just saying, come Monday, we'll both pretend it never happened." I paused. "Deal?"

"I can if you can."

In theory, it sounded so good.

But the reality turned out to be very different.

CHAPTER 48

For a long moment, we stared into each other's eyes, as if the reality was finally hitting home. *Holy hell. We were seriously going to do this.*

I heard myself say, "I like your office."

Hint, hint.

He smiled. "Yeah? You're gonna like it a lot more in five minutes."

I breathed, "I am?"

Silently, he turned and strode toward his office door. He opened it wide and then turned back to face me. He flicked his head toward the interior and said, "On the couch."

"What?"

The corners of his mouth lifted. "Unless you want to talk about it some more."

"No," I blurted. "I just mean, it's all settled, right?"

He moved toward me. "We'll see."

My stomach fluttered. "We'll see what?"

He never did answer. Instead, he closed the distance between us and pressed his lips to mine. If I'd thought our first kiss had been amazing, this one almost put it to shame. His lips were warm and sweet, and his arms wrapped so perfectly around me, cradling me against him as his lips moved against my own.

When his tongue darted between my lips, I gave a muffled sigh of pure bliss. He tasted like sin and candy – or maybe that was just me and my own emotions running wild like the feel of my heart racing in my chest.

By the time he pulled back, my knees were weak and I was having a hard time catching my breath. This was so wrong. But it felt so very right.

He smiled. "On second thought..."

I froze. *Oh, crap. He wasn't going to change his mind, was he?* I reached out and yanked him closer. "If you tell me 'no' now, I swear, I'm gonna..." I tried to think. *What could I do?* I didn't know, and I was far too distracted to come up with a decent threat. Lamely, I finished by saying, "I'll do something, that's what."

He laughed. "Got that right."

I pulled back to glare up at him. "What?"

"I was saying, 'On second thought...'"

I held my breath.

He leaned close and whispered in my ear, "I'm gonna fuck you on my desk."

I sucked in a breath. *Wow.* Did he *know* that was my fantasy?

Oh. Of course. I'd actually mentioned it, hadn't I?

I wanted to say something coherent in return, but nothing broke through my addled, lust-filled brain. So instead, I gave a slow nod and murmured, "Okay."

Okay?

The word didn't begin to describe how I felt. Then again, it probably *would* be unseemly to say, *"You'd better. Or else."*

He pulled me close once again and kissed me until I was a breathless, quivering mess. His hands on my back slid lower until they reached my ass. His hands crept under my skirt and caressed my cheeks through my panties.

His hands were big, and my body felt small and tight in his firm grip. Almost before I knew what was happening, he was lifting me up against his muscle-bound body. My skirt hiked high, and on raw instinct, I wrapped my legs around his waist as he turned, still kissing me, and moved us through his open office doorway.

Using his foot, he yanked the door shut behind us and then headed straight for his desk. Gently, he set me on the edge, facing the door we'd just come through. My thighs were parted on either side of his waist, spreading me open and ready.

Yes, I was still fully dressed, but inside, I was warm, slick, and waiting.

In a low voice, he said, "Don't move."

"What?"

He pulled back, leaving me staring up at him. Self-consciously, I began to close my legs.

"Don't," he said.

I didn't ask why not, because whatever he had in mind, I was willing and ready.

And then, to my endless surprise, he knelt down in front of the desk and kissed me first on the inside of my left thigh, and then my right.

He looked up to meet my gaze. "I've been thinking of this, you know."

I was almost too excited to breathe. "You have?"

"Oh yeah." He lowered his head and pressed his lips to my thigh again, higher this time.

I sucked in a ragged breath. This wasn't what I'd expected, and I almost didn't know what to do. But then, there wasn't much I *could* do, because with a trail of tender kisses, he reached the intersection of my thighs, where the crotch of my panties was the only barrier between his mouth and my aching need.

Through the silky fabric, he ran his tongue lightly across the surface of my clit. *Oh, my God.* I wasn't even sure how he'd found it so quickly. I mean, I hadn't been with a ton of guys, but Jaden was the first one who'd known exactly where to go – and *holy hell*, what to do.

I was still fully clothed, and so was he. But already, I felt dangerously close to losing it right there in his office.

He nudged aside the crotch of my panties and slipped a long finger inside me. My hips rose and I gave a little moan of encouragement. I was slick and ready, and even moreso when he further nudged the panties and took my aching clit into his mouth. He suckled it gently and then moved his tongue in maddening circles around the outside and then over the tip.

I murmured, "Oh, wow."

Wow?

What was I saying?

I hardly knew. But I *did* know that I didn't want him to stop. My eyelids drifted shut as his tongue danced across my aching nub, making me moan and squirm against the smooth surface of his desk.

I wasn't even sure how he did it – timed the motion of his finger and tongue and lips so perfectly in tune with what I wanted – or rather, what I hadn't even realized I wanted.

Already, I was the feeling the pressure building deep inside me. I should've felt self-conscious. He was still my boss, and technically, we were at work, even if it *was* after hours.

My hands were behind me, with my palms pressed flat against the desk. Otherwise, I might've simply toppled over from raw excitement. Heaven knows, my stomach muscles wouldn't be keeping me upright, not with him turning my whole body to jelly.

And yet, I was so desperate to touch him. Keeping my left hand in place, I lifted my right hand and reached out in his direction. I ran my fingers through his thick hair, letting it sift through my fingertips as he continued to drive me absolutely crazy with his mouth and tongue.

It was like he knew my body almost better than I did. And even in my addled state, I had to admit that he was right. *It wasn't bragging when you delivered.*

And boy, did he deliver. Almost before I knew it, my stomach muscles contracted, and I couldn't stop the waves of pleasure washing over me, even if I wanted to, which I totally didn't. As I shuddered my release, he didn't stop. Instead, he kept on going, teasing and coaxing more shudders out of me as I whimpered and ground against his face.

It was almost too much, and yet I loved every moment of it. Already, I felt almost too breathless and dizzy to stay upright, and I had to wonder if this was all just a dream.

If it was, it was very, very good.

When he pulled back, I gazed down at him and murmured, "You didn't have to do that."

He smiled. "Yeah. I did."

With a smile of my own, I asked, "Why?"

"Because I wanted to." He stood and gazed down at me. In a low voice, he said, "*And* because I want you to be ready."

"For what?" And then, I gave a nervous laugh. "Oh. Never mind. Stupid question."

But was it any wonder? In truth, I was almost surprised that I could speak at all.

Even so, it suddenly struck me that both of us were still fully clothed. Cripes, I was still wearing my panties, even if they *were* slick and soaked with the product of my desire.

I was ready and then some – and beyond eager. I pushed myself forward and reached for the button of his jeans. A few fumbling motions later, I had his pants open, and his erection in my hand. He was massively hard and even larger than I'd realized.

I felt myself swallow. Maybe it *was* a good thing I was so ready.

I encircled his length and smiled as it pulsed in my hand. I looked up to meet his eyes and was surprised to see him gazing at me with a look that I couldn't quite decipher.

He looked almost like a guy in love – but of course, that was beyond crazy. He didn't love anyone, and besides, this was just a one-time thing.

I looked back to his erection and felt my tongue brush against my lips. I knew I'd never be able to take *all* of him into my mouth, but I was *so* tempted to try.

I made a move to get off the desk. But he stopped me saying, "Don't move."

"Why not?"

"Because," he said, "remember what I told you?"

He'd told so many things that I had no idea what he meant. I shook my head. "Actually, I'm not sure."

He smiled. "I *said*, I was gonna fuck you on the desk." He made a show of looking down. "And look, there you are."

My pulse quickened. *Yes. Here I was.*

And there *he* was, so achingly close. Even now, my hand was tight around him, stroking him, feeling him, and anticipating how he'd feel inside me.

Oh, boy.

Suddenly, I couldn't wait another moment. With my free hand, I tugged at his jeans, shoving them further down. But my panties – they were still on. I didn't want to move, but I didn't want them between us either.

I murmured, "A knife."

"What?"

"A knife," I repeated. "I wish you had one."

Sounding mildly amused, he said, "Oh yeah? Why's that?"

I glanced down to my panties. "So you could cut these stupid things off me."

"Hang on," he said.

"What?"

But already, he was reaching down into the pocket of his half-removed jeans. A moment later, his hand emerged with some sort of pocket knife.

With a smile, he said, "You asked for it." He flicked the blade open and nudged it under the flimsy waistband of my panties. One flick of the knife, and the panties fell away.

I almost giggled. "I can't believe you just did that."

"Hey, you asked."

He was right. I did. And now, there was something else I wanted. I smiled. "So, about that promise…"

A moment later, I was guiding him to my opening – not that he'd need any guidance, obviously. But it felt good to have him in my hands as he first entered me, slowly at first, and then with one long smooth motion.

The fit was tight, almost too tight at first, but then, as his hips moved backwards and then surged forward yet again, I welcomed the fullness. It was unlike anything I'd ever felt, even in my fantasies.

I wrapped my legs around his waist and leaned back to enjoy the view of him. It was silly, really, because both of us were still mostly clothed, which meant that I wasn't seeing nearly as much of him as I'd planned.

But this, like everything else tonight, felt vaguely wrong but oh-so right.

As he drove into me – filling me again and again – I couldn't stop looking at him – his face, his physique, his eyes.

And then, there was the feel of him, sliding in and out, even as his hand caressed my face more tenderly than I might've expected.

By the time we shuddered against each other, I felt like I'd died and gone to heaven.

And that's when I knew – he was the best cookie I'd ever had, maybe the best I'd *ever* have, which made me love it all the more when we moved to the sofa for round two.

By midnight, he'd made nearly all of my fantasies come true – and all without leaving the office.

Afterward, we lay naked together on his office sofa. Now that our lust was spent, I should've felt uncomfortable or at least a little embarrassed at how I'd practically thrown myself at him.

But there *was* no embarrassment, just a deep satisfaction with zero regrets.

He was stretched out on his back, and I was cradled naked against him. With a laugh, I lifted my head to say, "I don't suppose you have any pizza?"

He made a show of looking around. "Not that I know of."

I snickered. "Oh well. Maybe next time." And then, I froze as the implication hit fast and hard.

Quickly, I added, "Not that there'll be a next time. I'm just saying, it's too bad I didn't think ahead." I gave a nervous laugh. "I would've packed a sandwich or something."

At that dreaded word, *sandwich,* I had to laugh for real. After all, sandwiches were nothing but trouble, at least when it came to Jaden.

With a warm smile, he said, "Would you settle for a candy bar?"

Oh man, a candy bar sounded nearly as blissful as, well, him actually. I nodded. "Do you have one?"

"Top drawer," he said. "But *you've* gotta get it."

"Why me?" I asked.

"Because," he said, "I want to watch your ass when you go. And then, when you return–"

"Oh shut up," I laughed, pushing myself up, and then off the sofa.

As I did, Jaden gave me a long, sleepy look. "That view's pretty good, too."

I gave an epic eye-roll as I turned to walk naked toward his desk.

When I reached it, he called out from the sofa, "But it's gonna cost you."

"Oh yeah? What?"

He gave it some thought. "A pen."

"What?"

"A pen," he repeated.

"Why a pen?"

"Because I see the way you mangle them."

I knew what he meant. When I got agitated, I tended to write a little too hard. I had to smile. If he didn't like what I did with pens, I could only imagine what he'd think of all the pencils I'd massacred over the years.

"Alright. *One* pen," I said, returning with the candy bar.

He pulled me back into his arms, and we shared it, feeding it to each other in small nibbles.

All of this felt surprisingly intimate, and there was a huge part of me that never wanted the evening to end.

But it had to sometime, right?

So, after the candy bar was gone, so was I, along with Jaden, too. *And why?* It was because he absolutely insisted on walking me to my truck, where true to his word, he demanded full payment in the form of the only pen I had on me.

It was a cheap ballpoint, and yet, I still put up a mock protest when he actually demanded the thing by reminding me, "Hey, *you* made the deal, remember?"

Yes. I had.

But when I handed over the pen, that *wasn't* the deal I was thinking of. Rather, it was the other deal – the one where we'd agreed that this would be a one-time thing.

Suddenly, the deal didn't sound so great after all. But it *was* smart, and so I said a silent vow to keep it no matter what.

Still, I had to wonder, *Would I be able to?*

In truth, I wasn't so sure.

CHAPTER 49

The next day I woke feeling totally cheated – not because the sex hadn't been Earth-shattering, but because already, I wanted it again. *With him.*

Talk about frustrating.

And stupid, too.

After all, the plan had called for me to eat that cookie and be done with it, not to make myself hungry for more.

It was just past sunrise, and I was lying alone in my double bed. Almost before I realized what I was doing, my hand had already strayed between my thighs. I was slippery with desire and slightly sore from the previous night. But it was the good kind of soreness, like a souvenir from the best theme park ever.

I loved souvenirs. And I wanted one again.

I wanted *him* again.

Damn it.

But it didn't matter. That *wasn't* going to happen, as I'd told both of us in no uncertain terms. So I tried the next best thing, replaying last night's events and letting my own fingers substitute as best they could.

My fingers were talented enough, but compared to the real thing? *Not hardly.*

By the time I finally crawled out of bed, I'd replayed last night's events two times and was craving a third.

What the hell was wrong with me?

He was wrong with me, that's what.

But it wasn't until I rummaged through my purse and discovered the metal-head T-shirt that I realized I'd need to pop into the office, even though it was a Saturday.

In all of last night's excitement, I'd forgotten to leave the shirt on his desk. Part of me said to forget it. But the other part – the oh-so sensible part – assured me that it would be weird to *not* leave it.

After all, it *was* my turn.

And besides, I wanted him to know that nothing had changed. With the sex out of our system, we were officially back to our regular employee-boss relationship.

It was such a perfect plan.

Unfortunately, it failed miserably sometime around noon when I swung by the office, only to find him there alone.

One thing led to another, and we ended up deciding that the deal didn't *truly* start until Monday morning, so there was no harm in some Saturday fun, right?

Saturday fun led to Sunday bliss, and by the time Monday rolled around, I was having serious doubts that I'd ever be able to resist him again.

It didn't help that he'd broken with tradition by leaving something for me to find on my desk, even though it wasn't yet his turn.

It was a snack wrapper from the same brand of candy bar that we'd shared on Friday night. Like everything else, it was annoying and funny, and made me smile in spite of myself.

But it wasn't until I actually picked up the wrapper – and realized there was something inside – that I actually laughed out loud. It was a pen, not *my* pen, but rather a new pen, still in its original packaging.

According to the promotional text, it was something called a tactical pen, supposedly for self-defense. But that wasn't the thing that made me laugh. It was the huge text proclaiming it to be virtually indestructible.

And it wrote beautifully, too. I knew this because it became my new favorite writing utensil – not for sentimental reasons, I told myself, but rather because it really *did* hold up to tons of abuse.

After that initial week, Jaden and I fell into a crazy new pattern. Every Friday, I'd announce that I didn't work for him anymore, at which point, we'd fall into each other's arms, or onto the desk, *or* into his bed.

Yes, I did spend an obnoxious amount of time at his house, usually sneaking in or out, to avoid running into Jax.

The whole thing was surprisingly easy.

Their house was massive, and aside from the common kitchen and living areas, each brother had his own wing. Plus, Jax spent a decent amount of time out of town, which gave me and Jaden run of the house in his absence.

The weirdest thing was, it wasn't just sex. We played video games, swam in the ocean, and even made sandwiches together.

And yes, we teased each other like crazy.

In truth, I was having the most fun I'd ever had. And if things were just a little better at work, I might've found absolutely nothing to complain about.

But the sad truth was, my co-workers were still avoiding me, and now, they technically had a reason, whether they realized it or not.

I was sleeping with the boss.

Still, it didn't feel that way. It felt like something else. I just didn't know what.

And maybe, neither did *he*.

CHAPTER 50

"Favorite food," Jaden said.

I *so* didn't want to say. With Jax out of town, Jaden and I were lounging out on the back patio of their beachfront mansion. It was a Friday evening, and we were watching the sun glimmer off the water.

In reply to his question, I tried for a casual shrug. "I don't know. I like lots of things."

He gave me a look. "You are so full of it."

I tried not to laugh. "I am not!"

"Yes, you are. You just don't want to admit it."

"Admit what?"

"That you've got a thing for sandwiches."

Okay, I did like sandwiches. In truth, I'd *always* liked sandwiches. When I was a kid, I'd been all about the peanut butter and jelly. But over the past few years, I'd branched out into all sorts of things – ham and cheese, pastrami on rye, turkey clubs, and the occasional meatball marinara with double parmesan.

Just thinking about them now made my mouth water. Trying not to show it, I said, "Yeah, I guess they're okay."

"Just okay, huh?"

"Yeah. Just okay."

He leaned back on his chaise lounge. "Oh, so *that's* why you make me order them."

I rolled my eyes. *Like I could "make" him do anything.*

Still, I knew what he meant. We ordered takeout all the time, even from places that supposedly didn't deliver. And Jaden almost always let me choose the restaurant.

And now, I didn't know what to say. In truth, I *had* been picking a lot of sandwich places.

When I said nothing in reply, his eyebrows lifted. "Unless you're doing it for *me.*"

I laughed. "Oh, stop it. *You're* the one who makes me pick."

He gave a low scoff. "That'll be the day."

"What do you mean?"

"Like I can make *you* do anything."

I gave a little start. This happened a lot, where he'd say something that I'd *just* been thinking – except that he'd have it all backwards, directing it at me instead of at himself.

As far as the sandwiches were concerned, I hadn't even realized I'd been going so heavy on them until today, when he'd started giving me a hard time about it.

Funny, he was *always* giving me a hard time.

And now, he was looking too darn satisfied for his own good.

I tried to glare. "What's *that* look for?"

"I'm just saying, we can order anything, lobster if you want."

This was true. Not only could he afford it, he could afford to have it delivered, probably on diamond plates with gold silverware.

But that was beside the point. "Yeah," I said, "but I don't like lobster."

"Uh-huh."

"I don't," I insisted.

"You liked that lobster sandwich."

I felt my gaze narrow. "It was a lobster roll, *not* a lobster sandwich." *And yes, it had been quite delicious.*

"Call it a roll all you want," he said. "It's still a sandwich."

"Well..." I hesitated. "Maybe it is to *some* people, but so what?"

His mouth twitched. "I'm just saying, you should admit it."

"What, like I've got a problem?"

He held up his hands in mock surrender. "Not with me. I'm a fan. But hey, if you want to hide your addiction—"

"Addiction?" I sputtered.

"Yeah. If you wanna hide it, maybe you should change it up once in a while, order something else." He paused as if thinking. "Like a chicken dinner."

A chicken dinner?

Like that day of our first lunch?

At the time, I'd *tried* to order a chicken dinner – not that I'd succeeded.

Oh yeah – he was definitely taunting me.

I didn't know whether to laugh or throttle him. "A chicken dinner, huh?"

He gave a tight shrug. "Just talking strategy here."

In reply, I grabbed a nearby throw pillow and hurled it toward his head. And of course, just like he always did, he batted it away without so much as a flinch.

"Hey now," he teased, "there's no need for violence."

"I'll give you violence," I muttered.

In what felt like a change of subject, he said, "So what's the deal with Hawaii?"

I wasn't following. "What do you mean?"

"You mentioned it a while back."

I tried to think. And then it hit me. During that awful conversation about transferring me to a new location, I'd made some crack about wanting to go to Hawaii.

At the recollection, my stomach clenched. *He wasn't thinking that again, was he?*

As if reading something in my expression, he said, "In case you're wondering, the answer's no."

"What?"

He gave me a wicked grin. "You're not going anywhere."

I couldn't help but smile back. Still, I had to give him at least *some* grief in return. "How do *you* know?"

"Oh, I know."

"You can't," I said. "*You're* not the boss of me. Remember?"

After all, I'd "quit" just a few hours ago. *Sort of.*

It was an old joke, but it never got old, at least not as far as I was concerned.

He said, "So, are you gonna answer the question?"

"About Hawaii?"

"Yeah. That."

"Well, you know my dad was stationed there, right? I guess I just really liked it, that's all."

I didn't bother rehashing my family history, because I'd already told him most of it in passing – how I'd been an Army brat, and had moved from place to place while growing up. One of those places had been Hawaii, where I'd spent some of the happiest years of my childhood.

And now, I was here.

With him.

At the thought, I took a quick glance around.

I was sitting on the back patio of a palatial beachfront estate, complete with its own palm trees. From here, I had a view of the ocean, along with an even closer view of the home's owner, who was pretty spectacular, too – well in some ways, anyway.

Other times, he was a royal pain.

When I looked back to Jaden, he said, "So Hawaii – it's your favorite place, huh?"

It was an odd question, and I gave it some thought. In truth, my favorite place at the moment was right here, with him, not that I'd admit it in a million years.

Dodging the issue, I said, "Well, it *is* pretty nice."

And it was. Back when I'd been growing up, I'd fallen in love with the sun and palm trees, not to mention the sight of the ocean so breathtakingly close.

But now, Hawaii was the furthest thing from my mind. I asked, "How about you? What's your favorite place?"

He shrugged. "Here's nice."

I gave him a long look. *Was he joking?* Honestly, I couldn't tell. I protested, "That's no kind of answer."

"Why not?"

"Because you didn't even think about it."

"Who says I have to?"

"Me. That's who."

He grinned. "Yeah? Well, too bad."

With another pillow toss, I said, "You're impossible. You know that, right?"

And he was.

In a million years, I'd never figure him out. Like tonight for example, we'd been hanging out for a couple of hours and hadn't yet jumped each other. It was unpredictable, and I liked it.

There were nights we'd have sex like two or three times, and other nights, we spent most of our time doing something else entirely.

At my insistence, all of this was a total secret, even from Cassidy and Jax. I had my reasons, most of which I didn't want to discuss. For once, Jaden didn't argue, and it was easy to guess why. No doubt, he was just as eager to avoid discovery as I was.

For secrecy's sake, we never went out. And for reasons that were a whole lot more complicated, we never talked about the future. But of course, I reminded myself, there *was* no future, as he'd told me on that very first night.

So for now, we were enjoying what we had and keeping it just between us.

Still, I realized that people *always* knew more than they let on. This included Jax, who couldn't have been truly blind to the fact that *something* was going on between me and his brother.

After all, Jax wasn't stupid. And neither was Jaden, even if he could still be a total jerk as he revealed yet again one Wednesday morning.

CHAPTER 51

"No you're not," he said.

We were standing in his office, and I'd just mentioned in passing that on this upcoming Saturday, I'd be helping Cassidy retrieve her things from her mom's place.

But now, he was telling me that I wasn't. *Was he joking?*

I shook my head. "Excuse me?"

From the look on his face, it was no joke. "You heard me."

Yes. I had. But I didn't know what exactly he was getting at.

A few months ago, Cassidy had moved in with her mom for one single week. Since then, she'd been having all kinds of trouble getting her stuff – mostly clothing and other essentials.

But finally, after weeks of delays and excuses, her mom had agreed on a scheduled time for Cassidy to stop by. That time was this Saturday at noon.

All Cassidy needed now was a truck and someone to help her. That someone was me, and I had no intention of letting her down.

I gave Jaden a look. "Yeah, I heard you, but I have no idea what you're getting at."

"Alright, I'll spell it out." His voice hardened. "You're not going anywhere near that place."

My jaw dropped. "And why not?"

"Because she hangs with the wrong kind of people."

I stiffened. "You don't mean Cassidy?"

"No. Her mom."

"Oh." On this, I was in total agreement. As far as I could tell, the woman made her living by trading her charms for money. It was one of the reasons that I'd been so horrified when Cassidy had decided to move in with her. "Maybe she does," I said, "but that doesn't matter. We'll only be there for a little bit."

"No. *You're* not gonna be there at all."

"Why not?" I demanded.

"Because you're working."

"This Saturday? I am not."

"Yeah," he said. "You are."

"But you never mentioned it."

"So I'm telling you now."

I felt my gaze narrow. "Do I *really* need to work? Or is this some sort of excuse?"

"Does it matter?"

"Of course it matters," I said. "I need to know."

"No. You don't. The only thing *you* need to know is that you're busy Saturday."

I was glaring now. In reality, I'd been busy *every* Saturday.

With him.

Was *that* the problem? That he didn't want our fun infringed on?

If so, I didn't like it. Regardless of whatever was going on between us, there was no way I'd abandon a friend when she needed help.

I edged closer and lowered my voice. "So what is it? Are you worried it'll take away from…" I hesitated. I really didn't want to spell it out, especially here at the office. As a rule, we kept our personal relationship separate from our work relationship, and I was very determined to keep it that way.

Oddly enough, this was the first time there'd ever been a real conflict.

Jaden said, "I'm not worried about anything, because you're not going."

I made a sound of disbelief. "Are you telling me this as my boss? Or as something else?"

"Both."

"You can't be serious."

"Alright, if it makes you feel better, I'm telling you as your boss."

Was he crazy? I didn't feel better. I felt worse. "So you're serious?"

"Do I look like I'm joking?"

No. He didn't. But I'd known that already. I crossed my arms. "So tell me, what's *so* important that I have to work?"

"I'll tell you Saturday."

This was too maddening for words. Trying hard to keep my voice under control, I said, "You know, I don't appreciate power trips."

"Yeah. And I don't appreciate carelessness."

"Oh come on," I said. "You're just bossing me around because you can."

"No, I'm 'bossing you around' because you don't know trouble when you see it."

I gave him a good, long look. "Oh, I know trouble, alright. And I'm looking at him now."

"Yeah? And we know how well you avoided *that*."

His words stung, and I drew back. He was right and wrong all at the same time. Yes, I'd utterly failed at avoiding the trouble that was Jaden Bishop. *But did he have to rub it in?*

I wasn't liking any of this.

And now, I had a choice. I could either let down my friend or risk losing my job. I paused. *Or maybe not.*

Very carefully, I said, "And what happens if I don't show?"

"If you mean Saturday, forget it."

"What are you saying? That you'd fire me?"

He didn't even hesitate. "If that's what it takes."

My mouth tightened. "And then what?"

"What do you mean?"

"On Monday, will you hire me back?" After all, that had been the pattern, even if it *had* been only in jest.

Jaden replied, "I wouldn't count on it."

A low scoff escaped my lips. "Thanks a lot."

"You're welcome."

My thanks had been purely sarcastic, as he surely realized. And now, I didn't know what to do – about Cassidy *or* Jaden.

Oh sure, I respected that he was my boss here at the office, but *this* situation felt totally wrong, like he was dictating what I did in my free time.

The jerk.

We argued back and forth until it became painfully apparent that neither one of us were going to change our minds. The argument ended only with me storming off to the ladies room before I lost my temper entirely.

I returned to my office a few minutes later to find a familiar male figure waiting just outside my office door.

But it wasn't Jaden. It was Jax.

Without preamble, he said, "The Saturday thing, it's covered, so forget it, alright?"

My gaze drifted to Jaden's office. His door was open, but I saw no sign of him. Still, it was pretty obvious that the brothers had been talking.

I looked back to Jax and asked, "Do you mean you found someone else to work for me?"

"No. What I mean is, *I'll* be the one helping Cassidy."

I bit my lip. "Did *she* ask for your help?"

"No. But I heard she needed it."

Again, my gaze strayed to Jaden's office. "Did you volunteer? Or did someone else ask you to do it?"

Jax said, "Does it matter?"

By now, I was beyond tired of that question. "Actually, yeah, it does."

"Why?"

"Because Cassidy asked for *my* help, not yours." I sighed. "Look, I don't want to be rude or anything, but don't you think she'd feel a little funny?"

He frowned. "Why's that?"

"Well, you know how parents are. They can be..." I hesitated. "...embarrassing sometimes."

When it came to Cassidy's mom, this was huge understatement.

Jax said, "You're forgetting, I already met her."

"Yeah, but—"

"But nothing. You're not going. And *I* am. So tell your friend, alright?" And with that, he turned and strode away.

Silently, I stared after him. I felt tired and ganged-up on, especially because I'd butted heads with *both* brothers in the span of a half-hour.

Plus, I had to break it to Cassidy that it wouldn't be *me* helping her on Saturday.

Knowing Cassidy, she wouldn't like it. Of all the people I knew, Cassidy had the hardest time accepting favors.

The only upside was, I had other things to tell her, too – things that might make her feel just a little bit better.

CHAPTER 52

I said, "You know he likes you, right?"

I meant Jax, of course.

It was the day after that argument with Jaden, and I'd finally caught up with Cassidy at the apartment. Between work and sleep, we'd been missing each other for the past day. But now, I simply had to give her the news about Saturday.

From her seat on the couch, she gave me a faint smile. "Sure. I mean, he must, considering all the favors he's done for me."

I almost cringed. *And he was about to do one yet again.*

I could only imagine how well she'd take it. Still, I tried to laugh. "I don't mean as a friend."

"That can't be true," she said. "Because if it was, he'd make a move or something."

I knew what Cassidy meant. But I also knew that both brothers were down on relationships. Even my thing with Jaden, I had no idea what it truly was.

Something twisted in my heart. Maybe it was over. After all, it sure seemed that way.

But I couldn't think about that now. Across from me, Cassidy looked so troubled that I just *had* to tease her. "What kind of move? The naked kind?"

"No." She sank deeper into the sofa. "Okay, well, maybe not at first, but he could at least ask me out or something."

It was funny to think that Jaden had never asked *me* out. Technically, we weren't even a couple, even if it *did* feel that way sometimes.

I longed to tell Cassidy was going on, but for her sake, I resisted. She'd be worried sick if she knew what I'd been doing with my boss – a guy who I'd always professed to loathe.

And besides, I reminded myself, my ill-advised fling – or whatever it was – was probably finished. So it was hardly worth discussing, right?

And yet, I stupidly wanted to cry.

Jaden and I had barely talked since that argument, and I was still livid that he'd resorted to a power-play to get his way.

It was so incredibly unfair.

With an effort, I returned my thoughts to Cassidy and Jax. "Wanna know what *I* think?"

"What?"

I forced a smile. "I think he likes you *too* much."

She gave me a dubious look. "What do you mean?"

"Well, from what I hear at the office, he's pretty down on relationships."

I'd heard this firsthand from Morgan, who was still popping into my office several times a week, trying to pump me for information. But the funny thing was, *she* always ended up doing most of the talking, whether I encouraged her or not.

In reply to what I'd said about Jax being down on relationships, Cassidy said, "Why? Because of a bad breakup?"

"No. Because of the thing with his parents."

"So, I take it they're not together?"

I nodded. "Exactly."

Her brow wrinkled in obvious confusion. "But lots of people have divorced parents."

"Yeah, but their divorce was weird. They don't even live in the same state." I leaned forward. "And get this. Half of the family hardly talks to the other half. It's like they don't exist or something."

She shook her head. "I'm not sure I get what you mean."

As she listened, I told her the little I knew. Apparently, Jax and Jaden had four other brothers who lived up in Michigan. Supposedly, their dad lived there, too. But as far as their mom, I'd heard nothing at all.

Jaden never talked about her, not even when I asked. In truth, he hardly talked about his family at all, and it was pretty obvious that it was a sore subject.

Pushing aside those gloomy thoughts, I looked to Cassidy and shared something about Jax that she might not know. "Do you know he hates coffee?"

She blinked. "He does?"

"Sure."

"But—"

I smiled. "But that can't be true, because you keep seeing him at that coffee shop?"

"Uh, yeah."

"Right. Because he only goes there to see you."

"Oh, stop," she said. "You're not serious."

But I was.

And finally, after filling her in on the details, I gave her the news that it wouldn't be *me* taking her to get her things.

She took it as well as could be expected, but I could still see the worry in her eyes. She was too nice for her own good and hated to cause trouble.

But me? I wasn't like that, which is why I found myself in the office late Friday night, long after everyone else had gone.

I wanted answers.

But all I found were more questions when I discovered the strangest thing on my desk.

CHAPTER 53

I stared down at the thing. *A ski mask?*

I tried to think. According to our secret schedule, this would've been the week for *me* to leave something for *him*, not the other way around.

After Wednesday's argument, I wasn't even sure that we were still doing that. In reality, I wasn't sure about a lot of things. Today was Friday, which meant that we'd normally be spending the evening together.

But neither one of us had mentioned it – probably because we were too busy glowering at each other over the past couple of days.

But the mask – it confused me, and not only because of the change in schedule.

All of the previous gifts – or whatever they were – had some hidden meaning, usually a private joke that only the two of us would understand.

But the mask meant nothing to me. As I stood silently behind my desk, I wracked my brains, trying to figure it out.

Last weekend, I'd mentioned that the weather was colder than I'd been expecting. Was *that* why he'd leave a ski mask?

Or was it a response to my crack about knocking over a liquor store?

I lifted the mask for a closer look. *Maybe it was something kinky that I didn't quite get?*

I was still trying to figure it out when I heard a noise coming from

Jaden's office. Startled, I looked up. His door was shut, and I saw no light coming from underneath.

But I'd definitely heard *something*, a slight rolling sound. It was the same sound his chair made whenever he pushed away from his desk.

My pulse quickened. *Was Jaden in there now?*

And if so, why wasn't he coming out?

Surely he'd heard me rummaging around in my office?

I waited for at least a minute, and then, when I couldn't stand the suspense any longer, I crossed the hallway and knocked on his office door. "Jaden? Are you in there?"

There was no response.

I tried the knob and was surprised to find the door unlocked. I was even more surprised when I pushed the door open and saw someone sitting behind that all-too-familiar desk.

It *wasn't* Jaden.

It was Morgan, and she looked nearly naked.

I couldn't help but stare. She was wearing a lacy black lingerie top that was so thin, I could see her nipples, even in the dim light.

I was so shocked, I hardly knew what to say. "Morgan?"

She made a sound of annoyance. "What are you doing here?"

I gave her a look. "That's a good question."

My mind was whirling as I tried to process what I was seeing. Already, I'd known that Morgan had a thing for both brothers, and lately, she'd been honing in hard on Jaden.

But this wasn't something I obsessed over, probably because it was pretty obvious that the interest was one-sided.

From behind the desk, she gave a loud sigh. "I know. So, are you gonna answer?"

It took me a moment to realize what she meant. Obviously, she was responding to my snide comment about her question. *What was I doing here?*

In reply, I murmured, "I work here."

"Yeah, but you're not supposed to be working *now*."

I gave a slow shake of my head as I tried to pretend that I wasn't seeing what I was seeing. Morgan had a nice body. She was long and lean with perfect boobs and legs that went on forever. I couldn't see her legs now, of course, but I'd seen them plenty during the last few weeks.

In fact, I'd been seeing more of them during every visit. *And why?* It was because her skirts had been getting progressively shorter.

Tonight, I feared, she might've skipped the skirt entirely. I didn't know for sure, but it seemed a fairly good guess.

And yet, she looked completely unashamed.

I could only imagine how *I'd* feel if the roles were reversed, if someone had caught *me* nearly naked in Jaden's office.

At the mere thought, I felt a rush of heat flood my face. Last Friday, I'd been fully naked. *And*, I'd been on that desk.

Multiple times.

Absently, I said, "Does he know you're here?"

She gave a toss of her long, red hair. "I don't know. Does he know *you're* here?"

The question made me pause. Obviously, she knew nothing about me and Jaden. But suddenly, I was almost wishing she did, because I was feeling very strange about the whole thing.

And, could I really judge her?

Just a week ago, I'd been wearing a lot less than that.

Lamely, I murmured, "Well, I *do* work here."

"Yeah, I know," she said. "You took *my* job."

God, I hated this.

I wasn't jealous. Or at least, I didn't *think* I was jealous. After all, I was nearly certain that Jaden had zero interest in Morgan.

But then, a little voice whispered, *"But what if he does?"*

My stomach lurched at the thought. Still, I gave myself a mental kick. *This was so stupid.*

Jaden and I *weren't* together. Even *before* that argument, we weren't together.

It was just a casual thing.

Right?

I shoved a hand through my hair and tried to think. Suddenly, I wasn't feeling so casual.

"Well?" she said. "Aren't you gonna say something?"

My mind felt slow and muddy. "Sorry, what?"

"I *said*, 'You took my job.'"

I sighed. "Yeah. So you keep reminding me."

It was true. She said this nearly every time I saw her. By now, I was getting so used to it that I hardly noticed.

And yet, I noticed it *now*, just like I noticed that she had perfect hair, perfect makeup, and perfectly perky nipples.

Were mine that perky? They didn't feel perky *now*. In fact, everything on me felt wrong and disjointed.

From behind the desk, Morgan looked to my hands and frowned. "What's that?"

Confused, I looked down. I was still holding that stupid mask. I heard myself say, "I don't know. I, um, saw it in my office."

She smiled. "Hey, toss it here, will ya?"

I froze. "What?"

She held up her hand. "Come on. Lemme see it."

For some stupid reason, I didn't want to give it up. "Why?"

Her eyes brightened. "Because I'm gonna surprise Jaden with it."

I gave a nervous laugh. "Oh, I think he'll be pretty surprised as it is."

Even now, the thought of him walking in and seeing *her* was a little hard to stomach.

In fact, the thought of him seeing *anyone* was hard to stomach.

Damn it. When did *that* happen?

I didn't know. It wasn't something I'd been planning on.

And it wasn't something I wanted.

Not with him.

He was a player. And bossy in more ways than one. Plus, he'd told me up-front that he didn't do relationships. *Maybe I should've listened.*

At the desk, Morgan was saying, "It's not for *me*, Silly. It's for *him*."

I swallowed. "What?"

"Yeah." She gave a little giggle. "I'm gonna make him wear it."

The mask?

Oh, God. That was an image I didn't need. In this little fantasy of hers, would he be wearing *only* the mask?

Beyond disturbed, I said, "So...are you expecting him?" I figured she'd say no, but it *would* be good to hear.

She smiled. "Oh yeah. Any minute."

My heart sank. "Oh." I hesitated. "Is he expecting *you*?"

"Well, I hope so," she said with a laugh. "Otherwise, I got dressed up for nothing."

Dressed up?

That's not how *I* would've put it.

She pointed to the mask. "So are you gonna give me that thing or not?"

Now, I didn't know what to say. I didn't know what to *do* either. I looked down at the mask. I'd already told her that I'd found it in my office, so I couldn't exactly claim it was mine or of sentimental value.

I almost scoffed out loud. *Sentimental value? Who was I kidding?* Even if I *had* developed feelings for Jaden, it's not like he'd ever return them.

He'd made *that* perfectly clear from the get-go. And like an idiot, I'd convinced myself that I'd wanted the same thing.

Now, I wasn't so sure.

The only thing I *did* know was that if I stood around, staring at Morgan for another moment, I'd surely say something I'd regret. So, with a bitter laugh, I tossed her the mask and said, "It's all yours."

After that, I didn't stick around. After all, tomorrow was the same Saturday that Jaden was forcing me to work, which meant that I'd be seeing him in just a few hours.

But now, I didn't feel like seeing him. If I was lucky, I decided, he'd either stay far away from the office or at the very least, be up for some sort of reasonable discussion so we could figure things out.

But when Saturday came, he was in no mood to be reasonable.

Or maybe that was just me.

CHAPTER 54

"Nice going," he said.

I looked up to see Jaden standing in my office doorway, looking vaguely amused. If I weren't so tense, I might've laughed, because I knew exactly what he was talking about.

Just now, his brother had practically sprinted from the office. *And why?* It was because he'd overheard me on the phone, telling Cassidy – and quite loudly too – that she'd be making a huge mistake if she tried to pick up her things alone.

In spite of what she thought, she *needed* someone to go with her. And she *had* someone more than willing – Jax, who'd obviously put some thought into today's mission. I knew this because he'd come into the office *not* in a suit and tie, but rather in ratty jeans and a generic T-shirt.

The way it looked, he'd been planning to look like a regular working stiff rather than the billionaire he was. It was a smart move, and it made me feel better about giving in and letting him handle the errand in my place.

But in typical Cassidy fashion, she'd been having a hard time accepting his help, so she'd called to let me know that she was thinking of going on her own. This was in spite of the fact that Jax had been scheduled to pick her up within the hour.

In a slight exaggeration, I'd told her that he'd already left. Thirty seconds later, this was no lie, because unless I was mistaken, he was now on his way.

Obviously, he'd overheard what I'd been telling her, which of course, had been my intention all along.

From the look on Jaden's face, he'd known exactly what I'd done, and he totally approved.

On any other day, we might've shared a secret smile. But today, I didn't feel like smiling – and not only because it was the Saturday he'd forced me to work.

Rather, the thing bothering me now was that scene with Morgan. It had haunted me all night for all kinds of crazy reasons.

The primary reason? Somehow, it had made me realize that whatever Jaden and I had, it wasn't nearly as casual as I'd thought.

Or more accurately, it wasn't nearly as casual to *me*.

Somehow, like a total idiot, I'd actually gotten attached to the guy.

Damn it. I should've known better. I'd never been the casual type.

Funny to think, it was only my loathing of him that had convinced me that I could have a little fling and be done with it.

No such luck.

Somewhere along the way, I'd stopped loathing him. And in fact, I was horrifyingly close to admitting – if only to myself – that my feelings might be quite the opposite.

Now, he was standing in my doorway with that look, the wickedly warm one that usually gave me butterflies.

There were no butterflies today. There was only a sick, leaden feeling that I couldn't seem to shake.

With no trace of a smile, I said, "Yeah, well, I'm glad it worked out." And then, I returned to my work.

I wasn't even sure what I was supposed to be doing today. Jaden had claimed that he'd tell me when I arrived. But other than a quick good morning, this was the first time we'd spoken all day.

Not wanting to just sit around, I'd been organizing some files.

From the open doorway, he said, "What is it?"

I looked up. "What's what?"

He wasn't smiling anymore. "What's wrong?"

I *so* didn't want to discuss it. I'd never been good at hiding my feelings, and I had a terrible hunch that if we started talking now, it would only end in an argument.

For once in my life, I simply wasn't up for it.

"Nothing," I said. "I'm just getting some work done. That *is* why I'm here, right?"

"No. It's not."

My tone grew sarcastic. "Oh, really?"

"We both know why you're here, and it's not to work."

I stiffened. So why *was* I here? *For a good time?* This might've been our habit in the past. But now, it was a habit that I'd be smart to break, for my own sanity if nothing else.

I gave him an annoyed look. "Well, I'm not here for fun, if that's what you're thinking."

His mouth tightened. "What kind of 'fun' do you mean?"

I made a scoffing sound. "As if you don't know."

He looked at me for a long, tense moment before saying, "That's what you think?" He stepped closer and lowered his voice. "That I made you come in so I could fuck you?"

I almost flinched. In spite of everything, his language shocked me. Oh sure, my own language could be just as bad, and normally, I liked it when he talked dirty. But to hear him put it like that, *now?* Well, it just made everything worse.

I lifted my chin. "Are you saying it *wasn't* the reason?"

His gaze met mine, and his tone softened. "You know it wasn't."

Okay, maybe I was being unfair. Even through my anger, I realized that he'd forced me to work today in order to keep me from away from all the trouble surrounding Cassidy's mom.

But I hadn't asked him to rescue me. In fact, I hadn't asked for anything. And I certainly wasn't going to start today.

I muttered, "Well, whatever the reason, it's too late to change it now, so…" I gave a loose shrug and didn't bother finishing the sentence. After all, what could I say?

Our last real conversation had been on Wednesday. And even *that* had been an argument more than anything. Since then, both of us had been professional to a fault.

No looks.

No smiles.

No talk of plans for the weekend.

Now, it *was* the weekend.

And I just knew it was going to be a bad one, because if I didn't get my emotions in-check, I'd surely lose it.

The executive suite was very quiet, with just the two of us facing off in my private office.

Normally, I'd be all excited, wondering what we'd end up doing, or where we'd be doing it. Now, I just wanted to leave before I made a fool of myself.

He reached back and shut my office door. "What is it?"

I shrugged. "What's what?"

"What's wrong?"

"Nothing," I repeated. "I'm just focused on my work, that's all."

At this, his voice grew eerily quiet. "Bullshit."

For some reason, this set me off. I pushed back my chair and stood. "You know what's bullshit?" I said. "*You.*"

CHAPTER 55

I hadn't meant to say it, but now that it was out there, I couldn't exactly take it back.

He looked annoyingly calm in the face of my wrath. "Yeah? How so?"

"Well, for one thing..." I bit my lip. There were so many things I wanted to say, but all of them were way too personal, especially considering that Jaden and I were nothing more than a fling.

In a flash of inspiration, I suddenly recalled something that he'd done a few months earlier – not to me, but to someone I cared about.

I gave him a challenging look. "There was that thing with Cassidy's job."

"What thing?"

"Oh, please," I said. "You *know* what. You stopped Jax from hiring her."

"If you're talking about *your* job, she did that to herself."

"I'm not talking about *my* job. I'm talking about a different job."

"Yeah? And what job's that?"

"I don't know," I said, "because she didn't get it."

I waited for a reply, and when none came, I sighed. "Aren't you gonna say something?"

"No. Because I don't know what you're talking about."

I felt my jaw tighten. *Did I seriously need to spell it out?*

Fine. If that's what he wanted.

Speaking very clearly and concisely, I said, "I heard that Jax wanted to offer her a job *here*. At corporate. But *you* talked him out of it."

"Yeah? So?"

I stared at him. "So, don't you feel bad?"

"Hell no."

"Oh, well that's nice." I wasn't even sure what I'd been expecting, but this *wasn't* it. "So I guess you're pretty proud of yourself, huh?"

"Proud? No. But I don't regret it."

"Why not?"

"Lemme ask you something. You think she would've liked that? Working here? In this building?"

"Well, it would've been better than waitressing."

He gave a low scoff. "You know her mom's a hooker, right?"

I was glaring now. Her mom wasn't a streetwalker or anything, but yeah, she definitely got paid for it. But that was beside the point. "That has nothing to do with Cassidy."

"I never said it did."

"Then why'd you bring it up?"

"Because I met her mom, remember?"

I *did* remember, even if I hadn't been there myself. But Cassidy had told me the whole story about Jax and Jaden rescuing her from whatever her mom had in mind. The way it sounded, Cassidy was just one limo-drive away from being forced into the family business.

I was still trying to think of a sharp comeback when Jaden said, "Your friend – does she want that?"

Un-freaking-believable. "What, to be a prostitute?"

Jaden gave me a look. "No. To be employed by my brother."

"Oh." I paused. "Well why *wouldn't* she want that?" Even as I said it, it wasn't lost on me that I *still* hadn't told Cassidy who owned the restaurant where she worked.

For *her* sake, I didn't plan on telling her either.

But that was totally different.

Wasn't it?

Jaden gave me a hard look. "*You* tell me."

"Why she wouldn't want a job here?" I gave a tight shrug. "I *can't* tell you, because I don't know."

He stepped closer. "Yes, you do."

Damn it.

Maybe he was right. Maybe Cassidy *would've* hated working for Jax, even in a roundabout way. But I was in no mood to admit it, and besides, Jaden had been awful from the get-go.

I made a sound of annoyance. "Oh, like you care."

"I care about my brother."

"Oh yeah? Well *I* care about Cassidy. And maybe if you cared so much about your brother, you'd realize how lucky he'd be to have her working here." I straightened in my seat. "And *you'd* be lucky, too."

"You think, huh?"

"Yes. I do. They're great together." My voice rose. "What, you think she's not good enough for him? Because of her mom? Is that it?"

Jaden gave a bitter laugh, but said nothing in reply.

I waited for him to explain, and when he didn't, I demanded, "What's so funny?"

In spite of the laughter, he looked anything but amused. "You think I give two shits about her family? Or what she came from?"

"Well, you obviously do, or you wouldn't have brought it up."

"No. I brought it up to make a point."

"Oh yeah? And what point is that?"

"Make that *two* points."

"Fine," I snapped. "Go ahead. I'm all ears."

"One," he said. "He doesn't *want* her as an employee, and mixing that up wouldn't've been good for either one of them."

The explanation – truthful or not – stung. It shouldn't have. But it wasn't lost on me that Jaden and I had been mixing up business and pleasure for quite a while now.

And it wasn't working out, at least not for me. *Not anymore.*

I crossed my arms. "And the second point?"

"We both know why I made you work today."

"Oh, really? Why?"

"So you'd stay the fuck away from that nut-job." His voice hardened. "And her pimp."

The so-called pimp was the boyfriend of Cassidy's mom. Oh sure, she called him her boyfriend, but it was beyond obvious that it was more of a business thing.

And the way it sounded, the business was expanding.

Still, I said, "But it wasn't your call. And besides, I can handle myself just fine."

"No," he said. "You *think* you can handle yourself fine, but that smart mouth of yours gets you into trouble."

I stood. "Hey! I've been the epitome of self-control."

He gave me a dubious look. "Is that so?"

It *was* – except when it came to *him*. The whole time I'd been working here, I'd shown a surprising amount of restraint, even as I'd been snubbed and insulted by practically everyone in the building.

There were friendly greetings that went unanswered, conversations that grew quiet when I entered the room, friendships that were destroyed in infancy by whatever Darla was saying behind my back.

And yet, through all of this, I'd maintained my professionalism, no matter how much it bothered me. Lately, it had been bothering me more and more, even though I tried not to show it.

I smiled when I wanted to frown. I greeted coworkers who seldom replied. I'd kept my chin up for months now in spite of the fact that Darla and her minions were obviously trying to drive me out.

But that wasn't the thing eating at me now. It was the one aspect where I'd shown zero self-control – *him*.

I had to be honest. A lot of this – cripes, maybe *all* of this – was my own fault.

I heard myself say, "You're right."

His gaze grew wary. In a careful voice, he said, "Alright. What's the catch?"

"Nothing. I just said you're right." I gave a hard scoff. "But trust me, I *can* do better." I sat back down and edged my chair closer the desk. "Now, if you'll excuse me, I've got work to do."

He didn't budge. "No, you don't."

I gave him a thin smile. "What are you saying? I'm dismissed for the day?"

His jaw clenched. "This isn't about work."

"Yeah, well, it is from now on."

His voice grew quiet. "What?"

"Our little fling – or whatever it is – it's over." Unable to stop myself, I stood again. By now, I felt like a jack in the box – up and down one too many times, just like my emotions. With a muttered curse, I grabbed my purse and then my phone. "I'm done."

He still made no move to leave my office. Rather, he merely stood there, looking at me like I'd just slapped him silly. "You serious?"

"Dead serious." I lifted my chin. "So if you wanna fire me, now's the time."

He looked at me like I was a crazy person. "What the hell? You think I'd fire you because..." He shook his head, but never finished the thought.

That was fine by me. In my current frame of mind, I was more than happy to finish it for him. "...because we're not gonna 'fuck'? That *is* how you put it, right?"

His voice was barely a whisper. "Allie."

It hurt to hear my name on his lips. I pushed aside the pain and said, "So if you're gonna fire me, you might as well tell me now so I can grab all of my stuff and go."

"You know it's not like that."

Maybe I *did* know. But I was in no mood to be fair. "So I'm *not* fired? Is that what you're saying?"

He shoved a hand through his hair. "You really think I'd fire you?" For the second time in thirty seconds, he murmured, "What the hell?"

"Great," I said, shouldering my way past him. "See you Monday."

I didn't look back, even as I strode out of the suite and then all the way to the parking garage, where the truck was waiting in its usual spot. I cried most of the way home, hating myself for every sniffle.

Life had been so much simpler when I hated him.

Regardless, I was officially done, at least with the personal stuff. And I meant it, too.

Jaden was my boss. But that's *all* he was. Now, I just needed to remember that.

Unfortunately, this became harder as the weekend rolled on, especially on Sunday night, when Cassidy dropped a new bombshell that only added to my confusion.

CHAPTER 56

As the weekend crawled to a close, I was utterly exhausted from trying to pretend that everything was okay.

It *wasn't* okay.

If I were lying to myself, I'd blame it on new drama with Cassidy's mom or the fact that I'd barely slept a wink.

But the truth was, without Jaden, the weekend had felt long and empty, in spite of the fact that he'd called me at least half a dozen times.

I hadn't answered, and he'd left no messages.

Maybe I *should've* answered, but I knew the folly of *that*. We'd either argue or end up naked in each other's arms. Knowing us, we'd do both.

I couldn't let that happen, not if I wanted crawl out of the hole that I'd dug for myself. This was, after all, my own fault.

All along, I'd known exactly what he was. Cripes, he'd even warned me up-front, telling me in his own words, *"I don't do relationships"*.

But had I listened?

No.

Now, my stomach churned at the certainty that I couldn't avoid him forever. Tomorrow was Monday, which meant that I'd almost surely be seeing him in less than twelve hours.

With a pang, I remembered that it would've been my turn to leave something silly on his desk – assuming that Morgan wasn't already there, lying nearly naked in wait, like she'd been doing on Friday night.

Now, I couldn't help but wonder if Jaden had seen her at all. He hadn't mentioned anything on Saturday, and neither had I – only because we'd spent our limited time arguing about other things.

I was so lost in my murky thoughts that I practically jumped out of my skin when Cassidy burst through the apartment door and said, "You won't believe what just happened."

She looked flushed and happy, like someone in love. This was no wonder, considering that she'd spent most of the weekend with Jax. Oh sure, there'd been some rocky moments with her mom, but it was easy to see that their time together had ended on a fairly high note.

Refusing to rain on her parade, I summoned up a smile. "Something happened? What was it?"

"You'll have to see it to believe it." And then, she practically dragged me outside, where a brand new vehicle was sitting in our driveway.

It was a little purple sports car – a gift to Cassidy from Jax. Apparently, he'd just bought it today.

I couldn't help but stare. "But it's a Sunday night."

Cassidy blew out a long, unsteady breath. "Yeah, I know."

"So, what happened?" I asked. "Did a dealership open up just for you or something?"

"Pretty much."

I gave a low whistle. "Wow."

"Yeah. No kidding."

"Sooooo..." I gave Cassidy a sideways glance. "Did you guys..."

"No." She sighed. "Not even close."

I turned to study her face. "You're kidding."

"I wish."

"Well, that's weird." I wasn't even sure what surprised me more – that he'd bought her a car, or that she'd actually let him. Normally, Cassidy was self-sufficient to a fault.

There had to be more to this story.

Next to me, she was saying, "Get this. He said the car was for *him*, not me."

I tried to think. "Oh. So it's like a loaner or something?"

"Not like *that*," she said. And then, she went on to tell me in a roundabout way that Jax had bought her the car so he wouldn't be worried for her safety.

Apparently, he'd seriously lost his cool earlier today when he'd discovered that she'd taken a ride share to his house.

On this, I agreed with Jax. In truth, I was more than a little horrified that Cassidy had done such a thing. I said, "You didn't seriously?"

"Do what? Take a ride-share? Yeah. I mean, people do it all the time, right?"

"Sure," I said. "But *you* shouldn't, not here, anyway."

"Why not?"

With a little shudder, I recalled that incident with her mom and the limo. With as crazy as things were, Cassidy shouldn't be riding anywhere with any stranger, especially given her mom's connections.

I said, "Because your mom's pimp—"

She stiffened. "He's not a pimp."

Yes. He was. But it was useless to argue. Already, Cassidy and I had argued way too much about the monster that was her mom.

I tried again. "Fine. Your mom's 'boyfriend' is big into that sort of thing. He's got that limo company, the taxi service, and he's a partial owner in that local ride-share, too."

Cassidy blinked. "He is?"

"Yeah. You didn't know?"

"No. I didn't."

"He's bad news," I said, "especially for you." As I talked, I realized that I sounded an awful lot like Jaden, who'd given me a similar lecture about the very same topic.

But this was totally different. After all, no one had tried to drag *me* into the world's oldest profession, thank God.

Cassidy asked, "Why me?"

"Hello?" I gave her a look. "He was trying to recruit you."

Cassidy frowned. "Technically, my mom was trying to recruit me."

I almost rolled my eyes. *As if that was an improvement.*

Still, over the next few minutes, I tried to drive the point home that Cassidy needed to be a lot more careful. She was gorgeous and vulnerable, too, especially since she was new the area and had no way of knowing who was connected to whom.

I was still making the point when Cassidy said, "But forget that. Wait 'til you hear what Jax and Jaden did."

Now, that made me pause. "They did something?"

"Oh yeah." She gave a humorous laugh. "And, they did it in ski masks."

My stomach lurched. "Ski masks?"

CHAPTER 57

We were still in the driveway, and I was still staring. Cassidy nodded. "Yeah, remember this morning, when you told me that Jaden had left a ski mask on your desk?"

I did remember. She'd been telling me about her date with Jax, and I'd been too down in the dumps to be decent company.

I'd tried my best to hide it, but had failed miserably. When she'd asked me what was wrong, I'd offered up some half-baked complaint that Jaden was always leaving stuff on my desk, including that ski mask on Friday night.

It was hardly the whole story, but lying by omission seemed a lot kinder than crying on Cassidy's shoulder, especially when she had more than enough problems of her own.

I gave a tight nod. "Yeah, I remember."

"Well," she said, "they went over to my mom's place and…" She bit her lip. "I'm not sure how to put this, but they, uh…" She paused, like she simply couldn't find the words.

Now I was dying to know. "They what?"

"Well, you know how Dominic's in the hospital?"

Her mom's boyfriend?

I *had* heard something to that effect. In fact, just last night, Cassidy's mom had called repeatedly to complain about it. But she was such a drama queen that I hardly ever took her seriously.

Last night had been no exception.

Next to me, Cassidy still hadn't replied to my question.

"Well?" I said. "What happened?"

She cleared her throat. "They, um, put him there."

They?

Meaning Jax and Jaden?

I felt myself swallow. "What do you mean?"

As I listened, Cassidy went on to tell me that on Friday night, the two brothers had apparently lurked outside her mom's apartment and jumped Dominic – that pimp of a boyfriend – when he'd ventured outside.

As she talked, I tried to put everything into context – the mask, the brothers, the fact that Jaden had made no effort to see me on Friday night.

Was that why? Because he had plans of a different sort?

Cassidy concluded by saying, "It was kind of a masked mugging, except they didn't really mug him, because they didn't steal anything."

My mind was still whirling. "Well, that's unfortunate."

"Oh, so you *wanted* him robbed?"

"Definitely." I thought of all the harm that could've come to my friend. "And roughed up, too."

Cassidy gave me a look. "Well, he *is* in the hospital, remember?"

Good.

I smiled. Maybe it was an evil smile, but I didn't care. Crazy or not, I was glad they'd done it. Absently, I said, "Oh yeah. I almost forgot."

In truth, I hadn't forgotten anything. Mostly, I was irritated that I hadn't thought of it myself. I despised Cassidy's mom. And I despised her so-called boyfriend even more – not that I'd ever met the guy.

But I didn't *need* to meet him to know that he'd surely bring my friend to harm if he ever had the chance.

Cassidy gave a shaky laugh. "Well, aren't *you* blood-thirsty."

Yes. I was. And with good reason. "Hey, he had it coming," I said. "But back to Jax, did he say *why* they did it?"

She winced. "He said he didn't want that guy near me."

I gave a slow, approving nod. "Good."

A few minutes later, sitting in our living room, she offered up more details. Apparently, on Friday night, the night before Cassidy was scheduled to pick up her things, Jax had driven by her mom's place to check it out in advance.

While there, he'd discovered by chance that Dominic was planning another sales pitch to recruit Cassidy. And Cassidy's mom, the selfish creature that she was, was doing nothing to discourage him.

Now, in the safety of our living room, Cassidy was saying, "But it's so strange. I mean, why would Jax do that?"

It was no mystery to me. "I'll tell you why." I smiled. "He's crazy." I meant it in the best possible way. My own heart ached just a little as I added, "Love makes you do crazy things."

Afterward, Cassidy went on to tell me that the two brothers had gotten together and decided to have an anonymous talk with Dominic before *he* could have a talk with *her*.

"Apparently," Cassidy was saying, "the talk didn't go too terrific, because it ended with Dominic in the bushes."

And in the hospital.

By now, I was half-surprised that Dominic hadn't ended up in the morgue.

Better luck next time.

Cassidy's story haunted me all night. I kept thinking about that stupid mask. I wasn't even sure whether Jaden had left it on my desk *before* that little adventure or afterward.

And why had he left it for me at all?

I saw no silly joke behind it. All *I* saw was a serious effort to protect someone that Jax cared for.

And Jaden had helped him.

That meant something.

I was under no illusion that he'd done it for me, or even for Cassidy. But he *had* done it for his brother.

I was glad. And thankful. And now, more confused than ever.

On Monday, I woke hours before dawn and lay there in the darkness for the longest time, feeling like I hadn't slept at all. Finally, when I couldn't stand it another moment, I got up and got ready for work.

When I pulled into the parking garage, the sun was barely peeking over the horizon. This was a good thing, I reminded myself, because it would give me some time to calm my nerves before anyone else came in.

But as it turned out, I hadn't come in nearly early enough, because when I walked into my office, someone was already there.

It was Jaden.

And unless I was mistaken, he'd been lying in wait.

For me.

CHAPTER 58

Yes, it was an ambush, plain and simple.

From the open doorway to my office, I stopped to stare at the sight of Jaden in my chair. He was leaned back with both feet propped up on my desk and his hands clasped behind his head.

I hadn't yet turned on my office light, and I squinted through the shadows. Everything about this was so strange. He wasn't even dressed for work.

Rather, he was wearing ratty jeans and a black T-shirt with some logo that I didn't recognize.

So far, he'd said nothing, and neither had I. As our gazes locked, I felt something stir in my heart. *Dread? Or something else?*

I waited for him to speak, and when he didn't, I finally blurted out, "What are you doing here?"

His voice was flat. "I own the building."

As if I needed the reminder. "I know, but what are you doing in my office?"

He gave me a look. "What do you think?"

"I don't know what to think."

"Yes, you do."

I made a sound of annoyance. "You know, I really hate it when you do that."

"Do what?"

"Act like you know what I'm thinking."

"It's no act," he said. "You know damn well why I'm here."

"Oh yeah? And why's that?"

"Because you didn't answer your phone."

"Well, so what?" I said. "I was off the clock. In case you forgot, you're not the boss of me everywhere."

His gaze darkened. "That's what you think? That this is about your fucking job?"

"Isn't it?"

His voice grew quiet. "You know it's not."

"Oh, really?" I said. "Then what *is* it about?"

"Us."

At that one single word, something twisted in my heart. But I knew all too well what he meant. "Us" meant sneaking around where no one could see. It meant secret smiles, but no public displays of affection. It meant hiding out from his family and keeping secrets from friends.

It meant no attachment whatsoever.

There was only one problem. *I'd gotten attached.*

Stupid me.

I forced a laugh. "Oh come on Jaden, there *is* no us." A long sigh escaped my lips. "Yeah, I mean, it was fun and all, but it couldn't go on forever, right?"

He was quiet for a long moment before saying, "Why not?"

"Is that a serious question?"

"I dunno," he said. "Give me a serious answer, and I'll let you know."

I was so confused, I could hardly think. "What?"

"You need me to repeat it?"

"Yeah, actually I do, because I have no idea what you're getting at."

"Alright," he said. "I'll make the question simple." His mouth tightened. "What happened?"

"What do you mean what happened?"

"Last Monday, things were good. *This* Monday, you're saying we're done. So I'll ask it again." His gaze bored into mine. "What. Happened?"

"Nothing 'happened,'" I said. "I just realized that we'd run our course, that's all." I gave him a faint smile. "I mean, come on, aren't you a little tired of sneaking around?"

"Yeah. I am."

"So, you see what I mean, right?"

"No." He pulled his feet from my desk and stood. "What *I* see is someone who got what she *said* she wanted, and now..." He looked away and muttered, "Shit."

Oh yeah. I'd gotten what I'd wanted alright. Unfortunately, it had been *too* good for my own sanity.

I recalled that very first night. To think, I'd only slept with him in the first place because I'd been oh-so sure that I could simply get him out of my system.

Now, months later, I was so addicted, I needed to go cold turkey or risk losing my mind.

And my heart.

Unfortunately, he was still my boss, unless I was willing to quit. I turned and glanced toward the suite's main door. I *could* walk out. But then what?

From behind my desk, Jaden said, "If you think you're leaving, forget it."

I turned and gave him an irritated look. "Oh, really?"

"Yeah. Really."

I made a sound of frustration. "I don't even know what you're saying."

"Yeah, you do."

"Oh, stop it," I said. "Are you saying you don't want me to quit?"

"No."

My stomach sank. *So he did want me to quit?* Probably, it was for the best, and yet, the whole thing stunk to high heaven.

But then he continued. "What I'm saying is that you *can't* quit. I won't let you."

"What?"

His voice hardened. "If you're worried I can't keep my dick in my pants, I can."

I stiffened. "Good."

"But you're not leaving."

"Why not?"

"Because that wasn't part of the deal."

"There was no deal," I said.

"Wrong. That first night, you told me we'd keep it separate. Matter of fact, you insisted on it." His jaw clenched. "Or, are you gonna tell me now that you don't remember?"

I *did* remember. I remembered a lot of things. And it wasn't only the sex. I glanced away and mumbled, "I remember."

"Good," he said. "Because I'm not having you quit on my account."

And with that, he stepped aside and made a grand, sweeping gesture toward my chair. "It's all yours." And with that, he strode past me, leaving me alone in the darkened office.

And where did he go?
I had no idea.

Rather than returning to his own office, he left the suite entirely. I didn't see him for the rest of the day, even though his schedule had been packed with appointments – appointments that I canceled one by one as the day dragged on.

When he returned Tuesday morning, everything was different. I never saw the hint of a smile – not to me, and not to anyone else either.

I tried not to flatter myself that he missed me just as much as I missed him. And even on the off chance that he *did* miss me, all I had to do was remind myself that he "didn't do relationships."

Still, the rest of that week was pure hell.

Jaden and I were obnoxiously polite to each other – more polite than we'd ever been.

And I hated it.

I missed the banter. And the teasing. And the feel of his arms. And the taste of his lips. And the feel of his body moving against mine.

I even missed that stupid car-racing game that we sometimes played on Saturday afternoons. I missed the sandwiches and even the jokes about my so-called addiction.

Still, I plodded along, trying my best to pretend that everything was fine as the week dragged on. By Friday afternoon, I was utterly exhausted.

On the upside, I had two Jaden-free days ahead of me. Maybe I could regroup and get a fresh start.

That didn't happen.

And why?

It was because all weekend long, his name kept popping up again and again. And like some kind of crazy addict, I couldn't seem to get enough.

CHAPTER 59

Cassidy was laughing. "So then, he torches the car, right there in the warehouse."

She was talking about something Jaden had done on the night she'd first met both brothers. Apparently, Cassidy hadn't personally seen the car go up in flames, but Jax had told her all about it during this past weekend – a weekend filled with sex and fun.

For Cassidy and Jax, that is.

According to Cassidy, there'd been plenty of both.

I was glad for her, and him, too. It was nice to see them happy, even if I wasn't feeling quite so happy myself.

For me, it had been a weekend filled with longing and humiliation – longing because I was missing Jaden like crazy and humiliation because I fully realized the stupidity of missing him at all.

Somehow, he'd burrowed under my skin and claimed a spot dangerously close to my heart.

How did *that* happen?

Hell if *I* knew.

Trying to sound casual, I asked, "So, this weekend, was Jaden around?"

"Yeah. For like five minutes." She made a face. "And he was in the *worst* mood, even more than usual."

I could *so* relate. "Really?"

She nodded. "Oh yeah. And he takes one look at me and says, 'Screw this, I'm outta here.' And *then*, we didn't see him all weekend. Honestly, I think he left town."

"Do you know where he went?"

With a little scoff, she replied, "Probably somewhere with Morgan."

My stomach sank. "Seriously?"

"Sure, if *she* had any say in the matter."

So it was a joke? I tried to smile and failed miserably. Morgan *had* been chasing him forever. *Had she finally caught him?*

On the sofa, Cassidy was saying, "Here's something that'll make you laugh."

If so, it would be a welcome relief. "Oh, really?"

"Yeah, last Saturday, when I stopped by their house, Morgan was there, waiting on their porch."

Already, I wasn't laughing. "For Jaden?"

"Oh yeah. And you should've seen her, too." Cassidy lowered her voice. "Her shirt was so small, her boob literally popped out."

I bit my lip. "But she *was* wearing a bra, right?"

"Not hardly," Cassidy said. "Really, she was wearing next to nothing. And you wanna know why?"

I was almost afraid to ask. "Why?"

"Because..." Cassidy laughed. "...she said that Jaden likes 'em slutty."

Of course he did. He'd told me so himself, along with his oh-so-smart reason. *He didn't want to get attached.*

Well, goodie for him.

As Cassidy talked, I couldn't help but recall that *I'd* seen Morgan nearly naked, too, waiting for Jaden in his office.

But had Jaden seen her? I wanted to kick myself for not asking.

Cassidy said, "And you should've seen her when Jaden got home."

"Oh?"

"Yeah. She practically sprints off the porch and throws herself into his arms."

I didn't *have* to see it. I could imagine it just fine. And like an idiot, I didn't like it one bit.

But what had I expected? Even when we *had* been seeing each other, we'd never insisted on exclusivity.

And yet, we *had* been exclusive. Of this, I was nearly certain – if nothing else, because we spent so much time together. Plus, during that particular timeframe, he'd received nearly no phone calls from other girls, at least not at the office.

My heart clenched. From now on, they'd probably be calling all the time.

But surprisingly, they didn't – except for one girl, who began calling at least once a week.

And apparently, she wasn't giving up.

CHAPTER 60

Sitting at my desk, I gripped the phone far too tightly for my own good. Trying to smile, I said, "No. He's not available. Can I take a message?"

On the other end of the line, she asked, "How about Jax? Is *he* there?"

By now, the routine was all too familiar, and I wondered why on Earth she kept calling in spite of the fact that both brothers were obviously avoiding her.

"I'm sorry," I said. "Jax is out of town."

This was true. He and Cassidy were on a weeklong vacation somewhere in the Bahamas. Even his assistant was on vacation, which meant – unfortunately – that it was just me and Darla in the office.

Oh yeah. And Jaden.

But I didn't want to think about *him*.

And why? It was because I'd thought about him all last night, and the night before that, and so on.

Now, other than business interactions, we almost never spoke. It was the strangest thing, because he seemed like a totally different person, devoid of any real emotion.

I could so relate.

And yet, I couldn't make myself regret the decision to end it when I did. After all, just like I'd told him, it *had* to end sometime, right?

On the phone, the caller was saying, "Well, just tell him that I called, okay?"

By now, I no longer needed to ask her name. It was Luna. She never gave a last name *or* told me why she was calling. The one time I'd asked, all she'd said was, "It's a family thing. Jaden knows what it's about."

By now, I was half convinced that he had a secret love child somewhere. I was dying to know more, but had no idea where to begin. Already, I'd asked Cassidy if the name Luna meant anything to her, but she had no idea either.

I'd even asked Morgan in a roundabout way, and all *she'd* said was, "Oh *her*? Trust me, you *don't* want to know."

She was wrong. I *did* want to know, even if it was really none of my business.

When I hung up the phone, I jotted down the message and added it to the stack. As I did, I wondered whether or not she was calling his cell phone, too. Did she even *have* the number?

Unable to stop myself, I took the stack of messages and crossed the hallway that separated my office from Jaden's. From the open doorway, I said, "I've got your messages."

He looked up and said, "Yeah, so?"

"So, do you want them?"

He eyed them with zero enthusiasm. "If I wanted them, I'd ask."

I paused. Ever since our breakup – or whatever it was – he'd been polite to a fault. Either those days were over, or he was in a seriously rotten mood.

Either way, I was determined to keep it professional. "Right. I know, but you haven't asked in like two days." I lifted my hand and gave the messages a little wave. "And they're sort of piling up here."

"So?"

"So, you *really* don't want them?"

His eyes were dark and hollow. They looked eerily similar to my own eyes whenever I looked in the mirror. But where mine were hollow from tossing and turning in my empty bed, his were probably hollow from tossing and turning with someone else, or a series of someone else's, assuming that he'd returned to his old habits.

I never saw these other girls, but I wasn't so naive to think that he'd suddenly become celibate. I mean, this was Jaden Bishop we were talking about.

From behind me, an older female voice said, "He already told you, he doesn't want them, so why don't you scuttle back to your own desk?"

Shit.

It was Darla.

I turned to her and said through gritted teeth, "Excuse me?"

"You heard me," she said. "Quit bothering him."

"I'm not bothering him," I shot back. "I'm doing my job."

I hated this. Whenever Darla filled in for Karen, she did everything she could to make my work-life miserable.

And yet, this was the first time she'd hassled me in front of Jaden.

Now, she gave a snort of derision. "Your job? *That's* what you call it? Prancing in here like he needs *your* attention?"

Prancing? Seriously?

I made a scoffing sound. "I wasn't trying to give him 'attention.'" Again, I lifted the small papers in my hands. "I was trying to give him these."

She crossed her arms. "Sure you were."

There were so many things I wanted to say in return, but most of them were laden with profanity of the worst kind. And the last thing I needed now was a scene at the office.

After all, things were shaky enough as it was.

I turned to give Jaden a nervous look, only to freeze in mid-motion at the sight of him standing directly beside me.

When did that happen?

He looked to Darla and said in a low voice, "I already told you, leave her alone."

"Why should I?" Darla said. "I see the way she looks at you."

I sputtered, "What?"

She looked to me, and her gaze narrowed. "What, you think I don't see you mooning over him? It's disgusting. Get a grip on yourself, will ya?"

I felt my fingers clench. *Oh, I wanted to get a grip on something alright.*

And now, Darla was saying, "*And* as long as I'm laying it on the line, stop cozying up to *my* daughter."

I stiffened. "I'm not cozying up to her."

"Yeah, well she's always in your office. You think I don't know what you're doing?"

I was staring now. "What are you talking about?"

"You're pumping her for information, aren't you?"

"Information? About what?"

Her gaze shifted to Jaden. "About *him*. And God knows what else."

My fingers were still clenched. "Hey, it's not like I'm *dragging* her into my office. She walks in on her own." *Uninvited, too.* But that was beside the point.

Jaden's voice cut through the noise. "Time to go."

Darla and I turned to look. I wasn't sure who he meant. *Her? Or me?*

Thankfully, his gaze was firmly trained on Darla. "You've got the rest of the day off," he said. "Use it to cool down, alright?"

Her mouth fell open. "What? You're kicking *me* out? For *her*?" She said "her" like I was some sort of contagious disease.

"No," Jaden said in an eerily calm voice. "I'm kicking you out because you can't control yourself."

Darla gave another snort. "Oh, like *she* can. Do I need to remind you, she jumped you the first day you met."

"Hey!" I said. "I did not. Nothing happened 'til later." As soon as the words left my mouth, I realized my mistake. Obviously, she'd been talking about the day of my job interview, when I'd taken a flying leap in Jaden's direction.

But I'd been so distracted by my own crazy, mixed-up feelings, I hadn't thought before speaking.

And now, there was dead silence.

Darla's gaze shifted between me and Jaden. Her lips pursed as the pieces slid into place.

I wanted to say something, but I didn't know what. Already, I'd said far too much.

My face was flaming, and my spine was twitchy. I looked toward my own office and mumbled, "I'll uh, just give you the messages later."

I turned to go, only to stop in mid-motion when Darla yelled, "You fucking tramp!"

Tramp?

Oh, for God's sake.

Something inside me snapped. I whirled to face her. "Yeah? Well so what?" My voice rose. "Yeah, I fucked him. And it was fabulous!" I jerked my finger toward his desk. "We did it *there*, multiple times. And just so you know, it was the best I ever had." My breath was coming in short, ragged bursts as I stepped closer and finished by saying, "There, you happy now?"

If happiness was a murderous rage, she looked like the happiest person on Earth.

Her fists were clenched, and her shoulders were tight. She looked dangerously close to punching me in the face.

If so, I was ready. "You wanna hit me?" I made a forwarding motion with my free hand. "Bring it on, granny-pants!"

She looked down. She *was* wearing a pantsuit today. And yes, the waist was quite high. *But since when did I care about that?*

I didn't.

It suddenly struck me that I'd not only insulted her, but semi-threatened her, too – or at least threatened to defend myself if she took a swing.

Fine. I didn't like this job anyway. *Much.*

And now, Jaden was reaching out toward Darla's elbow. His voice was very calm as he said, "C'mon, I'll walk you out."

"Walk *me* out?" she sputtered. "Why don't you walk *her* out? Or better yet, have security do it."

He smiled. "Hey, I *am* security."

That might've been a joke, but I was too distressed to laugh. None of this was funny. *Not at all.*

As I watched in stupefied silence, Jaden gently, but firmly, began leading Darla toward the suite's door.

She protested, "But what about my purse?"

He replied, "I'll have someone deliver it."

"No!" Darla said. "I need it *now*. It's got my keys."

Jaden caught my eye and said in an overly calm voice, "Allie, would you mind retrieving her purse?"

Unsure what else to do, I gave a silent nod.

But already, Darla had yanked her elbow out of his grip. "Fuck that!" she yelled, turning all her fury on Jaden. "If you want me to go so bad, *I'll* get it." Under her breath, she added, "Like I'd want her filthy hands on my stuff."

I looked down. *Filthy?*

Talk about insulting.

True to her word, Darla marched back into her office – or rather, Karen's office – and emerged a moment later with her purse slung over her shoulder. She stalked back to where Jaden and I stood, and then glared up at him to say, "If you want me, I'll be at home."

And with that, she marched out of the suite without looking back, leaving behind her a silence so heavy, it made my knees go slightly weak.

Or maybe that was just nerves.

I felt terrible for all kinds of reasons. I'd revealed something that was supposed to be a secret. I'd almost gotten into a fist fight with someone older than my own mother. And – this was the worst part – I was dangerously close to crying.

This totally sucked.

CHAPTER 61

I didn't want to cry. I wasn't the crying type. And I certainly didn't want to cry in front of Jaden.

I mumbled something about getting back to work and turned away, only to pause when he said, "Don't."

I looked back. "Don't what?"

"Don't run off."

"I wasn't running off," I said. "I was getting back to work." I lifted my chin. "Unless I'm fired."

His gaze darkened. "Fuck that."

I wasn't sure what he meant. "Do you mean my job, or...?"

"Forget your job." With two long strides, he closed the distance between us. "That's not what we're talking about."

I stared up at him. He was so close, I could feel the warmth of his body. I could smell the scent of his favorite soap. Most of all, I could see something in his eyes.

I didn't know what exactly it was, but I knew what it *wasn't*. It wasn't lust. And it wasn't indifference either.

Other than that, I could only guess.

I heard myself say, "I didn't mean to say that."

"Say what?"

I cleared my throat. "Any of it, actually."

He smiled. "So, I'm the best you ever had, huh?"

I glared up at him. "Oh, stop it."

"Stop what?"

"Stop looking like it's funny. It isn't." My mouth twitched. "Really."

This was so maddening. I wanted to laugh. *And* I was still in serious danger of crying.

It was official. He was driving me crazy. *Again.*

In front of me, he said, "You wanna know what's funny?"

"What?"

"You."

I bristled. "Me?"

"Yeah. You, thinking you could end it."

My breath caught. "What does *that* mean?"

"It means," he said, "we're not over."

His words sparked an embarrassing surge of hope, followed quickly by a new dose of despair. It would be so easy to fall into his arms, to pick up where we left off, to pretend that I could be happy with a casual thing.

But I had to be honest. I *wouldn't* be happy.

I blinked back tears. Then again, I wasn't happy now.

Into my silence, he said, "It was a mistake. You know that, right?"

Yes. I did.

All of this was a mistake, a big, giant mistake that would keep growing if I was stupid enough to give in to the temptation that was Jaden Bishop. And now, my eyes were burning with unshed tears. I took a useless swipe at them and murmured, "I know."

"No." His voice was very quiet. "I mean, it was a mistake to listen to you."

I gave a confused shake of my head. "What?"

His gaze met mine. "You said we wouldn't get attached."

I tried to smile. "And we didn't." Of course, this was only half true. I'd gotten far too attached for my own good. I just prayed that he couldn't see it, because how humiliating would *that* be?

"Wrong," he said. "Maybe you didn't. But *I* did."

I swallowed. "You did?"

"What, you didn't know?"

"How would I know?" I said. "You never said anything."

"Yeah? And you wanna know why?"

"Why?"

"Because I was a dumb-ass."

In spite of everything, I laughed. "You were not."

His eyebrows lifted. "Oh, so *now* you're being nice?"

"Hey, I'm *always* nice." I hesitated. "Okay, maybe not always-always. But most of the time."

"No, you're not." He edged a fraction closer. "You're a pint-sized ball of trouble."

"Me?" I sputtered. "What about you?"

"I'm not pint-sized," he said.

On this, he was correct in more ways than one. But that was beside the point. Speaking very softly, I said, "Well, you're *still* trouble."

"Yeah, and you love it."

I looked away and mumbled, "Yeah, well. Maybe sometimes."

"I've been thinking," he said.

I returned my gaze to his. "About what?"

"Us."

There was that word again. My breath caught. "Us?"

"Yeah. You know what we're gonna do?"

"What?"

"Start over."

It was such a pretty thought. And yet, I made no reply.

Desperately, I wanted to throw myself into his arms and pretend that everything was fine. But it wasn't. It couldn't be, not unless his ideas about relationships had miraculously changed.

Or maybe that's what he was telling me in that crazy way of his.

Was it?

When I said nothing, he asked, "What is it?"

I hesitated. "Well, I just think that maybe you and I want different things, that's all."

"Yeah? Like what?"

"Well, I mean, you told from the start that you weren't a relationship type of guy."

"Yeah. I wasn't."

Wasn't? As in the past tense? "What does *that* mean? That you *are* one now?"

"That depends," he said.

"On what?"

His gaze softened. "You."

CHAPTER 62

It would be wrong to say that we picked up right where we left off, because this time, it was different, with one exception.

We were still sneaking around.

It was my call, not his. After that whole scene with Darla, I saw all too well that I didn't want to be *that* person – the girl sleeping with the boss.

I'd even half-heartedly suggested a transfer, but Jaden wouldn't hear of it, telling me, "Forget it. I want to keep an eye on you."

Whether he'd been joking or not, I had no idea. But I *did* know that I didn't truly want a transfer anyway. I liked seeing him during the day, and I loved spending time with him at night.

We'd been back together for just a week, and already, I was getting spoiled on what had blossomed into an actual relationship.

Somehow, Jaden had convinced Darla to keep quiet about what she knew. As for myself, I'd been dying to tell Cassidy the whole crazy story. She was my best friend and the closest thing I had to a sister.

But she was also Jax's girlfriend. Oh sure, Jax might suspect that something was going on between me and Jaden, but he never said so.

For that, I was grateful. I had more than enough trouble at the office already, which also meant that unburdening myself to Cassidy was out of the question.

Sure, I realized that she could keep a secret, but I hated the thought of asking her to. More than anyone I knew, she deserved a little peace and happiness – happiness that I'd never risk by asking her to lie to the guy she loved.

Unless I was mistaken, they were hurtling pretty quickly toward something serious – at which point, I'd simply have to tell her, whether I was ready or not.

In the meantime, I was seeing Jaden on the sly – for now, anyway. Still, the clock was ticking.

Jaden had told me in no uncertain terms that he wasn't willing to hide it much longer. Even though I didn't quite agree, I loved the sentiment, just like I loved the way he made me laugh, even as he drove me insane in more ways than one.

Did I love him?

Maybe.

Okay, make that *probably*.

No. Definitely.

Still, the bigger question was, *did he love me?*

I wasn't sure. When we were together, he *looked* like a guy in love, but even *I* realized that looks could be deceiving.

We'd been back together for exactly one week when that girl – the one named Luna – called yet again.

I did the usual thing and told her that he wasn't available. But then, breaking with tradition, I didn't write the message down. Rather, I crossed the hallway, entered Jaden's office, and shut the door behind me.

He looked up and gave me a wicked grin. "Yes."

I frowned in confusion. "Wait, was that a question? As in 'yes, what do you want?'"

"No," he said. "It was the answer."

"To what question?"

He made a show of eying me up and down. "Whether I want a quickie." He smiled. "And the answer's yes."

I rolled my eyes. "I didn't come in here for a quickie."

"Good," he said, "because you weren't gonna get it anyway."

I scoffed, "Oh, really?"

"Yeah," he said. "I was gonna take my sweet time."

A stupid giggle escaped my lips. "Oh, so the quickie was a bait and switch?"

"Pretty much."

"You're impossible. You know that, right?"

"Hell yeah," he said. "And you love it."

No. I loved him. But I'd die before I'd say it first. So all I said was, "I have a different question, and no, it's not related to a quickie."

"You mean a longie," he corrected.

"Whatever," I laughed. But then, my laughter faded when I recalled why I was here.

Jaden said, "Alright, what is it?"

"I'm just wondering..." I hesitated. "Who's Luna? Is she like an ex-girlfriend or something?"

And just like that, he wasn't smiling anymore. "No."

"So..." Again, I paused. "Can I ask who she is?"

His expression softened. "You can ask me anything."

I gave a nervous laugh. "Yeah, but will you actually answer?"

"Alright," he said. "She's my brother's wife."

I froze. "Oh, my God, you don't mean—"

"No," he said with something like a smile. "I'm not talking about Jax."

Relief – along with a good bit of embarrassment – coursed through me. I gave a nervous laugh. "I keep forgetting, you've got more than one brother."

Funny though, he never talked about them.

And why was that?

Later that night, I found my answer, but it wasn't from him.

It was from Cassidy.

CHAPTER 63

Cassidy had just walked in through the apartment door when I said, "Hey, I know who Luna is."

Shutting the door behind her, she said, "Luna? Who do you mean?"

"C'mon, you remember," I said. "A while back, I asked if that name meant anything to you?"

"Oh, right." She laughed. "Sorry, it's been a crazy few weeks." From the look on her face, that so-called craziness was a very good thing. She came in and joined me on the sofa and then turned sideways to face me. "So? Who is she?"

"Get this. She's their brother's wife."

"Oh." Cassidy hesitated. "I guess I should've known that, huh?"

"I don't know," I said. "Does Jax talk a lot about his family?"

She shook her head. "Not if he can help it."

"What do you mean?"

She frowned. "It really *is* awful."

I wasn't liking the sounds of *that*. "How awful?"

"That depends," she said. "Do you know which brother Luna's married to?"

I recalled the little that Jaden had told me. "Yeah. Someone named Jake."

Cassidy made a face. "Then the answer to your question is 'Really awful.'"

"So, they don't get along?"

"Not hardly," she said. "Remember when I told you about Jaden torching that car?"

How could I forget? Still, I sifted through the details, trying to recall exactly what she'd said.

Apparently, one of their brothers had shown up here in Florida looking to reclaim an old car of his. One thing had led to another, and Jaden had torched the car right there in the warehouse, in front of the visiting brother.

I said, "So that was Jake?"

Cassidy nodded. "Yeah. There's a lot of bad blood between them."

"Do you know why?"

"Well, for starters, there's the car thing."

I tried to laugh. "Well yeah, I can see where torching a car might cause a *little* brotherly friction."

"But that's only half of the story," she said. "There's a lot more that I left out."

"But why?" I asked.

"Because it's so depressing. And honestly, I wasn't sure you'd want to know. I mean, you're not a huge fan of Jaden."

Oh, God. How awkward was this?

I forced another laugh. "Okay, now you've *got* to tell me or I'll go crazy wondering."

And so she did.

When she finished, I almost didn't know what to say. She was right. The story really was awful.

Apparently, when Jax and Jaden were barely teenagers, their mom had abandoned their family without so much as a goodbye. They'd been living in Michigan at the time, and had no idea where she'd gone until Jax and Jaden discovered on their own that she was in Florida with who-knows-who.

Even though they'd been far too young to drive, they'd stolen their older brother's car and then drove over twenty hours south all by themselves. But then, when they'd arrived at their destination, all they'd found was their mom living with a rich new family.

The saddest part was the picture Cassidy painted of Jaden, the guy I loved, standing on the unfamiliar doorstep, telling his mom that she had to come home.

But she hadn't.

She hadn't even offered to help Jax and Jaden return home.

So there they were, stranded in Florida with no money, no plans, and apparently, no one even looking for them.

It was almost too horrible for words.

I asked, "But what about their dad or older brothers? Didn't any of *them* come looking?"

Cassidy shook her head. "The only one who showed up was Jake." She grimaced. "And the only thing *he* wanted was his car."

I winced. "Ouch. You mean the one they stole from him?"

"Yup, that's the one." She gave a weak laugh. "It was the same car that Jaden torched a few months ago."

I blew out a long, shaky breath. "I can see why."

And I truly could.

The way it sounded, the only thing Jake cared about was his car. If so, I was glad Jaden torched it. I was just sorry that he hadn't done it years ago – the *first* time Jake had shown up looking for it.

I murmured, "I can't believe I'm just hearing this story."

"Why?" Cassidy asked. "I mean, it's not like you and Jaden are friendly. And even with Jax, it was like pulling teeth to get the full story out of him."

"But what about the rest?"

"What do you mean?"

"I mean, they're obviously living here in Florida. Are you saying they just never went home?"

"That's exactly what I'm saying," she said. "And if it weren't for Darla taking them in, who knows what might've happened."

At the mere mention of that dreaded name, I stiffened. Still, I was curious. "So she's not related to them at all?"

Cassidy shook her head. "No. But she happened to see them hunkered down in that car. The way it sounds, she invited them for dinner, and then just sort of adopted them."

"Really?"

The story made me feel funny in more ways than one, but it certainly explained a few things. Now, it was easy to see why both brothers were so down on relationships – *and* why they cut Darla so much slack.

My thoughts zeroed in on Jaden. In my mind's eye, I could almost see him, just a kid, begging for his mom to come home. He must've loved her, whether she deserved it or not.

And she'd totally abandoned him.

No wonder he'd turned out so jaded.

Suddenly, I hated all of them – the mother, the dad, and even the stupid brother who cared more for an old car than for his little brothers.

God, what a tool.

And now, the guy's wife was calling Jaden at the office? I could only imagine why. Probably, it was to give him grief about the car or to ask for restitution.

Talk about nerve.

Silently, I vowed that the next time she called, I'd tell her what she could do with that husband of hers.

But the strangest thing was, she *didn't* call – not that week, nor the week after.

Soon, a whole month had passed, and she slipped almost entirely from my mind.

And why? It was because things with Jaden were keeping me blissfully busy.

Almost every day, I was learning something new about the guy I'd fallen for. But it wasn't until the day I found something in his laundry room that I knew beyond all doubt that he cared for me just as much as I cared for him.

CHAPTER 64

Both Jax and Cassidy were out of town, which meant that Jaden and I had the run of the beachfront mansion. It was a Sunday night, and the weekend had been pure bliss, with plenty of sex, laughs, and sandwiches, too – just because, hey it's sort of how we met.

Now, I was borrowing his washing machine to catch up on some laundry before the workweek ahead. I was in his laundry room folding my towels when I happened to look up and see something sitting on a nearby shelf, atop some gloves and scarfs.

It was a ski mask – a very familiar ski mask.

The last time I'd seen it, I'd been tossing it to Morgan as she sat nearly naked behind Jaden's desk. I'd never asked him about it, mostly because I'd been so eager to put all of that behind us.

But now, with the mask in sight, I was dying of curiosity.

When I returned to the kitchen where Jaden was making us a couple of club sandwiches, I set aside my laundry basket and held up the mask. With an embarrassed laugh, I said, "I see you got it back."

He gave the mask a perplexed look. "From who?"

"From Morgan."

He grew very still. "What do you mean?"

Obviously, I'd hit a nerve. "Well, the last time I saw it, Morgan was..." *Gosh, how to put this?* "... holding it for you."

Now, he was frowning. "Where?"

I cleared my throat. "In your office, actually."

He muttered, "Shit."

"Sorry, what?"

"You saw that?"

"If you mean, did I see Morgan waiting for you, yeah, I did."

With a low scoff, he looked away. "No wonder you were pissed."

I gave it some thought. That whole weekend had been a definite downer. In fact, the day after I'd seen Morgan lying in wait, I'd ended it with Jaden. But at the time, Morgan's obvious interest had been only a minor factor in the big scheme of things.

I tried to laugh. "Actually, it was funny more than anything."

He gave me a look. "Bullshit."

"What?"

"You weren't amused. You were pissed off."

"I wasn't *that* pissed off," I said. "I mean, I knew she liked you. But I never really saw you two together, at least not romantically."

"Got that right." His gaze met mine. "And lemme tell you something, if you were pissed, you had every right to be." He gave me a rueful smile. "If *I'd* found someone waiting for you, I probably would've kicked his ass."

From the look in his eyes, there was no "probably" about it.

"Honestly," I said, "I wasn't *that* angry, at least not about that."

"Wanna bet?" he said. "You dumped me two days later."

"Oh come on," I laughed. "I didn't 'dump' you. I was just..." I struggled to find the words. "...ending a temporary thing."

"Temporary to *you*," he said. "Not to me."

His words warmed my heart. "Really? Even then?"

He left the kitchen counter and circled around it until there was nothing standing between us. He pulled me into his arms and said in a quiet voice, "You know it."

I leaned into him, loving the feel of his arms and the hardness of his chest. Still, I had to ask, "So, what happened? I mean, did you actually see Morgan that night?"

He stiffened. "Yeah. I saw her."

"And?"

"And I told her it wasn't gonna happen, not then, not ever."

"How'd she take it?"

He was quiet for a long moment. And then, he said, "Not great. But Morgan, she'll be alright, as soon as she figures out what she wants."

I pulled back to meet his gaze. "Oh, *I* know what she wants, or rather, *who* she wants."

But already, Jaden was shaking his head. "Nah. She just thinks that's what she wants. Trust me, I'd make her as miserable as Jax did." He grimaced. "And shit, who wants sloppy seconds after their brother?"

He looked so disturbed that it made me laugh. "Sorry," I said. "It's just the look on your face."

"If you think *this* look is bad," he said, "you should've seen me when I found her."

I winced. "That bad, huh?"

"Well, it wasn't good."

"Can I ask you a question?" I said. "Why'd you leave the mask in the first place?"

"You mean in my office?"

I shook my head. "No. Not *your* office. *My* office."

He frowned. "What do you mean?"

"I mean, I found it on my desk that night, so I guess I'm just wondering what the joke was."

"The joke?"

"Well, you know how we were leaving things on each other's desks. I guess when it came to the mask, I didn't quite get it."

"That's because it was no joke."

"What?"

"You want the truth?"

I nodded.

He gave me the hint of a smile. "I didn't know I left it."

I stared up at him. "So you *didn't* leave it on my desk? Is that what you're saying?"

"No. If you say it was there, I believe you. I'm just saying, I don't remember leaving it."

"So who did?"

He gave a rueful laugh. "Probably me."

"But wait, you just told me—"

"That I didn't *remember* leaving it. But that night, I *was* in there."

"You mean in my office?"

His voice grew quiet. "Yeah."

"So, what am I missing?"

"That Friday, you know what Jax and I did, right?"

It was funny to think that we'd never discussed this. But I knew exactly why. Everything about that whole weekend had been such a nightmare that I hadn't really wanted to re-live it.

But suddenly, this discussion felt long overdue.

I said, "You, um, roughed up Cassidy's mom's boyfriend." I almost shuddered. "Or should I say pimp?"

"Either way, you're right. And you know *why* we did it?"

"To keep him away from Cassidy, right?"

"Right."

I felt my eyebrows furrow. "But what does that have to do with you leaving the mask in my office?"

"After it was over," he said, "I got to thinking what I'd do to keep *you* safe. And before I knew it, I was standing in your office, wondering what I'd do to someone who ever hurt you."

His words melted my heart. "Really?"

Again, he pulled me close. Into my hair, he said, "I would've done a lot worse than 'rough him up.'"

That sounded vaguely ominous, and yet, I wasn't disturbed. Instead, I was feeling warm and gooey all over. "So, *that's* what you were doing?" I teased. "Plotting someone's demise?"

His arms tightened around me. "If anyone hurt you? Fuck yeah." He paused. "Allie?"

"What?"

"I love you. You know that, right?"

And just like that, the world stopped spinning. I pulled back to say, "You do?"

"What, you didn't know?"

"How would I know?" I said. "You never told me."

"Yeah, well, I'm telling you now."

I smiled. "And I'm telling *you*, too."

He smiled back. "Yeah?"

I leaned into him and said against his chest, "I do love you." I gave a happy laugh. "As if you didn't know."

Whether he knew or not, he never said. But suddenly, I wasn't in the mood for sandwiches. I was in the mood for something else. And as it turned out, so was he.

Lying in his bed afterward, he told me the rest of the story. Turns out, on the night of their masked adventure, Jax and Jaden had already returned home when Morgan called, claiming to be locked in Jaden's office.

He'd arrived to find her in the same condition *I* had – nearly naked and ready for action.

But the only action *she'd* received was a cold shoulder, along with a stern warning to never pull that kind of stunt again.

When he finished, I snuggled tighter against him. "That was probably a good thing," I said with a laugh, "since you'd never want to violate the sanctity of your office and all."

"Violate it, huh? So *that's* what you're calling it?"

"Definitely." And then, I pulled back to ask, "Just curious...have you ever done that with anyone else?"

His eyebrows lifted, but he made no reply.

I gave him a playful swat to the arm. "I mean *in* your office."

With a laugh, he yanked me close and kissed hard, leaving me nearly breathless. When the kiss ended, he murmured, "No. Just with you."

Just with me.

I was really liking the sounds of that.

And from the look on his face, so was he.

Unfortunately, just a couple of months later, everything was thrown into a sudden disarray – starting with an unexpected visit from an overly familiar name.

CHAPTER 65

It was a Monday afternoon, and I was the only person left in the office. Jaden was in Hawaii on business, and Jax had left early for the day. Even Karen had the day off, and unlike previous times, Darla *wasn't* filling in.

In fact, I'd seen Darla barely five times since that ugly scene a couple of months ago. Since then, we hadn't said a single word to each other – not even a passing "hello" or in Darla's case, "Up yours, you filthy-handed tramp."

Still, I hoped that eventually, we'd find some way to get along. Darla was important to Jaden, and Jaden was important to me.

On top of that, I had a new appreciation for everything she'd done for him, especially at a time when he needed it most.

But that was an issue for another day. Now, the most important thing on my mind was getting ready for my upcoming trip.

Technically, it was for business. In reality, the business didn't start until next Monday. But at Jaden's insistence, I'd be flying out this Thursday to meet up with him for some pre-business fun in the sun.

Yes, I was going to Hawaii.

In a lucky break, the company was acquiring some property there, and Jaden was handling the transactions personally. As for myself, I'd be helping him in whatever way I could.

He'd left early to get a jump on things, but I'd be with him soon enough. Already, I was counting the days.

It was just past four o'clock when the suite's door opened, and a pretty blonde walked in, wearing a white sundress and sassy sandals.

She looked to be near my own age or maybe even slightly younger.

She caught my eye through my internal office window and gave a friendly little wave.

As I waved back, I wondered who she was. She didn't look like she was here on business, and that made me just a little bit nervous. Between Jax and Jaden, they had more than their share of female admirers, and every once in a while, those admirers ended up here, looking for one or both brothers.

I rose from my desk and met her at my office door. "Can I help you?"

She smiled. "Yeah, I'm here to see Jaden. Is he in?"

I couldn't bring myself to smile back. Her voice sounded familiar, *too* familiar. I gave her a long, penetrating look. "You're Luna, aren't you?"

Her smile widened. "Yeah, how'd you know?"

I stiffened. "I recognized your voice."

At something in my demeanor, her smile faded to nothing. "Is something wrong?"

God, I hated this.

Right now, I was technically acting as Jaden's assistant. But in reality, I didn't *feel* like his assistant. I felt like someone who needed to tell this chick *and* her selfish husband what they could do with their concerns about a stupid car.

Abruptly, I asked, "Why are you here?"

Now, she was frowning. "To see Jaden, just like I said."

"Oh yeah?" I crossed my arms. "About what?"

"Family stuff." She hesitated. "He'll know what it's about."

"So you said."

Her eyebrows furrowed. "Excuse me?"

"On the phone," I clarified. "You said that he'd know what it was about. But he never took your calls."

"So?"

"So, don't you think it was a bit presumptuous to just pop in?"

"Maybe." Her chin lifted. "But isn't that for *him* to decide?"

"Yes," I said. "And he did."

"Sorry, what?"

"I'm just saying, if he didn't take your calls, what makes you think he'd want to see you in person?"

Yes, I realized that I was being horribly rude, but I couldn't shake the image of Jaden as a lost kid screwed over by his family. He didn't deserve that. And now, years later, he didn't deserve to be hassled about a torched car.

Luna edged closer to me and said, "Listen, I don't know who you are—"

"Fine, I'll tell you who," I replied. "*I'm* the person who loves him."

She blinked. "What?"

"Yeah, that's right," I said. "And I think it's pretty crappy that your stupid husband cares more about a car than about his own brother."

She was bristling now. "Hey! You don't know anything about it."

"I know enough to realize your husband's a jerk."

"Yeah, well maybe yours is too."

"Hah!" I shot back. "We're not even married."

"Oh, shut up," she muttered. "You know what I meant."

She was right. I did. And in hindsight, bragging that Jaden and I weren't married seemed pretty darn stupid. We'd never even talked about marriage even if he *had* said those three magical words.

I might've smiled at the sentiment if only I didn't have a bristling blonde glaring daggers at me.

I squared my shoulders. "I'm just saying, maybe you should've called first."

"Why?" she said. "So you could keep claiming that he wasn't in?"

"Well, he's not in *now*, so what difference does it make?"

Her gaze narrowed. "Did you even give him my messages?"

"What?" I sputtered. "You think I didn't?"

"Well, you *do* seem to have an attitude."

"This?" I said. "This is nothing." I straightened to my full height – which granted wasn't terribly high. "I've got a lot more attitude where *that* came from."

She gave a dismissive wave of her hands. "If you think you can scare me off, forget it. I've got brothers who are twice as scary as you."

"Yeah, well I've got brothers too. And they'd make mincemeat out of yours."

Mincemeat? What the hell was I even saying?

She gave me a perplexed look. "What's mincemeat?"

"I don't know," I admitted. "I'm just saying, you're not gonna intimidate me."

"I didn't think I could," she said with a little frown. "You're kind of scary."

"Hey!" I said. "I am not. I'm just..." I hesitated. "...mad at Jake, I guess. I mean, seriously, how could he do that to his own brother?"

Abruptly, Luna turned and looked to her right. I followed her gaze and stifled a gasp. Standing just inside the suite's door was – *damn it* – Darla of all people.

Well, this was just great.

CHAPTER 66

I'd been so focused on Luna that I hadn't seen Darla come in.

I hadn't *heard* her either.

But the way it looked, she'd seen and heard plenty. Her eyes narrowed to slits as she eyed me and my unwanted visitor. "That's it," she announced. "I'm getting security." And with that, she turned and marched out of the suite, leaving me and Luna staring after her.

Oh, crap.

This wasn't what I wanted. Cripes, I wasn't even sure who Darla would be reporting. *Me? Luna? Both of us?*

Regardless, this wasn't good.

And now, I didn't know what to do. I looked toward the phone on my desk. *Should I call security myself in hopes of heading off a scene?*

Probably too late for that.

This was, after all, Darla we were talking about.

I was still looking at my phone when Luna said something that took me completely by surprise. "Hey, you wanna get a coffee?"

I turned to stare. "What?"

"Coffee," she repeated. "If you really *do* love him, you'll want to hear what I came to say." She gave me a tentative smile. "I'll even treat."

It wasn't the promise of free coffee that convinced me to go. It was the fact that yes, I did love him, and I was beyond curious.

Plus, there was the little matter of avoiding security.

Turns out, I made the right decision.

An hour later, I sat in stunned silence as she finished the story of what had really happened over a decade ago.

"So," she concluded, "Jake *did* come for them. But when he saw how much better they had it *here*, he only *acted* like he'd come just for the car."

I shook my head. "But why would he do that?"

She gave a wistful smile. "You'd have to know him to understand."

"Understand what?"

"That he wanted his brothers safe and happy, even if it meant they hated him for it."

I thought of everything I'd learned from Cassidy. What Luna described was surprisingly believable.

In fact, I could almost see it, Jake showing up to retrieve his brothers, only to discover that they'd landed in a better place. And then, rather than dragging them back to Michigan as planned, he'd acted like a total jackass so they'd stay where they were.

I asked, "But why didn't he just tell them?"

"Tell them what?"

I tried to put it into words. "Like, he could've said, 'Hey, you look pretty happy here. Why don't you stay?'"

Luna leaned forward across the table, and her voice became earnest. "Because what happens if they say no? Or worse, what happens if the lady they're staying with kicks them out because they've got someone waiting at the door?"

I thought of Darla. No matter what, I couldn't see her kicking them out. She loved them, just like I did – or rather, just like I loved *one* of them.

As for Jax, I'd grown pretty fond of him, too. He'd been spoiling Cassidy like crazy, whenever she let him, that is.

Now, I glanced down at the table. My latte was long gone, and it was already past five. Earlier, on my way out, I'd locked up the office so I wouldn't need to return.

Still, at this point, I wasn't quite sure what to do. I looked back to Luna and asked, "So, why'd you tell me all of this?"

"Because I was planning to tell Jaden." She gave a rueful laugh. "Lord knows, Jake never would."

"He wouldn't?"

She shook her head. "He's funny like that. He never wants to take credit for anything. And…" She hesitated. "…Well, you want the truth?"

I gave a silent nod.

She smiled. "Sometimes, he needs a little nudge."

"What do you mean?"

"I'm just saying, I know he misses his brothers. He never says it, but I can tell."

"So, *that's* why you were calling?" I said. "To broker some sort of peace?"

"Yup. And guess what?"

"What?"

Her smile widened. "*You're* gonna help me do it."

Now, I was smiling back. I liked that idea. *A lot.*

After all, I knew how I felt about my own brothers. It was true that I didn't see them as often as I liked, but I couldn't imagine cutting them out of my life.

I left Luna with a solemn promise to do whatever I could to help mend all of those brotherly fences. And actually, I was feeling pretty good about everything until just a couple of hours later, when Cassidy shared a discovery that had both of us reeling.

CHAPTER 67

I'd just walked into the apartment when Cassidy said, "I've got a question. Double J – does that mean anything to you?"

I shut the door behind me and dropped my purse onto the nearby side table.

Double J? Oh yeah, it meant something alright. It was the name of a Bishop Brothers subsidiary, the one that handled their various real estate and side ventures – restaurants, bars, and tons of commercial real estate.

I said, "Yeah, why?"

"Well?" she said. "What does it mean?"

I gave her a puzzled look. "You know what it means. *You're* the one who got me the job." More to the point, she was dating one of the owners.

She groaned. "So it *is* them?"

"If you mean Jax and Jaden, yeah." I tried to smile. "What, you didn't know?"

"No. I didn't. I mean, I knew their initials, and I knew the name of their regular company, but I didn't know they had that whole other side thing going."

"You mean the real estate?"

"Yeah," she said. "It's like they own half the city."

I gave a casual shrug. "Not just *this* city. They've got property all over."

Now, she was frowning. "Yeah. Including *this* place."

What? I studied Cassidy's face. She didn't look like she was joking.

I shook my head. "No." Still, I took a quick look around. "They don't, do they? Are you sure?"

"Definitely," she said. "And get this, they *also* own the restaurant where I work."

Oh, crap.

I almost didn't know what to say. "Oh. Um, no kidding?"

Her gaze narrowed. "You knew?"

"Me?"

She gave me a serious look. "Yes. You."

I winced. "If I did, is that bad?"

"Yes," she said. "It's bad. *Very* bad."

"Why?"

"Oh, come on," she said. "You didn't tell me. What does *that* tell you?"

The truth was, yes, I'd deliberately avoided the whole topic. But I had a good reason. I knew exactly how she'd take it.

Lamely, I murmured, "Huh?"

"I'm just saying," Cassidy continued, "you *had* to know it was bad, or you would've mentioned it."

"Alright, fine," I said. "I knew. But I figured you'd feel funny if you found out."

"Of course, I feel funny," she said. "I work for my freaking boyfriend."

Funny, I knew the feeling.

I gave her a nervous smile. "Well, technically you don't *really* work for him. I mean, he's not the manager or anything."

She made a scoffing sound. "Yeah, because it's worse. He's the manager's manager with a whole bunch of people in-between." She gave a little gasp. "Oh, my God. I bet *that's* why I never work weekends."

"Oh, stop," I said. "Now, you're just being paranoid."

"I am not," she insisted. "Do you know how rare it is for a waitress to get weekends off?"

"Yeah, but you've worked weekends."

"Not lately," she said. "And get this, if I ever *am* scheduled for a weekend, someone always begs to take my place."

"Well, maybe they need the money. You *did* say those shifts were the best, right?"

"Sure, but don't you think that's odd? I mean, to be asked every single time to switch?"

"Maybe a little," I admitted. "But hey, they've gotta make their rent somehow, right?"

At this, she gave a hard scoff.

Obviously, there was more to the story. With growing concern, I asked, "What now?"

"Rent," she said. "How much do we pay a month?"

"Twelve-hundred." I smiled. "As if you didn't know."

"Yeah. Twelve-hundred. Wanna know what the *last* people paid?"

"I dunno. A thousand?"

She gave another scoff.

I tried for a joke. "You should probably stop that or you're gonna hork up a lung or something."

From the look on her face, she wasn't amused. "Ha ha. Now, guess again."

I gave it some thought. "Nine hundred?"

She shook her head. "You're going in the wrong direction."

No, I couldn't be. That made no sense. "Sorry, what?"

"The last person – or who knows, maybe a few persons ago – *they* paid more."

Now, I was really confused. "How much more?"

"A lot."

"How much is a lot?"

"Eighteen hundred."

I was beyond stunned. "Wait a minute, so they paid eighteen hundred for this place?"

"No, it's worse," she said. "They paid three thousand. I meant the *difference* was eighteen-hundred."

The numbers hit hard and fast. I heard myself say, "No."

"Yes."

Silently, I took a slow look around. The place was absolutely fabulous, and only a block from the beach. The first time I'd seen it, I'd been blown away by our good luck.

But apparently, luck had nothing to do with it.

Still, I was having a hard time processing what she'd just said. "But I write the checks," I murmured. "They go to that realtor."

"Yeah," Cassidy said. "A realtor who manages the property – on *their* behalf."

"Are you sure?"

"Oh yeah."

"And you learned all of this, how?"

Cassidy went on to tell me that her favorite barista happened to recognize the address from Cassidy's new driver's license, and then had gone on to mention that her cousin used to live here.

Apparently, this cousin had moved out because the rent was more than she could afford.

I felt myself swallow. It was more than *we* could afford, too. Okay, maybe *I* could've afforded it, given the fact that my job paid amazingly well. But even then, it would've been tight.

But that wasn't the thing bothering me now. It was the fact that all this time, Jaden had never mentioned it.

As I listened, Cassidy went on to tell me that she'd made some phone calls to double check. "But trust me," she concluded, "the information's good."

I blew out a long shaky breath. "Wow." And then, trying to process what all of this meant, I walked to the nearest chair and fell back into it. "Shit."

Cassidy claimed the chair opposite me. "Is that good or bad?"

I had no idea.

It was easy to see how all of this had started. Obviously, Jax had been worried about Cassidy and had already realized that she hated to accept help. So he'd sent us out with his own realtor, who'd shown us exactly one place, *this* place, which was owned by the two brothers.

This included the brother I was sleeping with – the brother I loved, the brother who hadn't mentioned a thing.

In reply to Cassidy's question on whether this was good or bad, all I could do was mumble, "I don't know."

She asked, "Should I say something? To Jax, I mean?"

"I don't know," I repeated.

She sighed. "I can't just pretend to not know."

I knew exactly how she felt. Already, I was doing the math. Since moving in, we'd underpaid our rent by thousands of dollars.

And counting.

Yes, I realized that all of this was pocket change to Jax and Jaden, but the arrangement still made me feel funny.

I worked for Jaden. And I lived in his property. Plus, aside from Cassidy, he was the only local person that I ever associated with.

Talk about having all of your eggs in one basket.

From the look on Cassidy's face, I wasn't the only one struggling to figure it out. She sank deeper into the chair. "Oh, my God."

"What?"

Now, she looked ready to be sick. "I'm turning into my mom."

Talk about ludicrous. "No, you're not."

"Sure I am," she said. "He pays for everything, even my rent."

"That's not true," I said.

And I meant it with all my heart. Cassidy was *nothing* like her mom. Even the mention of such a thing set my teeth on edge. That woman really *had* done a number on her daughter.

But that was an argument for another day. With forced cheer, I said, "I mean, we pay *some* of it."

Even as I tried to make Cassidy feel better, *I* was feeling worse. And it wasn't just about the apartment.

It was everything, especially my job.

It paid *very* well. Even from the beginning, it had seemed too good to be true. Now, looking back, I realized there was a very good chance that the salary had been inflated as a favor to Cassidy from Jax.

But then, like some clueless interloper, I'd stepped in and claimed that favor for myself. I hadn't meant to, but the end result was the same either way.

It was a sobering realization.

Still, as best I could, I tried to reassure Cassidy that the whole thing was nothing to get upset over. I told her that Jax was simply looking out for her, and that she was wrong to feel like some kind of loser for not paying her own way.

Probably, I should've *also* given that lecture to myself, because when it came down to it, Cassidy and I were in a very similar boat.

We both worked for the guys we loved. And both of us were receiving more financial support than we'd ever realized.

But in my case, it was even more egregious because I worked directly for Jaden rather than through a series of middle-managers. Plus, we mixed business with pleasure all the time.

Unless Cassidy and Jax were doing it on the restaurant prep table, they were miles ahead of us as far as behaving themselves on the job.

I almost sighed out loud. If anyone should feel awkward, it was me, not Cassidy, and I couldn't help but wonder if I was making a huge mistake, at least where my job was concerned.

All of this was too confusing for words, which is probably why early the next morning, when I encountered Jaden's brother, I blurted out something that I'd been mulling all night.

"Maybe I should quit."

CHAPTER 68

The office was empty except for me and Jax. I'd come in early in hopes of clearing my head. But all I'd found were memories of Jaden everywhere I looked, along with the appearance of his brother, who sauntered in mere moments after my own arrival.

As Jax passed my office, he greeted me with a basic good morning, only to stop in mid-step when I blurted out those four surprising words.

He turned and stopped in my open doorway. "What?"

It was too late for me to take it back, and besides, I was desperate for some insight. I cleared my throat. "I *said*, 'Maybe I should quit.'"

His eyebrows furrowed. "Why?"

It was such a simple question, but the answer was beyond complicated. The only upside was that *he'd* been the one to hire me, so he knew exactly where all of this had started.

"For one thing," I said, "I think I'm overpaid."

"And that's a problem?"

"So I am?" I looked away and muttered, "I should've known."

"I didn't say you were," he clarified. "But I *am* saying, why complain?"

I chewed on my bottom lip. "Well..."

"What, you want a pay cut?"

If only it were that simple. "That's not what I mean."

His lips twitched at the corners. "So you *don't* want a pay cut?"

"Honestly, I don't know what I want." I tried to smile. "I bet you're wishing you'd just listened to my old boss, huh?"

"What do you mean?"

"Well, I know he gave me a horrible reference."

"Yeah. And it backfired."

I shook my head. "It didn't backfire. You just hired me anyway."

"You think so, huh?"

"Well, yeah. But I'm sure you had a good reason."

"Oh yeah? What's that?"

I sighed. "Alright, you want the truth? I think you did it to keep Cassidy from leaving." I hesitated. "I mean, I know you offered *her* the job first, so you obviously had some interest in getting her to stay."

"I might've," he admitted, "but that's not why I hired you."

I gave him a dubious look. "So you *weren't* doing it as a favor to Cassidy? Is *that* what you're saying?"

"It was a favor to someone," he said, "but not Cassidy."

"Who then?"

"You can't guess?"

"Well, it couldn't be Jaden."

"Why not?"

I almost laughed. "Because he hated me on sight."

"Nah. He only thought he hated you."

That didn't make any sense. "Sorry, what?"

Jax gave a rueful laugh. "Alright, you wanna know what happened?"

I gave a silent nod.

"On the day of your interview, I call your old boss, and what does he tell me?"

I frowned. "Nothing good."

"Yeah, that's what *he* thought."

"What do you mean?" I asked.

"I mean, he tells me that you're a temperamental pain in the ass, says you're kind of scary, too."

"I am not," I said. "I just...well, try not to be intimidated, that's all."

Now, Jax was smiling. "I know."

The smile caught me off guard. "Okay, what am I missing?"

"My brother."

Oh yeah. I was missing him, alright. He'd been in Hawaii for several days now, and I was dying to join him. The only problem was, I wasn't quite sure that I should – at least, not as his assistant.

From the open doorway, Jax said, "It might surprise you to hear this, but my brother? He's not the easiest person to get along with."

In spite of everything, I almost snickered. *Talk about a massive understatement.*

I recalled how much I'd despised Jaden when we'd first met. But now that I knew him better, I realized that he was absolutely perfect in his own way. Or, at the very least, he was perfect for me.

I murmured, "He's not *that* bad."

"Yeah? Well, the previous five assistants might disagree."

"What?"

"Before you, he went through five in two years." Jax flicked his head toward Karen's desk. "Including mine."

"What? You mean Karen used to work for him?"

"You didn't know?"

No. I didn't. But then again, I didn't know a lot of things, being the office pariah and all. In reply, I gave a silent shake of my head.

Jax said, "He drove her nuts."

I had to smile. Jaden drove *me* nuts, too. But the funny thing was, I actually liked it.

Go figure.

Switching gears, I said, "But what about Morgan? *She* would've liked working for him."

"Yeah, but her work sucked."

I tried not to laugh. As the person who'd inherited some of her work, I had to agree.

"And," Jax continued, "Morgan working here..." He shook his head. "Let's just say it wasn't good."

I knew exactly what he meant. Even when she stopped by, she went out of her way to distract both brothers regardless of what else was going on.

I considered everything Jax had told me. "So, let me get this straight," I said. "Are you telling me that you hired me for the job, because you thought I could handle your brother?"

Handle?

His brother?

At this unfortunate phrasing, I felt color rise to my cheeks. *Oh, I'd handled him alright, in more ways than one.*

More quietly now, Jax said, "You're good for him, you know."

"I am?"

"Yeah. You are." He gave me the ghost of a smile. "And I hope you stay on."

I bit my lip. "So you're saying you don't want me to quit?"

"Yeah. I am." He gave me a penetrating look. "But I'm not talking about the job." And with that, he turned away, leaving me staring after him.

What did he mean by *that?*

Did he know about me and Jaden?

But of course he did.

Jax wasn't stupid. And unlike Cassidy, he saw me and Jaden together all the time. Apparently, all of those secret smiles weren't so secret after all.

Our conversation haunted me all day. There was a lot that we hadn't discussed – such as the situation with our rent or my recent run-in with Luna and Darla.

But those were things I needed to discuss with Jaden first. I just didn't know if I'd be discussing them on the phone or when I joined him in Hawaii – assuming that the trip still happened.

By four o'clock, the odds of this were looking decidedly grim because like a total idiot, I mentioned far too much when Jaden called in for his messages.

CHAPTER 69

On the phone, Jaden asked, "What are you saying?"

I sighed. "I don't know what I'm saying. It's just that I'm starting to wonder if I shouldn't be working for you."

"Why not?"

"Oh come on. You know why." Even though my office door was shut, I lowered my voice. "We don't have a purely professional relationship."

"Yeah? So?"

"So, I think people are noticing."

"Good," he said.

"No. It's *not* good."

My conversation with Jax had only confirmed what I'd been trying to deny. Apparently, Jaden and I weren't nearly as subtle as we thought.

Maybe *that* was the reason no one ever talked to me.

Then again, the cold shoulder had begun on my very first day, long before Jaden and I even liked each other.

On the phone, he was saying, "It's been eight weeks."

"What?"

"Eight weeks," he repeated. "That's how long you've been putting me off."

I knew what he meant. A couple of months ago, he'd told me that we were taking our relationship public. In response, I'd practically begged him to give it more time.

At work, things were awkward enough already. And the sad thing was, Jaden never saw it. Whenever I was with *him*, everyone was just terrific. They not only spoke to me, but occasionally smiled, too.

But when it was just me on my own, well, let's just say my reception was frosty at best.

I'd had plenty of jobs over the years, and I'd never experienced anything like this. Lately, it had been weighing on me more and more.

To Jaden, I replied, "Well of course *you* wouldn't mind. There's no downside for you."

"Meaning?"

"Well no one's gonna hassle *you* about it."

"Wanna bet?"

I frowned in confusion. "So someone's hassling you?"

"Yeah," he said. "And I'm talking to her."

"Oh, stop it. I'm not hassling you. I'm just letting you know how I feel."

"Yeah. And I'm letting *you* know that you're full of it."

"I am not," I said. "I just don't know if we should be doing both."

"Both what?"

"I mean sleeping together and working together." Desperately, I tried to think. "Remember way back, you offered me a transfer?"

"Yeah. So?"

Reluctantly, I said, "So maybe it's something we should consider."

"Or maybe," he said, "you should stop giving two shits about what other people think."

I wanted to scream. This was just like him. "That's easy for you to say. You're the boss."

"Of you?" He gave a low scoff. "That'll be the day."

"I didn't mean of me. I meant of everyone else."

"If they don't like it, fuck 'em."

I tried again. "But what about Darla?"

"What about her?"

"Well, you can't be so blasé about *that*."

"I already told you," he said, "we'll work it out. She's family. It's different."

"I know, but…" I hesitated. "Don't you think it would be better if I didn't work here?"

"I'm thinking plenty," he said, "but that's not it."

"Okaaaaay. So what *are* you thinking?"

"I'm thinking, you need to get over it."

I felt my jaw clench. "Get over it?"

"Yeah," he said. "Get over it."

Now, I couldn't help but scoff. "Thanks for your understanding."

"You're welcome."

I made a sound of annoyance. "I wasn't serious."

"Good."

"What?"

"Good," he repeated, "because you're not quitting."

Through gritted teeth, I said, "I *meant*, I wasn't serious about thanking you."

"Yeah? Too late now."

Normally, I'd find this amusing. But between the rent thing and what Luna had told me, I realized that things weren't nearly as simple as he made it sound.

I still hadn't told him about Luna's visit, but there was a very good reason for that. The more I thought about it, the more I realized that it *wasn't* a conversation for over the phone.

Cripes, maybe I should've waited for *this* conversation, too. But in all honesty, I'd figured we'd be able to discuss it like reasonable adults.

Apparently, I'd figured wrong. "You're impossible. You know that, right?"

"Yeah. And you love it."

"I don't love it *now*."

"Eh, you'll love it when you get here."

Here. Meaning Hawaii. That was another issue.

I bit my lip. "Can I ask you something?"

"What?"

"About the Hawaii thing, am I coming as your assistant, or...?" I waited for him to fill in the blank. And when he didn't, I added, "Well, *you* know."

"No. I don't."

I felt my fingers clench around the phone. Jaden was *not* stupid, so why wasn't he reading between the lines? Did he *want* me to spell it out?

When he said nothing else, I tried again. "I just mean, is this trip something that I'd be coming on either way? Or are you just bringing me because there's something going on between us?"

"Does it matter?"

"Yes. It does, actually."

"Why?"

"Well, maybe I don't want you paying me for that."

He gave a hard scoff. "That?"

Again, I lowered my voice. "*You* know."

He paused for a long moment before saying, "You think I'm paying to fuck you?"

Heat flooded my face. "God, do you have to be so crude?"

"Yeah. I do. And you wanna know why?"

"Why?"

"Because that's what you were getting at. And it's bullshit."

"It is not 'bullshit,'" I said. "It's a valid concern."

"Not to me."

I felt like we were going around in circles. "Of course it's not to you. *You're* the one paying."

This was true in more ways than one. Not only was he paying me on the job, he was also subsidizing my rent and paying for my vehicle. Until now, I hadn't given it much thought. But of course, I'd only learned about the rent situation yesterday.

Was that the tipping point?

Abruptly, he said, "What is it?"

"What's what?"

"What's eating you?"

I made a sound of frustration. "I've been trying to explain, but you're not listening."

"So try again."

I was losing my patience. "Maybe *you* should try again."

"What are you getting at?"

"I'm just saying, I've explained it already, but you're refusing to understand."

"Alright," he said. "Let me cut to the chase. Are you coming or not?"

I swallowed. "Do you mean to Hawaii?"

If he'd asked me that question even ten minutes ago, the answer would've been a quick and easy yes. But now, I wasn't so sure. This conversation hadn't gone anything like I'd hoped.

When he made no reply, I asked, "Do you want me to?"

"Just answer the question."

"Why should I?" I said. "You didn't answer mine." For his benefit, I repeated it. "Do you *want* me to come?"

"If I didn't, I wouldn't've invited you."

As far as a reply, it wasn't warm and fuzzy. Cripes, it wasn't even welcoming. I murmured, "Then the answer is...I guess I don't know."

His voice grew flat and cold. "You don't know."

"No. I don't."

"Yeah? Well, tell me when you do." And with that, he hung up. Afterward, I pulled the phone away from my ear and stared at the receiver.

What had just happened?

I wasn't quite sure.

But whatever it was, I didn't like it.

CHAPTER 70

The next two days were horribly tense. At least twice a day, Jaden called in for his messages. And, at least twice a day, I gave them to him with only minimal commentary. At the end of every call, he'd ask me the same maddening question. "Is there anything else you want to tell me?"

I knew what he wanted me to say – that I wasn't quitting *and* that I'd be there in Hawaii as originally planned.

But there were things that I wanted *him* to say, too – that he understood my concerns and that the trip to Hawaii was nothing in the big scheme of things. But the way he was acting, like it was some do-or-die thing, well, it made me feel a little strange.

After all, he'd practically admitted that it wasn't truly a work trip. And if he only wanted me there for my company, then why wasn't he being more understanding about it?

On top of that, he wasn't even calling me at night, in spite of the fact that we usually talked all the time, even when he was out of town.

By the time Wednesday afternoon rolled around, I was feeling seriously stressed about the whole thing. Supposedly, my flight left at six o'clock tomorrow, which meant that I was running out of time to make an official decision.

On top of that, I hadn't even packed, mostly because I wasn't sure whether or not I'd be going.

As the afternoon dragged on, I kept glancing at my phone – meaning my work phone, where Jaden would be calling in for his messages. Normally, he called by four o'clock, but already, it was nearly five.

Still, I waited.

Five o'clock came and went.

No call.

Finally, at six, I began gathering my things to leave for the day.

Whether Jaden realized it or not, the last two days had only confirmed what I'd been thinking all week.

I couldn't continue to work here.

Everything was so twisted up with my own personal feelings that I was having a hard time acting remotely professional. I couldn't help but recall how I'd acted when Luna had shown up out of the blue.

I'd almost lost it.

Was that how a normal employee behaved?

No. It wasn't.

I was just heading out of my office when I heard the phone ringing at my desk. I dropped my stuff and practically sprinted to pick it up.

It was Jaden.

Thank God.

But then, he skipped the whole message thing entirely and went straight to the point. "Time's up."

I frowned. "What?"

"The flight leaves tomorrow. Are you gonna be on it or not?"

I felt my jaw clench. "Well, hello to you, too."

In a tight voice, he said, "Hello. Now answer the question."

Even for Jaden, this was *so* unacceptable. I said, "And what if the answer's no? What then?"

His only reply was a muttered curse.

I said, "Oh, that's nice."

"If you want nice," he said, "you've got the wrong guy."

I squeezed my eyes shut and tried to think. It was true that part of the reason I loved him was that he *wasn't* Mister Softie, but did he *have* to rub my nose in it?

I heard myself say, "Or maybe *you* have the wrong girl."

"What?"

"I'm just saying, it cuts both ways."

"Alright. If that's the way you want it."

I made a sound of frustration. "No. It's *not* the way I want it. Haven't you been listening?"

"I've heard plenty."

His attitude was beyond infuriating. It was like talking to a brick wall. "Alright," I said, "here's something you *haven't* heard. Do you know that no one here ever talks to me?"

He paused. "What?"

"Yeah. That's right. Oh sure, they're perfectly lovely whenever I'm with *you*. But when I'm on my own? Cripes, they might as well spit on me." My voice rose. "Haven't you noticed that I have no friends? That no one except Morgan ever stops by my office to pass the time? That I'm not invited to any party for cake or whatever?"

Sounding genuinely surprised, he said, "What are you talking about?"

"Well, like for Tessa's baby shower, the one they held in the break room – only *one* person on the whole floor wasn't invited." At the memory, my voice grew very quiet. "Me."

Jaden was silent for a long moment. And then, more gently now, he said, "Come on. You couldn't've been the only one."

"I was too," I replied. "Name one other person who wasn't invited."

He gave a low scoff. "Me."

I felt like screaming. "Was that a joke? You *do* know they only invited women, right?"

In a way, it was a real shame they'd done it that way. If they'd invited guys, too, I *definitely* would've been invited, if only because I'd be at Jaden's side.

They'd never snub *him*.

As the silence stretched out between us, a horrible thought occurred to me. Maybe *that* was the reason they'd had an all-girls shower in the first place, so they wouldn't need to include me at all.

Oh, crap.

It probably was.

On the phone, Jaden said something that I didn't quite catch, probably because somewhere along the line, I'd stopped listening. Absently, I murmured, "What?"

His voice softened. "Allie, just get on the flight, okay?"

It was the closest he'd come to actually asking me. Unfortunately, I was too far gone to care. "No."

"What?"

"No," I repeated. "And you know what else?" Before he could respond, I'd already said it. "I quit." And with that, I hung up.

CHAPTER 71

I didn't know what I was expecting, but utter silence *wasn't* it.

Yes, I realized that I'd been the one to hang up, but stupidly, I'd been thinking that he'd at least call later on, if only to ask if I was serious about quitting.

And the answer to that question?

Yes. I was.

I had to.

Unfortunately, this meant that now, I'd need to find another job.

But that wasn't the thing that had me crying into my pillow. It was the idea that Jaden and I might be finished. In spite of everything that I'd believed and felt for last few months, maybe it *was* just a work fling.

I mean, it wasn't a fling for *me*. But everything about this past week had served as a grim reminder that Jaden held all the cards. He was my boss. And my lover. And, aside from Cassidy, my very best friend.

Now, I didn't know if he remained *any* of these things.

At least a hundred times that night, I debated calling him to ask. But each time, I stopped myself at the recollection that I'd already tried repeatedly to tell him how I felt. And he simply hadn't cared.

It was beyond heartbreaking.

Now, I wasn't sure what to do, even about work. Sure, I'd already quit, but it was standard practice to give at least a two-week notice. *Should I keep working until the two weeks were up? Or stop showing up immediately?*

In the end, I decided that I'd keeping working at least until Jaden returned, at which point, we could discuss some sort of transition –

assuming that we'd be talking at all.

The next morning, I slouched into the office bleary eyed and somber. Maybe it was something in the air, because a definite gloom had settled over Cassidy and Jax, too.

Over the last few days, she'd been nearly as grim and quiet as *I'd* felt. Meanwhile, in the office, Jax wasn't looking much better. I didn't know what exactly was going on, and I didn't dare ask – because I was pretty sure that if I did, I'd only end up crying about Jaden.

And I definitely didn't want to do that – at least not where anyone could see.

The day dragged on with no call from Jaden whatsoever, not even to get his messages. Then again, I reminded myself, he probably didn't even realize that I was at my desk.

I tried to think. If he stuck to his original schedule, he wouldn't be returning for at least a week. *It felt like forever.*

All day long, I kept glancing at my office clock. If it weren't for those arguments, I'd be leaving for Hawaii at six. Now, I was going nowhere fast.

I hadn't even mentioned to Cassidy that the trip was off, mostly because she obviously had troubles of her own. But she'd discover the change soon enough when she returned from work to find me *not* in Hawaii, but rather, sulking on the sofa.

Or my bed.

Or wherever.

A sad sigh escaped my lips. If only I'd kept my mouth shut until Jaden and I could talk in person, maybe things would've turned out differently.

Then again, restraint had never been my strong suit.

At five o'clock, I gathered up my things and began the lonely walk to my truck.

It's not that the building was empty. In fact, it was bustling with people leaving for the day. But it was lonely for me as everyone I passed avoided making even basic eye-contact.

Fine.

They could snub me all they wanted. And in two weeks – or maybe less – they could forget me entirely, because I wouldn't be around.

So I did what I always did. I kept my chin up and eyes straight ahead – trudging down the hall outside the executive suite, standing silently on the elevator, and finally, crossing the main lobby on the ground floor.

In spite of my resolve, I felt dangerously close to losing it. Between Jaden, the job, and everything else, I felt like a giant loser who'd made Florida my own personal train wreck.

Still, I kept on going until – *damn it* – I spotted a gaggle of familiar faces gathered near the main doors.

One of those faces was Darla's, and she was laughing it up with several of her closest friends. Oddly enough, they were the same friends who'd shown up with coffee and cake on my very first day – not that *I'd* been offered any.

At the sight of them, my steps faltered.

I'd have to pass directly by the whole group unless I wanted to make for the emergency exit, where an ear-splitting alarm would announce to everyone that I was a freaking coward.

Sadly, I was almost tempted.

And then what?

Enjoy some nice mockery tomorrow?

As if I needed any more grief.

Finally, I squared my shoulders and marched straight ahead, ignoring them just like I'd been ignoring everyone else who refused to make eye-contact.

As I passed, I said a silent prayer that Darla would just ignore me entirely and get on with whatever she was doing.

But she didn't.

Instead, she called out the strangest thing. "Have a good night."

I was so surprised, I almost fell on my face. I turned to look. "Um, excuse me?"

Darla repeated it, louder this time. "I *said*, 'Have a good night.'"

Stupefied, I glanced around. "Were you talking to me?"

One of her companions snickered, and I felt my body go stiff. *What was this? Some sort of joke?* Who knows, maybe they *knew* that I'd quit, and this was their way of rubbing it in.

If so, it would be the perfect ending to a crappy workday.

I turned to glare at the person who'd snickered, only to pause when Darla turned to the woman and demanded, "What was that?"

The woman – whose name was Robin – froze in mid-snicker. "Sorry, what?"

"That noise," Darla said. "You weren't laughing, were you?"

The woman glanced around. "I, um..." She lowered her voice. "Wasn't I supposed to?"

"No," Darla said. "You weren't."

As I watched from the sidelines, I wasn't even sure what I should do. *Leave? Stay? Dig a ditch and throw myself into it?*

Finally, I settled on mumbling, "You have a good night, too," before turning once again toward the exit.

"Hey!" Darla said.

Startled, I turned around. But as it turned out, she wasn't even looking in my direction. She was glaring at her companions. In a voice so loud, it carried throughout the whole lobby, she said, "Aren't you gonna tell Allie goodnight?"

The women exchanged glances. The one standing closest to Darla whispered, "Are we supposed to?"

"Hell yes," Darla said, "and not just when I'm around either." Darla gave me a quick sideways glance. In a quieter tone, she mumbled, "I mean, she's not *so* bad."

Coming from Darla, this was high praise indeed.

But I had no idea what it stemmed from, until I recalled that just yesterday, I'd been whining to Jaden that no one would talk to me.

Obviously, he'd had some sort of chat with her.

At the realization, I wanted to die of embarrassment. I appreciated it. Really, I did. But how humiliating was this? Now she – and heaven knows how many other people – would know that I'd been complaining to my boss-slash-boyfriend.

Shit.

As thankful as I was, this wasn't what I'd wanted. Stubbornly, I'd been hoping to win them over on my own – without threats or cajoling from Jaden or Jax.

Too late for that.

And yet, through my discomfort, a new hope kindled in my heart.

If Jaden cared enough to convince Darla to be nice to me, what did that mean?

Maybe it wasn't over, after all?

As my mind whirled with this new possibility, the women awkwardly wished me goodnight while I returned the sentiment as best I could, even as my face burned with the certain knowledge that they were only doing it under duress.

When it was over, I was beyond relieved to get out of there. Soon, I'd be home, and then, I could crawl into my own bed and try to forget about this whole mess, if only for a few hours.

But that didn't happen.

And why?

It was because when I rounded the corner and spotted my truck, there he was, Jaden, leaning against passenger's side door, just like he'd done on the first day we'd met, all those months ago.

I stopped to stare, and our eyes met across the distance.

And then, he did something that sent my heart straight into my throat.

He smiled.

CHAPTER 72

Almost in a trance, I walked slowly forward, never taking my eyes off him. He was dressed casually in jeans, a dark T-shirt, and a red hoodie. Unless I was mistaken, it was the same hoodie that he'd been wearing when I'd first shown up on his doorstep all those months ago.

Unlike *that* time, he strode forward, meeting me more than halfway in the bustling parking garage. We practically collided into each other's arms, and he cradled me tight against him.

Into my hair, he whispered two words that caught me totally off-guard. "I'm sorry."

With a laugh, I pulled back to look into his eyes. "Really?"

His gaze was warm and wonderful. "Is that such a surprise?"

"Yeah," I said.

He gave a tight shrug. "Eh, just goes to show…"

When he didn't finish, I said, "It goes to show what?"

His eyes filled with humor. "What *you* know."

I tried to glare, but failed miserably. The truth was, I was so insanely glad to see him that I couldn't even pretend to be angry.

But I *was* confused. "What about Hawaii?"

"What about it?"

"You were there."

"Yeah. And now I'm not."

I was still soaking up the sight of him. "But why'd you come back?"

His gaze met mine. "You've gotta ask?"

Suddenly, I felt like crying, but they weren't tears of sadness, not this time. They were the other kind, the *better* kind.

In a softer voice, he said, "You should've told me."

"Told you what?"

"That people were giving you grief."

"But they weren't," I said.

His eyebrows lifted. "Is that so?"

"Okay, well maybe Darla and I had a few spats, but honestly, nobody was giving me grief. They were just..." I tried to laugh. "...pretending I didn't exist."

"Say the word, and I'll fire them all."

Now, I laughed for real. "Oh stop it. You wouldn't."

"Wanna bet?"

From the look on his face, this was a bet I'd surely lose. The thought was more than a little unsettling.

I looked down and murmured, "You know I'd never want that." And it was true. I didn't, especially when most of them probably thought they had good reasons to hate me.

He placed a gentle finger under my chin. "Hey..."

When I looked up, he said, "If anyone hurts you – and I mean *anyone* – they'll have me to answer for. Got it?"

At the intensity of his gaze, I sucked in a quiet breath. "Is that what you told Darla?"

His eyebrows furrowed. "What do you mean?"

"Well, just now, she was actually pretty nice." I gave a nervous laugh. "So whatever you said, it obviously made an impression."

But already, Jaden was shaking his head. "Sorry, I haven't talked to her."

I felt my brow wrinkle in confusion. "Are you sure?"

"Oh yeah." His expression darkened. "But I will."

"No," I blurted, and then softened my tone. "I just mean, I think it'll work out on its own." I paused. "Or maybe it already has." With a sigh, I waved away the distraction. "But forget that. You didn't *really* come back because of me, did you?"

"Hell yeah."

"But what about Hawaii?"

"Say the word, and we'll leave tonight."

I laughed. "Oh, stop it."

"You think I'm joking?" he said. "The jet's waiting at the airport."

"The jet? You mean your private jet?"

He gave me a crooked smile. "You didn't think you were flying commercial, did you?"

Actually, I did. But looking back, I should've known better. After all, he'd mentioned sending a car to take me to the airport, and when I'd asked about plane tickets, he'd said that the driver would have everything I needed.

But this was something to ponder later on, when my mind wasn't already whirling. Still, I had to point out the obvious. "But I already quit."

"Yeah. About that…"

I held up a hand. "Just hear me out, okay? I've been giving it a ton of thought, and you're *really* important to me – a million times more important than any job."

I gave him a tearful smile. "And if quitting is what it takes, then I'm happy to do it, honest."

His eyes filled with mischief. "Happy, huh?"

"Well, not thrilled," I clarified. "I mean, I'd miss you during the day, but…" I sighed. "I just feel that it's a little awkward, trying to hide how we feel."

He shrugged. "Alright, so we won't hide it."

I stifled a laugh. "You're impossible. You know that, right?"

"Me?" he said. "I'm an angel compared to you."

"Hey!"

"And," he said, "I'm not just saying that as your boss."

I rolled my eyes. "But you're not my boss, at least not for long."

"We'll see…" He pulled away and gave me a look that I couldn't quite decipher. And then, he did the strangest thing. He sank down to his knees, right there in the parking garage.

With a laugh, I reached out and tried to pull him back up. "Oh, stop it. Like you'd actually beg me to come back."

His eyes were filled with humor. "I might."

I hesitated. *Something was definitely up.* "So, are you?"

He smiled. "No."

My heart was racing now. "Then what are you doing?"

"You can't guess?"

"I, um." *Oh, my God.* With my heart in my throat, I managed to say,

"I'm not sure I should."

"Good."

"Why is that good?"

"Because there's only one word I want to hear."

Breathlessly, I said, "What?"

Still on his knees, he reached into the pocket of his red hoodie and pulled out a little black jewelry box. As I watched in stupefied silence, he opened it to reveal the most dazzling diamond I'd ever seen.

And then he said it, "Allie Brewster, will you marry me?"

CHAPTER 73

Oh. My. God. He was serious. I felt myself swallow. My lips felt dry, and my eyes grew wet.

I knew exactly what word he wanted me to say. Happily, it was the same word that I felt like hollering to the whole world. But instead, with a heart filled with love and longing, I said it in a breathless whisper. "Yes."

With a look that warmed me to the core, he pulled the ring from the box and slipped it onto my finger. It fit perfectly, too, like it was made just for me.

Who knows, maybe it was.

Soon, I was in his arms, soaking up the feel and scent of him. I'd missed him so very much, and now, the thought of having him forever was almost too wonderful to be real.

But it *was* real, just like the feel of his arms and the taste of his lips as he kissed me like I'd never been kissed before.

Suddenly, the only thing I wanted was to be alone with him – *really* alone, where we could make up for lost time.

Breathlessly, I pulled back to say, "We should go."

He smiled down at me. "Yeah?"

I gave an enthusiastic nod. "Yes. Definitely."

He chuckled. "Alright, Hawaii, it is."

Suddenly inspired, I said, "That sounds amazing, but do you think we could leave tomorrow instead?"

"Why tomorrow?"

"Because…" I gave him as sheepish smile. "I was thinking that now, we could go to my place." Technically, it was *his* place, but that was a conversation for another time. More importantly, Cassidy would be working until ten, which meant that we'd have all the privacy in the world to catch up.

His eyes lit with interest. "Why yours?"

I laughed. "Because it's a lot closer than the airport."

He gave me a mischievous grin. "So, you wanna pack? Is *that* what you're telling me?"

"No." I hesitated. "Well, yeah, maybe that, too, but..."

With a look that was all innocence, he said, "But what?"

"Oh, you know what," I laughed. With that, I reached for his hand and began tugging him toward the truck.

Behind me, he was saying, "You're pretty strong for someone so small."

Now, I couldn't stop laughing. "Oh stop it. If I weren't dragging you, you'd be dragging me."

"Got that right."

Giddy with love and laughter, I rushed us toward the truck. But when we reached the passenger's side, my laughter faded. "Oh, no." I pointed through the window. "The keys, I left them in the ignition."

It shouldn't've been surprising. This morning, I'd been so distracted, it was a wonder that I'd made it into the office at all.

From behind me, Jaden said, "So?"

I turned around to face him. "So, how are we gonna leave?"

He eyed me with obvious amusement. "Is that a serious question?"

"Oh. Right." I glanced around. "So, where'd you park?"

"Nowhere," he said. "I had Hank drop me off."

Hank was his regular driver – the one who ferried the brothers to the airport whenever they weren't driving themselves, which granted, wasn't very often. I said, "So....should we call him now?"

"Screw that." Jaden left my side and vaulted himself into the truck bed.

I asked, "What are you doing?"

Already, he was reaching toward the rear window, or, as he'd called it, the slider.

Now, I couldn't help but cringe. "Sorry, it's locked." And it was. Ever since that first day, I'd been excessively careful. In truth, I never used the slider at all, for fear of accidently leaving it open.

But Jaden was grinning. "We'll see."

From the sidelines, I watched in amazement as he slid open the rear window and began climbing, head-first, into the vehicle. My mouth fell open. *What the heck?*

I *had* locked it, hadn't I?

I couldn't help but stare as he tumbled into the passenger area and then reached out to unlock the passenger's side door. He pushed the door open and said, "And just so you know, I'm driving."

I was too stunned to move. "Wait, it wasn't locked?"

"Not anymore."

"So....you had a key?"

He grinned. "Get in, and I'll tell you."

I was too giddy to argue. With a laugh, I climbed into the truck and shut the door behind me as Jaden settled himself into the driver's seat.

As he fired up the engine, I said, "So...? What'd you do? I mean, it didn't even have some sort of secret key, did it?"

He gave a low scoff. "Keys are for pussies."

I stifled a giggle. "So you *broke* in?"

"Nah." He gave me a sideways glance. "You *see* anything broken?"

"No," I admitted. "But I can't see the outside from *here*."

"Good."

"Wait, why is that good."

"Because there's nothing to see."

I felt a goofy smile spread across my face. In a voice filled with love, I murmured, "There is too."

"Yeah? What's that?"

I was still smiling. "You."

When we reached the garage's exit, he turned to face me head-on. With a wicked grin, he said, "And don't you forget it."

As if I could.

We were halfway to my apartment when I suddenly realized something. "Hey, wait a minute..."

"What?"

"A few months ago, you gave me a ride home."

"Yeah, so?"

"You remember the reason, right? It was because just like today, I'd locked my keys in the truck."

"So?" he repeated.

"So, if you were able to get in, why didn't you then?"

He was smiling again. "Why do you think?"

I couldn't help but smile back. "It wasn't just to give me a ride home, was it?"

"Hell yeah, it was."

I laughed. "No."

"Yes."

"But you didn't even like me."

"Wanna bet?" he said. "You drove me fucking crazy."

"Yeah? Well you drove *me* crazy, too."

"Good."

"No," I laughed. "It wasn't good. It was terrible."

"Admit it, you loved it."

I tried to glare. "I did not."

At the next stoplight, he turned and gave me a long secret look. "You sure about that?"

Woah. With that look alone, I felt primed and ready. *What was it about him, anyway?* Happily, I'd have years and years to find out.

Still, I insisted, "Of course I'm sure." I paused. "Well, most of the time, anyway."

"Uh-huh. We'll see about that."

That sounded vaguely ominous. "What do you mean?"

"I mean," he said, "you're gonna tell me everything."

"Like what?"

"Everything," he repeated.

"Oh yeah?" I teased. "And what if I don't?"

"Trust me, I've got ways of making you talk."

And oh, boy. Did he ever.

CHAPTER 74

When we reached the apartment, we were naked in like two minutes flat. Or rather, *I* was naked. As for Jaden, he was annoyingly clothed – at least below the waist.

But it wasn't my fault. Every time I'd tried to take off his jeans, he'd been totally uncooperative.

I might've objected more strenuously except for the fact that his lack of cooperation where his jeans were concerned was completely overshadowed by his fingers dancing over my naked body.

I was lying face up in my double bed, and already, I was a breathless, quivering mess. He was lying next to me, propped up on his elbow, giving me a view that was pure bliss, even if it wasn't nearly as complete as I wanted.

His pecs were hard and defined. His biceps bulged. His stomach was a work of art, with its sculpted washboard lines and ridges.

Again, I reached for the button of his jeans. Again, he pulled back, even as his fingers toyed with my nipple, worrying it between his smooth fingertips.

I stifled a little moan. "What are you doing?"

With a slow smile, he released the nipple and trailed his hand slowly down my torso. Softly, he asked, "Is that a complaint?"

I knew where his hand was heading, and my hips rose in response. On a ragged breath, I said, "Yes."

His tone grew teasing. "Sure, I believe you."

His hand moved lower still, trailing down my stomach. His fingers brushed the tip of my clit, and I gave a whimper of need.

He whispered, "Say it again."

"Say what again?"

"*You* know."

In my addled state, I wasn't quite sure that I did. "You mean..." I was almost too distracted to think. "Yes?"

Again, his fingers brushed my clit. "That sounded like a question." In a playful tone, he said, "You're not having second thoughts, are you?"

I wasn't even sure what he meant.

Second thoughts about saying yes to his proposal?

Or second thoughts about my complaint that he wasn't naked?

I wasn't sure, and I was finding it hard to think. I had to ask, "Second thoughts about what?"

"This," he said, teasing that special spot with his fingers.

I gave a little whimper. "Nope. No second thoughts here."

"So... say it."

I breathed, "Yes."

He rewarded me with a series of little circles up and around that swollen nub. "So," he said in a tone that was almost conversational, "tell me what happened."

My mind was growing fuzzier with every passing moment. "What do you mean?"

"I want to know..." he said, stroking me just the way I liked, "... just what upset you."

Right now, our stupid argument was the furthest thing from my mind. Somehow, I managed to say, "You mean aside from the work thing?"

"Yeah, aside from that." His fingers were still working their magic. "I wanna know."

With renewed desperation, I lifted my hips. Already, I was wet and aching for him. Cripes, I'd probably been wet from the moment he'd undressed me and lowered me onto the bed with a kiss that had me yearning for more.

In my mind, I could still taste his lips, warm and sweet against my own. Somehow, I managed to say, "Upset? Me?"

Jaden gave a slow nod. "Yeah. And I wanna know why."

I breathed, "I'll tell you later."

He shook his head. "No. You're gonna tell me before." He didn't need to say before what. I knew exactly what.

What a total tease.

I protested, "Why before?"

"Because I wanna know."

"You mean *now*?"

"Yeah," he said, rewarding me with more of those little circles, followed by a long finger deep inside me. I loved every single one of his fingers, but they weren't what I wanted. Or at least, they weren't the *only* thing I wanted. With renewed desperation, I reached for the button of his jeans.

He edged back and teased, "No cheating."

"That's not cheating," I protested. "You're the one playing dirty."

He lowered his head and pressed his lips close to my ear. In a voice filled with sin, he said, "If you think this is dirty, you ain't seen nothin' yet."

A warm shudder ran through me, and I blurted out, "I know that you and Jax own this apartment. And…" I took a deep breath. "…The rent." I shook my head. "It's too low, like *way* too low." My hips rose when he rewarded me with another finger. In the middle of a moan, I murmured, "And I'm pretty sure I'm overpaid, too."

He gave a low chuckle. "Is that it?"

"What do you mean 'Is that it?'"

"That?" he scoffed. "It's nothing."

"I, um…" *Oh, God.* What was he doing now? It felt so damn good. I murmured, "It is, too."

"Nah," he said. "That's pennies."

"It's not pennies. It's…um…" *Oh wow.* Now, he was tracing my clit with his thumb, even as his fingers moved inside me.

"It's nothing," he repeated. "But you know what?"

"What?"

His voice was a warm caress. "You're everything."

"Me?"

"Yeah. You." He smiled. "Everything I never knew I wanted." With that, he lowered his head and took my nipple into his mouth. His teeth closed ever so slightly, giving me a nibble that made me ache in the best possible way, *below* my waist.

If I didn't have him like *now*, I felt like I'd explode into a million pieces.

Against my skin, he asked, "Anything else?"

"Yes," I laughed. "If I don't have you now, I think I'm gonna die."

He sounded highly amused. "Die, huh?"

"Yes," I insisted. "And it'll be messy, too, like with blood and guts and, I dunno, brains and whatever other stuff."

He pulled back to gaze into my eyes. "I love it when you talk dirty."

His fingers were still moving so enticingly inside me. As my hips rose and fell, I reached out with one hand. "How's this for dirty?" I snagged the waist of his jeans and yanked him closer. "If you don't take off those jeans right now, I swear, I'll..." *Oh, God.* His thumb brushed my clit, and my words ended on a low whimper.

He smiled. "You were saying?"

He looked so smug, that I couldn't help but laugh even through my desire. "You're awful."

"Nah," he said. "I'm the best."

And he was.

Soon, he proved this beyond a shadow of a doubt by shedding his jeans, along with his briefs, and giving me exactly what I wanted.

Him.

His body was warm and hard, and when our hips met, I gave a happy sigh. "Finally."

He pulled out half-way and teased, "Was *that* a complaint?"

"No," I blurted. "Definitely not." I reached around with both hands and grabbed his ass. I yanked him tight against me and gave a little moan of pleasure when his length filled me completely.

He lifted his head and whispered, "I love the way you sound."

I smiled up at him. "I love the way you look. And sound. And feel."

Now he was smiling, too. "Yeah? Well, there's more where that came from." And with that, he kissed me hard and moved against me in earnest.

Over and over, our hips collided, and our lips met, and the world seemed to stop spinning as he delivered on every cocky promise he'd ever made.

I loved him.

And he loved me.
How on Earth did that happen?

With deep, trembling breaths, we climaxed at nearly the same time, leaving me warm and tingling all over.

Afterward, as he cradled me in his arms, I couldn't resist saying, "You owe me, you know."

"Oh yeah? What?"

"Well," I began, "I told *you* all sorts of things, so you should tell *me* something in return."

With a smile in his voice, he asked, "Like what?"

"I'm not sure," I said. "Something that I don't know."

"Alright," he said, smoothing a stray lock of hair from my face, "you remember when we met?"

"How could I forget?" I laughed. "You were awful."

"Yeah. And you wanna know why?"

"Why?"

"Because," he said, "you were so fucking cute."

I made a sound of exasperation. "Cute? Not hardly."

"You were, too," he said with a laugh. "You looked like you wanted to kick my ass. It was so fucking adorable, it scared the shit out of me."

"I was *not* adorable," I protested. "I was a mess."

"Yeah, a hot mess." His voice warmed. "Shit, I wanted to gather you up and take you home."

"But you *were* home."

"Yeah, and I left the door open, didn't I?"

"Oh sure, to torment me." I gave him a playful swat to the shoulder. "Like that whole thing about you and Jax taking turns with Cassidy. You were such an ass."

"Eh, that was bullshit," he said. "Something to get a rise out of you."

"Well, you certainly did that."

"Yeah, and I'll be doing it again." With playful doom in his voice, he added. "For years."

Now, I couldn't help but giggle. "You promise?"

To my infinite delight, he did.

CHAPTER 75

We were still lying naked in my bed when I heard the door to the apartment open and then slam shut a moment later.

I tensed. "Oh, crap."

"If that's another guy," Jaden teased, "he's about to get his ass kicked."

"Oh, stop it," I whispered. "You *know* who it is. She must've gotten off work early."

For weeks now, I'd been wanting to tell Cassidy about me and Jaden. And yet, I'd kept putting it off – sometimes to spare her the worry, and sometimes, if I were being totally honest, because I wasn't quite sure how to break it to her.

After all, she *still* thought I hated him.

And now, I didn't know what to do.

I especially didn't know what to do when I heard another voice join hers. "Oh, my God," I said. "It's your brother."

I pulled back to give Jaden a look. "Be honest. Does he know about us?"

Jaden grinned. "I might've mentioned it."

"When?"

"I dunno. Maybe a month ago."

Now, I was staring. "A whole month? And you never told me?"

"Hell no," he said. "You were crazy enough as it was."

I knew what he meant. I *had* been pretty crazy in my determination to keep our relationship a secret. Still, I gave him a playful push and then stifled a gasp when something on the edge of the bed slid off and thudded to the floor.

A shoe?

I didn't know, and it hardly mattered now, because the voices in the living room had gone suddenly silent.

I whispered, "Do you think they heard?" Before he could even think to reply, I said, "Oh, crap. The door."

"What door?"

I pointed. "My bedroom door. I didn't lock it."

As I made a move to get up, Jaden said, "Stay. I'll get it." True to his word, he climbed off the bed and headed straight toward the bedroom door.

He'd gotten barely halfway when after a single knock, the door flew open, and Cassidy stood in the now-open doorway.

She gasped.

I gasped.

Whether Jaden gasped or not, I had no idea. If he did, the sound was completely drowned out by Cassidy's frantic apology, followed almost instantly by the sound of her slamming the door shut so hard that the walls literally shook.

Soon, that wasn't the *only* thing shaking. Embarrassed or not, I was shaking with laughter, especially when Jaden turned and gave me a look that said it all. *"You're in big trouble."*

I *was* in trouble, because I was about to marry the most impossible person I'd ever met, who, as it turned out, was absolutely perfect.

For me, anyway.

EPILOGUE

We were married in Hawaii the very next month. Aside from it being one of my favorite places in the whole world, it apparently was *supposed* to have been the site of Jaden's proposal – or so he told me the day after we'd gotten officially engaged.

Yes, *that's* why he'd invited me to Hawaii, to pop the question in a place that I'd always loved. It was sweet and wonderful, and yet, I felt awful for ruining it, until he reminded me that I could always make it up to him on the honeymoon, if I were so inclined.

Oh yeah. I was inclined, alright, as Jaden learned for himself.

In the end, I decided that the proposal was perfect just the way it was, especially after Cassidy gave me happy news of her own regarding a certain somebody whose last name was also Bishop.

During the month between the proposal and our wedding, we finally had the chance to get our families together – his *and* mine.

Mine was the easy one. Oh sure, they were scattered across the country, but at least we all got along. And, with Jaden insisting on paying the way, getting everyone together was easier than ever before.

When it came to Jaden's family, that was a little more complicated, even *after* I explained everything that Luna had told me during that fateful visit over coffee. But in the end, the brothers worked it all out, and I was delighted to see all of them not only attending our wedding, but also catching up after all those years apart.

As far as Darla, I finally learned why she decided to like me after all. It wasn't because of anything Jaden told her, but rather because in a strange twist of fate, my telling off Luna had earned me a special place in Darla's heart – a place reserved exclusively for people who stick up for anyone who Darla happens to love.

And she definitely loves "her boys."

Does she love me? I'm still not sure. But she *did* mention on our wedding day that I was almost like a daughter to her – in *her* words, "maybe a niece, because it takes a while to work up to daughter-level."

That was fine by me, having been blessed with amazing parents of my own.

As for Darla's *real* daughter, she finally gave up on both brothers and set her sights elsewhere – on a local musician who loves Morgan just the way she is.

Heaven help him.

As far as my job, I never did officially quit. Rather, I stayed on, at least for now, if only to make my new husband crazy.

Or should I say crazier?

Just like he's always made me.

THE END

Other Books by Sabrina Stark

(Listed by Couple)

Lawton & Chloe

Unbelonging (Unbelonging, Book 1)

Rebelonging (Unbelonging, Book 2)

Lawton (Lawton Rastor, Book 1)

Rastor (Lawton Rastor, Book 2)

Bishop & Selena

Illegal Fortunes

Jake & Luna

Jaked (Jaked Book 1)

Jake Me (Jaked, Book 2)

Jake Forever (Jaked, Book 3)

Joel & Melody

Something Tattered (Joel Bishop, Book 1)

Something True (Joel Bishop, Book 2)

Zane & Jane

Positively Pricked

Jax & Cassidy

One Good Crash

ABOUT THE AUTHOR

Sabrina Stark writes edgy romances featuring plucky girls and the bad boys who capture their hearts.

She's worked as a fortune-teller, barista, and media writer in the aerospace industry. She has a journalism degree from Central Michigan University and is married with one son and a pack of obnoxiously spoiled kittens. She currently makes her home in Northern Alabama.

ON THE WEB

Learn About New Releases & Exclusive Offers
www.SabrinaStark.com

Printed in Poland
by Amazon Fulfillment
Poland Sp. z o.o., Wrocław